DAVID EBSWORTH is the pen name of writer Dave McCall, a former negotiator and Regional Secretary for Britain's Transport & General Workers' Union. He was born in Liverpool (UK) but has lived in Wrexham, North Wales, with his wife, Ann, since 1981. Following his retirement, Dave began to write seriously in 2009.

To find out more about on the author and his work, visit his website: www.davidebsworth.com.

Also by David Ebsworth

The Jacobites' Apprentice
A story of the 1745 Rebellion. Critically reviewed by the Historical Novel Society, who deemed it "worthy of a place on every historical fiction bookshelf." It was also a finalist in the Society's 2014 Indie Award.

The Assassin's Mark
A political thriller set towards the end of the Spanish Civil War. "The characters are so incredibly vivid – there are characters you adore, others that annoy you and all of these are so expertly devised that you simply cannot help but miss them all when you finish the book, and you will finish it; this is not a novel you will be able to put down."
– Rachel Malone, Historical Novel Society

The Kraals of Ulundi: A Novel of the Zulu War
Picks up the story of the Zulu War where Michael Caine left off. "An accomplished, rich, beautifully produced and very rewarding read that brings a lesser-known era of history to life."
– Cristoph Fischer, Historical Novel Society

The Last Campaign of Marianne Tambour: A Novel of Waterloo
A novel of action and intrigue based on the real-life exploits of two women who fought, in their own right, within Napoleon's army. "Superb! David Ebsworth has really brought these dramatic events to life. His description of the fighting is particularly vivid and compelling."
– Andrew W. Field, author of *Waterloo: The French Perspective* and the companion volume, *Prelude to Waterloo, Quatre Bras*

Each of David Ebsworth's novels has been awarded the coveted B.R.A.G. Medallion by the worldwide Book Readers Appreciation Group

The Song-Sayer's Lament

DAVID EBSWORTH

Published in 2016 by the author
using SilverWood Books Empowered Publishing®

SilverWood Books Ltd
14 Small Street, Bristol, BS1 1DE, United Kingdom
www.silverwoodbooks.co.uk

ISBN 978-1-78132-511-7 (paperback)
ISBN 978-1-78132-512-4 (ebook)

British Library Cataloguing in Publication Data
A CIP catalogue record for this book is available from
the British Library

Set in Bembo by SilverWood Books
Printed on responsibly sourced paper

Dedicated to the memory of Rosemary Sutcliff, who first inspired me to write about sixth-century Britain, and in the hope that she would forgive my interpretation

Glossary of Place Names

As with the maps, this is a list of mostly imagined names by which speakers of the Cousins' Tongue may have known the places to which the story takes them, along with their modern equivalents.

Across-the-Sea – Armorica/Brittany
Bear Fort – Bryn Euryn, Colwyn Bay
Benin's Cross – High Cross, Leics
Black Pool – Dublin
Broad-Hand – St. Albans
Bridge-Fort – Cambridge
Bright-Place – Gloucester
Cairn of the Twenty – *Crib y Ddysgl*, Snowdon
Clud's Rock – Dumbarton
Clud-Vale – Strathclyde
Corin-Mound – Cirencester
Dark-Pool – Lincoln
Dark-Water Vale – Thames Valley
Defile-Fort – Bodfari, *Varis*
Eidyn-Fort – Edinburgh
Fairwater Maw – Aberffraw, Anglesey
Fast-River's Run – East London (Cousins' Tongue)
Fort Overmon – Caernarfon, *Segontio*
Fortress of the Hammer-Fighters – Dinas Dinorwig, Snowdonia
Gallaecia – Galicia, Spain
Gazing-Hold – Din Sylwy, Anglesey
Giant's Tomb – Snowdon, *Yr Wyddfa*
Great Forest – The Weald
Great Hurdle – Clwydian Range

Headlands – Conwy Coast, *Rhos*
Laigin – Leinster
Land of Hosts – Kent
Legion-Hold – Chester
Long Battle Bay – Beaumaris Bay, Anglesey
Lug's Ditch – Carlisle
Lundenwic – West London (Saeson)
Moon's Glow – Lancaster
Mud-Fast River – River Teifi
Ogfran's Ring – Oswestry
Narrow Strait – Menai Strait
Peak Fort – Birdoswald
Legion's Neck – Holyhead
Red Fort – Ruthin
Red-Tops – Richborough, *Ritupis*
Reed-Hold – Conwy, *Conovio*
Ridge-End – Stretton, Staffs
Ridge River – River Cegin
Ridgeway's Gap – Dunstable
River-Port – Sea Mills, Bristol
Ruddy Bank – Rhuddlan
Saeson Shore – Sussex
Solon's Hill – Brockley Hill, Greater London
Southern Sea – English Channel
Sulis Wells – Bath
Three Bridges – Cave's Inn, Warks
Twin Sisters – Deganwy Castle, Conwy
Uric's Hold – Wroxeter
War-God's Fort – Colchester
Yew Grove – York, *Eboracum*
Zeugitana – North African Province

Glossary – General

Bangor – An enclosure with palisade
Calends – First Day of the Month
Carrio – Chariot, or war-cart
Cruth – Stringed instrument, a *crwth*
Currock – Sea-going boat, a *currach*
Follis – Coin, translated as "purse"; *purse*, worth forty nummi
Gathelic – Language of the Incomers, *Gaelic*
Guisers – Mummers
Liliacum – Aloe Vera
Mansio – Way-station on Roman road systems, approximately 30km (a day's cart journey) apart
Mensis – Month
Mithras – Roman and eastern deity, birthday celebrated on 25th December. Mithraism was one of the Empire's principal faiths until Christianity became Rome's official religion in the fourth century
Nones – The seventh day of March, May, July or October, and the fifth day of all other months (Roman Calendar)
Nummus – Roman coin of the smallest denomination, like a farthing, translated in the Cousins' Tongue as a *number.* Colloquially, also means "small change"
Pagus – Rural district
Papaver – Opium
Rhetor – Teacher of rhetoric, and much more, in the Roman education system
Rómhánach – Incomer (*Gaelic*) word for Romans
Sun Standing – Solstice
Solidus – Roman coin, translated in the Cousins' Tongue as a *solid*, and worth 150 folli, or *purses*
Tribole – Threshing board, a *tribula*

Preface

The Song-Sayer's Lament is simply a story. A fiction.

In the Westerlands of those isles once named Britannia by the Empire and its vanished Legions, the brother of Ambros Skyhound is killed in a kinfolk-feud, which will ignite a vicious civil war. There are warlords who follow the new ways of the Christ-followers – those, too, who still defend their belief in the old order of the Oak Seers and the Great Melody. But the natural ravages of both Yellow Pestilence and the Endless Winter's hunger may attack each side equally. And, in the midst of all this, Ambros has a dream: to unite all the territories of the four former provinces – to form a new Britannia Magna. It's a dream shared by his teacher and mentor, Meridden of Sea Fort. And also by the blind song-sayer, Morgose. The journeys and struggles of Ambros, Meridden and Morgose through duplicity, betrayals, conflict, plague and famine, will become the stuff of legend. Yet that same legend, which should be shining a light on the road ahead is, through collective folly and the implacable forces of nature, paving the way for a terrible darkness.

It's a story set in sixth-century Britain and, as such, this poses a significant problem. An unusual one. For, in practice, we know virtually nothing about that lost hundred years of our history, and especially the history of those indigenous folk we would generally describe as the "Celtic" Britons. For those who may be interested, I have set out, in the historical note, a few more details: of the actual resources available to us for the period; of the obvious flaws in those resources; of a possible interpretation for their meaning; and of my own largely irrelevant conclusions.

It is customary, when writing about the period, to use location names handed down to us by the fragmentary annals. So, for example, the story opens in the area generally known as the Kingdom of Gwynedd – northwest Wales – and inhabited by descendants of the tribe known to the Romans as the Deceangli. It is unlikely that anybody in those years would have used the term "kingdom" and, since English stands here for the language of the period – which I have chosen to call the Cousins' Tongue throughout the novel – I tried to find English words, which might at least conjure the meaning that those place names would originally have conveyed. Hence, Gwynedd becomes the White-Wilds, and the descendants of the Deceangli call themselves the Bough-Gatherer Clan. So I have merely used my own imagined version of sixth-century Britain as a setting, and the maps I have provided are no more to be taken as factual or historically accurate than, say, those in *The Lord of the Rings*, or *Game of Thrones*. The fifth of these maps simply shows the invented tribal clan names, using the Cousins' Tongue, and the territory they occupied, while the sixth map is a speculative reconstruction of a map, an itinerary, for the old Roman road I have called the Eleven.

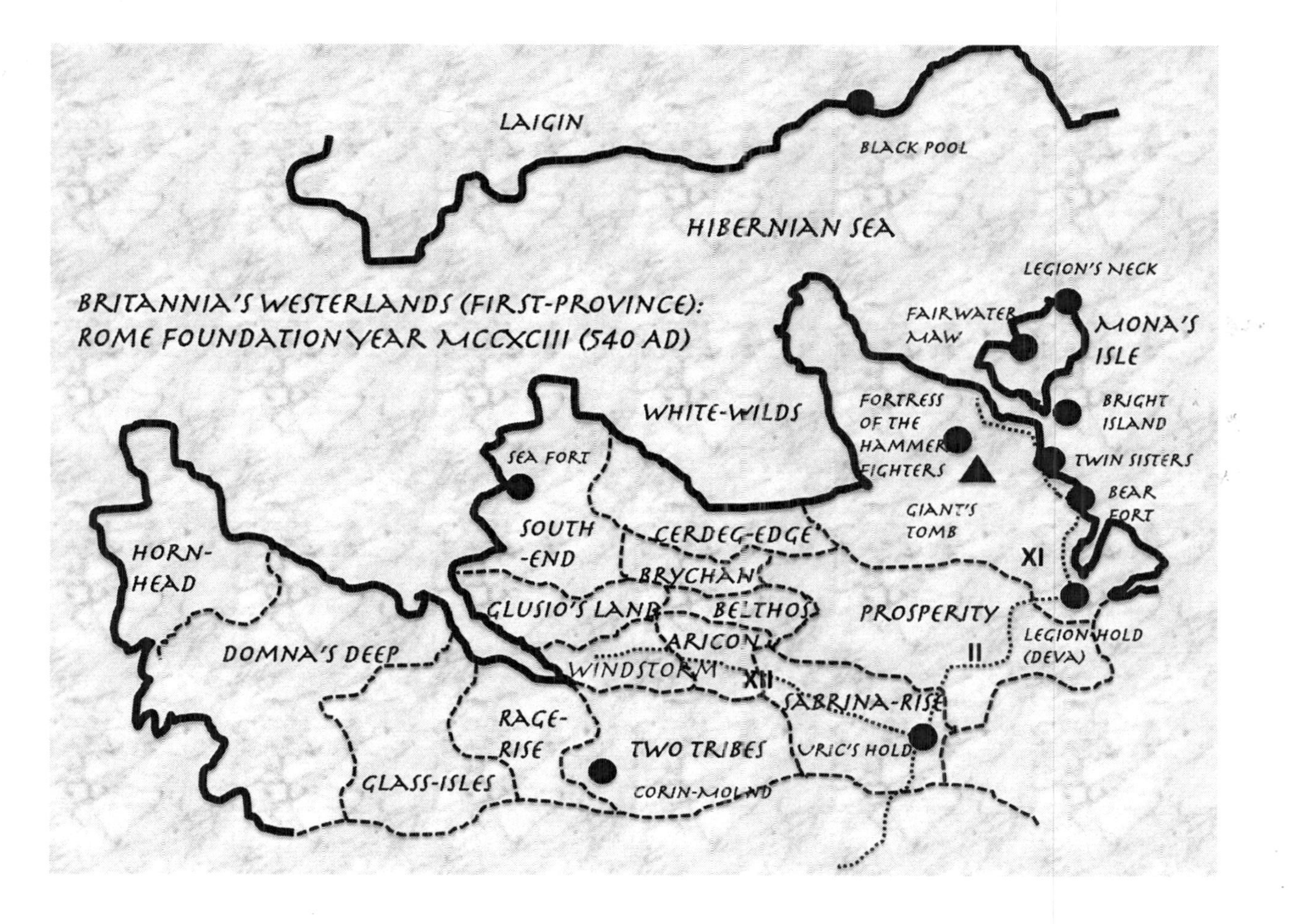
BRITANNIA'S WESTERLANDS (FIRST-PROVINCE):
ROME FOUNDATION YEAR MCCXCIII (540 AD)
LAIGIN
BLACK POOL
HIBERNIAN SEA
LEGION'S NECK
FAIRWATER MAW
MONA'S ISLE
BRIGHT ISLAND
TWIN SISTERS
BEAR FORT
FORTRESS OF THE HAMMER FIGHTERS
GIANT'S TOMB
WHITE-WILDS
SEA FORT
SOUTH -END
HORN- HEAD
CERDEG-EDGE
BRYCHAN
GLUSIO'S LAND
BELTHOS
ARICON
WINDSTORM
PROSPERITY
XI
XII
II
LEGION HOLD (DEVA)
DOMNA'S DEEP
SABRINA-RISE
RAGE- RISE
TWO TRIBES
URIC'S HOLD
GLASS-ISLES
CORIN-MOLND

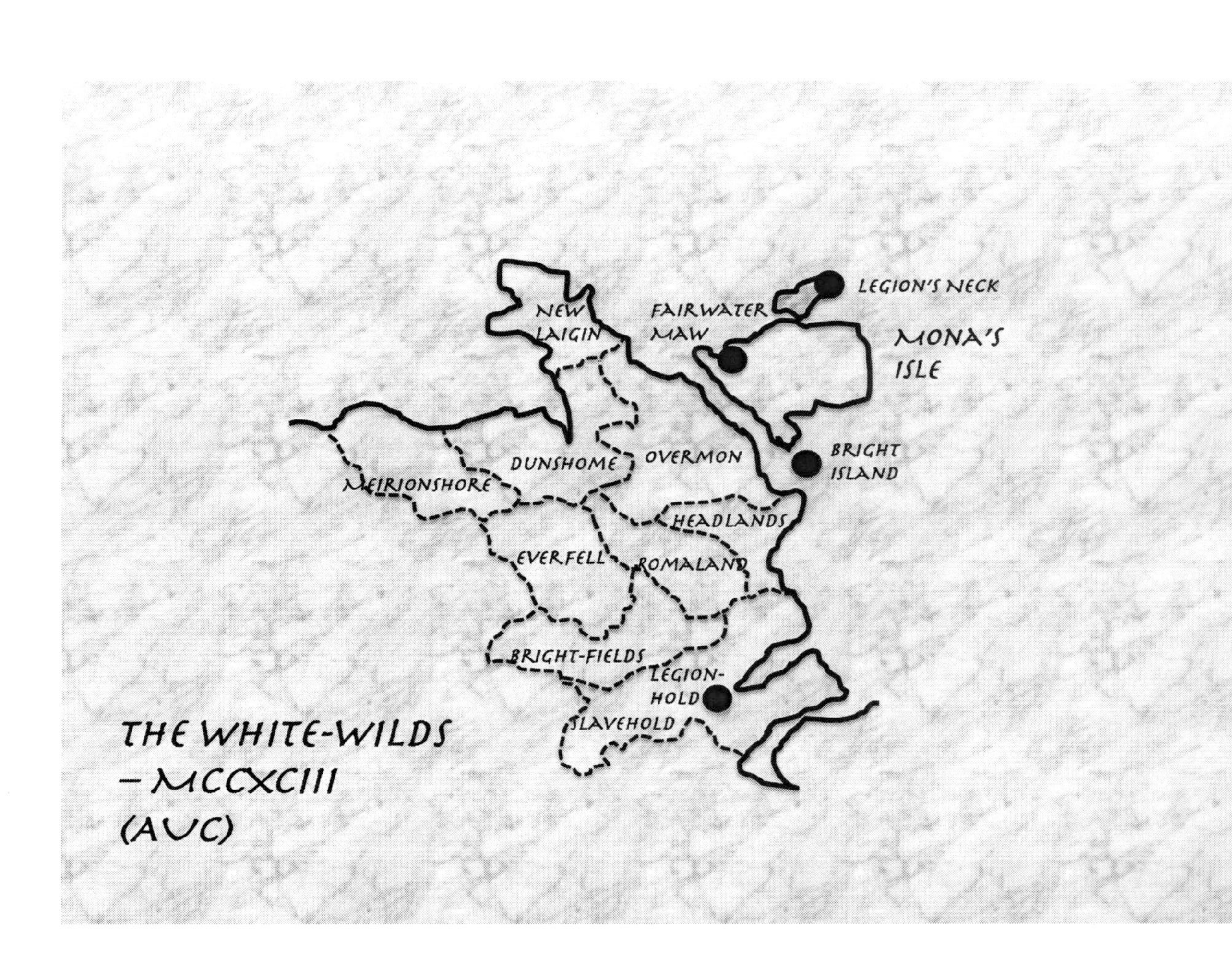
LEGION'S NECK
NEW LAIGIN
FAIRWATER MAW
MONA'S ISLE
DUNSHOME
OVERMON
BRIGHT ISLAND
MEIRIONSHORE
HEADLANDS
EVERFELL
ROMALAND
BRIGHT-FIELDS
LEGION-HOLD
SLAVEHOLD
THE WHITE-WILDS
– MCCXCIII
(AUC)

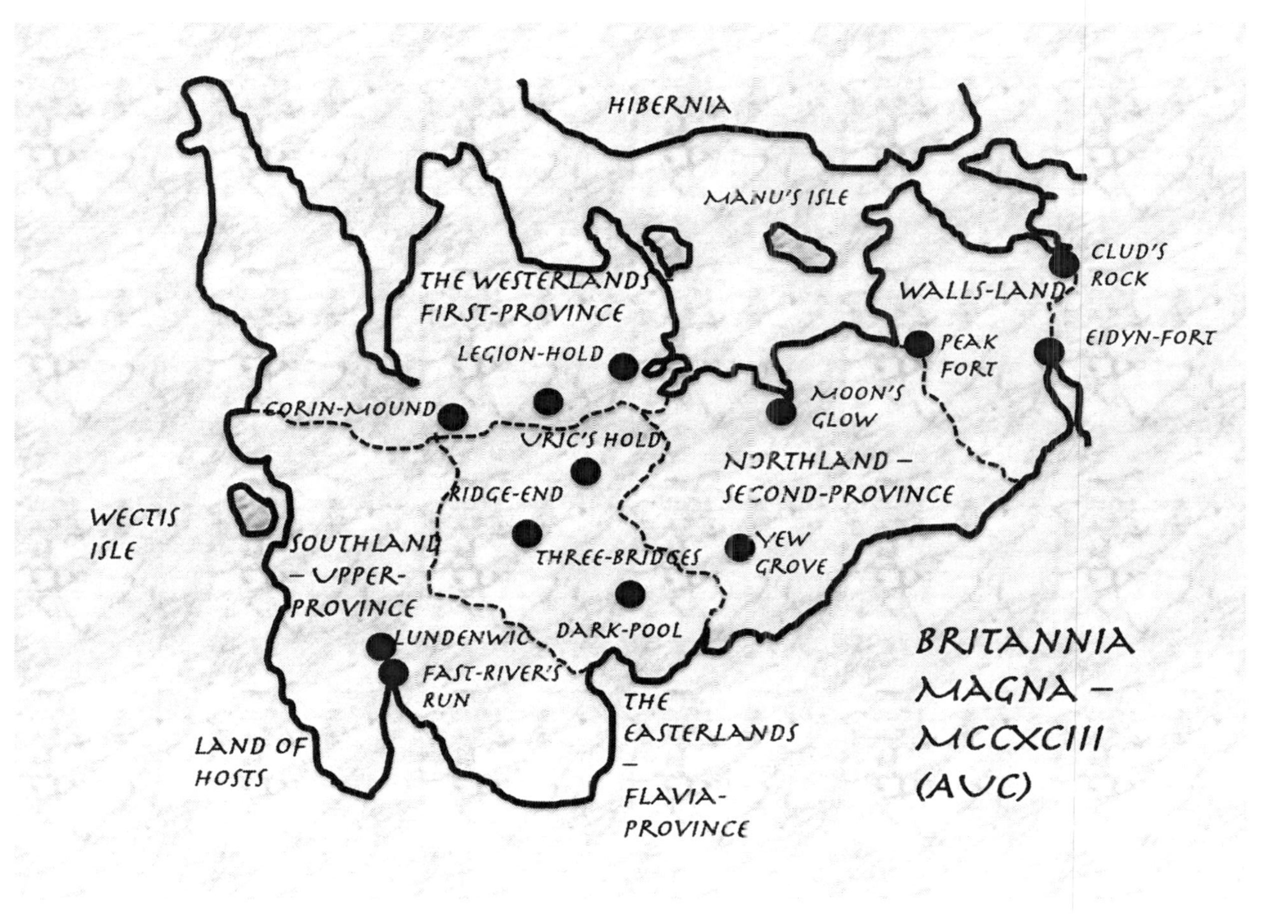
HIBERNIA
MANU'S ISLE
CLUD'S ROCK
WALLS-LAND
EIDYN-FORT
PEAK FORT
THE WESTERLANDS FIRST-PROVINCE
LEGION-HOLD
MOON'S GLOW
CORIN-MOUND
URIC'S HOLD
NORTHLAND – SECOND-PROVINCE
RIDGE-END
WECTIS ISLE
SOUTHLAND – UPPER-PROVINCE
THREE-BRIDGES
YEW GROVE
LUNDENWIC
DARK-POOL
FAST-RIVER'S RUN
LAND OF HOSTS
THE EASTERLANDS – FLAVIA-PROVINCE
BRITANNIA MAGNA – MCCXCIII (AUC)

NEWLANDS
CHANNEL
MANU'S
ISLE
CLUD'S ROCK
THE SEVERANUS
CLUD-
VALE
NEWLANDS
GIFT-GIVEN
VOTAN'S
LAND
EIDYN-FORT
BATTLE-
FOREST
GLITTER-
WATER
WHITE
HAVENS
ABUNDANCE
WESTWOOD
CRAVEN-
PEAK
ELM-
WOOD
HIGH-PASS
WALLS-LAND
(VALENTIA)
MAMMARY-
MAMUCIO
SOUTH-PEAK
EAST-
HAVEN
YEW GROVE
THE WALL
NORTHLAND – BRITANNIA'S
SECOND-PROVINCE: ROME
FOUNDATIONYEAR MCCXCIII

TRIBAL NAMES FOR BLOOD-KIN PEOPLES OF THE COUSINS' TONGUE, THE LANDS THEY OCCUPIED, AND PRINCIPAL SETTLEMENT AREAS OF INCOMERS AND OUTLANDER FOLK
1. HARD-FEET
2. BLOOD-SHEDDER
3. STAG-SON
4. KINDRED-HOUND
5. HORSE-HOLDER
6. DEEP-WORLD
7. FAST-POWER
8. HUNT-CHASER
9. VOTAR-LAND
10. HIGH-BORN
11. CAULDRON-BURNER
12. HORN-GOD
13. BOUGH-GATHERER
14. HAMMER-FIGHTER
15. LOUD-VOICE
16. ISA-RIVER
17. META-LAND
18. BATTLE-FIGHTER
19. GRAIN-RICH
20. TWIN-BROTHER
21. WORLD-GOD
22. PLAIN-DWELLER
23. RAGE-RISEN
24. INLAND-RUNNER
25. RIGHT-WIELDERS
26. HOST-HUNDRED
27. THREE-NEWLANDS
E. ENGLOI OUTLANDER FOLK
L. LAIGIN INCOMERS
S. SAESON OUTLANDER FOLK
Y. YUTI OUTLANDER FOLK

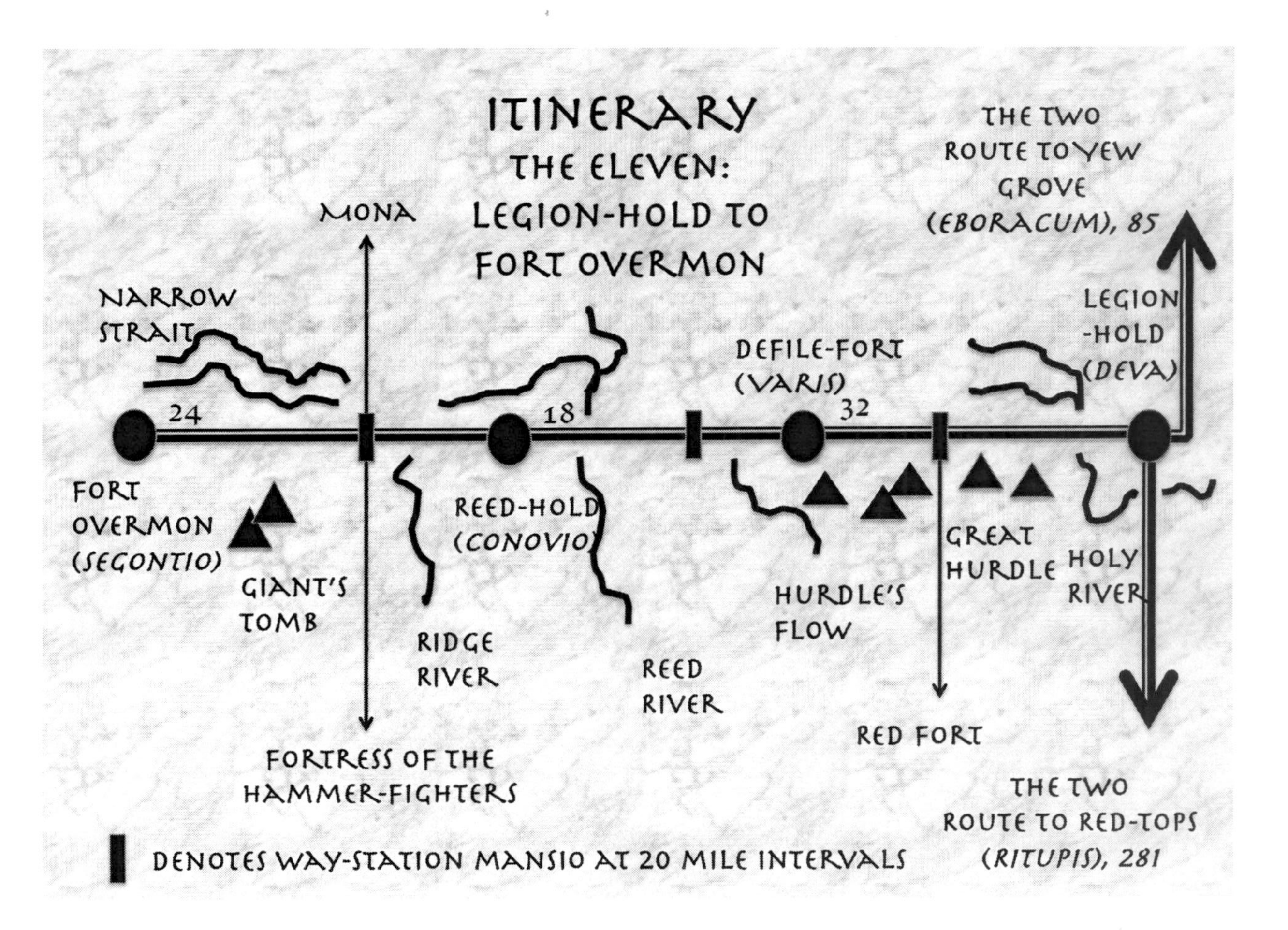
ITINERARY
THE ELEVEN:
LEGION-HOLD TO
FORT OVERMON
THE TWO
ROUTE TO YEW
GROVE
(EBORACUM), 85
MONA
NARROW
STRAIT
LEGION
-HOLD
(DEVA)
DEFILE-FORT
(VARIS)
24
18
32
FORT
OVERMON
(SEGONTIO)
GIANT'S
TOMB
REED-HOLD
(CONOVIO)
RIDGE
RIVER
REED
RIVER
HURDLE'S
FLOW
GREAT
HURDLE
HOLY
RIVER
RED FORT
FORTRESS OF THE
HAMMER-FIGHTERS
THE TWO
ROUTE TO RED-TOPS
(RITUPIS), 281
DENOTES WAY-STATION MANSIO AT 20 MILE INTERVALS

PART ONE

The Song-Sayer

Hear now my tale of time before time.
An endless sea's Great Rhyme.
Melody's threads, creation's chime.

Seas, in which a brine-foam
creature's born. Shapeless and free to roam,
until she finds the oak-grove home.

Lonely, lost, she sups on
milk-white seeds. Innocence flies, all gone,
brings forth Kernuno, Hornèd One.

Kernuno, first child – lost,
lonely too – grows to manhood, storm-tossed,
seeds his mother's brine-foam womb of frost.

She spawns them, gods of old.
Epona. Teutates. Herne the Bold.
Lug. Mapon. Taranis Storm-Cold.

Tugri Iron-Brow
Song of the Great Melody

Chapter One

It began where it would also end. In death. At a fording place on the Ridge River.

The waters still heavy with the melt menace of the new year's first fall of snow. Summer End's Eve and the Calends of November only recently behind us. Timid sunlight on mail-shirt and buckler boss, the rust-red rays barely piercing the filthy famine clouds that seemed hardly to have parted for a generation. Trees so bereft that the Oak Seers would have wept for the gods' blessings, beseeched promises of new beginnings. Forty foemen across the stream and blocking our advance. Spears shaken. Warriors shaken too: that chill-laden quaking as each man tested the depth and strength of his own mettle. Ash shafts crashing together. War hounds baying. A mortal challenge. While those on the further margin raged and ranted in return.

The Empire of the Caesars was fallen apart. Dread had been bred in the bones of my father and many of his lineage before him at its loss. The bereavement still whimpered within us, all this time later. The word swarms sang of turbulent histories, while we struggled to fill the emptiness we had been bequeathed. Blood lines broken, divided. The weather gods turned against us. Pestilence across the Hibernian Sea. South too, among the Horn-Head folk. A *pharmakos*, ritual blame-beast, sought. And who better than the Outlanders and Incomers? So the Saesons scourged for our uncertainties. At least until they learned to savage us in turn. Yet, for some little while now, a collective intake of breath. Pause taken. Hope for the future, I thought. A tally of our stock, and just the normal cattle raids and cross-border squabbling – like this foolish venture – to provide so much of our entertainment. A time of relative peace.

'Well, Master,' said the gleaming youth mounted alongside where

I stood, and his bare legs hanging down the pony's flanks, toes almost brushing the heather. 'Any lesson here for us? Apart from the obvious.' The weary sweep of his arm encompassed the frost-patched moorland before us, while his own hound, Charger, swung its great shaggy head at the movement, anticipating an instruction to hunt.

'If I owned a gold *solidus*,' I replied, looking up into those smoke-grey eyes, 'for every time I stood in the shield-press, I should now be the richest teacher in all Westerland. Though I've not yet fought in one that added even a jot to my betterment.'

The lad scratched at the red thatch inherited from his Incomer mother, wiped his fingers down the ring-mail coat that was one of his few conceits. It was always a delight to look upon his face, for his features shone, the skin translucent as though he were the living embodiment of Mithras himself.

'Perhaps you have always chosen the wrong side, Mentor.' He patted his pony's neck to hide the smirk I knew he was wearing. 'Or the wrong cause.'

'Puppy!' I snarled. His father, Owen White-Tooth, had enticed me from my previous post at Moon's Glow, on the strict mutual understanding that, in all matters pertaining to the education of this younger son, Ambros, my authority should be unquestioned. But reaching the pinnacle of one's career, or almost so, is a bittersweet affair. I had brought my body slave south with me but, unsure of the future, I had recently sold him into Owen's own service. Besides, boredom sits easily alongside even short-term success. Hence my willingness to stand in the battle line once more, though Lord Owen would have expected me to be present anyway, available to lend the lad guidance. Or protection.

'Insolence seems to be my birth right Master,' he laughed, holding up his hands as though to ward away some imaginary thrashing. 'But my father would hardly thank me if such a wealthy commodity as yourself should be lost for so little gain.'

He was certainly correct in this too. For, with the demise of so many schools and colleges, there was great demand for Mentors of my experience. There were plenty of lower-rank mentors, *rhetors*, as the Empire named them – Grammarians and Literators still ten a silver number. Plenty of our Oak Seers too, though the scope of their teachings no longer conferred meaningful status on their students. But Mentors? A prized symbol since most of my peers had taken their skills to Across-the-Sea – *Armorica* in the Common Speech – and beyond. But the current scarcity of Institutes in these nearer lands meant there was no way for me to progress.

'It would take more than those in-bred braggarts to bring us harm,' I sneered. 'Look. Not a horseman among them.'

Another fact. Our own force may have mustered no more than ten war ponies but, as things stood, those were more than enough to redress the imbalance in our overall numbers. If it ever came to blood, of course.

'There must be *something* to learn from this nonsense,' murmured Ambros.

Ahead of our outnumbered line, the elder of White-Tooth's sons, Einion, was riding back and forth, just beyond the enemy's bow and slingshot range, crowing his own Praise Names and rattling his javelins.

'No,' I said. 'Unless, perhaps, a finer detail about public speaking. Defective style, look. Your brother has agitated his great-uncle's men well enough. Fair play to him. Though where's the effect he seeks? To provoke an attack across the stream? It's Quintillianus's most essential point. The best of rhetoric is doomed to failure if the oratory is flawed.'

'They've been ordered to hold, for some reason,' said Ambros, the brightest of my disciples. 'But I'm disappointed, Mentor. That you didn't seize upon logics and philosophy for your theme. Contemplate the virtue of our expedition, maybe?'

'Ah, my Lord Skyhound,' I said, choosing to use his own Praise Name, 'you know very well that I hold no brief for the teaching of philosophical arts. Entirely beyond me. But since you seek to test my intelligence, let's look at the situation in which we now find ourselves. Your brother's wife runs back to her mother for reasons on which we shall not dwell. She seeks sanctuary from her mother's husband – who, sadly, happens to be your great-uncle. He arranges for her to take the Christ-followers' vows, though she's already a Song-Sayer for the Oak Seers. A fine one too, they tell me. And your brother chooses to invade the lands of her sanctuary rather than attempt diplomacy, arbitration or domestic reconciliation as his optimum solution. I think I might need to attain a Chair of Eloquence before I understand this one.'

Ambros leaned down so he could whisper in my ear.

'Besides all that,' he said, 'we have to face this too. That she's hardly a prize worth the shedding of any blood.' But suddenly he straightened, pointed across the Ridge. A group of horsemen more numerous than our own had crested a rise to the west, where a wooden wall could just be seen under construction. 'There,' Ambros sneered. 'The reason we're kept waiting.'

'Can you make them out?' I asked.

Below us, Einion Iron-Anvil had stopped his useless cavorting, drawn rein to also peer at the newcomers.

'Not much doubt about that one,' said Ambros, and I followed the direction of his finger to the absurdly tall rider trotting a little apart from the rest, towering above his pony's neck, knees bent sharply, his ankles almost touching his own buttocks, gripping the creature's hips. 'Rhun,' Ambros smiled. 'He'll have been taking a blessing from those piss-ditch Christ-followers up there.' The hilltop palisade marked the outer boundary of Bishop Deniol's newest hermitage, another *monasterios* to supplement those for which White-Tooth's uncle – the father of this Rhun the Tall – had already gifted several land grants. For my own part, I tended to follow whichever religious trend suited the politics of the day, though I had no great trust in any of them. Unlike Ambros, who whispered for the blessing of Mithras, even as we watched.

Rhun had dismounted now. Or, rather, he had allowed the pony to slip from between his legs, a warrior running forward to lead the beast away while its rider shook the cramps from his arms and legs. He carried a wicker shield, a broad-bladed spear in the same hand and, in the other, three well-crafted javelins.

'If this is a kin-visit, Einion Iron-Anvil,' he bellowed across the stream, 'why come you with so many hall-guards at your heel?'

'You know why I'm come,' Einion shouted back. 'To take home my wife from the Christ-followers.'

'My father's wife-daughter may come and go at her own will,' called Rhun the Tall. 'The monks do not hold her. And you, it seems, are incapable of doing so.'

'Now that,' I said to Ambros, 'was a clever combination of both rhetoric *and* oratory.' For Einion, stung by Rhun's barb, had slapped knees to his mount's flanks, running the pony into the Ridge's icy flow and, without warning, casting the first of his own javelins, which the other man knocked easily aside.

'Pits of the Dead!' Ambros groaned. 'No way back for us now.'

'Well, no blood spilled yet,' I replied. 'You never know.' Owen White-Tooth might hold his lands as a client lord to Rhun's father, Malco Battle-Shield – Malco Dragon's Isle – but the two men shared the same political aims just now and would not want their alliance sundered so easily.

'I offer the Champions' Challenge,' cried Einion, shattering my own optimism but to a collective sigh of relief from our own battle line. For a duel of that sort was rarely followed by further fighting, each side accepting, by unspoken agreement and custom, that a single combat should settle matters. Only Ambros, it seemed, shared no enthusiasm for the thing.

'Einion lacks the skill to deal with a bull like Rhun,' he said. 'Hold the hound!' And he kicked his pony forward, while I grabbed for Charger's war-collar. Ambros was gone before I could stop him and I should, by rights, have stayed at his side, but three of us clustered at the water's edge would have been absurd. Bad enough that we now seemed to have not one potential champion but two. A further provocation. And Rhun knew it.

'Ah,' he shouted, 'a brace of brothers. At least that will make for a more balanced bout. I will dedicate the double kill to the Mother of our Lord Christos.' And he made that shape of a crucifix that the Christ-followers favour though, when he sketched the crosstree, he did so by drawing the flat of his hand across his throat.

Surely, I thought, wrestling to keep the dog in check, *Rhun cannot intend this to be a death-match!* To be honest, I still expected the thing to end in a flurry of insults. A few cuts and bruises. The Champions' Challenge often ended in no more than a wound or two, but I feared then for the brothers. I imagined Ambros arguing that Einion should withdraw gracefully and, while Rhun may have taunted them both, everybody knew this could only be a contest between two individuals – so that, as I watched, the younger brother was sent packing, trotting back to my side, the lad's face grim and set.

'He means to go through with this,' Ambros muttered, and reached down to settle Charger's raised hackles.

'It takes only one,' Einion called out. 'And when you are defeated, Rhun Malco's Son, our path to my wife shall not be impeded.'

'May my soul be denied entrance to the Province of Heaven should it not be so,' Rhun replied. 'But now, unless I'm mistaken, you owe me a javelin.'

I barely saw the shaft leave his hand and neither did Einion, until too late. He made some effort to move the pony, but it had taken no more than a single backwards step before the pilum's tip pierced its chest. The creature screamed and staggered, collapsed in a fountain of pink-puked water, with Einion jumping clear only to stumble, fall splashing upon his arse as the shallow torrent turned to deeper red around him, bleeding away towards the winter sea.

Ambros raised a hand to cover his eyes, began to recite a litany from the Mystery.

'And I was become one with the Lion,' he murmured, 'at the Fourth Circle, in my alignment with Great Jupiter...'

He continued with the catechism, refusing to watch as Rhun swatted away each of his opponent's remaining javelins while Einion, for his part, was forced to leap about in an effort to dodge the incoming barbs that crooned his death dirge each time one flew from Rhun's cast.

'Look now,' I told Ambros, 'they're closing for the fight.'

'He's better with the sword at least,' said the lad, as his brother advanced to the middle of the ford and pulled from its sheath a blade of the legionary fashion, short and broad. It was, they said, the same that his ancestor, the Great Maximus, had carried into battle. All swords are precious, but this one had history too, a Manhood Blessing of great potency from their father, a symbol of White-Tooth's faith in his older son. A faith that, to me, now seemed misplaced.

Einion carried no shield, because he was capable of wielding a blade equally well with either hand – an unnatural gift, though one he employed to the confusion of any enemy foolish enough to come within its range. Though Rhun was no such fool, preferring to use his fighting spear to keep Einion at bay, feinting, probing his defences, using the wicker shield delicately, despite his bulk, to contain any thrust or slash that might penetrate inside his reach. And I had never before realised the depth of Rhun's ugliness. Yet it was perhaps his snarling battle-wrath that exaggerated the crooked, overlapping teeth, the hog-spawn eyes too tiny for the boulder block of his head. But every grunting backhand sweep of the spear shaft brought a chorus cry from his followers and even, it seemed from the black crows that wheeled about his head.

The Sword of Maximus sang its own response too, sighing, mocking the foe's efforts and then, at times, as Einion sprang from the water with the Dolphin Spin, it howled high and loud as though it would steal Rhun's soul long before it had any chance to approach that Province of Heaven which he seemed to value so much.

'The oaf is tiring,' I observed, as Rhun edged back towards his own bank.

'Is he?' said Ambros, through gritted teeth. 'Look how carefully he places his feet.'

And I saw that he was correct. Saw too, that Ambros would have given anything to go and drag his brother away. Their enemy stood now in deeper water, up to his knees, and giving Einion the appearance of a height advantage for the first time. An opportunity too good to miss, so that Einion drove forward. A crosscut with his right. Sleight of hand that transferred the grip to his left. And an overarm hack that would have cleaved Rhun's head like a marrow. A yell of triumph rose then in the throats of all our war-band. But it stuck there like a chicken bone, choked them all, as we saw Rhun crouch beneath the sword's swing, Einion falling onto the spear. He flopped upon its point like a hooked fish. And any premature victory cries turned to outpourings of grief, a howl of deepest pain from Ambros, so despairing that the roots of the Death Halls must have trembled.

'No, Ambros,' I told him, grabbing for his reins to restrain him, prevent the lad from riding to his brother. There was ritual and honour law involved in the Champions' Challenge, the danger of being oath-broken if he interfered.

He sobbed then, the last occasion, I think, on which I ever saw him do so. And Mithras be praised that the lad could not watch the following moments as Rhun cast Einion's still thrashing body down into the stream, put a foot on the convulsing throat and prised the Sword of Maximus from the twitching fingers.

'I too,' Rhun laughed, 'give Einion Iron-Anvil the Manhood Blessing.'

I only wish that Ambros had kept his gaze averted, but he looked up then, in time to see Rhun grab a handful of Einion's hair and, pulling the head clear of the water, sever it with a single stroke of the blade, so that the lifeless torso and limbs were released back to the Ridge's embrace, hot gore gushing into the freezing stream. But Rhun was not yet finished, took the sword and plunged it through Einion's chest before making the sign of the cross once again.

'I swear by my Lord Mithras,' Ambros groaned, 'that I shall take that sword and avenge my brother's death – against Rhun the Tall and every other Christ-follower who crosses my path.'

Rhun could not hear him, of course, for the chanting of his men, the calling of his Praise Names, though it almost seemed as though he responded to the Skyhound's pledge, his own voice carrying clear above the tumult.

'Know this, Ambros,' he bellowed, 'that the worthless land on which you stand today, you may keep. At least, until my father, Malco Battle-Shield decides to claim it back. Or call your clan to account for this breaking of the client-oath. Yet should any of your kin, or any of your blood-fellows, attempt to cross the Ridge without authority, their fate will be the same as this worthless piece of crow-carrion.'

He held up Einion's head for emphasis, pulled free his spear, but left the sword in place. A strange thing to do, I thought, considering its worth. Yet I wonder now whether Rhun had some inkling, even then – as neither myself nor Ambros had yet discerned – of the curse that hung around that weapon.

'I swear by the Seven Circles,' Ambros was saying, 'that, one day, we'll be done with all this foolishness. No more petty lordships. Those lands across the Ridge part of a united whole once again.'

'No wider ambition?' I murmured.

'Oh yes,' he snarled. 'One day, a common cause. A cause for which standing in the shield-press may bring betterment to us all. A cause to bind us fast against this god-cursed Endless Winter. A start to driving the Christ-followers all their long road back into the sea.'

Wild dreams, on all counts. For even his own father, old Owen White-Tooth, had moved from initial ambivalence to active enthusiasm for that faith. And Lord Owen was, after all, my patron. Besides, the Christ-followers seemed as thick upon the ground as all the devotees of the Elder Faiths combined.

'Perhaps the Christ-followers –' I began, thinking to suggest that they may also by now be too defensively ditched to be so easily shifted. But Ambros was already kicking his pony to the reed-line. He could be reckless at times. It came, I supposed, from having lived a charmed life so far, in which he had never once taken any wound or injury. Yet he was safe enough, I saw. For Rhun the Tall, with Einion's head hanging by its hair from his belt, had gathered his javelins and was leading his warriors away towards the Narrow Strait and their homes, while Ambros dismounted and splashed to his brother's side.

And there he set both hands around the sword's heavy hilt, used all his considerable strength to pull the blade free from the body of Einion Iron-Anvil while, for my part, I thought I saw a flock of bats startled from their caverns and filling the evening sky with beating, leathered wings that carried away any hope I might have nurtured for a bright new future.

Chapter Two

A whole year and more had passed. The year Twelve Hundred, Ninety-and-Four, City Foundation Year, *Ab Urbe Condita*. Another in which the crops grew sparsely and game was scarce. A year in which the Light Six-Month was barely distinguishable from the Dark, and we asked ourselves how long this could continue. The sky still hung with those mysterious pastel clouds that occasionally rained ash and dust upon our heads. Crops failed. Gales blew hard. The snows came ever earlier, lasted longer. And there was little appetite even for the Midwinter Sun Standing that was almost upon us. It seemed like some poor jest to still be celebrating the Invincible Sun, or even the Birth of Mithras, when we had seen so little evidence of blessing for so long from either one or the other.

But there had been, at least, some brighter news since, from the Middle Sea, merchant ships brought words of hope. To some of us, though not all. For the Emperor of the East, Justinian of Constantinopolis, had sent that renowned commander, Belisarius, to reclaim the Diocesis Africanus and the island of Sicilia, then taken Rome itself back from the Gothi. Surely the Empire would now be made whole once more. Starvation banished. The sickness healed.

Yet every man, woman or child it seemed, had their own opinion on what was ailing in our own world. In the Headland territories of Owen White-Tooth, however, there was little doubt that the cause lay with just one man – Owen's uncle, Malco Battle-Shield – but more than just one event to blame. There was the death of Einion Iron-Anvil, naturally. The grief that had hung over us all ever since. This ignored the obvious fact that the summer-starved years had begun long before the Champion Fight at the Ridge Ford, or even the problems that had developed between Einion and his wife, Morgose. So another reason must be found.

'Ah,' folk said, 'it all began those years ago when Malco decided to extend his own lands beyond Mona's Isle. To murder his first wife, Rhun's mother. Then to lust after another's woman, the bride of a Laigin nephew.' And they recalled instances when the gods may have been offended during the warlord's acquisition of neighbouring turf, this side of the Narrow Strait. A shrine of Isis desecrated here. A well of the Great Mother Cybele poisoned there. The mark of Bacchus smashed somewhere else. Curses accumulated.

Yet, even setting this aside, Einion's death still cast a long shadow. Ambros, of course, had pondered ways of taking Rhun's head as payment for that of his brother in a way that would not further rupture relationships between Malco and Lord Owen. And there were bitter days as Lord Owen himself consulted with an Arbiter, checked whether there might be some other way to seek justice. But the codes were all clear. It was Einion who had issued the Champions' Challenge and, while Rhun may have used excessive brutality in his reaction, excessive zeal in taking matters to the death, he had certainly not infringed any stricture, regardless of whether it may have been the Incomers' Judex Laws, or the Oak Seers' Missives, or the Empire's Twelve Tables. Nothing. Not even the Table Seven dictum about mutilation. And then, to add insult to injury – so far as Ambros was concerned – that same Bishop Deniol came calling, pouring some sanctimonious words of their Christian scripture to remind Lord Owen about the value of meek forgiveness. He was impressive too, and I wondered whether his own training included lessons in rhetoric.

As things transpired, I had a chance to ask him in those days before Midwinter, by which time Ambros had taken Rhun at his word and remained on our own side of the Ridge, yet occupying afresh the long-abandoned Auxiliary Camp that still stood at the river's estuary. The lad had inherited the much more impressive holdfast, previously his elder brother's birthright, at Bear Fort. But, for now, Ambros chose to leave those comfortable halls, our *ludus* and library there, in favour of this wind-swept relic of the Legions. The repair work was watched closely by one of Deniol's monks, set to spy on us, and we feared a trap when, one morning, the bishop sent the same fellow down to issue an invitation. A visit to the *monasterios*.

'Perhaps,' Ambros suggested, 'you could slip some poison in his cup while you're there.'

'You think I should accept the invitation?' I was surprised that he had not lapsed into another fit of rage, as he had become prone to do since his brother's death.

'What reason has he given for the invitation, Mentor?' he asked.

'Apparently the Christ-followers' Papa Bonifatius Secundus has died and they have chosen a new head for their Church, in Rome,' I replied. 'Some cause for celebration on their part, though I suspect he has other reasons for seeking our company.'

'Well, you do not require my blessing, Master,' Ambros smiled. 'And I'll not go myself. But be careful. They're a dangerous breed those Christians. The sooner we're rid of them, the faster we'll shift this cursed weather.'

'I must have failed in my duties if you truly believe it so, lad,' I told him. 'I was more impressed when you believed we might all make common cause against our trials.'

'With the Empire back in Rome,' he said, 'it makes that cause even more pressing. With Britannia restored, we might enlist the Emperor's help too. Perhaps you could ask your new friend, the bishop, to put in a good word.'

I considered the proposition carefully as I travelled to the *monasterios*.

'The new Father has decided to adopt the name Yohannes Secundus,' said the bishop, as he showed me the hermitage's chapel. Though, in truth, there was little enough to boast about in its wooden architecture.

'Adopted?' I asked. 'Shamed by his own name?'

The bishop may have laughed, but the eyes betrayed his annoyance that I showed no rapture at the scale of his timber temple. Yet I had seen more elaborate cattle byres in my time – with less shit in them too. And he vented his spleen upon the sow and her piglets that had gained access to his sacred hovel and defiled it with their ordure, lifting the skirts of his undyed woollen robe, kicking the beasts' soiled arses until their defiance turned to resignation and they finally grunted and snuffled an exit.

'It would hardly serve, Mentor,' he said, breathless but using my title to drip some sarcasm into the conversation. 'His birthing name was Mercurius.'

He pronounced the words with that distinctive dialect of the north-east, even though his family had lost their lands there two generations earlier, during the High-Pass Blight that we still sang about. And even his time in the south had done nothing to blunt the accent. Yet it was the significance I did not fully understand. Could it be such a bad thing? To be named for the messenger of gods? The patron of eloquence too, of course.

He led me outside once more, as though he possessed the local blood, like the dunghill's cockerel. Out into the open precinct that had been gifted by Lord Malco Battle-Shield. The precinct, therefore, now provided something of a sacred rampart between the feuding rivalries of the White-Wilds and Headland, while its woven perimeter fence also offered some protection for the religious community from the smoke-smeared wind and seabird song that rubbed relentlessly along the Straits beyond. Whether it would provide shelter from plague and hunger was another matter, but thought of the Narrow Strait caused me to glance cautiously beyond the palisade, still thinking of traps and not wishing to be caught on the wrong side of the Ridge. Yet Bishop Deniol steered me safely through a cluster of miniature huts that served the monks as cells, and towards the only ambitious building on the site, a rectilinear barn with a very fine tiled roof that I initially mistook for a gather house or dining hall.

'For a sect that eats the imagery of all it encounters,' I told him, 'would it not have made sense for the Father of the Church in Rome to keep the name of Rome's own deity?'

A carpenter was finishing some repair work to a corner post, not one of the holy brothers but an in-bred fellow come, I guessed, from the settlement, the *vicus*, that had sprung up alongside the bangor. As I spoke, Deniol was whispering something in his ear and the gap-toothed fool began to pack tools into his bag, all the while avoiding any eye contact with me. But I could do nothing except watch the carpenter scuttle off and wonder what words Deniol might have passed him.

'Sect?' the bishop replied, at last, lifting his fingers to his lips, his eyes to the heavens. 'There is but one god, Mentor Meridden, and one faith. Praise the Lord that the world is now learning this simple truth at last. I only wish you could have brought your young disciple with you.'

'To which of them do you refer, Bishop?' I tried to make it an innocent query, for I knew he could only be talking about Ambros himself. That young man had developed a certain reputation as a monk-mauler, and Deniol's raised eyebrow was all he needed to demolish my attempt at dissembling.

Go on! I thought. *Say the name. Speak the profanity.*

'*Puer Cuneglasus nomine, credo.*' You know the Latin, I assume? He was telling me that he believed the lad to be called *Cuneglasus*, and he smiled, having lapsed into the Common Speech, knowing the pitfall and stepping around its edge since, in our shared Cousins' Tongue, *Ambros* was synonymous with the word Divine, or Immortal – a heresy that the bishop was keen to avoid. So he chose the Latin word that spoke my disciple's Praise Name. *Cuneglasus*. Skyhound.

The bishop pushed open the heavy oaken door as if it offered access to my better understanding, inviting me across the threshold to enlightenment within. And I did, indeed, find illumination that day, even though the full thrust of revelation might not have dawned upon me all at once.

'Ah, yes,' I said. 'I left him busy at his studies.'

'The pagan art of rhetoric?' Deniol sneered. 'I wonder that a man of your intelligence should waste your time on such matters.' It seemed that I had my answer, then, without asking, to whether he might himself be a student of Cicero or Quintillianus. 'And he finds sufficient time,' the bishop continued, 'to molest and harass my holy brothers. Two of them are confined to their mattresses from the beating he gave them.'

I pretended to admire the carvings that adorned the vestibule's main braces and beams.

'A positive identification, Bishop, is it?' I muttered over my shoulder. Ambros had caught the monks on his own side of the Ridge, netting there for trout, beaten them senseless. Open and shut case. But Deniol ignored my cross-examination.

'They say the lad will seek revenge for the death of his brother,' said the bishop as we passed through the vestibule and into a large study room.

'He is a young man educated to understand the realities of life,' I replied. 'His brother issued the challenge and paid his price. And my Lord Skyhound is son to a client-chieftain. He knows his duty.'

'Yet he still pursues the so-called Mystery of Mithras too, I'm told,' Deniol sneered. 'Despite the epiphany of his own father. Does the lad possess no filial respect?'

There were a dozen lectern tables, crown-shaven monks perched at half of them, candle-lit and labouring with goose quill on vellum. A scriptorium.

'It is a faith that has survived five hundred years,' I told him, though I did not press too hard. Young Ambros was a staunch believer. It was one of his two passions. A dream that, one day, there may be a new congress of the world's great theologians, proofs provided that, despite the ravages of these Christian fanatics, the Mithraic faith was still alive and well. Yet a congress on that scale would require an imperial edict, and such a thing was unlikely. Well, impossible I should say. For each Emperor since Constantine had affirmed belief in the Christos as the official religion of Rome and Byzantium. And why should he not? It was quite a promise the Church had made him. All despotic deeds to be forgiven when Caesar finally entered the afterlife, while his citizens were being taught to tolerate all and any earthly deprivation on the basis that they would receive their reward in Heaven. And nobody ever came back to complain of being cheated, did they?

'Then he should visit this scriptorium, Master Mentor,' said the bishop, 'and he shall understand the reason for the success of our One True Faith and the demise of his Mithraism.'

'Its demise and its burial,' I smiled. For the monks and priests already had licence to systematically eradicate their rivals. They had even begun to claim that this Midwinter season marked the birthing day of their own so-called Saviour, rather than that of Mithras. It was partly the reason Ambros hated them so much. Indeed, I knew I was standing on the very spot where, beneath my feet, the local Mithraeum had now been filled with rock and rubble. And they had done the same everywhere they went, nowhere so spectacularly as in Rome itself, where one of the largest temples had been destroyed and the Christian Basilica of their Saint Peter built upon its ruins at the Vatican Mount.

'Oh, we shall bury that pagan aberration indeed.' It was the bishop's turn to smile. He normally walked with bandy-legged weariness, yet there was now a spring in his heavy step as he paraded from table to table, pausing at each to nod his approval at the quality of the work in progress. 'The new canon shall have only four testimonies to the Messiah's life. Saints Matthew, Mark, Luke and John. No more Pelagian heresies. No more interpretations. A single *biblia sacra*, a scripture that, by its very existence, shall scatter our seed over the entire world.'

'Each *monasterios* has such a scriptorium?'

'That is the instruction to every bishop of the Church. And I count myself blessed at the generosity of Lord Malco for providing this ground to our purpose.'

Given Malco's reputation as a wife-killer, this seemed something of a hypocrisy, yet I tried to ignore the mention of that Lord, my discomfort at being here on his lands, attempted to calculate instead the scale of the project that Deniol had outlined. But though my role as a Mentor required that I should teach geometry and other advanced forms of reckoning – in addition to geography, literature, music and public speaking – this particular test of the *arithmetica* was beyond my capability. Yet I understood, in general terms, the sheer enormity of the thing. It was masterful. Borrowed directly from the philosophy of the Empire itself, naturally. A single image of Rome had been exported and adopted across all lands. The concept planted that everywhere outside the borders of those lands there was merely *barbaricum*. The idea that those on the outside were the unfortunates. Those inside, the blessed. All members of one common family. In truth, like many of my generation, I still considered myself a citizen of Rome, even though the last of the Legions had marched away more than a hundred years before. And, despite the way they had abandoned us like orphaned children, to fight their own failed wars against the Gothi and Hunnoi, the image continued to shine bright. Yet was it possible for the Christ-followers to pull the same trick?

'And tell me, Bishop,' I said, for want of anything more intelligent, 'does your new Scripture finally reconcile the enigma of your Lord's name?'

It was a favourite taunt of the Mithraists. For, while they could recite the antecedents and history of Mithras with ease, these priests and monks still struggled to explain how they could not even find a better name for their own deity than *Christos*, the Greeks' word for *Anointed*. And *Yesu*? Another Greek translation, this time of a Hebrew name, Yeshua.

'You have not read the four testimonies, Mentor?' said the bishop. 'And you claim to be a scholar? They make the thing clear. That our Lord lived here upon the earth, though He was the Son of God. Lived among us in humble guise. As Yesu of Nazareth. Yet also as the Christ. The Anointed One. They tell me that one of our monks in Rome has now even been able to extrapolate from those testimonies the precise year of His birth, and that His Holiness has commissioned the development of a new calendar for the Empire. An *Anno Domini* calculation. When we celebrate that birth, in a few days from now, it will be the most glorious of moments.'

I did not press him on exactly when these testimonies may first have been taken down, for I knew that it mattered little. I admired them, these zealots. Yesu the Christ was now firmly planted in place and time, though I had never found trace nor mention of him in any of the excellent contemporary histories for that era that adorned our libraries. It was a wonder of modern invention and I marvelled at it. And then the development of these workshop scriptoria, the mass production of those holy books, churning them out like tiles from a factory kiln and, for each copy, a new missionary or martyr somewhere to help spread its doctrine. Such a clever use of communication. The modern world was changing fast, though this concept of a new calendar was ludicrous nonsense. Yet these Christians had established their own man-myth. Then built upon it in a way that it, too, like the Mystery of Mithras, might stand for five hundred years. Perhaps more.

For, wherever I travelled, their churches had sprung up along the way. They sprang up among those of our kindred blood, in all the lands from the Holy River to the Mud-Fast. They sprang up among the settlements of those Incomers who shared our boundaries and, latterly, our culture, but whose roots rested with the *foederati* transported across the Hibernian Sea to work the mines here when pestilence depleted our own folk – the mother of Ambros was such an Incomer, and the second wife of Malco another. The churches sprang up among the clans of their original homeland in Laigin and its neighbours. They sprang up among the other kindred of our Westerlands – the old First-Province, *Britannia Prima* in the Common Speech – and the other provinces, even those that are already riddled with the Saeson Outlanders, now so numerous that, in their own harsh tongue, they have the nerve to call *us* the foreigners, the *Welish*. They sprang up even across the Southern Sea – among all the other territories of the west, among the lands of the Frankoi too. And I recall those I had seen in my younger days, completing my education in the City of Clovis, in Parisius itself, or in the village of my lodgings there, upon the Hill of the Martyr.

The scale of it all!

I think it was then that the madness first entered me. For what if I, Meridden of Sea Fort, now Mentor of Headland, could do the same for my disciple? For young Ambros, who already dreamed of stellar futures.

'So tell me, Bishop,' I said, suddenly realising the lad's suggestion might not be such a bad idea, 'do you think that, with Rome itself now back under Justinian's control, we might see its blessing back upon our shores once more? Might your Holy Father Mercurius see his way clear to suggesting some help for us? Food supplies, perhaps? It would be an impressive miracle.'

'The Lord helps those who help themselves, my son,' he replied. 'And I understand the whole peninsula of Italia to be in a state almost as parlous as our own. The Gothi have not been kind to the land, they tell me. In any case, much of our current condition is a punishment by God for the heathen ways of so many here.'

It was hardly an answer that would pacify Ambros. Yet, of course, that was all before I felt the ground shake. There were hoof-beats, the noise amplified within those walls of studious silence. I had known, of course. From the moment Deniol had sent his tradesman off with the whispered weasel words in his ear. Yet my curiosity about the workings of the *monasterios* had lured me like a moth to a flame. And I remembered Rhun's threat. Any kin or blood-fellow of Ambros found on the wrong side of the Ridge, he had said, so that my Mentor's mind began to formulate my defence even as I turned on Bishop Deniol, gripped his flabby jowl between my fingers and squeezed until the self-satisfied smirk of treachery slipped from his face, eyes bulging as I pushed him back towards the door. He howled, his terrified monks tumbling from stool and table, scattering like hens away from our clumsy passage.

'You and your Christ be damned!' I snarled. 'Or have you just paid a debt to your true master? Well, I hope he appreciates it enough to give you a decent burial.'

'But you are a man of logic and learning—' he began, until I slammed him up against that door, drove all the breath from his bulbous body.

In truth, I had no plan. There was no other exit and I could now hear the pounding of feet, raised voices, barked commands outside. And my rage ebbed a little with the knowledge that, while killing the smug Christ-follower might be satisfying, it would not help me. So I threw the stuffed sack of wind aside, hauled open the door, and sprang forward to meet whatever fate might await me.

'There he is!' cried Rhun the Tall, squinting at me through those pig-like eyes. It seemed a superfluous statement, for the others of his party, all spears and shields, had plainly seen me too, spread in a half-circle that would afford me no escape route.

'What is this, Rhun Malco's Son?' I thundered, folding my arms and standing tall in that way I had been taught in order to assert authority over a crowd, an audience or even over wayward students. And, for a moment, it gave him pause.

'My father wants you,' he said, when he had remembered his mission. 'You can come quietly, or have it the hard way. Your choice.' And, in the end, I went quietly.

Chapter Three

And, so, I spent that particular Midwinter Sun Standing and Mithras-Birth confined in the most remote of Deniol's other hermitages, at the opposite end of Mona from the Narrow Strait. Rhun had dragged me there with no real damage done, and left me in the charge of the Christ-followers. He had refused to answer any of my questions though. Why was I held? To what purpose? For how long? Did he have no respect for my place in society? And, for pity's sake, why here?

The place was its own dungeon, a snow-capped island mountain beyond the main island, egress only possible at low water and then a full day's hard march through deep drifts to reach the Straits. And, by that time, the *monasterios* bell would have set every islander and his dog upon my trail. Thus, once I had given up waiting for the rescue that I knew, in truth, would never come, I resorted to exploring the ice-rimmed cliff tops of that haunted headland, a place of great beauty. It was my only salvation and blessing as I dreamed of the feasting that would have warmed my days had I been left at liberty among my own. I was no great observer of Mithras-Birth as a religious event, but I loved the sense of family and community it generated. In truth, I remembered little of my own early family life in Sea Fort. My mother had died in a house fire when I was small and my father, more interested in his business than my upbringing, had fostered me to a cousin in Calunium at an even younger age than was normal. A painful separation from my sister, Mirian, but I remembered those Midwinters at Calunium with huge affection. Nostalgia. Blazing fires. Food a-plenty. Fears set aside awhile since, Midwinter behind us, there was now the prospect of the sun's return once more. Songs of the Invincible Sun. And I had expected that, here in the *monasterios*, some of that joy and optimism would have transferred itself to the Christ-followers' own celebrations. If they had now determined that this was, indeed, also the birthing day of their Yesu, surely it might warrant some special attention. Yet the pattern of the monks' day seemed little changed from its normal routine. Their singing in the Latin may have been a little longer than usual, the form of their *missa* extended, but the message seemed much the same.

Even the Januarius Full Moon brought little additional joy among them, though, for me at least, it delivered word that I was finally to be moved – to the halls of Malco Battle-Shield. A propitious moment, I hoped, yet you would hardly have known it from the sombre mood of these monks providing my escort along the white-shrouded road. They had been my only regular companions since my imprisonment, several weeks earlier.

'I shall miss the cliffs of the Cauldron,' I said to the nearest of the monks – and searching for at least an intimation of whether I should be returning there – as we crunched through the last miles towards the Fairwater's Estuary. But he would be no more drawn into conversation than throughout my time with them. The food, of course, had been even more bland than their company, and no dietary reprieve at the large settlement nearby either. Legion's Neck. Three Roman walls remained intact there, with the sea itself serving as the fourth angle of their defences. The buildings were occupied within, beside the new housing erected between the stronghold and the still just functional bathhouse. Yet the citizens less welcoming even than the monks and, besides, I had not a silver slug with which to purchase supplies. Nor bathhouse services. Nor even a whore's smile at the port's crumbling quayside.

I was not sure what fate might await me at Malco's court but, by this time, I had put myself into that state of resignation that I normally reserved for travelling, in which the senses were suspended. Yet, as we drew near to the Fairwater, the roads on that blanketed landscape became busier. A gathering had plainly been convened, though the traffic had nothing of celebration about it, no feast day anticipation.

We passed through a thicket of sparkling silver birch and there, before us, stood Fairwater Maw, Malco's metropolis. It was still some distance away yet dominated the promontory on the northern side of the dune-studded estuary, protected by a double wall of timbers and sheer ditches on its seaward sides, and an additional brace of ring-works on the nearer eastern flank with its bronze-bound entrance gates and watchtowers. A road snaked from the gateway too, past the old Legion walls, now mostly abandoned, down towards the harbour pool that sheltered in the citadel's lee from almost any direction of foul weather. Yet today brought only a slight south-westerly, a few benign flurries of snow, salt and shore-wrack on the breeze that did little more than ripple the surface around those craft still resting gently on the tide or sitting in the sands above the sinuous high-water mark, while harsh-voiced gulls navigated their way between a maze of spectral masts, swooping towards the shallows in hopes of scavenging whatever the fisher-folk toiling at the nets there might throw away. And such variety of boats. Countless shapes and sizes of fishermen's pot-bellied river craft. A score of coastal currocks with their oars and sails stowed safely. And even one of those wood-sided merchant gazelles that carried the restored trade from Carthago on the Middle Ocean to the Hibernian Sea – and, presumably, stranded there for the winter.

Yet the nearer we came to the Maw, the faster my air of resignation slipped away and my guts began to heave. It may be one thing to stand in the shield-press, a good companion at your shoulder, the rage-mist in your eyes, but this was something else entirely, and I was hardly cheered by the sight of Malco's Memory Stone set below his gates. It stood twice my height, the rock smoothed, then carved with eternity knots, depictions of heroes, rows of battle trophies, weapons and human skulls – the whole finished in sapphire blue, in ruby red, in amber yellow, in emerald green, and in nacre white. It was an ancient memorial and, once upon a while, Malco's bloodline that ruled before him would have hung here the booty from their raids and conquests, the severed heads of their foes. Yet now there was only one such souvenir, and the enthusiastic grin of Einion's desiccated, eyeless face was there to greet me – the first friendly features I had seen for some time. The poor fellow had not been well used, although there was at least a tiny garland of early winter-blossoms on the snow beneath. Somebody cared, it seemed.

The monks crossed themselves, of course, but I merely nodded my greeting to that foolishly fallen young man, turned over in my mind some long-neglected blessing for the dead, while the oldest of the Christ-followers continued up the hidden path, passed through the false-way, and stopped beneath the gatekeeper's watchtower, where he began that ritual game of craving admittance. Yet we were not long delayed before

Rhun was summoned and arrived to greet us, heavily cloaked against the bitter weather.

'Brother Flavius,' he boomed. 'This learned guest has been handsomely accommodated, I trust?'

The old monk seemed confused, stammered something about his instructions, to such an extent that I felt the need to rescue him.

'Handsomely indeed,' I said, without any trace of sarcasm. 'I was remarking earlier that I should miss the place.' Well, it was worth another try.

'If today does not go as my father wishes,' Rhun sneered through those crooked circle-stone teeth, 'you may have the chance to take root there.'

I doubted that he meant a place to settle down and live in peaceful retirement.

'Today?' I ventured, as we wound up through the four lines of defences; the dead and deep-blanched grounds between; the succession of lifting bridges across each sharp-sided ditch; the inner gateway towers; and past the townsfolk moving in the opposite direction to go about their daily routine – until we finally entered the holdfast's heart with its randomly placed thoroughfares, its mix of hut, workshop and housing styles cluttered around the central palisade and Malco's inner *sanctum*.

'It seems that Owen White-Tooth and his second brat place some value on your hide after all, Mentor,' he said.

'They're here?' I asked him, knowing there was fear in my voice, from the dread that I had been used as bait. And to what purpose I dared not think.

'You disappoint me, Mentor,' said Rhun. 'I'd expected a more impressive display of indifference. Or perhaps concern for their fate has wiped away your training.'

I said nothing further as we approached Malco's Great Hall, part from fear of betraying myself once more, part from awe at its dimensions. It must have measured fifty paces by twenty, its snow-crusted thatch thick and sloping almost to the ground and when we were at its threshold, the portal guards thrust open the deeply carved doors and sang Rhun's Praise Names. Rhun the Tall. Rhun Malco's Son. Rhun Long Cast.

Rhun Einion's Bane, I thought, as my eyes began adjusting to the interior's flickering light. A fire smouldered and smoked in the central hearth pit, while raucous conversations sparked and crackled about the long-benches, from which vine-etched ribbing crooks rose to support the tie-beams, purlins and ridge tree. At night the whole space would fill with the exaggerated passions of the Bacchus brews, and then I should have feared for my life, since these wild folk of Mona, more Incomer than blood-kin, became easily crazed in their cups – something else that Ambros had inherited from his mother. Yet, for the moment, the gathering seemed sober enough, almost intense, as though summoned for a senate meeting, though making more noise than a flock of starlings.

Rhun pushed me forward and I added the extra offence to that tally of debts that, one day, I would settle with the man. But I chose to make my way, as required, between the hounds, past the crowded platforms of the long-benches where my monkish escort was abandoned, while Mona's duty-holders observed my passage, pointed fingers, grunted, or spat upon the straw. Their noise was certainly not diminished by my presence, however, and it must have been only the keenest of them who could discern anything of the proceedings. Yet I pressed towards the draped wall and its raised gallery that separated this public chamber from Malco's private domain. And there, on the gallery's high throne, I could make out the exaggerated bulk of Malco Battle-Shield himself, holding court, shouting, thumping his fist against the chair's dragonhead handholds.

'Proof?' he was yelling at somebody within his audience, spittle flecking his gorse-bush beard. 'You demand proof?' The pale robes of that deceiver and web weaver, Deniol, showed at Malco's left side and, at his right, the ash-pale feline features of his second wife, the White Lady of Laigin, Murgain. And as, at Rhun's insistence, I pushed between the council members growling before the gallery, Malco noticed his son's presence as well as my own. 'At last,' he sneered. 'Here's your damned proof.'

Heads turned. Movement among the crowd. Somebody spoke from the gathering's core.

'Master!'

Ambros. So it was true. He had been lured here. And presumably requiring some evidence that I still lived. Gratifying, though I merely nodded a curt and formal greeting. Nothing more. Just a simple reminder that we must remember our respective positions, maintain our dignity until we each understood the purpose of this gathering. Perhaps he already knew – though from the wary caution in his eyes, I doubted it very much. And my doubts were strengthened when the lad's father gripped at his tunic sleeve, urging the son to be still.

'Easy, Ambros,' said Lord Owen. His head, apart from the drooping moustaches, was smooth as a lead sling-almond, the upper lip cleft to reveal the prominent tusk that gave him the Praise Name, White-Tooth. I offered him a salute, right fist upon my heart.

'My Lord,' I said to him, though again keeping my voice flat and level.

'I told you, Nephew,' Malco sneered him, 'we have kept your investment safe. A simple security to underline the sincerity of my invitation.'

A young woman spoke from away to my left. Her voice carried clear, a ringing bell above the babble, and despite the low rumble that emanated from the throat of the hound around which she was draped – the largest deer-chaser I had ever seen.

'Why should anybody want such a thing?' she said. I wondered at first what she meant, then realised she meant *me*. I knew her only by reputation. Malco's wife-daughter, Rigantona. I had never seen so much hair upon one person in all my life, so thick and crimped that her face was almost entirely hidden. How old? About the same age as Ambros, I calculated. Strange accent too, that betrayed the Gathelic she must have learned as a child in Laigin, though her grasp of our Cousins' Tongue seemed flawless.

'Sadly, my dear,' said the girl's mother, Lady Murgain, 'my husband's people surrendered the teaching of their children to the *Rómhánach*. They are now reliant on such as this one.'

Well, I thought, *that's only part of the story*. There was still as much thirst for education as there would always be, but I had spent long enough in other lands to see how the wind was blowing. Other influences. From the Outlanders. From the Frankoi. From Deniol's Christ-followers. The learning fashions of the Empire fading fast.

'Not entirely, Lady,' I offered, perfectly capable of controlling my tongue when any other danger threatened, but a fool to precipitate folly when my profession was under attack. 'The Bard and the Oak Seer are respected here as equally as in your own former homelands. Song-Sayers like your second daughter.' It was a stinging reminder of Einion's fate. 'But a mind closed to the learning of other cultures,' I pressed on, 'is a book shut upon life.'

She flicked a dismissive hand in my direction – this enchantress for whom Malco had already slain one nephew – while I became aware that there was also a murmur of quiet translation taking place, though I did not know the language. Some form of Aramaic, I imagined, and shared between a brace of richly robed merchants, grown fat on the over-priced grain on which so many folk depended, and the under-valued gold, silver or tin that we traded in return – and now seemingly stranded here as surely as their ship.

'That is well-said,' one of them declared in the Common Speech, the *sermo vulgaris*, that form of the *lingua Latina* we each learned at our mother's knee.

'What did he say?' asked the girl, Rigantona.

Well, it made the point of itself, did it not? The rest of us could have used the Common Speech to converse anywhere from the Wall to the borders of Parthia. Yet, fortunately, not all the Incomers were so insular and the mother of Ambros, as well as his father, had embraced the need for him to enjoy the most complete of educations. But after Ambros? After my current crop of disciples? My future work prospects looked less than secure. All the same, it was the here and now that troubled me for the moment, though the presence of these merchants eased my concerns a little. It could be neither normal council nor judgement meeting if such outsiders were allowed to take part in the proceedings.

'Never mind!' bawled Malco, and slammed his fist upon the chair's arm again. 'Here is your Mentor. And we're not gathered to discuss the price of his release. Only to settle some related matters.'

'The price of our Mentor's release is already paid, Uncle,' said Lord Owen. 'Is it not? You promised that if we danced attendance upon you, he would be freed.'

'I think,' Rhun smiled at him, 'we promised he would rot within the bishop's hermitage at Legion's Neck if you did *not* come to us.' He turned to me then. 'That's not the same thing, is it, learned Mentor?'

'He's a Mentor,' snapped Lord Owen, 'not a bloody Grammarian. But why insult me with this ransom demand when all the other lords of the White-Wilds are come here in free council? Do you dishonour me, Uncle, by doubting my allegiance oath?'

I looked around at the others who were present, each with his own entourage of duty-holders. Mabon Modron's Son, Lord of New

Laigin. Custain, of Dunshome. Kei of Meirionshore. Alios of Everfell. Cullough of Bright Fields. Bran of Romaland. Yet I saw that Lord Owen was mistaken. Or overlooked the fact that one, at least, was missing. Cundruin from those wide lands of Slavehold that rose above the Holy River. Lands rich with lead, copper and silver. Though perhaps there was some already acknowledged reason for his absence.

'I considered some leverage might be necessary,' said Malco. 'That's true. But if I really doubted your allegiance oath, Nephew, it would have been more than your Mentor I would have taken. Besides, there are greater things to concern us here than family squabbles, Owen.'

'Greater things than the desecration of my brother's body?' Ambros cried. 'His head now adorning your Memory Stone as though we were the Hunnoi. Tell him, Father, that Einion's head goes back to Bear Fort or, by the gods...'

I recalled the garland of winter-blossoms.

'You challenge us in our own Hall?' spat the White Lady of Laigin.

'Shut your mouth, woman,' Malco screamed at her. 'When I want your interference, I'll bloody tell you to speak.'

The woman's eyes narrowed, the muscles clenching around those high cheekbones. Yet she complied.

'If I may, my Lord...?' said Deniol. 'Perhaps I might act as Arbiter here?'

'Does your court not possess the real thing, Uncle?' said Owen White-Tooth. 'If I'd known, I would have brought my own.'

'Our lands are well-served with Arbiter and Judex alike, old man,' laughed the girl, Rigantona. 'But in this Hall...'

'In *this* Hall,' Malco cut across her, 'the bloody women speak when they're spoken to. And I choose my own Arbiters here. Go on, Bishop. You were saying?'

Malco's second marriage was plainly not to his liking, and these Incomer Laigin women were a different creel of fish to the compliant mouse, now three years slain, who had birthed his son. Yet I sensed that Rhun was bristling at my side, unhappy at the way his father had spoken to the girl.

'Simply, my Lord,' said Deniol, 'that no civil law has been breached here, and no commandment of God infringed either. Yet I agree with your great-nephew. I hear the Voice of the Lord Yesu singing in my ears.

Render unto Caesar that which is Caesar's, he reminds me. Perhaps restore the Mentor to the disciple? The head of Lord Einion to the father? And let us proceed to the grave concerns of which you speak.'

Well, that was magnanimous of the bloated blusterer given that, at our last meeting, I had handled him so roughly. There was a complaint from Rhun, of course. To hell with Caesar, that sort of thing. The head belonged to him, he said. A legitimate battle trophy. A yell of agreement from the spear-hawks in the body of the hall, those younger men who served others in the hope of earning land of their own; or while waiting to inherit from their fathers; or seeking cattle-wealth as a prelude to taking a wife; or in payment for freedom from bondage; or, in rare times of need, called out as a militia.

'The advice of Yesu the Christos is good,' shouted Malco, waving aside his son's objection and hammering at the dragonhead handgrips for order among the crowd. 'It pleases me to grant these tokens.' But he sought in vain for any sign of gratitude from Owen White-Tooth or young Ambros Skyhound. *Render unto Caesar*, indeed. 'And now I call upon this council to understand the blight that is upon us,' Malco continued. 'Two pieces of news brought to us by our merchant friends.'

The first part of their story was simple enough. Their fleet had set its normal course for the southern coast, to pick up their cargo of tin from the folk of Horn-Head, but they had found the ports closed to them. The Yellow Pestilence. And I saw a space open around the two captains, the crowd drawing back from them even at just the mention of the Black Hags.

'Closed to us,' said the merchants' spokesman. 'The ports. Each of them. Delayed us so badly that we could not make the journey home before the blizzards closed in. Do you think we would still be here to tell the tale if we'd made contact with the infected?'

I doubt that anybody was fully convinced but he was right enough. Three days voyage here from Domna's Deep, their subsequent forced stay at the Fairwater Maw, and they would have shown the signs, plain enough, many weeks ago.

'So we know what to expect,' said Deniol. 'The wrath of the Lord is upon these islands and there are always those who try to run before the plague's storm. Always fail too.'

The normal trade restrictions were therefore to be put in place.

Word spread. Watches strengthened, wherever possible, at the obvious territory markers, at the way-stations on high roads, at the mountain passes, and at fording places. We were far to the north of Horn-Head but the Black Hags were no respecters of distance.

'And what word from Cundruin?' asked Cullough of Bright-Fields. The question was put rapidly, pressed hard upon the heel of the previous discussion. Almost unseemly haste, I thought.

Malco seemed troubled, considered his words carefully before he spoke them.

'That brings us,' he said, 'to the second purpose of our council. It seems that Cundruin no longer considers himself a part of this federation. And you know nothing of this, Lord Cullough?' Cullough grovelled, begged to be believed. He had heard not a word. Not a single word, he swore. 'Well, we shall see,' Malco continued. 'But you all know what this means. Slavehold has broken its bond and that cannot be allowed to stand. Too many threats that face us. And the collective strength of the federation is the very key to our defences. Yet every year there's something new. One lord or another will tell me how his people cry out for independence. They belong to this tribe or that. They complain about paying taxes to meet the needs of the whole. Our grain grows strong while another's crop fails, they say. Why should we help them? We have our own mines, they tell me. Rich enough to stand alone. But they forget that the Empire is back in Rome once more. How long will it be before the Legions return? How will we then be seen to have failed in our own duties? The *civitates* in ruins about our ears. So I have reached a decision, my friends.'

He spoke for a long while, then. About the problems of holding his federation together, his territory of the White-Wilds, in this somewhat isolated corner of a former Province. But he had spent the year in dialogue with others. In the South-End lands. In Sabrina-Rise. Elsewhere. There was support, he said. Not universal, but enough. Sufficient allies to forge the western-most province anew. Rebuild First-Province. Common trading pacts. A defence plan. Sufficiently strong to hold off any threat. And doubters like Cundruin of Slavehold to be dragged kicking and screaming back into the fold, or pay the price for their refusal. It was ambitious, but I wondered how the plan would sit against the even greater dreams of Ambros Skyhound. The forging of not one former province but all four, into a single entity. Greater Britannia. *Britannia Magna.* A goal that even the Empire had never achieved. Malco's basic concept was sound enough. We needed to all pull together, pool our resources, if we wished to survive. But the collective strength of Westerlands alone would surely fall short of our needs. I saw Ambros shake his head in dismay. And then the lad's father stood forth.

'Then tell me this, Uncle,' said Lord Owen. 'You said we were not gathered to discuss the release of my Mentor, but to settle related matters. If you plan to unite the Westerlands once more, you shall have the support of Headland in that worthy endeavour. But how else is that a matter which requires settlement between us?'

'Because, dear Nephew,' Malco sneered, 'the normal bond of blood between our families was plainly not enough to prevent Einion from breaking his wedding vows and then rampaging across my lands while my attention was turned elsewhere. So we shall correct that wrong. The support of Headland in uniting First-Province I demand as a right. But how do I also guarantee the fidelity of this second son, this Ambros Skyhound?'

'Father...' Ambros burned red with indignation, turned to Lord Owen, the insult against his integrity spurring him to protest, though the words were never spoken, his father's fingers raised, pressed against the lad's lips.

'Quiet, boy,' said White-Tooth. 'Hear him out. It's only fitting.'

'I think we all know why the marriage between Einion and my wife-daughter could never succeed,' Malco sneered. Yet the council members and the spear-hawks at our back remained largely silent. After all, a man's sexual preferences were not to be made the stuff of public jest, and especially not when the man's father was Owen White-Tooth. But few of us had been able to understand the match, and there had been many who thanked the gods for Morgose's blindness, that she might not be able to see what was happening under her very nose. Yet she was an Oak Seer Song-Sayer and, sightless or not, I well knew their capacity for perception – though, of course, I still had no inkling about the true extent of Morgose's power. 'So the next one...' Malco continued, allowing the four words to penetrate even the thickest skull, '...shall be hedged about with more guarantees.'

I believe that both Ambros and the girl, Rigantona, must have seen what was coming next at the same time, for the cry of outrage, which each of them emitted, was perfectly attuned to that of the other. Almost a happy omen, a portent of harmonious understanding, of empathy between the couple. Yet I knew, that in the case of Ambros Skyhound, the protest was driven by a bitter memory. For he had already been wed. Some years earlier. To Brock of the Tusk's young daughter. She had seen just fifteen summers, then died in childbirth. The babe too.

'Guarantees?' Lord Owen asked his uncle. He was always a man to get straight to the matter's crux. Though it was Deniol who provided his answer.

'This time,' said the bishop, 'it shall be a wedding that unites these young people in a bond derived from God, permanent and indissoluble, consummated in the eyes of God, one that shall redeem the evil and carnal act by the procreation of children.'

And that, I imagined him reprimanding young Ambros, *shall pay you back for the beating, which you gave my brothers.*

Yet I imagined something else too. The possibility that all this talk of unity might lead to another thing entirely. For the chronicles of our library still spoke to me of our recent past. A hundred years of civil war. Holdfast against town dweller. Town dweller against Saeson Outlander. Outlander against Laigin Incomer. Incomer against holdfast. For each had been convinced of the path forward and had pushed that path down the throat of any who believed otherwise. And we might have continued doing so had the new realities not intervened. That brace of Titans, which had towered above our sad, internecine self-destructions. First, the Ice Demon of the Years Without Summer and the hunger that followed in his wake. And, second, the Black Hags of the Yellow Death.

So we had paused. Drawn breath. The hardships multiplying, but at least there had been peace, of sorts, while we pondered the tracks we must tread to survive. It is good to ponder. Though, as Quintillianus had taught me: "*While we deliberate how to progress a thing, sometimes it grows too late to even begin.*" And time, I knew, was no longer on our side.

Chapter Four

We fought. Once Einion's head was returned to his father. The now reunited remains interred afresh. And we fought as part of Malco's war-band of retribution. Against a still non-compliant Cundruin. All through the Light Half. Or whatever passed for summer in that year of yet more stunted crops, rib-thin cattle and half-starved ponies. But the folk of Slavehold did little to resist. For we avoided their high places. The holdfasts that sat astride the Great Hurdle. The earthworks and the wooden walls. Those knuckles, which gave that fist of their land its spine. So we stole their livelihood instead. Closed the mines. The Venus-blessed red-running cuprum shafts. Those leats and galleries of the black lead still yielding Luna's precious silver – though we left them with the dark ore itself, for the arse had long since dropped out of that particular market. And we ran off their livestock, held it against their better behaviour. Or blocked the drove roads. Fed fear to their cow-hands, even the toughest of them. Until we ran Cundruin to ground at Legion-Hold. At Deva's Ridge. Or just Deva, as both the Cousins' Tongue and the Empire had once named it, for the goddess. But it had become such a prominent fortress that it had earned the simple name Legion-Hold, setting it above all others. And, beyond Legion-Hold, the Holy River's incessant tumble of fresh flood finally tasted salt brine and was devoured by the tides of the Redstone Firth narrows.

Rhun the Tall had taken his own followers downstream, following the river's edge as it curved north and widened, across from the walls, past the old harbour, towards the ferry that Cundruin had negligently failed to destroy and which, we hoped, might allow us to cross the sacred waters, complete an encirclement of this difficult colony and prevent our enemy's escape. Lord Owen's spear-hawks were left at this southern bank, holding the nearer end of the town's only bridge, its farther side barricaded strongly against us and protected by the great walls of the fortress, three hundred paces beyond. They dwarfed the houses between but not the Arena, despite its crumbling. The village was a pleasant enough place to hold, though. An industrial settlement of brick-chambers, smelting furnaces, filled with the hammering of copper-beaters. All honest Minerva worshippers, not a Christ-follower in sight. A few good pot-houses too – in one of which Ambros and myself had become fond of taking the occasional jug of heather-beer.

'I don't suppose I need to be there for the bloody ceremony itself,' he mused, unable to take his eyes from the serving girl's wine-dark lips. 'Just a letter, d'you think, Master? With my own vows?' Ambros reached down and scratched the wiry hair between his hound's ears.

'There might be a problem with that, lad,' I replied. 'Apart from anything else, you'd have to write it in the Common Speech. And the *sermo vulgaris* doesn't seem to have been on the curriculum for your bride's schooling.'

He was gazing out past the rolled shutters to the Paved Way beyond.

'Or I could just ride,' he said. 'Out of the door, turn south and follow the Two all the way from here to Red-Tops. Then across the Channel.'

'By way of Ogfran's Ring?' I asked him. For there stood the tomb-mound of the girl he still counted as his wife. White-Blossom. And the boy-child who had died with her, never even named.

'I think of her every day,' he told me. 'I buried her with the silver body-chain she loved so well. And the little one wrapped in a tiny mantle. Cloth of gold. Then laid him on the skin of a boar I hunted for him. My first.'

He looked awful, had not shaved for more than a week, and his red thatch, normally so carefully cropped in the imperial style, was matted and filthy. Nothing to do with our raiding, either.

'I thought you had a repair plan for the roads,' I reminded him. 'We can't restore Greater Britannia for the Empire if you're away wenching in Across-the-Sea.'

'Just a stupid dream,' he said. 'Not even clear to me any more. Now that I'm trapped in this waking nightmare. And what does it involve, this Christ-followers' ritual, that makes it so binding?'

Well, there it was. Trapped. That was how he saw himself. The honour-oath given by his father to Malco Battle-Shield.

'I have asked,' I assured him. 'But it doesn't seem much different to the normal Gaius and Gaia stuff. Nothing to get excited about. Just the bishop's holy words upon the contract once it's signed.'

'A sacrifice?' said Ambros.

'Perfectly acceptable, so far as I understand it.'

'We can still slaughter the bull?'

'I think you may need to settle for a pig,' I told him, and he grimaced. Mithras set no real store by pigs. Not the cleanest of creatures. But the killing of a strong bull, or ox...now *there* was a commitment.

'And the fasting of hands?' he asked.

I shrugged, beckoned to the serving girl for another jug, wondered from which part of the world her forebears had originated.

'The same,' I said. 'More or less. They use the Roman Ribbon but we could always substitute that for a ropen ring. A closed loop. It will stand perfectly well for the Eternal Serpent.'

'That hair-strewn Christian bitch will know the difference,' Ambros snarled.

As things happened, Rigantona appeared at the wedding – they had chosen the Nones of Octubres for the ceremony – neither hair-strewn nor, apparently, especially concerned about the occasional Mithraic symbolism. Indeed, her personal gift to Ambros was a gold and jewel-encrusted cloak brooch in the form of a scorpion, with all that it signified for the faithful. Her difficult hair had been tamed in the six-braid *tutulus*, piled into its traditional cone, and the cone parted by an ornamental spear-head from which, in the present style, her veil hung down – yet only so far as to lend modesty to her eyes. And such eyes! Green as emeralds. Set in features that the hair had protected so long from the weather they were purest alabaster. Quite exquisite. And the scarlet diaphanous cloud of the seductive *flammeum* veil only served to enhance her surprising beauty, so I could see Ambros considering his situation from completely new angles. Thinking laterally, as I had taught him to do in our sessions on problem solving.

Apart from anything else, we had each expected that the girl's mother would insist on a ceremony more in tune with the customs of the Incomers. But he had at least made an effort, using the bathhouse facilities at Fairwater Maw to have himself oiled and scraped, shaven, his hair wreathed and scented. His clothes were simple, white to match those of his bride, and the only time I saw him flinch was when our small family procession reached Malco's doors. Praise Names were recited; the Lord and his own party called forth; the initial jolting shock when Rigantona's beauty was revealed – though she still clung to that monstrous deer-hound; and it then dawned upon us that there had been no discussion about a Matron of Honour to preside over the rituals. I have no idea what we expected, but never that the duty would be performed by the White Lady of Laigin herself. And I saw Ambros make the horn signs then, to ward off whatever evil he perceived in the role she had chosen.

We had returned safely from Legion-Hold, of course, travelling the Coastal Eleven in a straggling column more than a hundred strong. The Slavehold affair was settled, with the good and loyal folk of Cundruin's walled bolt-hole having slit the fellow's throat rather than risk either a siege or Rhun's wrath. And Rhun had been rewarded by his father with the lordship of Slavehold itself. A good excuse for him to avoid the wedding though, for myself, I suspected he might have more personal motives.

It had taken no more than a couple of drinking sessions with Rhun's own hall-guards to pick up the rumours, the raging arguments they had overheard between father and son about Rigantona's future, about Rhun's thwarted expectations that, one day, the girl should be his. Well, I suppose I should have mentioned all that to Ambros, but his bride did not seem to have any reciprocal fondness for her mother-husband's son, so it seemed best to let sleeping dogs lie – though I realise now that this was perhaps not the best of courses, let alone, as I was later to discover, the best choice of epigrams.

But everything went well enough on the day itself. The contract was signed and Deniol did indeed act as Auspex, delivering a stinging sermon that he claimed as a blessing.

'Chastity,' he stormed, 'is the only path designed by the Almighty for the avoidance of all evil. Chastity!' He pointed his finger at the astonished family members gathered before him. 'Yet the Lord also sets His blessing upon the procreation of children, and therefore redeems the performance of the Great Sin for that purpose. And that purpose alone. Alone!' he glowered at each of us in turn. Slowly. Seemed to spend more time on me than anybody else. But maybe that was just my own guilty conscience. Too many women in my past. 'So I tell you this,' he went on. 'That the Lord has looked into the hearts of these two young people. And He sees transgressions there.' Heads turned, puzzled expressions. Transgressions did not seem too bad, did they? 'Trespass.' Again, nothing wrong with a little trespass here and there. 'And lust!' Smiles of relief, particularly from the bride and her groom. Another good omen. 'But those lusts,' Deniol raged on, 'can only be constrained within the boundaries of a union between one man and one woman, sanctified in the eyes of God. Yet let either of them step outside the boundaries of that bond and the Wrath of the Lord shall pursue the fornicator into eternity.' *Shades of Hades*, I thought, *that's quite a curse.* But Deniol was not finished. Heads were nodding. Malco and Owen White-Tooth exchanging silent agreement on the wisdom of the bishop's Christian words. Bloody hypocrites. 'Yet the Lord,' spat Deniol, 'has also looked into the hearts of all those others gathered here today. He sees all our own misdeeds.' Owen White-Tooth, I saw, shifted uneasily from foot to foot, and his wife – the Skyhound's mother – cast a questioning glance at him. 'Our wrong-doings.' Malco and the Lady Murgain hung their heads. 'Our veniality.'

Well, to be fair, I think that few of them understood veniality. But by the time Ambros made his vows, the sermon had literally put the fear of Deniol's god into each of those who believed, and the bishop seemed well satisfied that he had somehow brought both bride and groom into that fold. So he stood with hands spread happily upon his paunch, while those of Ambros and Rigantona were joined by the spliced rope circle, as we had planned, and held above the oathing stone.

'I pledge you always the first taste of my wine,' Ambros intoned, 'the first breaking of my bread, the first portion of my feast. My spear and my shield for your protection. My lips sealed to strangers upon anything that may pass between us. My body for you alone. My honour to cherish you in this life and the next.'

I had heard more eloquent speeches, yet it was more than I had expected from him. More than pure duty to his father demanded. It dealt adequately enough with the marital requirement for a man to provide physical care for his wife, though it was thin on the *affectio* side.

No poetic words of love. Yet Ambros seemed happy enough as our little procession paraded to the nearest cliff edge so that the stone could be cast out into the waters. And, strangely, I envied him. There was something about Rigantona that fascinated me.

Then it was back to the hall for the First Feast, financed by Ambros himself, and the transfer of the *dotum*. And it was a generous gift. For, with Rhun now Lord of Slavehold, Malco was free to bestow the lordship of Overmon upon his new wife-daughter's husband. A brace of new slaves too. And I could see that Ambros was both surprised and delighted. Personally, I was shocked. The lands of Overmon are rich, a base from which ambitions may be nourished – as, you will know, they had been nourished and grown in the past.

'In any case,' Malco told him, without the slightest hint of irony or humour, 'your brother had already snatched a slice of it, and you've planted your own holdfast upon the ground at the Ridge's Mouth. So let's see how you manage the rest of it.'

Though why trust him to do so? I wondered.

It was Owen White-Tooth's role to respond, however, to reciprocate on behalf of his wife, the Lady Uithera, and their blood. I swear that I had no idea about his intentions. Though I thought, for a moment, that the ghost of Einion stood there among us, offered some words of advice. For Lord Owen hesitated, sucked at that cleft upper lip like a hare scenting the wind, then walked towards the threshold where the door-keepers had just lit the evening's first torches. He took one, as Malco, others in the hall too, tensed and rose from their places, unsure what was happening. For trust is thinner than faith, is it not? And White-Tooth stepped outside, began to wave the guttering flame back and forth, howled out the war-cry of his followers.

'Bear-Brothers!' he yelled. Then he laughed, loud and long, as the Fairwater Maw became riven by chaos and confusion, warriors running to gather weapons against whatever threat might be wrought upon them, the ground beyond the earthworks trembling, Ambros and his mother seized, myself and our retainers surrounded, threatened. And suddenly there were ponies everywhere. Lord Owen splitting his sides as our wild stock riders drove home the gift-herd into Malco's beast pens, a spectacle and libation that would have honoured the horse-lords of the Hunnoi.

*

Lord Owen and his uncle were still slapping each other's backs at the jest's audacity, the various ways in which it might have gone badly wrong, and the newly-wed couple were still accepting lesser tokens, though still fine gifts. From this past year's merchant captains, for example, their business circuit now completed and long since returned south again for the fleet's journey home. A matched set of red-glossed flagons, with intricate motifs, which they had picked up in Zeugitana. But the gifting over, Ambros had been escorted with his bride to the bedchamber among all the usual ribaldry, or downright obscenity, that always accompanied such occasions. Bishop Deniol had made himself scarce for this part of the celebration. And fair enough. The custom and practice of the deed shared little in common with that which his faith seemed to think might be redeemed by procreative good intent.

Then the versing began and, for the first time during the various stages of the wedding, the two families and factions began to mingle more harmoniously. To relax, I suppose. Favourite refrains shared. The riotous and raucous. Those with a gift for flute or frame-drum or lyre providing accompaniment whenever the singers could be kept to a rhythm long enough. That slow drift into the magical and the melancholy while, without anybody really noticing, Deniol slipped back into the gathering. I only spotted him again when, during a brief pause in the proceedings, the sweet notes of a twin-stringed cruth began to pierce the smoke and I knew that we had a true song-sayer in our midst.

'What's she doing here?' mumbled Lord Owen from deep within his cups.

In many ways, she had started all this, although that was an unjust thought. It was Einion who had pursued her. Some reason that only he could have understood. Yet she stilled the hall now as I had seen her do before, that first time, not long after I came south.

'Foes of Pagus, terror spoke; faithless Saesons, pledges broke; raven feeders, fire and smoke.'

Well, it was still a favourite, even though nobody in this place, nor anybody within a week's march or more, had seen any cause to name the Outlanders as "faithless" throughout our entire lifetimes. Nor those of several generations past. But we stamped our feet and thumped our horn-cups to the beat, while Morgose conjured living visions of pillage and rapine from the soft breath of her singing, and the gentle weaving of her fingertips on the cruth strings.

'Faithless foe, red ruin wrought, to Cadell's borders. Death they brought, until Ambrosius vengeance sought.'

She wore the pale robes of the *monasterios*, the front of her head shaved of hair in the same fashion as the monks, and I realised why I had been so surprised at seeing Rigantona's features. For this sister was almost as distinct as may have been possible. Dark-browed where the younger sibling and mother were whey-faced. Charcoal and chalk.

'Thick lies Saeson slaughter dew, on Breiddon Hill, a bone house brew. Spear clash, war blades, straight and true.'

And what does she see, I wondered, *with those eyes born blind?* That single point of similarity. The milky shade of Rigantona's cheeks reflected in the sightless pupils of Morgose.

'Ambrosius bore the Christos sign, upon his shoulders, through their line. The pagans' bane. The living shrine.'

Ah, here it came. The latest version. No mention of Ambrosius being a Christ-follower in any of those we ever heard before, but most seemed to approve the addition. Even Lord Owen. A sign of the times as their new faith insinuated itself into all aspects of our society. The inventions made fact by simple repetition. I thanked the gods though that my young disciple was not there to listen. It was not the best time to discuss my career prospects, but thoughts of the lad and an over-indulgence had loosened my tongue.

'And me, Lord,' I said to Owen White-Tooth, 'you won't be needing my services any longer, I'm thinking. Your son has reached his Manhood and his second Bridal Bed at much the same time.'

'Still much to learn, that boy,' Lord Owen slurred. 'And more than fancy words he'll need from now on, to keep that young witch warm and moist. But you've the right of it, Master Mentor.' He tried to thump my arm but missed. 'No point wasting more of my silver on your salt-fee now. Done good though. Good!'

As terminations of contract go, it was less than I might have desired, but I was too fugged to calculate how long I might survive on the paltry amounts I made from my lesser disciples.

'No, Lord,' I said, and wishing that I could think of something more eloquent. 'I'd been thinking of travelling in any case. To find the sun again. Gallaecia, perhaps.'

'South, you mean?' he said. 'No. Won't do! Been talking to my uncle. Traders say there's some physician. From the Africanus dio…'

'Diocese?'

'Correct. In Laigin. Cure for the Black Hags. Sending the lad there. Before the Yellow Death comes for us. Ready for it!' He slipped from the bench we had been sharing, his horn slipping from his fingers and showering him with the Middle Sea's finest red wine. 'See?' he grinned again. 'Still needs you. Go with him. But he can bloody pay. Not me!'

I was getting too old for this. A whole night of wine and heather-beer, hoarse from singing, and then the breakfast feast to face. Once the happy couple appeared from their adventures, of course. And they kept us waiting long enough. Good sign, though it was hard to confirm the extent to which they might have fulfilled Bishop Deniol's procreative encouragements, for Rigantona's hair now hung long once more and the face of my young disciple showed nothing but his manly bearing, no display of juvenile boastfulness. Yet he took her hand politely enough and led his bride to their places at the table where they accepted still more gifts, and we accepted further platters of pasted fish or honeyed flesh.

By then, Deniol and the blind song-sayer had gone, presumably back to whichever *monasterios* she now called home and, long before noon, the wedding procession was gathered for the march towards Rigantona's new bridal place. The road west to the Narrow Strait first, in time to catch the evening's low water slack for the crossing into Overmon, and then to the Eleven again, stopping for the night at the way-station *mansio* still functioning near the junction of the Fort Overmon and Mona sections. From there, the couple would head inland. Towards the twin peaks of the Giant's Tomb and Cairn of the Twenty. To Overmon's capital, their new home, at the Fortress of the Hammer-Fighters.

But before that there was the Narrow Strait to negotiate, those afoot, or Rigantona herself in her fancy ox-cart, taking the eastern route – the causeway to Dog Island, then the rafting ferry to the mainland. But the rest of us, those a-horse, kicking our ponies into the shallows just three hundred paces west, where we must swim the beasts across the deeper though narrower waters of the cattle ford.

'What was it you'd said about your bride-sister?' I asked Ambros at our first chance to exchange a private word. 'Hardly a prize worth the shedding of any blood. Wasn't that it?'

'My brother should never have wed her,' he replied. 'And certainly not pursued her when she ran from him.'

'Pride, I suppose,' I said. 'But she certainly raised the rafters last night.'

'Deniol showing off his latest acquisition?' said Ambros. 'He'd do well to remember how she served the Oak Seers, before ever she found this Christos. But at least she might help to keep the lads' spirits up.' I must have looked puzzled. 'Didn't my father tell you? I'm being sent on some fool's errand to search for the magic cauldron.'

'The plague-cure you mean?'

'What, Mentor?' he laughed. 'You think it exists? I would have expected better from you. I don't know what Malco's got in mind but I'm damned sure it's nothing to do with a potion for the Black Hags.'

'And Morgose?' I said. 'What's she to this expedition?'

'It's Laigin, of course,' said Ambros. 'Not the safest place for strangers. And certainly not strangers without the Gathelic.'

'You never learned from the Lady Uithera?'

'Mother tried to make me use it, but I never saw much point,' he said. 'And Malco insists that I take along a family link.'

'Your wife doesn't fancy the trip?'

'Not the best of sailors, apparently,' he said, his voice flat.

'And Rhun the Tall?'

'Too busy with his new territory.'

'You'll not be similarly occupied with your own then?'

I had the uneasy feeling there may be more than met the eye to the lad's mission abroad while Rigantona and Rhun remained at home. And something about the prospect burned me.

'Rigantona assures me she can cope adequately without me,' he said. 'But so long as I still have you with me, Master, for guidance and diplomacy, I am sure we shall fare well enough.'

'I'll stay so long as you need me, lad,' I replied. *Contract or no contract*, I thought. But I was focused more on how I might more immediately test whether I had genuine cause for concern about the uncomfortable news

I had gleaned. 'But how was it?' I asked him, trying to make the query sound as licentious as possible. 'You know what I mean. Last night.'

It took him some time to reply, until our ponies' hooves were gripping ground again, floundering a little in mud of the Overmon shore, but across, all the same.

'Her heart seems to belong elsewhere,' he said, at last, but betraying no emotion.

'I heard rumours,' I replied. 'But they seemed one-sided. Does she return his affections after all?'

'Whose affections?'

'Rhun's.'

'Rhun?' He smiled, though there was no humour in it. 'Oh, I should not have minded that so much.'

'Then…?'

'The deer-hound,' he said. 'She will not be parted from the thing.'

I began to see the problem. Or thought so.

'Off-putting, I suppose,' I sympathised. 'It sleeps on the bed?'

'No,' he shook his head. 'You don't understand.' Ambros bit his upper lip. 'She has trained the creature. To…to lick her. And Mithras knows what more besides. The bitch thought it might amuse me to watch.'

Chapter Five

There was little further news about the Black Hags and it seemed safe to assume that the pestilence had been contained within the lands of Horn-Head, a comfortable distance to the south. All the same, we were still diligent about border precautions at the fords and passes. Yet if we had taken the extra trouble to brave the Hibernian Sea, over the months after the wedding, so much more that followed would doubtless have fallen out very differently. But other things intervened.

Construction work for Ambros. The restoration of his Fortress of the Hammer-Fighters to its former glory. The transfer of *armaria*, my small scroll and codex collection to a new library cubicle there, along with those copies upon which Ambros himself had worked, as well as his slave scribes. His determination to open the harbour at Fort Overmon again so that Overmon should have its own trading port. For Malco Battle-Shield, the consolidation of the White-Wilds, diplomatic missions dispatched to each district and *pagus* beyond his own borders that had once belonged to First-Province. Though only so far as the Sabrina Estuary. With proposals for the convening of a Provincial Council meeting – the first time such a thing had been held in almost fifty years. And nobody wanted to invite the disease-ridden Horn-Head folk from beyond the Estuary to *that* gathering.

Well, when somebody gifts you a pony, it is impolitic to examine its teeth. An ambassadorial bounty would keep the wolf from my door a while longer. So I found myself dispatched to the extensive South-End territory of Lord Fergna Urcol's Son, whose own capital and stronghold happened to then be at Sea Fort – my own birthplace. What more could I have wanted? A reunion with my sister, Mirian, who had recently lost her husband, Willowbane Cutren's Son. And her son, Cador, grown almost to a man and longing to take up the spear.

But the principal gain from my journey was the chance to distance myself from Rigantona's hearth, which was especially welcome. For I wished every day that I had kept my curiosity to myself and never asked Ambros about their damned nuptials, and I would certainly have preferred him to be less forthcoming in his reply. I could hardly look the woman in the eye now. Nor the hound neither, if truth be told. But, with Rigantona, my feelings had become confused, went somewhere beyond the obvious disgust.

'Why should I come at Malco's beckoning?' Fergna snarled when I was finally granted an audience, separated from the prying eyes of his hall by a thick curtain of woven hunting scenes. Food had been served and a Throne-Sense board set out for our use. 'And will you attack or defend?'

I sensed that attacking Fergna in any form might be dangerous. He was, I knew, in his sixtieth year and, while somewhat bent and black-robed, he seemed more than capable of mayhem still.

'Might I defend, Lord Protector?' I replied using the title he had taken for himself, though he often preferred to call himself *Vorteporigas*, after the Gathelic of his ancestors. 'And simply an invitation, I think. A discussion between peers. About co-operation. A collective front against common perils. Possible recreation of the Province.'

'For what?' he demanded. 'So that we're all neatly packaged up ready for the Legions' return? Ready to be pressed under the Empire's thumb again?'

His opening move squeezed one of my shield pieces from the board.

'I believe that Lord Malco sees the possible advantages of having our own political and governance structures in place should, as you say, the Emperor Justinian decide to reclaim these lands. But would you not agree, Lord Protector, that a trading pact with New Rome – with any state beyond the boundaries of the Endless Winter, for that matter – is precisely what we need just now? And a trading pact attractive to such a state requires a certain economy of scale, perhaps.'

'Well, Master Meridden,' he sneered, 'will you listen to yourself, now? A trading pact, is it? We let them have our tin and copper, and they let us have their Yellow Death.'

'You cannot believe...' I began.

'What? That it's a deliberate act? Of course not, Mentor. But nor do I believe it to be pure coincidence that every time trade through Carthago is renewed, the Black Hags appear immediately in its wake.'

He was right about that. But nobody had ever worked out how crews sailing all that distance could themselves be immune from the pestilence if they were, at the same time, its bearers. It made no sense, though there were plenty of theories – and none of them worth a single drop of lamp oil.

'Yet the trade still continues, Lord Protector,' I reminded him. Then paused while I took my king a point closer to the board's edge and safety. 'Regardless of the threat. But a fractured trade, a fractured Province, serves none of us.'

'Let me tell you something, Mentor,' he said. 'I would not serve a day under a Christ-followers' fool like Malco if my life depended on it.' My face must have betrayed a sense that, perhaps, his life was precisely the thing at stake here. 'And you may tell him so, if it pleases you to do so. Tell him that the lands of the South-End are very far from Slavehold, and that the *Vorteporigas*, Lord Fergna Urcol's Son, is a far cry from weaklings like Cundruin. There is none here that would slit my throat. And neither Malco, nor his son, is capable of the deed. So he must stay that which he has always been, and shall always remain – a large fish in a small pool.' He laughed. 'First-Province, indeed! I tell you, Mentor, that if I were a younger man I should have broader ambition than that.'

'Greater Britannia?' I asked him.

'If only Mithras would send us somebody capable of the task,' he said.

I waited for a moment before speaking again. The king was in my hand and I could see the move that would guarantee its escape route. But instead I laid the piece on its side, conceding defeat.

'Then I fear, Lord Protector,' I said, 'that I may be acting as diplomat for entirely the wrong master.'

I made a brief stop at the Fortress of the Hammer-Fighters on my way back to the Fairwater Maw, but only for a quiet word with my former disciple and to collect my codex copy of *Instituto Oratoria*, part for company on the onward journey, and part because I might need some inspiration from Quintillianus to help explain the failure of my diplomatic mission. I made enquiry with the Lady Rigantona, and found Ambros supervising work at the grotto he had discovered, no more than five hundred paces beyond the holdfast's steep earthworks.

'An ideal site,' I told him, as I admired the painted tiles just being set in place around the cave's recently constructed entrance arch. A new Mithraeum to give thanks for his blessings. 'Your wife seemed hardly enthusiastic about your efforts here.'

'Rigantona refuses to follow the normal *matrona* protocols,' he said. 'The idea that she is now part of a new family, and should follow the cult favoured by her husband, is completely lost upon her.'

'I doubt it helps,' I said, 'that your own father and mother have been turned.'

'There's barely a day goes by without her reminding me. But how did you fare with Fergna Urcol's Son? As though I could not guess from your demeanour.'

'It was good to see the old place again,' I said. 'My sister and her boy too. But the Fergna won't be coming to Malco's Provincial Council. You'd like him. Says he won't serve a Christ-follower. Won't settle for anything less than a single Province again either.'

'You will doubtless receive the sharp edge of Malco's tongue when you reach the Maw,' said Ambros.

'He will have been informed?' It was a stupid question.

'Another protocol that Rigantona regularly ignores,' he said. 'Confidentiality. She will have read those troubles painted on your face too. Sent a runner to her mother. But Fergna. Like him or not, this will mean another war-trail.'

I could see that it was already eating away at him, the thought of raiding into South-End, against a Lord who shared his own beliefs.

'Well,' I said, 'a blood-oath is a blood-oath.'

'Yes,' he said, 'but South-End is not the same as Slavehold.'

'And that,' I told him, 'is exactly the message the Prefect Lord Fergna Urcol's Son would have me relay to Lord Malco.'

The Federation Council meeting was held seven days later, and Malco's hall was almost full to bursting with the hundred duty-holders elected to serve in its deliberations. Like most of his kind, Malco saw his hereditary right to rule as superseding any opinions that the council members might hold, but in a world where that right might itself be wiped away with the thrust of a stronger rival's spear, it was always sensible to at least go through the motions of attentive advice-seeking and action plan endorsement. Always best to keep as many of the duty-holders on your side as possible. It was a lesson I had tried to instil in Ambros, yet I saw that, even now, while the other Lords Prefect – of Cerdeg's Edge, New Laigin, Meirionshore, Dunshome, Everfell, Romaland, Bright-Fields, as well as Owen White-Tooth and Rhun the Tall – were almost inseparable from their own knot of councillors, the new Lord of Overmon still stood somewhat apart from all but his closest spear-hawks.

I had already reported to Malco Battle-Shield and endured the raging invective with which he damned Lord Fergna to eternal torment. But at least there had been the distractions of the monthly market to enjoy between that interview and the full council meeting. Not that the market demonstrated any great bounty, of course. A flock of underfed geese being driven by a small boy with a stick. Bearers of half-filled baskets and thin bolts of linen cloth. Strings of narrow-shouldered ponies. Unhappy pigs. Carts with clay jars of watered heather-beer, or with sagging sacks from Mona's once-bountiful granaries. Pack animals staggering under the produce of smelting ovens. Hapless hawkers of iron-ware. Vendors of skeletal chickens, pigeons or partridge. The monks with their blackened final stocks of last winter's vegetables. And me. I felt like a sub-standard commodity too. But along the upper shore, on a terrace of flat turf, the market's stalls had at least been erected. Faded awnings and holed rain covers. A few braziers smouldering. Greasy meat fats fouling the air. The town's animal byres, hardly full but loud with grunting, lowing beasts and stinking from five hundred paces distant. A whistle being played somewhere among the crowd. Yet it was none of these things that entertained me, but the number of strangers that I observed among the market-goers.

There was another gazelle in the port, from Carthago, and bringing a further welcome cargo of grain, though this time the vessel had been hauled on timber rollers to sit upon the hard, while its swarthy sailors made repairs to the hull and steering gear, or mingled in the market with a group of swaggering Outlander barbarians. There was much muttered speculation about the Outlanders' presence here, all flaxen hair and wisping beards, though none of us spoke their harsh tongue. In any case, they were outnumbered by the Incomers who had arrived to help work the mines now that trade was increasing again. These had actually been at the Maw for some time, apparently, though Malco had insisted they spend at least a week penned away from the holdfast, in a separate detention stockade, until he was certain they carried no disease. Similarly, the sailors and their merchant master were required to confirm that they had not landed in any of the infected lands, and the Saeson Outlanders… well, the truth was that they all seemed so robust it was possible to believe the rumour of their complete immunity from the pestilence. And the reason for their presence among us was finally made clear during Malco's opening address to the council meeting.

'Only Fergna!' he cried. 'Self-styled Lord Protector, *Vorteporigas*, of the South-End. I send him one of the most renowned Mentors in the land. One of his own. The famous Meridden of Sea Fort. And what? He rejects my proposal as though Malco Battle-Shield – the whole of the White-Wilds, in fact – was nothing but an irrelevance.'

It was a slight on my professional expertise, of course, but I was in no position to argue. Besides, the long journey home had left me feeling less than my usual self. And the dwelling-place that had been made available for Ambros and his entourage – me included – left much to be desired. I hadn't stopped itching since I arrived in that flea-infested midden. Not that I'm averse to a few fleas, you understand, but this particular hovel seemed to have more than its decent share.

'I hear, Lord,' said Bishop Deniol, 'that Fergna Urcol's Son proclaims openly he would never ally himself with any that believes in our Saviour, Yesu.'

Well, the old bone-crow had been a little more specific, in fact. Less than helpful though, for Fergna to be so publicly forthright. Not the best trait for somebody with political responsibility.

'And why should that be an issue for the man?' said Malco. 'It is hardly as though all those gathered here have yet seen the light.' He looked directly at Ambros. 'But that does not blind them from understanding the greater needs of our people.'

'But impossible to rebuild the Province, Lord,' Deniol reminded him, 'without the lands of the South-End at its heart. Should we therefore let one man stand in the way of your God-given vision? When all those others have lent their blessing.' He counted them off on his pudding fingers. 'Prosperity. Belthos. Breconis. Glusio's Land. Windstorm. Aricon. And Sabrina-Rise.'

I knew that this was untrue. Most of us did. Gereint Six-Fingers of Windstorm had promised only to give Malco's proposal careful consideration. And Iago, Morn's Son, in Sabrina-Rise, was merely non-committal, being another who still preferred to follow the old gods than this new and joyless faith of Deniol and the Emperor in far Constantinopolis.

'But, Uncle,' said Owen White-Tooth, 'Fergna is strong in spear-hawks and we, here, need all the folk we have, simply to keep ourselves fed. War against the South-End would be a long affair. It would cost us dear, my Lord.'

The White Lady of Laigin shrieked with laughter, there at Malco's side.

'You see, Bishop?' Murgain sneered. 'You may baptise some of them, but the act does not always endow them with the True Faith. Do you not see, husband-nephew,' she pointed directly at Lord Owen, 'that such a war-band would go in the name of God? That the Almighty would lend them strength for a speedy victory against Fergna and his heathen hosts.'

'Enough, woman!' shouted Malco. 'For pity's sake, can you never be still? I lack no faith in the Almighty, but our nephew is right. And all the God-spells in the world could not give us an easy victory over Fergna Urcol's Son. But there is one here who *can* do so.' He shifted in his chair, gripped the dragonhead handholds and heaved himself to his feet. 'Step forward, Osla Big-Knife,' he bellowed.

Osla was smaller than I had imagined from his reputation. Wind-scoured Saeson features and a cruel squint to those tiny eyes. Good at his work, I imagined. For where the White-Wilds was rich in mineral wealth, but currently poor in home-grown food, and entirely starved of working hands, the Land of Hosts and the Saeson Shore – each controlled respectively by Osla's father, Henga White-Stallion, and Osla's older brother, Octan Oxen-Strong – enjoyed precisely the opposite economy. That thriving First Corner of Britannia's Southland, *Maxima Caesariensis*, Upper-Province, around the Saeson Shore, with its mingled population of Cousins' Tongue Host-Hundred, Common Speech Frankoi, and the Outlander languages of Frisians and the Saesons themselves. So they earned good money by hiring out as *foederati*, as they had always done. And it was this that brought such a sharp intake of breath from the gathered delegations. For there was a belief abroad – ill founded, in my opinion – that bad fortune always favoured those who turned to *foederati* for their services.

In the feasting that followed, it was probably fortunate that Osla seemed to know so few of our words. For here was *Breiddon Hill* again. No Morgose for tonight's performance but another song-sayer, this fellow recently returned from Across-the-Sea and travelling north to visit his family. And I was filled with wonder that he had picked up precisely the same version.

'Ambrosius bore the Christos sign, upon his shoulders, through their line. The pagans' bane. The living shrine.'

'The power of modern communication,' he explained, when we shared a horn of wine later. Though an aching head warned me that I should not take too much of the stuff. 'I make a fortune these days, carrying news, wrapping it up with a few good rhymes. Mind,' he sneered, 'they're a weird bunch over there. And the food's shit.'

'You could always find the same work here?' I suggested, rubbing at my temples.

'Piss off!' he replied. 'Bloody place is on its knees. Half of it can't understand me any more. Some of those stretches in the south, you have to ride for days before you hear the Cousins' Tongue. And the Common Speech? Forget it. Sodding savages. We're overrun with Outlanders. Sodding barbarians. Just look at that one.'

Well, Osla might not be good at holding his heather-beer, but he was no worse than the spear-hawks with whom he seemed to be in competition.

'And news from Horn-Head?' I asked. 'What word of the Horn-Head folk?'

'What?' he said. 'The Yellow Death, you mean? I stayed clear of them too. But I had it from a reliable source that the outbreak's been contained. No problem any more. That's what I heard anyway.'

I slept badly that night, wild dreams and demons disturbing my rest and, when I woke before sunrise, my stomach was heaving. *Something in the food*, I thought. *The fish. Almost certainly the fish.* And I barely managed to get outside before I spilled my guts against the dwelling's wall.

Better. But only for a few moments. Then the sweating began upon my face, though I was shivering with cold, and the sea roaring in my ears, the whole world swimming in it, back and forth. Until I fell.

Ambros caught me, I think.

'Mentor,' he cried, though his voice came to me from a great, empty distance.

I knew, of course. Tried to send him away.

'Not inside,' I told him. Never inside. Not near the others. Not near to anybody. I struggled weakly, trying to keep my head averted. Trying not to breathe upon him. For, surely, it must be transferred that way. From person to person. Must it not? Or carried upon the foul and humid vapours of the Sunless Years.

Yet he carried me back into the dwelling house, where the darkness was some comfort. Laid me near the hearth fire and covered me with pelts to keep the chill from my bones.

The pains in my head became worse until I thought it would split in half, made it impossible to sleep, despite the draughts that Ambros insisted on trying to force between my lips. Even though they did nothing except induce the cramps and spewing once again. So that I soiled myself. Wept with the indignity. Until somebody took my clothes and burned them in the flames.

And the pain spread. Oh, how it spread. Through my neck and shoulders. My back. Arms and legs. Until I was aflame all over. Unable to move, nor yet to sleep. A few lucid moments though. For the rest, I know that I raved like one who was wine-soaked. And such waking visions that I hardly dare speak them. But in those lucid moments, I knew I was travelling. There was open sky. Jolting discomfort of a cart. Then nothing but the burning agony. And the terror.

Chapter Six

The Black Hags had come upon us. And as my pains subsided, as lucidity slowly returned, Ambros told me the horror of it.

He had brought me from the Fairwater Maw to the former way-station *mansio*, which sat exactly mid-way between that place where the Eleven's branch left the main highway and cut across Mona to reach Legion's Neck, that three-walled port and fortress where I had previously been entertained by Brother Flavius and his monks. The *mansio* was largely abandoned now, though in its glory, exactly placed at the end of a day's ox-cart journey, it would have provided shelter, rooms, food, lodging, drink, a bathhouse and a toll collector – precisely the same as all other such stopping places at each twelfth milestone on every principal road in Britannia and throughout the whole Empire. So, a hospitable place, though now turned more to a Quarantine Temple, where some of the sick could be safely ensconced until, after a few prayers mumbled to whichever gods might be available, they passed away without causing too much distress to those they left behind.

'We should have sailed to Laigin when we had that first warning,' he said, holding my head and touching the water cup to my lips.

'You should not be here,' I croaked.

'Where else should I be?' Ambros replied. 'Malco had the good sense to close the crossing of the Strait, so there's nowhere else to go, Master.'

'Many dead?'

'So far? At the Maw, it has taken a third, I should say. Then it spread across the island like a forest fire, but slowly burning itself out. All told, I should say that a large proportion of all Mona's folk have perished. Five hundred, at the least. You were lucky, Mentor.'

Five hundred. In what? Ten days?

A couple of monks, their faces tightly wrapped with cloth, carried a corpse past the open doorway of my cell. A child. Its fingers and nose eaten away by the filthy necrosis that gave the pestilence just that one of its many names. The Black Hags. I pulled back the covers, expected the worst, but saw only the fading rash. None of those pus bags that nobody survived.

'Lucky,' I nodded. 'You?'

'Nothing,' he said. 'Nor my father, Mithras be praised. Though three of his duty-holders gone. Four of my own.'

Well, I might have known the lad would be safe. Ambros, he who had never taken hurt in battle. Ambros, whose name the Christ-followers' holy men could not speak. Ambros. Divine.

'And Osla?' I said.

'That weasel still lives,' Ambros replied. 'But a couple of his men came down with it. One of them pulled through. So all that nonsense about them being immune – oh, and a gazelle's crew too, by the way. It went through them like a batch of bad fish paste. Deniol says it's a punishment sent by his god, of course. A curse upon all those who deny their faith. He's been having his monks scratch crosses for all they're worth. Look, even you've got one.'

He pointed at the wall, showed me where a crude crucifix had been gouged into the stone.

'They've all escaped the pestilence?' I asked. 'The monks?'

'Master, really!' Ambros laughed. 'The pestilence has struck his hermitages as hard as anywhere else. Though he's been fairly silent on the point. Or claims that any Christ-followers who've died must have been less than sufficiently devout.'

'But you'll go to Laigin now? In case of another outbreak.'

'We'd not receive the best welcome, I think,' he said. 'Not now. It's not just the Yellow Death, is it? It's the madness it brings in its wake. The good folk of Fairwater Maw took it into their heads that the pestilence must have been brought by the new Laigin Incomers. Rounded them all up. Women and children too. Then they stoned them to death. From a nice, safe distance. Oh, and the song-sayer too. That one from Across-the-Sea. They decided he must have lied about travelling through Horn-Head.'

*

Yet, despite the risk of reprisal, Ambros was required to sail to Laigin anyway. And he required me to sail with him. A foolish desire.

First, because I had only been safe from the Black Hags for just over a full moon. New cases were being reported, here and there, across Mona, the island itself still far from free of their grip. So there was risk, surely, that we might carry the pestilence in our breath – if that was, indeed, how the thing was spread. Yet, overall, my concern about the sickness aspect was that I yet felt far from fully recovered.

The second reason for viewing my participation with disdain, though, was the lad's insistence that my rhetorical skills might help him in his mission. It was hard to understand how this might be. I spoke none of the Gathelic language with which Hibernia is blessed, and I knew little about the riven politics of our destination. No more than the next man. The tribal clans and septs of one family – in the Cousins' Tongue we called them the Grandsons of Dunlain – in the north, with their great holdfast at Dun Aulin; and the more powerful Grandsons of Kinsell in the south, with their capital at Ferna – and ruled there by Corpre Cormac's Son, to whom the White Lady Murgain was kin. Corpre styled himself King of Laigin, in the way of that land. For they said there were more kings in Hibernia than a hound has fleas. But that was the limit of my knowledge.

And the third reason? Well, I had a fear of water. Unlike Ambros – who seemed to think it some duty to Mithras that he should swim daily in lake or river or sea – I had learned the skill of sinking at an early age and never quite broken the habit. More importantly, I was a poor sailor. He had insisted that I accompany him on occasions in his fraught and wallowing, wind-blown, small boat ventures along our own coastal shoreline, or once when he had circumnavigated the whole of Mona between one sunrise and the next. Yet I had never done so without being miserably ill.

'This will be easier,' he told me, with unconvincing self-assurance when we had taken ourselves to Legion's Neck, and thence to the bath-house. 'At this time of year, the winds come regularly from the north-east during the morning.' He blew gently upon the surface of the warm pool in which we were immersed. 'Tomorrow, at first light, at slack water, we head out past the Cauldron. We take a back-bearing, keeping the Cauldron's Tip here…' He spread the first and second dripping fingers of his right hand, squinted between them, wriggled the middle finger. '...and the Grey Seal Rocks there...' He repeated the gesture with the first finger. '...and we keep following it until they're both out of sight.'

'And then?' I said, trying to keep the panic from my voice.

'By then the sun will be above us and heading precisely the way we want to go. We follow it. The flood tide will drift us northwards for six hours. Then the ebb will take us south for another six. But so long as we keep pointing for the sun, we'll end up precisely where we want to be – in sight of Edar's Head.'

'You're happy that the boat-master's got that all right?'

'Boat-master?' he smiled. 'Who needs a boat-master when you have Ambros the Divine?'

My heart sank, as surely, we would all sink very soon.

'Yet isn't there a small flaw in the logic of your plan?'

He shook his head, water spraying from his red thatch.

'I don't think so, Master,' he said. 'Have you thought of one?'

'Just this,' I replied. 'That we have barely seen the sun for five summers now.'

Later, we surveyed the flimsy tub, which was supposed to protect our small crew from all that the Hibernian Sea might throw against us. She was pulled up on the port's shore while her belly was being carefully filled with ballast stones.

'The locals call her a puffin,' said Ambros.

I could see the reason. The currock was short, squat, and the wicker shelter built upon the boat's aft half-deck gave her stern all the appearance of that bird's unusual beak.

'I should have preferred the Carthago gazelle,' I told him. Though that craft and her depleted crew had long since left these shores. 'At least she had a decent timber hull.'

'You can't beat leather, Master.' He slapped his hand against the sheep-greased hide. 'Tight as a drum. You should know that. You've sailed with me often enough.'

I ignored that.

'And if, by some miracle, this thing gets us there safely,' I said. 'There's the language problem. The Laigin Lord's likely animosity towards us, too. Perhaps we should have brought your wife, after all.'

It was intended as a jest.

'The Straits are still closed,' he replied. 'And she will not sail.' He was perfectly serious. Almost sad. 'At least, not without the dog.'

I wished he had not said that, and swallowed yet another unfortunate image. Besides, Ambros had been forced to leave his own hound, Charger, in his wife's care for the duration of our journey. I just hoped the beast would not pick up too many bad habits.

'Dog or no dog,' I said, 'Rigantona would have served us well by her presence.' And the truth? I had rather hoped that she would join our expedition.

A woman's voice startled us both, and we spun about.

'They say that more than one dog on a ship is a certain recipe for disaster, do they not, Skyhound?'

I knew my mouth was gaping open as I struggled to understand how she had managed to cross the shingle so silently, regardless of the background noise of waves that sighed and suckled at its margin – and I clamped my lips shut, though knowing that Morgose could not see them, one way or the other.

'Well met, wife-sister,' said Ambros, his dislike for the woman loud in every syllable.

'Ah,' she replied, 'no longer entitled to brother-wife, then?'

'You left him. Led him to his death.'

'He left me before we were even wed, though I did not understand it then,' said Morgose. 'And none led him to death except his own rashness. Though perhaps he could have relied more on family or wiser friends to take him on a different path.'

It was a thought that had plagued us many times already, without any help from Morgose.

She touched fingers lightly to the shaven section of her scalp, and sadness filled her features so that I knew, suddenly, who it was that had placed the garland near Einion's head as it rotted below Malco's Memory Stone.

'And now?' said Ambros. 'Here to spy on behalf of Bishop Deniol? You're a long way from your own *monasterios*, Morgose.'

'I am here at the bidding of my father,' she replied. 'To resolve this problem you face. But the bishop would doubtless expect me to do my duty to the Church also.'

'Problem?' said Ambros.

'The thing you were discussing.' She rubbed a knuckle into her eye socket, a self-conscious gesture. 'It was difficult not to hear. You need an intermediary. And it seems I am your solution.'

I turned my head, not wanting to see the expression on the lad's face.

'Laigin?' he said. 'You?'

'You object? It seems you have more than one problem then, Skyhound, sister-husband.'

'I hadn't counted on taking the Voice of Deniol with me.'

'Problems upon problems,' she laughed, and it was a surprisingly pleasant sound. 'You have no Gathelic. You hate Christ-followers. And, it seems, despite your birth-mother, no great liking for the Laigin either.'

'I have nothing against the Laigin, neither in their homeland nor as Incomers, lady,' he snapped. 'Except for the indecent haste with which they've flocked to follow this Yesu after so many ages in which most of the world did not even know the fellow's name.'

'It seems our voyage promises some lively debate then,' she said. 'I look forward to it. But with eyes or without them, only a fool would fail to see that this Faith of the Christ-followers is here to stay.'

Strangely, her words seemed to imply that this faith was a thing apart, rather than something in which she was personally enmeshed.

'And in that case,' I said, 'what advice would you give to one with ambitions to become a prince among men.'

She smiled, sniffed at the sea's breeze.

'The wind may favour that journey tomorrow,' she said, 'which it would fracture today. But you can never set out without knowing which way the winds shall blow.' Morgose paused, then added, 'Ambros, do you not agree?'

Somewhere to the east, beyond the Giant's Tomb, the sun must have been coming up, though we could not see it from the waters of the port. Simply a paler shade to the darkness of the clouds. Enough light to just make out the even deeper black hills that encircled the bay. But the wind was exactly as predicted, and we needed six strong backs to row into its face a while to clear the old harbour, twelve of us to the crew, including Ambros and myself, as well as Morgose the monk-sister.

It was amazingly pleasant, the seas gentle and remaining so even after Ambros had split the crewmen into two tent-sections, assigned duties, and shouted orders for the yard to be hoisted aloft. The square sail was set and trimmed as he took the steer-board himself and swung us around until the flax-cloth filled, the oars were brought inboard, and the waters whispered faster, louder, along the hull's length. There were moments when it felt as though we flew, the currock fairly skimming atop the waves, and time itself suspended, the morning endless, eternal, yet full of peace, the wind rubbing at our necks to ease away all care.

'Well?' I said to Ambros when we finally took our turn in the shelter to share some food – a little cheese, some smoked sausage, and a handful of oatmeal mash laced with hazelnut. 'Have you thought any more about what she said?'

'You still think she was being prophetic?'

'She was a respected Oak Seer long before she became a Christ-bride. Long before she married Einion too. I suppose she simply echoed something I had thought about myself.'

'What? That I should use the power of their Church, rather than oppose it?'

'It's a strategy which has served the Emperors very well. And I think she's right. Like it or not, they're here to stay. For some time, at least. They have answers that pacify people.'

'Dishonest answers.'

'Useful answers, Ambros.'

There was excitement out in the ship's waist, a pack of dolphins came leaping and cavorting amidships, the men all laughing at the sight of them. But Ambros was peering up at the clouds, at the translucence that showed where the sun was hiding.

'Bear away a little,' he shouted to the man who now held the steer-board.

I looked towards the prow, where Morgose had wedged herself, her head tilted towards the dolphins, and she began to sing. Beautiful. Clear.

'*Spread our wings, wind-tasted, stowed the oars. Set course and bear the load. For Skyhound rides the whale-road.*'

'Have you heard this before?' I asked him.

'Never. And where's she going with this?'

'You could almost think she was making it up as she goes along.'

'Heave, lads. Haul. Salt-scented, goad the waves. Take fear, Sea Lord's abode. For Skyhound rides the whale road.'

The other men had the rhythm of it now, and it employed all the cadence of a sailor's song, so that they joined in at every last line.

'Holy Mithras,' he said, 'she *is* making it up.'

'You'll soon be famous if she can write a few more.'

'*Brother-friend, foe-bender, showed the blade. Tremble, debts that are owed. For Skyhound rides the whale-road.*'

'That verse for Einion, d'you think?' he asked. It was two full years and a Dark Half since the death of his brother. But Ambros was more relaxed now, enjoying the moment as verse followed verse, dozens of them. Brilliant.

'You never told me,' I said, by way of reply, 'does this tub have a name?'

'She does now,' he smiled, though he was still looking at Morgose. 'The *White Enchantress*.' Though he used the old word of the Incomers' Gathelic. '*Uindabhair*,' he said.

Chapter Seven

Epicurus said that, for every happiness in life, we must pay with an equal measure of pain. The greater the happiness, the more pain we must endure at its end.

And so, with the sun's ghost at its zenith, the sail's tortured convulsions announced that the wind had dropped. Stillness. A gannet overhead, gliding in lazy circles above the mast. The very last of the flood tide still drifting us northwards in that heaving emptiness until even that ceased and the *White Enchantress* could do little but wallow nauseously in the residual swell.

'Oars?' shouted one of the crew, Custyn Banon's Son, a boyhood friend of Ambros, like most of those on board. And, for a short while, Custyn had also been a disciple of mine.

'Yes,' said Ambros, 'and Second Section to me. Get that yard down and the sail furled. But watch! The wind will be up again soon. And swinging around.'

He was right. Every few minutes it would whip at us erratically from a new direction, while those of us not at the rowing struggled clumsily with the yard braces, the flapping sheets and the furling ties, and the First Section cursed us for fouling the stroke as we stumbled over their perches. And all the while, Morgose sang from the prow, some of our favourites but, more often, crooning a foot-tapping rhythm for the rowers in her own Gathelic.

It seemed to me that we had no sooner managed to lash everything away than the wind freshened again, and steadied, this time against our left cheeks, almost the exact reverse of its earlier direction, and bringing with it a towering anvil of purple cloud laden with rain. Back to the ropes, the yard raised again, more or less fore and aft on the steer-board side of the mast, the sail unfurled but flapping harmlessly, then the sheets pulled home so that the forward half of yard and sail were swung across the prow, the spar's pointing finger pulled down slightly until the rig began to draw us obliquely across the face of the gusting breeze and the rowers' Section could stow their oars again.

'It never ceases to amaze me,' I yelled. 'This process of sailing into the wind.'

'Not into it, Master,' Ambros called back. 'That's not possible. This is about as close as we can come.' He looked behind, to the helmsman. 'Remember,' Ambros shouted to him, 'the ebb's starting to carry us south so she'll be trying to edge us upwind. You must keep her pointing just so…' He jabbed with the flat of his hand. '…or we'll lose all our way. Or worse. And be ready to wear about. On my word.'

Then the rain started. Great driven slingshots of the stuff, while the wind went from strength to strength and the waves steepened. Foam gathered atop the crests. We no longer slid across them now, but rose and fell, the hull slapping against the downhill faces, and the vessel wearing each hour at the Skyhound's command.

'Do we not lose ground every time we do that?' I cried, wiping away the salt water that dripped from my nose and bearded chin.

'We need to be where the wind's coming from,' he told me. 'But we can't get straight there. So we weave our way back and forth, trying to head into it as much as we're able on each tack. If the wind wasn't so strong, we'd turn across it, but in this blow we'd never have the strength to pull the yard around. So we have to wear like this, let the wind help us swing the yard about too. We lose some ground, you're right. But it's our only choice.'

And so, for every pleasant morning hour we had passed, each of those for the remainder of the day was a nightmare. Sickness. Half the crew entirely debilitated with it, myself included. Moments when it seemed the boat must surely founder. Whistling through the ropes. Those still capable bailing with buckets, Morgose in their midst and working with the best of them. That terrible instant when we first heard breakers crashing upon rock. The Eye of Edar's Head suddenly rearing out of the rain, impossibly close. Ambros kicking each of us into action, despite our languor. Three of us heaving at the steer-board until, finally, we found ourselves once more in calm waters and a welcome shoreline ahead.

*

Morgose licked at the air, there above the tidal line.

'Home,' she said. 'Can you not taste the difference?'

To me it seemed little different from the lands we had left behind. But it was my first time in Hibernia and I was happy not to rush the judgement. All other considerations aside, I needed to wait until the world ceased its swaying.

'Well,' said Ambros, 'here we are. Right on target.'

'The Mentor may be fooled by that bravado, Skyhound,' said Morgose, 'but I can smell the relief in your voice.'

'Relief?' he said. 'Simply, Lady, my unbridled delight that we have succeeded in keeping my wife-sister safe.'

'I made my first sea crossing before you were even born,' she sneered. 'Long before.'

I realised this was possibly true. She was certainly older than Ambros. But by how many years? Five? Ten? I could not tell and would not ask. Yet it was not age that showed in her dark features but the ripeness of maturity, to which the shaven, oil-polished scalp lent only mystery.

We rigged a shelter that night from the sail-cloth and found sufficient driftwood for a fire. But in the morning Ambros left Custyn and one other spear-hawk to guard the boat, while the rest of us packed minimal provisions and began to trek south and west for Ferna, soon finding a decent rutted road, which forked inland, away from the coast. Yet we had completed no more than an hour's march before we heard the drumming of hooves, the bouncing clatter of iron wheel rims, coming towards us. A war-cart, a *carrio*, I realised, as it came into view around the woodland bend. I had heard of these legendary vehicles, but never seen one. Matched white ponies strapped to the yoke, the charioteer balancing upon the pole and driving the team like a madman while a youthful warrior with flowing hair and cloak sat casually on the side arches, leaning on a heavy spear that he had wedged against the opposite frame.

'Jupiter's Balls,' said Ambros. 'I must have one of those, Mentor.'

The driver shortened his reins so quickly that the ponies reared in their traces, the *carrio* slewing sideways, scattering stones and dust in a cloud through which the warrior vaulted lightly to the ground, planting the butt of his spear shaft before him, leaning upon it once more, as nonchalantly as he had previously kept his seat aboard the vehicle. He was armoured, though with modesty, his boiled leather tunic strengthened by small square plates of iron stitched about the body, and we could now see that, while he carried that single heavy spear, the war-cart itself bristled with other weaponry, javelins and long darts. Yet it was the Christ-cross dangling from his neck that caused Ambros and myself to exchange glances.

'Who is he, wife-sister?' Ambros asked, then grimaced, realising – I thought – that Morgose had no way of knowing. But she was already taking steps towards the war-cart, her palms and fingers clasped flat together in a gesture of supplication until the charioteer held up a warning hand, shouted to her, indubitably an instruction to stay where she was. Morgose called back, and I heard her speak her own name among that stream of Gathelic that was otherwise beyond me. Her mother's name too, I thought. And on it went. Questions from the driver. A gesture towards our party. Explanations from Morgose. An occasional comment in response, and a final lengthy speech. But in all that time not a single word from the Laigin warrior. And not even a sign of farewell when he eventually leapt back upon the *carrio*, and allowed his companion to lash the ponies, turn a tight circle and disappear again down the track.

'The warrior is Fingal of the Five Stallions,' explained Morgose, when she retraced her steps to us without faltering. 'First among Laigin's Champions. Guardian of this North Shore. And that was his charioteer, Eochain Storm-Rider. But I'm sorry to tell you, Skyhound, that we seem to have wasted a journey.'

I groaned inwardly.

'He's not here?' I said. 'The Mauri physician? But they must still have the plague-bane. A knowledge of how to make it, at least.'

'Eochain says that their bishop denounced the brew as sorcery,' she answered. 'Called down the wrath of God upon all who would turn to some heathen potion rather than trusting in our Lord, Yesu the Christos. They would have put the sorcerer to death, but he escaped. Took ship, he thinks, to the lands of Elidyr of Clud-Vale.'

'Elidyr is a good man, I think,' said Ambros. 'I know his reputation.'

'Not according to Eochain,' Morgose replied. 'He says that Elidyr is another enemy of the True Faith. A man with ambitions to see himself installed as Imperator of all Britannia.'

'Does he now?' mused Ambros. 'Well, that is news, indeed.'

'Yet something we could have learned without travelling so far, I think,' I reminded him. 'And what about us, lady? There'll be no welcome for heathens like ourselves either, I'm thinking.'

'On the contrary, Mentor,' Morgose smiled. 'Eochain says that any who travel with a Christ-bride will always be welcome in the lands of the Laigin, and especially those so well connected to the kin of Corpre mac Cormac. They've gone back to send a cart for us. So you see, Skyhound,' she said to Ambros, 'how you might sometimes bend the power of the Church to your own advantage, rather than always oppose it?'

I was astonished that he seemed to take her advice. Even more astonished that Morgose did not expose him. But he accepted Corpre mac Cormac's hospitality with alacrity and avoiding any inference that he may not share the King of Laigin's beliefs.

'It's a strange title, is it not?' he mused one day when we had passed a full sennight within Ferna's wooden walls, lodging on the sleeping benches of his own hall.

'No stranger than Lord of This, or Ruler of That,' I replied. 'And there were once kings in Rome itself. You've read your Livy. The story of Tarquinius Superbus.'

'All the same, it feels as though time has passed this place by.'

'At least they have a High King,' I said. 'Some sense of cohesion.'

'Symbolic,' said Ambros. 'Purely symbolic. They spend more time feuding among themselves than even our own clans. Fingal says so.'

'You've mastered the Gathelic then?'

'Of course not,' he snapped. 'But a few words here and there. And Morgose has been translating.'

'Morgose?' I said. 'Morgose? Ah, you mean that sightless wife-sister of yours? The woman you said was hardly a prize worth the shedding of blood?'

'We all make mistakes, Mentor. And I'd like you to do something for me. That war-cart of Fingal's. Can you copy its design? I would have one built for myself. A few adaptations perhaps.'

'And you think you will have need of a *carrio*, when we get back to the White-Wilds?'

'Morgose has been translating some of those tales we've heard at Corpre's Feasting Fire. Those stories of their heroes. And their charioteers. They spark my blood. Does that sound foolish?'

'A man with ambitions must make his mark,' I said. 'Racing around the Westerlands in a war-cart – well, it's as good a way as any other. And imagine the rhymes that your new friend, Morgose, can weave around it for her song-saying.'

Ambros shook his head, as though dismayed by my sarcasm.

'There are these too,' he said. He looked around the hall, checked that we were not observed, then pulled a long cloth-wrapped bundle from the deeply-shadowed recess against the low wall, where it joined the roof. He unfastened the cords that bound the bundle, showed me the three spear shafts within, each very different from the other. 'This one they call the *gae*. Or *birin*.' It was short, slender, barbed, with a brace of triangular fletches at its lower end. 'You see? Lead-weighted too. Like the Legion's darts. Fingal carries three of these beauties.' He set it down. 'And this.' Ambros picked up a longer spear, rigged with a throwing loop. 'A *sleag*,' he said. 'Equally useful as a javelin or for thrusting. But look at this.' He lifted the third weapon, heavy shaft and the blade wickedly barbed. Buried in a man's guts, it would have been the very devil to pull free again. 'The *craiseach*,' he smiled. 'We have nothing like this. They use them in phalanx, to force an enemy back through sheer weight. But sometimes from horseback too.'

'There is much to learn here,' I said.

'My apologies, Master,' he frowned. 'You were pursuing your own enquiries. Any news of the potion?'

'None. There are precious few here who use the Common Speech, and those few had no enthusiasm for talking to foreigners.'

'Christ-followers?'

'Yes.' But it was the hollow-eyed signs of starvation that had struck me most about the citizens of Ferna. It was more than six summers since the Black Hags had struck here, killed so many – Corpre's father, Cormac, among them. And that on top of the failing crops, the sickly livestock, which seemed even more of a blight here than in our homelands of the Cousins' Tongue. I had spent as much time as possible wandering the local glens to see the devastation. And it seemed no more than a matter of luck that this clan of Corpre's, this *Ui Cheinnselaig*, had been devastated only marginally less than their rival *Ui Dunlainge*, just down to the north. 'Though it seems strange,' I continued, 'that they should have taken so against the Mauri's medicine when Malco's own bishop remains so intent on its discovery.'

'Do they communicate, one with the other?' said Ambros. 'I expect not. And the Christ-followers are adept at playing the one game by two entirely different sets of rules, depending on their mood, or to suit the occasion. Perfectly feasible that they should see the potion here as a heathen brew and, over there, as a gift from their god. Hypocrisy seems to be their by-word.'

'You'll not say so too loudly?' I said. 'Not here.'

'I thought you would have been impressed,' he smiled. 'I have been playing the cross-bearer with the best of them.'

'Hypocrisy, I see,' I told him, 'is not simply the preserve of the Christian bishops, then?'

'Well, it was my wife-sister who planted the seed. I took her words as a blessing.'

'It doesn't strike you as strange that she has not noticed?'

He coloured, I saw.

'I've been careful not to rub her nose in it,' he said. But I knew there was more to the story, for his voice softened now when he spoke her name. He spoke it almost apologetically.

'Ambros,' I said, 'I am no longer engaged as your Mentor, but if I may speak as a friend?'

'Old habits die hard,' he replied. 'I suspect you will speak whether I give you leave or not. But if you intend a lesson on marital fidelity, Master, you should know that my readiness to wed Rigantona was more calculation on my part than mere compliance with Malco's demands or concern for my father's honour.'

And, to be fair, I thought, *a calculation that did not reckon upon the hound.* Still...

'But this other one,' I began, hardly able to believe that he should be so open about the thing. 'Your wife-sister. The implications. If marriage to Rigantona was a political decision then why risk the goals you hoped to achieve? And tomorrow, or the next day, we must away once more to the White-Wilds.'

He rolled the bundle of weapons afresh, tied the cords carefully back in place.

'We're not going back to Mona, Master,' he said. Not yet awhile.

I have a task to fulfil. To find that Africanus physician and his potion. We've a good crew, a sturdy boat. And Elidyr of Clud Vale sounds like a man worth visiting.'

My heart skipped several beats.

'But you have no charts.'

'You had that fine codex at Bear Fort,' he smiled. 'Did you not memorise the *formae* that it contained of our coasts?'

'It's still there, but my old *Geographia* would hardly have helped us navigate,' I replied. The topographies had been compiled by the High-Born surveyor, Martius Nobilis, under a commission from Flavius Stilicho during the latter's campaign against the Pictoi which, if my memory served me correctly, must have been in the Rome Foundation Year, Nine Hundred and Fifty, or thereabouts – though they were still largely up-to-date. As it happened, I had rubbed my copy from the bronze original that still hung in the great library at Moon's Glow.

'How difficult can it be?' he said. 'We keep sailing north down the coast and stop each night at a fishing village, take instruction there on the next day's journey. At some point, when we reach Ulaid, we'll pick up word about the Newlands Channel, and how to cross to Clud-Vale.'

'And your wife-sister?'

He laughed.

'By the time she realises we're not heading home,' he said, 'there'll not be much she can do about it. Besides, I fancy she's not quite the Christ-follower she pretends.'

Chapter Eight

There seems little point in telling the entire tale of that voyage and its immediate aftermath, since you will know the outline well enough from the song-saying. The latest version I heard, of course, set us aboard three vessels rather than one, so I have restricted myself to the details as they pertain to the Skyhound's true story, and leave you to recall those riddling verses that are more a product of the fertile imagination of those who wished mainly to entertain the young ones around a winter's night-fire.

'Three sails, three sows and three spears. Nine times nine, his crewmen's fears. Who now past the maelstrom steers?'

The sows? I have no idea. But it was certainly a journey of mixed blessings.

Fingal's sailing master – indeed, Fingal of the Five Stallions himself – accompanied our party as we retraced our steps at first light to the *White Enchantress.* Fingal made us promise that we would return, and soon, to help Corpre mac Cormac in his struggle with the *Ui Dunlainge.* A struggle to be fought in the name of the Lord God, he said. Ambros swore a Kinfolk Oath that he would do so, and he even made the cross-sign to seal the bargain. Then we boarded the currock again, heeding the sailing master's entreaty that we should clear the Black Pool at once, reach Edar's Head while the water there was still at low slack. Ambros played his role well, confirming that we should then ride the gathering flood tide, as measured by the liquid dripping of the *clepsydra*, the water-clock, into the still-veiled sun for six hours, before using a back-bearing upon that timid orb and allowing the ebb to carry us south for a further six and, thus, back to Legion's Neck. Reasonable weather was promised, from the feel of the clouds and the sea-wrack omens, and a fair breeze was likely. But we were well past the limits of their vision by the time we rowed out beyond the head's reach and, with a steady gust coming up from the south and west, Ambros ordered the yard hoisted, the sail set – though, to everybody's surprise except my own, he then took the steer-board, called out the hempen hawsers to be bent or secured, and swung us about so that we rounded Edar's Head rather than put it behind us.

Surprise. Each man of the two crew-sections – whether they were today's oarsmen or, like myself, part of the five set to tame sail and spar – cast his glance at Ambros, then at the Christ-bride, yet quickly back again to his duties. But it seemed she could sense their attentions, for Morgose cocked her ear towards them before turning her face to the clouds.

'That's a clumsy course you've set, Skyhound,' she yelled. 'Even for you.'

'I go where my fates take me, woman,' he called back, and Morgose laughed into the weather's breath.

'Now,' she said, 'is that not the truth!' And she settled again in the prow, chanting a tune that touched each swell and every caress of brine on hull-hide.

There were plenty of other vessels in these waters too, I saw. Fishermen for the most part, but a few heavier trading boats too, broader-bellied. They made the passage of that first day easier, set a line for us to follow. Inland of a reef-fringed islet; the next cape; a broad channel between mainland and a larger island; skirting the westward fringe of wave-washed granite fangs that could have been the twins of the Grey Seal Rocks at the northern approaches to Legion's Neck; a third headland; chasing a vast pod of those short-finned whales that we called Blackfish, pursuing them across the mouth of a wide bay; Morgose pressed to shouting for guidance from a fishing boat; and following the fellow's advice to find an estuary with the village and holdfast that he named as Green Mantle.

These humble folk fed and housed us for the night there. Meagre fare, but spurning our silver in favour of news and an hour of host-hearth entertainment from our on-board song-sayer. And always a saga to the glory of Ambros Skyhound. I caught him humming one of the tunes next day as we threaded further north in cold and rainy weather, huddled low in our square-weave from Green Mantle to Firth's Head in Ulaid. A less hospitable welcome, but a respite all the same. And another pleasant passage on the third day, north, north again, until we raised the Obsidian Head. One more fishing village, the locals busy hauling their small boats far beyond the high-water line, lashing their gear securely against the storm which, they swore, would keep us all ashore on the morrow. Yet next morning saw one of those rare spells of clear sky, fingers of true sunlight thrusting down to scatter golden dust upon a gently-rippled ocean where a curlew cried its lost lament.

'How far?' I asked, searching the heavens for any sign of the tempest.

'According to our hosts,' Ambros replied, 'it's no more than six hours across the Newlands Channel to the coast of Clud-Vale.'

Yet those hours must have been the longest of my life. I was never, by nature, a timid man. More through some want of wits, I think, than any hint of heroism. Or brute defiance of danger. As prone to the chancing choice between fight or flight as any other, though once my mind was set on the former, I tended towards a mindless and stubborn stupidity. So I clung to a mast-shroud with a rictus grin stitched to my face and weathered that endless day. In any case, flight was never an option once those seas rose up and crashed around us. The wind whipping into our eyes. Tack and tack about, though with the stomach-churning certainty that we were making no headway whatsoever. The *clepsydra* tipped so violently that there was no measurement of time. Just a lurching eternity of terror, until even the terror melted into monotony. Heave and fall. Hull-hide smashing down as though it must surely tear apart. Heave and fall. Vats of salt-spray flung into our faces. Dripping wetness. Frozen beyond all feeling. Simply perpetual pitch and puke. All of us. Except Ambros, of course. And Morgose the song-sayer.

'*Sea-wings cry, Black Backs sweeping. Gannet soar, Red Beaks leaping. Wind-race pass, shoreline creeping.*'

They came at her summons. Flocks and droves of seabirds in all their variety, dancing with the updrafts, diving into the eddies, like starling-swarm but driven here across the gale until, at once, they were gone, the wind gone with them, and the sweet sight of Cairn Point, at the tip of Broad Nose Loch, in the precise place to which the Christ-bride's stretching fingers were pointed.

In those days of pestilence, it would have been negligent to admit us without a period of waiting, of careful observation, yet it was almost a sennight before we were finally admitted through the gates of

Broad Nose holdfast itself, and then only after we had been carefully interrogated.

'*What man guards the Lugos gate? Nine times nine their names must state, praise their talents, foes berate.*'

I cannot speak for the Lugos gate, but I know that the gatekeeper there in Elidyr's southern capital was a surly traditionalist who demanded our names and our genealogies more than once during that week. And we were proud to fling them back at him, high over the rampart's wooden wall.

'Ambros Owen's Son,' cried the Skyhound. 'Ambros that is called *Cuneglasus* in the Common Speech. Ambros the Red. Ambros, Lord of Overmon. Ambros, from the Bear Clan of the Bough-Gatherer Blood.'

And the rest of us. Myself – Meridden of Sea Fort, Mentor of Moon's Glow; Gwri Powell's Son – Gwri Golden Hair, Gwri the Lost; Senent of Elios; Mabon Meleth's Son; Custyn Banon's Son; Anwas the Winged; Gareth Grim's Bane; Amron of Headland; Cai the Blood-Taster – Cai of the Nine Lives; and Birch Strong-Arm – Birch of the Spirit-Lance. All, apart from myself, boyhood companions and spear-hawks, or foster-brothers, to Ambros. Except for Birch too, the old weapons-master, with his own family and holdfast at the Vale of Wood-Temple.

'And the woman?' the door-porter would cry down at us. 'Whence comes the Christ-bride?'

'Guard your tongue as well as you guard your gate, old fool,' Ambros replied. 'For this is no mere Christ-bride. A song-sayer too. Lore-keeper of the Oak Seers. Morgose by name, and daughter to the White Lady Murgain of Laigin, wife-daughter to my Lord, Malco of the White-Wilds.'

The delay in our reception was also due, naturally, to the fact that Elidyr himself was not there at Broad Nose. And why should he be? His main stronghold lay many days to the north, at the Clud's Rock, though Elidyr was not at Clud's Rock either. Rather, he was hunting, they told us, with his brother, Rhodri, in the ancient forests of Newlands, between the two locations. But he came, at least, riding a pale pony decked with small bells, like some lord of the Sithian Folk from the Mystic Mounds, a tail of hounds and hunters at his heel, with enough slaughtered game to fill his larders for the winter. He was the smallest man I had ever seen that was not truly a dwarf, and he had lost an eye – to a wolf's claw, they said, so that he sported a patch, encrusted with sparkling jewels and fine enamel. Elidyr the Generous, he was called, though the donor of his Praise Name must have been something of a humourist – a description that could never have been applied to Elidyr's sour brother, Rhodri.

'And why precisely,' said Rhodri, 'should we deem it necessary to share the secret of the plague-cure with you, Ambros Skyhound, when Corpre mac Cormac cast it aside so frivolously?'

I had taught the lad better than to fall back on trite appeals to human kindness, or to be beguiled by simple titular generosity.

'Because those who would share great ambition,' Ambros replied, 'must sometimes provide tokens of faith, one to the other.'

Elidyr looked about him, at the forge-faced warriors and brooch-bright counsellors crowding behind his couch, at the jet-dark eyes of the Mauri physician's glistening ebon features. He was not Mauri at all, of course. Nor even a physician. We knew that now, for our time waiting beyond the gates had been well spent. And it transpired that he was Numidian, Masul by name, and had learned his many skills at Carthago Africanus. A man of letters.

'Will you listen to him, now?' Elidyr cried to the assembly. 'Whatever this great project might be, in which Ambros of Overmon seeks to partner me, it seems that I should also pay for the privilege.'

His followers were dutifully amused.

'The entire world knows Elidyr's ambition,' said Ambros. 'The wind whispers the thing abroad, in all four corners of the world. The creation of Greater Britannia. An empire of our own.'

Elidyr buried his face in his hands.

'Empire?' he said. 'Perhaps. But created from what fragments, Skyhound? Does anybody now even remember what we called ourselves before Rome? Before the Legions. The Isles of Fair Presence? The Mountain Lands? What was it, boy?'

'Does it matter, Lord?' Ambros replied. 'It is enough to know that pestilence and famine have stolen our ability to stand fragmented any longer. There's barely a state or federation left with enough trained officials to maintain order. We slip steadily into chaos. And we all know it.'

'Not here, Skyhound,' said Elidyr. 'Not here. Not in Clud-Vale. But if we *did* share such an ambition, what might you bring to the table for your own token?'

Ambros was silent for some time before he spoke, and I saw him glance at Morgose.

'I would bring you the White-Wilds,' he said, at last. 'And I would bring the finest song-sayer in all the lands of the Cousins' Tongue to glorify our names when we succeed.'

Morgose laughed at that. Sarcastic laughter. Though she did not gainsay him.

'Truly?' Elidyr sneered. 'The last I heard, the White-Wilds was ruled by Malco Battle-Shield. Malco the Christ-follower. Malco whose own ambitions rest within the borders of First alone. And himself set to be its High Ruler. He would see us with four Provinces, not one. His own he would cut off from any form of commonwealth, seeking the freedom to starve in splendid isolation. But with his Province established as a *Diocesio*, power shared with his bishops and the Christos Church. A gift for his new god.'

'These things are true, Lord,' said Ambros. 'Yet not entirely. His house cannot stand forever. And it is a house divided. By those who will support nothing but the city-state and Hibernian kingships.'

'Like his wife, you mean?' Elidyr thrust out his chin. 'Or the wife's daughter perhaps. Your own woman, is she not?' He pointed at Morgose. 'And what form of token is *that* which you drag here, Skyhound? Did you not know that I have sworn to purge Clud-Vale of the Christ-followers? And if I should dream of Greater Britannia at all, it would be a dream that excluded those faith-stealers.'

'Your gate-porter must have told you, Lord,' said Ambros, 'that the Lady Morgose is no simple Christ-bride. But also a lore-keeper of great note. She has a view that, where we may be able, we should bend the strength of the Christ-followers to our own purpose rather than simply oppose them. But where that might not be possible...'

It was not possible, in Elidyr's opinion, across the settlements and homesteads of his eastern frontier. There, where his domain touched the farthest north-eastern corner of the Northland, old *Britannia Secunda*, the lands of High-Pass and its Lord, Morgan Thunderbolt, who was creeping his borders and his Outlander *foederati* ever westwards, a whole flock of bishops making trouble as quickly as they made converts, calling down damnation on faithless heathens like Elidyr the Generous, or dripping poison-laced honey into the ears of the district's duty-holders and elders, promising the earth – and the Christ-followers' Heaven too. The bishops brought them the *biblia sacra*, and Morgan took their taxes. Elidyr's revenue!

So there was the token with which Ambros must pay for the plague-cure and his alliance for the future. Three weeks of shared raiding along the borderlands, the holdfasts that sat astride those dark and sinister ridges of the Battle-Forest. Three weeks in which those who had been pressed to change their faith were easily turned back again. Either that, or they found their way to whatever Heaven might exist much faster than they may have anticipated. We had our first brush with the Outlanders there too, groups of Engloi farmers and warriors in Morgan's pay that we put to flight on the slopes below the Three Peaks. And it was that day we found the monks building a new *monasterios* on Elidyr's own side of the river. If they had simply done as they were told, all might have been well. But, as it happened, they refused to leave, barricaded themselves inside the shell of a new temple – so that Elidyr ordered the timbers to be fired. I still hear their screams. I still smell the roasting pig-flesh stench of their deaths.

'Lugos Silver-Hand commands, search the weathered westerlands, where the blessèd cauldron stands.'

And there *was* a cauldron in the tale, as you might have guessed. For, as we rode north to Clud's Rock – Elidyr insisted that any treaty should be sworn there, at his own Mithraeum – Masul the Numidian was finally permitted to share his secrets with us. We had already spoken many times about other aspects of natural philosophy and, predictably, he was fluent in the *sermo vulgaris*, lacking a single trace of the distortions with which our own Cousins' Tongue dialects had so corrupted the Common Speech.

'I have a theory,' he told me. 'Simply from my own observations, you understand? Yet I believe that the pestilence is carried by rats.'

'Rats?' I laughed. 'What, they breathe their ill-humours upon us while we sleep?'

'The thing that they carry,' he replied, with scorn etched upon his words, 'is fleas. And I have never seen a victim yet who was not also riddled with the bites of those creatures on some part of their body. At least, in the early stages. Before the flesh becomes consumed by other symptoms.'

'We all have fleas, my friend,' I reminded him, and scratched involuntarily.

'You must speak for yourself,' he scolded me, and preened himself. He made a notable figure, the exotic finery of his Numidian robes and headgear mingled within the bear's pelt cloak that he used to protect himself from our northern chill, and this interminable winter.

'Then we all have hounds – and the hounds have fleas. Does that appeal more to your sensibilities? Why rat fleas, and not those of my hound?'

'I have no idea.' He flashed me an extravagant smile from those impossibly white teeth. 'And it seems that not all rats may be culpable either. Yet the three things are always present. A propensity of rat dropping. Flea bites. The early symptoms.'

'And the cure?' I asked.

'First and foremost,' he said, 'an attempt at prevention. The practice of cleanliness. Regular washing of one's body. Three times each day. Or four. And the regular application of clean clothing. Ah, where is the faith that would teach such practical codes rather than make false and superstitious promises?'

'And where prevention fails? Is it possible to actively heal those who fall to the Black Hags? Or is survival a matter of pure chance, as in my own case.'

'Chance, you say? From all you have told me, it seems you were placed in the best of circumstances to survive. Whether by chance or not, I cannot say. But cleanliness again. Isolation of the infirmed, where that is possible. The chewing of garlic by those who must be exposed to the sick. And the regular administration of a potion. A brew of garlic and cone flowers, with oil of origanum and sweetened by heather honey. But it must be brewed long and slow in a silver cauldron. Only silver.'

I explained all this to Ambros later, when we had settled for the night in a strongly fortified *mansio* standing in the shadow of the Lugos Fortress, on the neglected remains of the Two's extension, West Way – that road which the Legions had driven through Clud-Vale, through the Province they would eventually call *Valentia*, to service their second great wall, the Severanus.

'So it seems I may owe you my life, Skyhound. For isolating me, at least.'

'He is certain this potion works?' said Ambros.

'Nothing is certain in life, my friend,' I replied, 'except eventual death. The physician says that the earlier the potion is consumed, the more likely its success. But once the pus bags appear, or the Black Hags have begun to eat flesh...'

'If he holds the cure,' Morgose interrupted, 'why is he here? He could be making himself rich in any of the Great Palaces between Parisius and New Rome.'

'Masul the Numidian seems to be making a decent enough living from his journey already, Lady,' I said. 'His travels are sponsored by the court of Justinian himself. One of many such emissaries, it seems. Sent to assess each of the lands where the fingers of Empire once stretched.'

'And Elidyr knows this, of course,' said Ambros. 'That he has the Emperor's eye at his back? Have you not noticed already that, whenever the Numidian is with him, the terms of his ambition change. An insistence that we must forge Greater Britannia in the name of Justinian, rather than Elidyr's own.'

'There would be no room in Elidyr's world,' said Morgose, 'for a High King *and* an Emperor too.' But she used the Gathelic term for High King, knowing that the phrase was common currency in the Skyhound's own lands also, where so many of the Incomer words had become embedded. *Arth Rhi*, was the term she used. And she was amused by it. Began to play and spin it around her song-sayer's tongue. 'And that bauble should not be for Elidyr,' she mused. 'You are Ambros of Bear Fort. *Dun Arth* in my kin-words. Ambros of *Dun Arth*. Ambros *Arth Rhi*. For *Arth Rhi* also means High King.'

There were many meetings. Judgements to be made about those Lords who might be trusted to share the vision – or those who would stand against it. Ambros and Elidyr weighed them all. Constantine of Horn-Head. Aurelius Caninus of Two-Tribes. Lord Protector Fergna Urcol's Son of the South-End Meta-Land Folk. Marcus Seahound of Domna's Deep. Urien of Gift-Given. All those countless others beyond the boundaries of First: the Northlands of Second-Province, where Lenocus of Yew Grove – father, they said, to some strange wolf-boy – held such sway; or Elidyr's own Walls-Land, *Valentia*. Yet what about those less well known to us? The Lords of the other former Provinces here –

the Southlands of Upper-Province and the Flavian Easterlands, those segments of our ambition that lay along the farther coasts, and where the Outlanders were woven so strongly into the mix. Like Henga White-Stallion from the Land of Hosts. And how would the Painted People react – the *Cruithni*, the Pictoi, from beyond the Severanus, where the Legions' Provinces had never stretched in the first place? But there were domestic matters to be considered too. Elidyr's brother, Rhodri, seeking a new wife, and the Oak Seers' matchmakers tasked with finding suitable options. So I naturally suggested my sister, Mirian, named Morning Star for her great beauty and, besides, carrying some significant wealth through her son, Cador Pale-Meadow.

We spoke not a word about the monk-burning, of course, not in earshot of Morgose, at least. Yet it was evident that she knew, for the nature of her song-saying had begun to change in subtle ways until, one night, there was a riddling line about that Sword of Maximus, which Ambros guarded so carefully at his Fortress of the Hammer-Fighters holdfast.

'*Who has let the wolf-fang slip? Magnus Hard-Blade at his hip, Plucked from Iron-Anvil's grip.*'

And as the rhymes unravelled, there was this...

'*Where may Oak Seer giants rise? Above their own and others' lies. Atone for flames and monks-hood cries.*'

Elidyr usually paid her scant regard, yet these lines caught him.

'Then tell me, Lady,' he called to her when she had finished, 'how can it be that one such as you may claim to stand for the Oak Seers when she has already vowed herself as a Christ-bride?'

'Because they are the same,' she said. 'As Christ-followers, we believe that all the heavens and the earth must have a creator, and that this creator, our God, must by His very nature, be eternal. As Oak Seers, we embody all the Life Force of the heavens and the earth in the form of other symbols. The Great Mare. The Horned One. The Long Arm. Yet we still hold that the Life Force they represent must also be eternal. It is a shared faith, do you not see? A belief that there can exist in the heavens some great unknown, which has always been, and which needs no creator of its own. An unknown from which all things emanate and to which all must one day return. The name that we give to such a power is the least important of all matters.'

'Well,' said Elidyr, 'it matters very little. We have agreed our plan. Greater Britannia will become a reality. And those who stand with us will be blessed – regardless of the creed they follow. But those who stand against us...'

I lay awake a long while that night, until all the hall had fallen silent in slumber. War was now inevitable. A war that would add to the woes of our people a while. Yet if those people could be united, wrought together to deal with both the Yellow Pestilence *and* the Famine Times, surely that must be a price worth the payment.

And, as I turned the thing over and over, I thought I saw an ashen shape flit silent beneath the eaves, gliding between the sleepers on the long-benches. A Ghost Owl, I thought, for it had the same form, white under-wings extended, tips never quite touching the ribbing crooks. But then the creature settled at the side of Ambros Skyhound, so that I saw the shaven scalp and heard Morgose whisper to him. She whispered the words that had been in my head since that visit I had made to Deniol's *monasterios*, realised the power of the *scriptorium*. She stole those words, as though she had reached into my own brain and taken them for her own.

'So, it is done,' she murmured – though the sound could have been no more than a breeze threading through the thatch. 'Your dream stands open before you. And you see, too, the myth that the Christ-followers have built. An unshakeable myth, Ambros. One that will stand for a thousand years or more. And we shall do the same for you, my sweet boy.'

There was much I had missed. I saw that now, as she lulled him back into sleep with the almost inaudible strains of the riddling rhymes.

'*What man guards the Lugos gate? Nine times nine their names must state, praise their talents, foes berate.*'

It was Ambros, I knew, who must be the gatekeeper. For he held the keys to all our futures. Yet Morgose sang with all the siren seduction of the small folk from the Hollow Hills. *And perhaps*, I thought, *there is more than one* Uindabhair, *more than just one White Enchantress, in this story.*

PART TWO

The Plague Lords

The brine-foam creature flees –
Senuna must go back to the seas,
her Endless Song abandoned breeze.

Kernuno pines, love-lorn,
ill at ease. Their child-gods pine and mourn,
long for fresh invention. New dawn.

They take the oaken bark,
chew the strips, then fashion boar, deer, lark,
all creatures of both day and dark.

The seeds they scatter wide,
forge woodlands, endless forest divide,
through which the gods may hunt and ride.

But still they lack a plan,
mould the bark. And then they fashion man.
First woman too, the kinfolk clan.

Tugri Iron-Brow
Song of the Great Melody

Chapter Nine

We raised the Draco's Head and our homelands again three full moons after we first sailed from Legion's Neck for Laigin. And I could still not rid myself of that stink in my nostrils. The smouldering monks of the Three Peaks. I said so to Ambros.

'No,' he replied, 'I can smell it too.'

There was smoke. Dark clouds of it that drifted towards us on a northeast wind when we lined up the transit withies marking the channel into the estuary. The smell of roasting pig. Or human flesh. And the smoke thickened, left oily flecks upon our faces as the oars were let fall and we rode the flood tide into the shadow of Twin Sisters, the stronghold of the Skyhound's father, and near the abandoned fortress which some call Reed-Hold for its place above that river's mouth.

'Tell me what you see,' cried Morgose, as we vaulted over the toprails and into the grey shallows, hauling the *White Enchantress* up the shingle and over the rockweed wrack.

'Deserted,' Ambros shouted. 'All the lower holdings. Not a hut still occupied. Some of them burned. Come on!'

I handed her down, steadied her as the Song-Sayer's sea legs found their balance afresh.

'If the Black Hags are still abroad,' she said, 'we should not stay here.'

Most of the crew members agreed, but Ambros was already striding up the track between the vegetable patches, towards the gate towers of his father's ramparts. To the gate which filled the saddle between Reed-Hold's two hills. The gate at which Owen White-Tooth's keeper, Braden Bronze-Ears, now kept the holdfast closed against us. Ambros leaned on his spear, hooked his heel against the lower shaft, and called to the fellow.

'My father?'

'Dead, Lord. This sennight past.'

'How, old Bent-Back?'

I heard no emotion in his voice, saw none in his eye.

'As all the rest,' called Braden. 'The Black Hags took them.'

'The Lady Uithera?'

'Your mother lies at the Hall.'

'She lives?'

'Barely.'

'How many more?'

'I've lost the tally of them. But not a family untouched. More than half of us already taken.'

Ambros looked around at us, knowing that his company had questions of their own, families for whom they, too, must fear.

'Beyond here? At the Bear Fort? Or at the Fortress of the Hammer-Fighters?'

'There is no news. Your father commanded the gates closed. As soon as the first signs appeared.'

'But I have the cure.'

'I fear it has come too late, Lord.'

The ancient gatekeeper turned his gaze towards the higher summit to our right, and he tugged at the heavy ornaments hanging from his ear lobe. A timber tower stood upon the ridge, a refuge of last resort against the possibility that the rest of the holdfast should fall to its enemies. But now it was impotent, redundant against this particular foe, and there were funeral pyres, bonfires of the dead, all along the winding path to the peak.

'It's madness. Why did my father order such a thing? The sick should have been taken beyond the holdfast, not kept within its walls. He should have sought isolation, taken himself and my mother far from here. What was he thinking?'

'He was simply following the instruction he had received.'

'Instruction?'

'From Lord Malco. He sent word with a couple of Bishop Deniol's brothers.'

'Monks?'

'I think so, Lord.'

'Then let us enter, Braden,' Ambros instructed him, 'for I must know more of this. And see my mother.'

'My instructions, Lord...' Braden began.

'My father is dead, fool. His instructions died with him.'

'Yet they came from Lord Malco, and he still lives,' the gatekeeper groaned.

I was close enough to hear Ambros murmur, beneath his breath.

'But not for long,' he said, soft as an arrow's flight. And I saw that Morgose heard it too.

'You know the laws, old one,' I called. 'With the death of the father, Ambros Skyhound is now Lord of Headland, master of this holdfast.'

It was a moot point and, in truth, I hoped that Braden would contest the thing, for none of us relished the prospect of following Ambros into the corruption, which must lie beyond the gates. But the ancient porter was worn down, seemed near to death himself, and after only a brief moment, the timbers swung open before us.

My own brush with the Yellow Death had left me surprisingly unprepared for the devastation we found that day within the palisade walls, and we each wrapped cloak-fold about our faces in a vain effort to keep the stench at bay, to repel the miasma upon which, we imagined, the plague was spread – despite the Numidian's wild contention about rats.

'Mentor,' Ambros called to me, 'you know what's needed. Prepare the brew, if you please.'

'And you, Skyhound?' I said.

'The hall. To find the Lady Uithera.'

'You risk too much, Lord,' Morgose told him, though he laughed in her face.

'Me?' he said. 'But no weapon may touch me. Have you not said so, Song-Sayer?'

'What web is it you weave, Lady?' I asked her, as Ambros continued his climb between the dwellings and plot-holdings to his father's hall.

'You mistake me for my sister, I think,' she admonished me. 'Now where, Mentor, do you think we may discover a silver cauldron in all this place of death?'

The hall itself was the most likely location for such a thing. Perhaps not a cauldron, precisely, but certainly there should be a bowl, a silver receptacle of some sort, capable of slow cooking. So I dispatched Mabon Meleth's Son in the Skyhound's footsteps to see what he could gather, while the rest of us began to forage for the other ingredients we needed – and mainly the wild garlic, which we would all chew for the duration of our work there. We still possessed the oil of origanum vials, which had been our parting gift from Masul, but I was keen that we should use these sparingly, here at least, for it was plain to us all that there were few at Twin Sisters who could possibly benefit from the potion. So we chose some huts, emptied them of everything we could move, then went among the villagers, selecting those still in the early stages of the Yellow Death's grip, helping them to our makeshift Quarantine Temple, sometimes forcing them at the spear's point when they refused to leave their kinfolk.

For the others, those already held tight in the embrace of the Black Hags, there was a separate section of the holdfast marked out, and we wasted no time on cleansing or succour for this group. Those who could no longer tolerate the daylight. Those who screamed at the torments of searing pain behind their eyes. Those with the burning lumps on their necks, within their armpits, around their groins. Those whose pus bags had blackened, sprouted open, to ooze blood and stinking slimes. Those whose extremities were already being eaten by the necrosis. All those, regardless of age or status, we herded beyond the ditch, bank and wooden wall at the base of the Second Sister, that higher hill upon which the funeral pyres already burned. Henceforth, it would always be known as The Hill of the Dead, and they say it is haunted still by the repugnant shades of our plague victims. But we felt foolishly safer with the Black Hags on one side of the palisade, and we on the other. At least, it took fewer of us to stand guard and make sure they remained there – until their own turn came for the flames.

We kept a third area for ourselves, Masul's brew simmering quietly over one small fire, in the hanging welcome bowl that Mabon had liberated from the main feast-hall. It must have been worth a small fortune. Far too ornate to serve, under normal circumstances, as a cook pot but the Numidian's requirement for a silver vessel had been very specific. I hoped that, one day the bowl could be restored to its former glory.

'Did you see the Skyhound's mother?' I asked him and, like all the others, I stupidly searched his face, in the flickering light, for any early sign of sickness. That was the way of it during an outbreak. You peered into the faces of those around you, seeking any of the tell-tales, knowing that if you saw them, it was likely too late for you already.

'Dead,' Mabon replied. 'And Ambros calling down the wrath of all the gods on those responsible for her passing.'

Cai the Blood-Taster knelt at a second fire, stirring contents of the more conventional cauldron, which had accompanied us on the voyage. It smelled good, though we were wary of the ingredients. Most of them we had found ready for use, prepared for other meals that had never been eaten. Soaked red lentils. Leeks. Thyme and mint. A couple of chopped rabbits. Some honeyed vinegar. More garlic, naturally. A round of bread, warming on a platter stone.

'Always somebody to blame,' said Cai. 'Madness.'

He was right. A familiar pattern. The Yellow Death knelt to no master. No logic to its coming and its going. Yet I knew of no case in which those afflicted by its touch had failed to allocate some human source for the *infectionem*. The curse of some alleged enchantress. The foul breath of the Outlanders. The evil eye of a holdfast's fool. A God-sent punishment for the unfaithful wife. A lord's failure to follow any number of local rituals. And if the hapless blameworthy were lucky enough to survive the sickness itself, they were unlikely to avoid either retribution or sacrifice in its aftermath.

'I fear that, in this case,' I said, 'Ambros has already cast Deniol's monks, and my Lord Malco, as the culprits in our little play.'

'For Mithra's Tears, Mentor,' snapped Amron of Headland, 'can you not feel the Black Hag's breath on your neck? This is no matter for bloody jest.'

'Well,' said Senent of Elios, 'whatever the cause, here's another parcel of land that won't be worth the holding any more.'

Amron had been supping from the communal feeding dish, but he flung it now across the floor, stood and stormed towards the doorway.

'May the gods damn your eyes,' he spat, as he disappeared into the darkness.

I suppose we could have shown more sensitivity. After all, this was Amron's birthplace, and much of his family was now gone, taken by the plague. For my part, I should not have made light of the situation. And Senent should probably have held his tongue too. But when death surrounds you, as it did, there in Reed-Hold, the tongue sometimes runs away with itself. A way to hide the terror, which gnaws at our toes. And only Morgose seemed truly free of it. She had unslung the cruth from her back, taken it from the hide bag and begun to pluck one of its strings. The same note. Over and over, punctuating her words.

'Cauldrons bright from iron broth-pots grow,' she murmured.

'You think this one will turn to silver too?' laughed Cai, chiming our wooden eating bowl against the pot's side, before ladling it with fresh stew again, handing it to Gareth Grim's Bane.

'Always some gain to be made,' Morgose told him, 'from even the deepest disaster.'

Somebody outside. A spear scratching against the thatch and rested there. The leather entrance flap pulled aside. Ambros ducking into the dwelling, twin-shadowed by the double fires, a mirror handle gripped between his fingers, the speculum's polished silver face flashing flames around the woven walls.

'You must indeed have the gift of far-seeing, Lady,' he said, 'to perceive any possible profit from this loss.'

'Here,' snarled Grim's Bane, holding out the wooden broth bowl to him. 'Your turn.'

Ambros took it gratefully, supped at the liquid and fingered a morsel of meat into his mouth.

'Mabon told us about your mother,' I said. 'I feel your sorrow, Skyhound.'

A ripple of echoed sentiment, though not from Morgose.

'There's profit to be had,' she said, 'for all those with the luck and determination to survive the Black Hags. To take the abandoned holdings under their own care.'

'And every time you turn around,' Grim's Bane replied, 'some duty-holder now calling himself the Lord of Here or Master of There.'

'Either that, else you find some Outlander or Incomer working the land,' said Gwri the Lost. Then he winced, recalled that the Skyhound's mother was such an Incomer. Morgose too, of course. He cleared his throat. Unusually, abashed. Spat into the straw.

'There are worse things,' Ambros replied. 'They could be Christ-followers too! My mother should not have died. Not like this.'

'Her pain and her fear live still in your voice, sister-husband,' said Morgose. 'Nobody deserves to die thus.'

'She blamed Deniol's monks too?' I asked.

'At the end,' he replied, 'she was beyond blaming anybody. But, earlier, she cursed this.' He held up the mirror, then rubbed its convex face upon his breeks, before studying his own reflection.

'And the Lady Uithera's ruin?' said Morgose. 'The thing of which you spoke. What is it?'

'Her looking-ring,' said Ambros. 'She awoke and found it uncovered on the stool at her bedside.' He ran fingers through his hair, burnished copper in this light. 'She screamed. Begged me to stop her soul from being trapped inside the mirror. Swore that she could feel herself being sucked inside the silver. I covered it. But too late. She was gone by then.'

'Is it covered still?' Morgose asked him.

'No,' he replied. 'You think...?'

Morgose said nothing, continued plucking at that damned string, and we all fell silent, knowing that the Lady Uithera's soul was now likely caught within the speculum, its journey to the afterlife halted.

'Where is your mother now?' I asked.

'You mean,' said Ambros, 'has she gone to the flames? No, Mentor, she has not. Nor my father. His remains are preserved, at Lady Uithera's command, until they can be shown the proper respect.'

'And who will you find to perform the rites?' said Custyn Banon's Son.

'Your mother and father had converted to the Christ-following, Lord,' Morgose reminded him. 'And the morrow is a memorial day for their Church. Fitting. I know the words of the Christos-blessings well enough.'

'They will be buried,' Ambros snarled at her, 'in the manner of our old faith and with the blessing of Mithras. Not this Christos nonsense. Each of them will be honoured with their own Flesh-Eater. *Sarcophagi* to suit their status. A tomb for each of them so they may guard the approaches and gates to this place forever. We shall rebuild Twin Sisters in their name. In that way will my mother's soul be freed again. And at each Day of the Dead we shall journey here to honour them. Those of us who survive this turmoil.'

'Amron will be pleased,' I said. 'I fear we angered him.'

'I saw him,' Ambros replied. 'But, for now, we need a tale to drive the Black Hags from our minds a while. What do you say, wife-sister?'

And she told us an Incomers' tale, about Arth, Son of Conn, and a High King of Hibernia; about how Arth had eventually banished a foul enchantress from his lands, and therefore ended the famine and pestilence she had brought in her wake; about the trials Arth had overcome in the process – the hideous creatures he had defeated and the enormous cascades of ice he had been required to scale in his quest; about the choices he had made – between the poisoned chalice and that which bestowed life; and about the sacrifices he had offered on behalf of his people.

'That's a fine story, Song-Sayer,' I said, 'for driving back the darkness.'

She acknowledged my praise with a rare smile, while the rest of the company wrapped themselves more tightly in their cloaks. Cai, meanwhile, made the cook-fire safe, and I doused the other, declaring the Numidian's potion ready for use at first light. But I heard Ambros murmuring as he settled himself for the night.

'It is a good name, is it not?' he said. 'Arth, I mean. The name I should have given my son. Had he lived. Arth of *Dun Arth*.'

'I did not intend to cause you grief, Lord,' Morgose replied. 'But will you now repay *me* with a tale, Skyhound? You talked about holding back the dark. Will you tell me about that thing, Lord?'

'How should I tell you about that within which you have spent your entire life?' I heard him say. 'A grief of your own with which to deal.'

'Darkness, Lord,' said Morgose, 'is something I do not comprehend. And I count you blessed who may experience its joy. Blackness is the way you describe an absence of everything else. The colour of death, perhaps. Or great loss. An absence of all other images. Yet, for me, there is no such state. I know that I cannot see. Not in the way you might mean. But my head is filled with those that you call colours, though I think there is no relationship between our names for them. For me, they have depth. And warmth. Or a lack of those qualities. Like words. Or music. Or smells. Images that I know as Birdsong, Flame, Earth, or Winter Wind. A thousand of them. And in every shape or form that I have ever handled. It matters not whether my eyes are opened or closed. Whether asleep or awake. They never stop. Never leave me. Sometimes I focus upon them. Try to believe that the gods will one day make something of them for me. Weave them together into the sense you know as sight. Or more. That the images may have meaning. Pointers towards the secrets of the future. Of an afterlife. But, mostly, I simply wish they would leave me in peace. In darkness, Ambros Skyhound. Oh, how I envy your darkness.'

I settled myself upon the floor, feet towards Cai's embers, Mabon's knees pressing into my back, nose nuzzling Gareth's grease-reeked cloak and over-close to the raucous spasms of his throat. The fellow could sleep anywhere. A skill I did not share. But I lay quietly, pretended to doze, yet listened as Ambros Skyhound lowered his voice, which was at once gentled. Unusually gentled.

'Envy?' he said to her. 'I had never thought about somebody being able to envy darkness. But I suppose there is comfort for us in that superficial state. A simple absence of light. Soft as a raven's wing, Song-Sayer. The warmth of oblivion. Though darkness comes in other forms too. Less healthy forms. The destruction of learning. Of knowledge. The bottomless pit of an enraged soul.'

'The cruelties in a man's heart to which only a wife may truly be privy?' she asked.

'You deserted a wife's duty to her husband,' said Ambros, 'and drove him to his doom.'

'It was rashness that killed Einion Iron-Anvil.' She spoke the words with sadness. 'Would you have me weave you the words, Ambros? About how it was between us?'

He was silent a while.

'I think I would have you weave a different tale now,' he said, at last.

'Then know this, sister-husband,' she told him. 'That unless you have a care, the same rashness will destroy you also. Either rashness, or the darkness of revenge.'

'Revenge?' I heard him whisper. 'Oh, I must drink from that particular cup for a while, at least. And I shall drink my fill, Morgose.'

Chapter Ten

Three full days had passed since any symptom-sign had shown. The potion dispensed from our silver cauldron seemed effective for many within the makeshift Quarantine Temple, so that the number of those dispatched to their fate beyond the pale had slowly diminished. Indeed, a few had even returned from that place, apparently cured, though still requiring care, of course.

From our own companions, only long-limbed Gwri Powell's Son – tall Gwri Golden hair – had succumbed to the touch of the Yellow Death. The head pains. Chills and fever. Exhaustion. Nausea and vomiting. I remembered it all too well. But no Black Hags. No pus bags. No blood in his piss. So we dosed him with the brew, observed each of Masul's other recommendations closely. And, Mithras be praised, within a sennight he had climbed back from the void.

'So why do they also call you Gwri the Lost?' I asked him. 'When you seem to have more lives than Hecate's Hounds.'

'No sense of direction,' he groaned. 'Couldn't find the way around my own arse!'

And it seemed to me that he was not alone in that regard. For Ambros had lost his way also, paid scant regard to the work at hand, and spoke largely in riddles, as though he, himself, was dribbling with delirium. It burned in him as fiercely as the stinking corpses we continued to torch, though there were less with each new dawn.

'What word from Bear Fort?' I asked him when I had finished ministering to the sick and taken my turn at the bonfire again.

'It seems they followed the Christ-followers' instruction too,' he shouted through the rags wrapped around his mouth and nose. Despite the best precautions, those snarling flames seared against our faces, and we were careful to stay upwind from their putrid smoke. 'I sent Birch,' he went on, standing back as we dragged a young woman's remains from the small mound of the dead. If she had hoped for dignity in the last agony-filled moments of her life, she would have been disappointed. For the strong breeze caught the hem of her woollen skirts as we lifted her, bared the shit-stained thighs and buttocks. And, as I averted my eyes, their gaze fell upon her own – or, rather, the sockets left by raucous crows. The skin of her face was blood-puddled, nose bitten by the Black Hags. 'I told Birch,' cried Ambros, 'to remain clear of the gates there. So he stayed at my brother's Memory Stone. And just as well. The Hags have eaten their fill of Bear Fort. Worse than here, Mentor. Birch says there are fewer survivors than dwellings.'

'He was always ready with a good tale,' I said, rubbing my palms on my breeks, vainly hoping to wipe away all memory of the young woman as she fried and split, her internal fats feeding the fire. Birch must be exaggerating, of course. The Fortress of the Bear was home to three hundred souls. Half of them gone? Surely that could not be possible.

'Well,' he said, 'tomorrow we lay my father and mother to rest, at the gate. For now, at least. Until we have time for the tomb. To free her fully from the mirror. Then we'll see about Bear Fort. But, true or not, I shall find Deniol and his monks, then nail them to trees like that imposter whose crucifixion they value so much.'

We slid like spectres through ground mist seeping from the salt marshes that spilt Draco's Head from the rest of Headland. A scant two hours march from Twin Sisters to the Bear Fortress on paths Ambros had known since childhood. Yet our ragged ponies feared the place: the treacherous ground on either side; the gulleys, which the sea still smeared with foetid sludge at every turning of its tides; and the courage-quaking curlew cries punctuating each of our wary whisperings.

'You will be Lord of Headland now,' murmured Senent of Elios. 'And whether we like it or not, the Christ-following has caught root here.'

'And there's wrong chance about them,' Mabon Meleth's Son reminded him. 'No doubt about it. Evil befalls those who stand in their path.'

'I shall be Lord of Headland in one of only two circumstances,' said Ambros. 'The first is by the grace of Malco Battle-Shield – and he would only grant such a thing if Deniol advises him to do so.'

'You're kin to Malco now,' said Senent.

'I am husband to his wife-daughter,' Ambros replied. 'That does not make me kin. Simply another hound for his pack. It places an obligation upon me as duty-holder, not on Malco as my wife's mother-husband.'

'And the second circumstance,' said Morgose, 'is one in which you simply seize the lordship without Malco's blessing.'

We had all been together for too long. Easy to forget the Song-Sayer's quiet presence at the best of times. Especially simple to lose our own sight of her divided loyalties.

'Perhaps best not to discuss such matters on this accursed swamp,' said Anwas the Winged.

'You mean,' Ambros laughed, 'not with my wife-sister in our company? Well. There's no secret to my intention. And Morgose could have returned to Fairwater Maw at any time. Fulfilled her obligation to act as Malco's ears. Is that not so, Song-Sayer?'

'Do the folk of Headland not have enough to occupy them, Skyhound?' she said. 'The pestilence. The hunger. The tragic deaths walking in their wake. And now you would have them at war once more? The Christ-followers speak of this thing. Four terrible horsemen. Apocalypse. We need the blessings of any gods we can muster. Peace. And if the Empire is truly building its trade routes anew, perhaps prosperity again in the comfort of that peace. Wealth flowing from your mines again, even.'

Most of us glanced westwards at her mention of the mines, to the bulk of Draco's Head, where the copper ore had lain unmolested far too long. A downturn in demand but a lack of folk to work the galleries, despite the Incomers we had thought might fill the emptiness.

'The Empire will not trouble itself with trade to Britannia,' said Ambros, 'nor send back the Legions to protect its interests, unless we have somehow succeeded in turning it back into one or more Provinces, rather than this fragmented patchwork of self-seeking primacies that remain.'

We trotted out of the haze and skirted the foot of the Jewel, the wooded mountain that cradled the Fortress of the Bear in the bosom of its eastern flank. And there we came upon the Memory Stone of Einion Iron-Anvil, bright and fresh-painted with the symbols of Skyhound's family and the images of his brother's life. Yet nothing here to create a link with Morgose. Worse, a desecration – and one that was uncomfortably close to Einion's monument.

'Are we at the place?' she said, aware that we had all fallen silent in the stone's cold shadow, and that only Ambros had jumped from his pony's dappled back.

'Will you not make peace with my brother, even now?' he asked.

She flinched at the question, as though he had struck her. Yet she made no answer. For she picked up the mood from the rest of us, I think. The utter silence, unbroken even by the Skyhound's passage through ryegrass and heath ling, past the Memory Stone, to the gulley into which a slurry of rotting humanity had been spread. From the weft of their wool and the hold of their hair, as we used to say in those days, they were all Incomers. There had been a large community of them here for many years. The same community from which the Skyhound's own mother had sprung. Just part of the mural. And I suppose that they were still thus. Only now their pigments stained the scene with a different image. They tainted the air too, of course, even though the breeze carried the worst of their odour away from us. But, as Morgose, sniffed at the stench, I sensed it was something else that her nostrils detected. Some essence of her homeland.

'Laigin folk?' she asked.

Ambros turned upon Birch Strong-Arm then.

'You said nothing of this,' he cried.

'I hardly knew how to tell you,' Birch replied. 'They were turned out of the holdfast, it seems. Blamed for the pestilence. Turned out on the mountainside. Left here to die.'

To be fair, the Incomers always seemed even more susceptible to the Black Hags than the rest of us.

'We slam our gates,' said Morgose, 'upon the fingers of those who helped to fashion them.'

It was an old saying, but true, often enough.

'They did not deserve this,' Ambros howled at the empty stone rampart above us.

'Did they not, Skyhound?' she taunted him. 'Even though so many of them were Incomer Christ-followers?'

'I have nothing against Incomer or Outlander. How could I?' he called back. 'Only against those that infect them with false faith.'

And there was not time, now, for holding those responsible to account. Just another episode of the tragedy. So we began the work afresh. Entered the Bear Fortress and unloaded the silver cauldron. A new Quarantine Temple. Fenced an area outside the main ramparts where we could exile the hopeless. Began to light the bonfires once more. For the folk of Headland, from inside the holdfast. For those Incomers left on the cold slopes. We observed the usual precautions. And took our own rest in the deserted main hall, that elegant space within which Einion and Ambros had both been fostered at the age of seven, and which each of them had subsequently inherited in different circumstances. It was here that I first met the boys when I came from Ialanus. In the small chamber, which served as our schoolroom. As *ludus* and library too. And it was here I now found myself reunited with those fine scrolls it still contained, along with that old, rubbed copy of my *Geographia*, the only part of my codex collection we had not moved to the Fortress of the Hammer-Fighters.

I was alone, studying by a constellation of oil lamps – one of the topographies written by that High-Born surveyor, Martius Nobilis – perhaps five nights later, when Ambros came to me.

'When I was first sent here to the fostering,' he said, 'just a cub, rolling in the dirt with Cai and some of the others, I used to stand out there, upon those limestone ramparts, and turn my gaze around all the paradise over which my father held sway. I wondered how one man could hold so much in the palm of his hand. Southeast, and that unbearable beauty of the mountains. West to the Reed River's estuary, to Twin Sisters and Mona's Isle across the sound beyond. North over the sun-blessed expanse of the Hibernian Sea. And east to the place where the hills of Slavehold plunge into the ocean.'

'And now it all seems like such a modest territory,' I replied. 'Its beauties marred by so much grief.'

'Will you travel for me again, Mentor?' he asked.

'You think me restless because I peruse these *formae*?'

'It's myself that's the restless one, I think,' said Ambros. 'But I need you to take a few of the company. Pick whomever you choose. Then off to the Fortress of the Hammer-Fighters with you. Take the cauldron. Act for me if the Yellow Death has struck there too.'

I fought down the emotions that raged within me for, while I relished the mission, it troubled me too.

'And you will gather a war-band,' I said. 'Try to pick up Deniol's trail.'

'As Mithras guides my steps.'

'He may guide you straight to Malco's spears. I shall have difficulty explaining this to your wife.'

'Perhaps best not to try it then. When you take the road, I shall still be here. You may tell Rigantona you left me here, tending to my fallen kinfolk. For that will be the truth. And, for whatever happens after you have gone, you cannot be held accountable.'

'I should prefer that you follow our counsel, Skyhound. And the Song-Sayer has it right. The people need to rest now. To recover from all this. Why not leave the Christ-followers be?'

He gripped my shoulder, shook that red thatch slowly, striving for patience with me. Our roles reversed. Ambros now the teacher. Myself, the delinquent student.

'My friend,' he said, 'the task we face is far more than a simple settling of scores. To forge afresh a province fit for the Empire's attention and wealth – an empire within the Empire – we need to bring together all those of like mind. Men like Elidyr and Fergna Urcol's Son. Others too. They will not do it without leadership. And they will not follow any they regard as a minor player. Master of Bear Fort? Lord of Headland? Lord of Headland and Overmon? None of these are enough. I need Mona and all the lordships that swim in its wake. If I speak for the whole of the White-Wilds, it is just possible that our natural allies may heed me. But Malco will not join us willingly. And Deniol? The other Christ-followers? They have their own empire to forge. They will not treat with any but their own. In which case I must create my own fate, Mentor. So go to the Fortress of the Hammer-Fighters. Distract Rigantona. Pay tribute for me at the new Mithraeum. Bring Charger back with you. And, when you're done, fetch me the Sword of Maximus. Find me at the Fairwater Maw.'

She sat upon an unfamiliar oaken throne, and all above her head hung garlands, freshly picked. The face held proud, masked by twisted tendrils of her hair. About her brazen, pale-fleshed feet, a dozen shields of fallen foes. Her father's, I imagined, from the patterns painted on their hides. It was a statement, spoken clear and loud. But here she was Queen Maeve, of whom the Laigin legends tell. The Lady Crow. All shrouded round with gauze-weave, shimmering black, though sheer enough to shame her modesty. And mistress of these lands, all held in Malco's name besides.

'I found the Mithras Temple closed, Lady,' I said. Not the most polite of openings. But I had waited over-long for the audience. And even the distraction of her openly displayed charms, the welcome essence of her scented body oils, made little impact on my impatience. Not then, at least. Not greatly. Though I recall the hazy hint of pleasure that I felt with the memory of Rigantona wedding-dressed in her scarlet diaphanous *flammeum*. I remember, too, the way I hefted the bulky satchel at my hip to help dispel the image.

'Upon the advice of our good Bishop Deniol,' she replied, and hardly to my surprise. 'He sent word of the Yellow Death creeping upon our borders. Stressed that we should close the gates, pray to our Lord Yesu of Nazareth. And to forsake all graven images, as our *biblia sacra* demands.'

She still spoke the Cousins' Tongue with Gathelic-laden accents of Laigin but her perfect use of the *sermo vulgaris* to describe their holy books was clear evidence that she had been studying under the monks or Christ-brides.

'My Lord Ambros will not be pleased,' I told her.

'My husband is returned then? Here? No, I thought not. Yet, you see? The bishop's advice, the blessings of God Almighty, have served us well. No trace of the Black Hags in my halls.'

It was true. All the way westwards, from Headland, along the Eleven, I had been dodging smoke-smeared settlements and malodorous *mansios*. But once I had turned my pony's head south into the passes of Overmon, in company with Mabon and Birch Strong-Arm, I had seen no sign of the pestilence until we reached the gate towers at this Fortress of the Hammer-Fighters. The gate-keepers had permitted us to erect a shelter there, to wait out the days in proof that we were free from threat.

'It pleases me to hear the news, Lady,' I said.

'I understand that my husband has not been so fortunate. They say he labours still at Bear Fort with some heathen potion, hoping its efficacy can match the Will of God.'

'You may recall it was Lord Malco who sent him in search of the elixir. With the blessing of Bishop Deniol, was it not? And it has, indeed, helped to deal with the sickness.'

'My mother's husband has a foot in two faiths, Mentor Meridden.' I could not plainly see her mouth, but it seemed to me she smiled, for her voice gentled. 'And I lack the wiles to play so many parts. Besides, the bishop has now received better guidance on the matter. Malco sent Ambros on a fool's errand. And, like a fool, my husband went. You claim the potion helps. Yet your eyes betray your uncertainty.'

In truth, I had not realised she could see my eyes. Foolishly deluded by the fact her own were hidden behind that veil of shifting hair, I was forced to recall them as they had been revealed so briefly on her wedding day. Emerald green and full of fire. I could not see their flame now, but I could sense them searing through my soul.

'The same eyes, Lady,' I said, 'that have witnessed the potion working. Not in every case, that much is true. But if you sense uncertainty in me, perhaps it simply stems from my doubts about the welcome we might expect at your gates.'

'Did you doubt it?' She sounded genuinely affronted. 'You are my husband's Mentor. A man of great renown in these lands. And there is the custom of my own people. To respect such learning.' You would not have known it from her words at our first meeting, at the Fairwater Maw. '*Why should anybody want such a thing?*' she had said about me. Well, she seemed at least to set some greater store by me now than on that occasion, though I chose not to remind her of the earlier outburst. 'Even if,' she continued, 'we may sometimes be at odds with those possessing that gift. Or did you expect some different salute? The legendary hero returned from the impossible quest. But I'm sure my sister will have done her best to fashion each of the Skyhound's loyal companions into her tale-telling. Where is she now, Master Meridden? Back with our mother at the Fairwater Maw?'

It struck me suddenly that danger lurked in telling her the truth. Morgose still at the Bear Fortress. With Ambros. For it also occurred to me, at the same time, that it would indeed seem strange for the Song-Sayer to still be there. Though not so strange for me. Not since that night in Corpre mac Cormac's hall at Ferna.

'When I left Bear Fort…' I began. My rehearsed speech. But she slammed her hand upon the arm of that oaken throne.

'Did I not just speak about the laws of hospitality, Mentor?' she sneered. 'Do not abuse them by licking your lips with some falsehood's helm. I know my sister better than she knows herself.' Her voice softened again. 'But never mind. Whatever the purpose for which my husband sent you here, your visit will provide a pleasant distraction.'

She must have tired of the deer-hound's company then, I thought, and immediately wished for a more worthy image of this woman. She shifted in her seat, stroked the fragile dusky film of a shimmering gossamer sleeve. And I recalled my disciple's words. Distract Rigantona, he had said. From what? More, perhaps, than just his ambitions.

'I should certainly welcome a visit to the library cubicle,' I said. 'I left some old friends in your *armaria*.'

'And brought your copy of Quintillianus back to rejoin them, I hope?'

I could not insult her by asking whether she truly knew his work, so I bowed graciously, acknowledging the acuity of her riposte, and patting the satchel at my side.

'I have kept it safe and dry all these months, Lady. For that very purpose. And perhaps we will find distraction a-plenty within this contentious codex.'

She slipped from the throne, gestured for her spear-hawks to remain at their station. Then she beckoned me to follow as she led the way from the gather-hall into the privacy of the chambers beyond.

'Your other friends,' she said, over her shoulder, the night-mist of her skirts whispering and floating about her shins, 'are they comfortable?'

'Mabon Meleth's Son only finds comfort,' I told her, 'when he has some god's token in his paw. He doesn't really favour one over any other. In a tight corner, I have seen him variously produce a Knot of Isis. Or Cybele's Crescent. Even a small wooden cross of your Yesu the Anointed. Hoping for a favourable result from one or the other. But it's the Dolphin of Bacchus that he favours most. And so long as he has a wine cup close at hand, he'll feel at home.'

'And the other? The one who looks like a bearded ancient oak?'

'That's Birch,' I said. 'They call him Strong-Arm. Or Spirit-Lance. He tutored your husband in weaponry when Ambros was fostered at the Bear Fort. He's always happy when he has some tale to embroider. So he'll either now be telling Mabon that he's never seen a lodging-space so fine and grand, or complaining that it's the worst pit into which he's ever been thrown. But pay him no heed, Lady. Your hospitality is generous enough.'

'I hoped you would not be disappointed, Mentor,' she replied, stopping in the passage at a place I remembered well. Rigantona had added her own refinements, of course. The wattle walls of the corridor had been clay-daubed and whitewashed, decorated with a woven hanging that spoke of her roots, and lit by the stone lamps of fish oil. The sparse luxuries of her bedchamber stood open to our left while, on the opposite side of the narrow corridor, she held back a different drape, covering an entrance to the compartment, which I had helped Ambros furnish with a honeycomb of wooden *armaria* shelves now holding our collection of scroll-books and codices. It was wonderful to be among them once more, and I filled with joy as I took down sections of one after the other, filling my nostrils with the seduction of their aroma. That codex copy of the *Iliad* with illustrations. Augustine of Hippo's *City of God*. The legal reference *Codex Theodosianus*. The *De Re Militari* by Vegetius on Roman military science. Cicero's *Orator*. My extracts of the *History* by Priscus. Another history text, this one by Ammianus Marcellinus. Martius of Mamucio, with a *Genealogy of Britannia's Prefects and Tribunes*. My own *Anthology of Northern Song-Sayers*. My rapture was so deep that I almost forgot Rigantona's presence. Until her milk-white arm stretched out and took down a more recent treasure. Presumably one of those on which Ambros had caused his slave scribes to work. 'And this one?' she said.

It was a codex. The *Metamorphoses* by Apuleius.

'You've read it?' I asked, failing to mask my incredulity.

'I think you mean, am I *able* to read it,' she replied. 'That bonded scribbler of my husband's finished his task a sennight past. Interesting boy. I pressed him to teach me more of the Common Speech.' I knew the lad. Ambros had purchased him a couple of summers previously. From the Great Market at Uric's Hold. He had somehow discovered that the young weakling, useless for all other purposes, was monk-taught, clever with the reed-pen. So he had been set to copying some of Owen White-Tooth's favourites for my disciple's own collection. Including this one, it seemed. 'But I could have understood it,' she told me, so that I could almost see her smirk, 'perfectly well from the pictures.'

It was not the complete work, of course. Simply a segment of Book Nine, which included that side-tale – the one about the Wife's Tub. You've read it? The one in which a faithless wife hides her lover in the bathing vat when the hapless husband returns early from his work. She convinces him that the lover is only there to purchase the vessel but has insisted that it should first be thoroughly scoured. The husband is persuaded it may be best to scrub the thing from inside, so turns it over and climbs inside with a lamp to undertake the work. Of course, the brazen woman takes the opportunity for one more moment of adulterous pleasure – on top of the upturned tub, while her lover shouts innuendo-filled advice and instruction to the husband slaving beneath them. So, here was the image. Beautifully executed. A glorious addition to the original. The lover straddling the tub. The wife straddling her lover's exaggerated phallus.

'It seems the boy has managed to expand your vocabulary considerably,' I said, though I wondered how the lessons had been conducted in practice. But I remembered, too, a description that Apuleius had also written. "*A witch,*" he had said. "*Power of a god. She could bring down the sky. Lift land into the air. Turn rivers into rock. Wash mountains to the dust. Bring the dead back to life. Diminish the stars. And brighten even the realm of Tartarus.*" He could have been describing Rigantona. For then I knew that here was yet one more White Enchantress, another *Uindabhair.*

'I think perhaps it was a mutual exchange of knowledge and experience,' she murmured, and traced a finger over the illustrated erection – prompting one of my own. It hardly helped when a fold of that black diaphanous gown settled upon my arm, stroked it with exquisite gentleness. She turned her head to me, so that some of those tangled locks parted a little, revealing the sweet dampness of Rigantona's lips. And, Mithras help us all, I gripped the edges of that veil, pushed back the braids until I could swim in the depth of her eyes, and far, far beyond.

In truth, I saw no sign of Rigantona's deer-hound until the final day of that guilt-smeared sojourn at the Fortress of the Hammer-Fighters. And I never even gave the beast a second thought after my first coupling with its mistress. It had been out with a forage party. The Skyhound's own dog, Charger, with them too. A productive hunt. So we feasted well on our last evening within Rigantona's walls. The deer-chaser, meanwhile, though plainly happy to be reunited with her, displayed not the slightest unnatural behaviour. So I began to wonder whether Ambros might not have told me the truth.

Rigantona, I convinced myself, though hardly innocent, was simply lonely. Understandable. A marriage of political convenience that she did not relish. In a land that was not her own. A husband still mourning the loss of his first love and who, at this very moment, was fulfilling his own ambitions, through the gods knew what mischief towards her mother-husband. She had turned to me in a moment of weakness and I had given her succour. Ambros himself had told me to distract her, had he not? Though I feared it was myself who felt the most distraction. So I crept away from Mabon and Birch before dawn, for one last tryst with Rigantona, wishing that I might stay but driven to leave by the men's increasingly difficult questions about why we tarried so long at the Fortress of the Hammer-Fighters. I crept away, expecting that Rigantona would share my reluctance to part. But I was wrong, of course.

'Just as well,' she said. Her arms were wrapped tightly around the deer-hound's neck, its head nuzzling into her crotch. 'Your stay here has been costly, Mentor.'

Costly? I wondered. But she would not be drawn further and we parted in that strange way. I felt as guilty and wretched as Aeneas in his abandonment of Dido. I saw myself having to endure the Clearing – that public and judicial confession of crimes, which the Incomers had originally brought across with them long ago, but now so much a feature of our own justice system in these parts too.

'Kernuno's Crown,' said Mabon, as we neared the Narrow Straight, with Charger running loose, just ahead of us, 'you've barely spoken ten words in two days, my friend. Are you sickening again?'

'More sickened than sickening,' I replied, and knew I had said too much.

'Indulged yourself too much at the table of that witch,' said Birch. I turned sharply towards him, dreading that he might somehow have discerned the truth, saw the suspicion in his eyes. 'That was some strange feast,' he sneered. 'Even for you, Mentor.'

Chapter Eleven

We found Ambros, as we had known we would, encamped around Malco's holdfast at Fairwater Maw. It would hardly have qualified as a siege, however. First, because the lad's forces were not numerous enough to make such a thing effective – he had no more than forty spear-hawks at his back, and barely a dozen of us mounted. And, second, because the Maw was impossible to blockade without a few ships to seal the estuary.

'The old monster has been sending out his boats for days,' Ambros told me, as soon as he had quietened Charger's unleashed joy at reunion with its master. But we each wrapped ourselves more tightly in our square-weave too. For the Light Half was nearing its end in those closing days of Octubres, and the approach of another New Year at Summer's End. Not that you could easily define the difference between seasons any more, of course.

'You don't seem too troubled,' I replied, delving into my pony's pack. 'Anyway, this should also bring you joy.'

I handed him the fleece-wrapped bundle.

'You brought it,' he exclaimed, and hefted the Sword of Maximus into the air. 'Bullock's Balls! Did my wife not query why I should be needing it?'

'She doesn't know I have it,' I replied.

It was true. After Rigantona had dismissed me so abruptly, I decided she was no longer worthy of my confidence. So, with Mabon and Birch, I had forced our way into the closed Mithraeum, discovered the blade in exactly that section of the grotto as described to us by Ambros, and stolen it away. It had made me feel better. As though the deliverance of the sword would somehow atone for my other misdeeds. My betrayal of his trust.

'And how did you find my wife, Mentor?' There was an edge to his voice. 'Pleasant?'

'Inseparable from that brute of a deer-chaser, for the most part,' I said, then moved swiftly to change the subject. 'And Malco. He's not taken to his boats also?'

'He has no real need,' said Ambros. 'Look at us. Forty men to take one of the strongest holdfasts in the White-Wilds.'

'It may once have been,' I replied. 'But not so hard to crack any more. He lost half his people too, remember. In the last outbreak. And not much activity up there.'

There was little activity in general. And I had been struck by the number of abandoned settlements we had passed since crossing the Narrow Strait. Fewer drovers than would be normal, bringing their beasts down from the summer pastures. Fewer harvest wagons.

'Not at the moment,' he said. 'But it won't take long for his messengers to get through. Then we'll see who answers his call. Unless I miss my guess, many of Malco's Client Lords will stand shy of this one. Until they've no other choice, at least. Rhun will come, naturally. And Osla Big-Knife.'

'The Saeson's not here?'

'There's been no sign of him. Nor that god-damned bishop.'

'Perhaps that's a blessing,' I said. For, while I still dreamed of building a myth around Ambros to match that of the Christ-followers, I feared them too. 'But even if only Rhun and Osla muster for him, we'll be trapped here.'

'And worse,' said Ambros. 'Malco sent a runner down yesterday. Offered a truce. Family should not be divided at Summer's End Eve, he said. Regrets for the fate of my father and mother. No difference so great that it cannot be resolved over a horn of heather-beer.'

'That buys him time for the War-Band to get here. What words of wisdom from our Song-Sayer about all this?'

'Not here either,' he murmured. 'Truth be told, she's with Deniol. At that liars' den where she took the Christ-followers' vows, it seems.'

The bishop's original *monasterios* still stood on Bright Island, which the Incomers called *Seiriol* in the Gathelic.

'Spilling her guts about monk-burning?' I said.

'You'd be surprised, Master,' he smiled. 'You should not judge her falsely. Did you not teach me that loyalty is what we seek from friendship?'

'It was Cicero, I think.' I had to turn my face away, pretended to watch a forsaken thunderhead sweeping over the wild uplands beyond the holdfast. 'But what will you do about Malco's offer of truce? Take his hand? Fall into the trap? Or simply walk away? Not too late for reconciliation, I suppose.'

'Far too late, Mentor,' he told me. That edge again. Yet honed now. Tempered. Sharp.

'It's good that you came, boy,' Malco roared, his great ham of a hand gripping the Skyhound's shoulder, hugging the lad close to his barrel chest. It was a strange sight, this embrace between the scarred old stag and the rutting red buck, there at the threshold of the gather-hall.

'I've seen twenty winters, Great-Uncle,' said Ambros. 'Hardly a boy any more.'

I made a note to myself, that I must remember this also, then tried my best to feign disinterest in their conversation. Instead, I peered into the darkness, watched as the guisers' parade made its triumphant approach. Each of the masked mummers with a torch blazing aloft, or his arms filled by the food collected from each dwelling, every surrounding homestead, for the night's feast. And, at their head, Grey Mare pranced and snorted. His dappled, pony-hide cloak billowed in the wind, neckpiece covering his outstretched arms, the back, flanks and buttocks flapping down behind. He carried an ancient stallion's skull in his hands too, with great skill, manipulating the movements as though the beast was real. And, at each child he passed, he caused the mare to snap at them. *Clack, clack, clack* went the jaws, and the terrified infant would leap back into the arms of a protective parent or older sibling.

'True enough,' Malco beamed. 'But in the name of Our Lord, I'm the only kin you have left now. So tell me about this grievance, my son. What were you thinking? Turning up here at my gates like some young Achilles. Haven't I always kept faith with you? Gifted Overmon into your care? And my wife-daughter too?'

'Grief, I suppose,' Ambros replied, 'is my only excuse. It had been a hard voyage, Lord. And in your name. To find a weapon with which to fight the Black Hags, as you instructed.'

The guisers were weaving their way between the holdfast's dwellings and, at every house, they paused, while those living within lit a west-facing light, to help guide home the spirits of the family's dead.

'I was wrong to send you,' said Malco. 'Wrong! The answer was here all along. Exactly as Bishop Deniol promised. We closed our gates upon the Yellow Death. Prayed with him for our salvation. And our god delivered us, Ambros. Do you not see? Why not renounce your false deceivers, allow the bishop to offer you the water blessing?'

'It saved neither my father nor mother. Nor all of those upon Mona, I think, from the newly abandoned homesteads we've seen.'

With each horn lamp lit, a modest offering of food and a small bowl of water was left beneath, to revive friendly spirits after their long journey back from the Halls of the Dead, or to placate any of the Fair Folk come visiting from the Hollow Hills – since both would be abroad that night.

'There are those among us who refuse to accept the protection of the Christos and are punished for their wickedness,' said Malco. 'You must understand that, surely.'

'I shall never understand any god who gathers followers by fear alone,' Ambros replied. 'But my father and mother had already taken this water blessing. Did it seem to you, Lord, that their wickedness outweighed the conversion?'

'I did not say so,' Malco snapped, 'and God knows I had sins enough of my own to confess.' Well, he was right enough in that. Wife number one and the first husband of his second to account for, apart from any other considerations. 'But I have done so, my boy. My tablet is scraped clean. I am promised a fine place in the Eternal City after I leave this life.'

And life could be confusing at times. For there we stood, watching the ritual for those who believed that our kin were left, lost and wandering through the cavernous Halls of the Dead, until we summoned them back among us upon that single night of the year, while the rest, the Christ-followers, looked forward to basking forever in the sunlight of some Heavenly Palace. Malco's confession of his crimes, meanwhile, would have been made in some private and whispered half-truth to his friend, the bishop, rather than the public arena of the Clearing, in which the people, and a Judex or Arbiter, might determine the criminal's reparations.

'Then who should I hold accountable for their deaths?' said Ambros. 'If not yourself, then Deniol perhaps, who ordered their gates shut when the Yellow Death had already crept within, and thus condemned them to its grip.'

'Why seek to blame any for the Will of God, Ambros?' said Malco. 'His ways are mysterious. But tomorrow sees the beginning of a new year. And the bishop tells me he has received a missive from the Holy Father in Rome. That we should use this time of Summer's End not only to welcome home the spirits of our lost kindred, but also to venerate the Sainted Martyrs of the Church. New beginnings, my boy. And with the New Year upon us, we can talk about your future. What say you?'

'I say,' Ambros shook free of the older man's grip, 'that the Church of this Christos is like the Ravager, the Swelling Sickness, which devours a body from the inside out. For your faith, Great-Uncle, consumes all that's healthy in the world, takes all the lore, all our traditions, and twists them to a shallow imitation that will eventually cause folk to forget each of our old values.'

'Beware the feast in times of famine', we used to say. In the literal sense, of course, the meaning was obvious. Bellies that had become accustomed to frugality rebelled violently when the hungry suddenly found themselves faced with relative plenty. But it also carried the image of Greeks bearing gifts, an offering almost too good to be true. The wooden horse, which deceived the Trojan.

'There are more blades in this hall than I should like,' I whispered to Ambros, reaching down to tickle Charger's ears, to cover my words. We were perilously close to Malco Battle-Shield and the White Lady Murgain of Laigin. Just along the bench from them. Too close for open dialogue.

'We seem a little thin on the ground, true enough.' He mumbled his reply against the pig's rib from which he was studiously picking the sweet meat. His previously infamous diet seemed to have waned since our return from the north. Or perhaps since the deaths of Owen White-Tooth and the Lady Uithera.

'So, my boy,' bellowed Malco, reaching along the table to slap the Skyhound's back. 'What d'you say? Will you stand at my shoulder while I drag this rag-arsed province back together again?' He turned to his wife. 'He's a good lad, this one. What did I tell you? He'll fill that girl of yours with some fine sons, unless I'm much mistaken.'

Murgain was finding it hard to eat too, her pale face badly bruised and the corner of her mouth swollen and bloodied. I assumed she was still having trouble controlling her tongue when in her husband's company.

'We met those on our travels, Lord,' I said, 'who would see that ambition stretched. Who believe that our own quarter of the land is insufficient for our needs.' And, however difficult it must have been, the sound of my voice seemed to push Murgain through her discomfort.

'This creature still in your pay, daughter-husband?' she spat through the operative side of her lips.

It was a raw nerve that she struck with me, too, for I had seen no fresh coin for some time now. I was living off a limited reserve of my own by then, but it could not last forever, and Ambros seemed oblivious to the fact. A problem with the young: this failure to understand the value of things.

'Mentor Meridden remains with me…' Ambros began, then paused as though the question had caught him off-guard. 'He remains with me,' he concluded. Answer enough.

'Should be rid of him,' said Murgain. 'I sense he has ideas above your station, Ambros Skyhound. Folly to reach too high. Be content with Headland and Overmon. With my daughter too. They are more than enough for you.'

'As Mona was enough for your husband, Lady?' I said. And she hissed at me, lynx-like. I saw Malco grip the table's edge too, restraining himself from some outburst, either towards me or the woman, I could not tell. But his eyes narrowed as he looked around the gathering. He seemed to be tallying heads.

'The blade you were carrying,' he said, at last, 'when you came through the gates. It was the sword of great Maximus, I think.'

'The very one bequeathed to my brother,' Ambros replied. 'That with which your son severed Einion's head. What of it, Lord?'

'They say it sings in battle,' said Malco. 'But also that it carries some curse. An ill thing for fetching to a Summer's End Eve. You have it here?'

A curious question, I thought.

'The same sword, Great-Uncle,' Ambros told him, 'though it hasn't been used in anger since that day. So I cannot vouch for either song or curse. But I left it in safe hands. Beyond your doors.'

Malco seemed satisfied, commanded the guisers to leave, Grey Mare too. Then he hammered upon the table for a song-sayer. Not Morgose, of course. Another. A monk, that I did not recognise, but with a nose so sharp that he must have inherited the thing directly from the Legions. Tiresome too. The sort of dirge that would make you think of opening your wrist veins, or swallowing hemlock. Another Christ-followers' distortion of fact.

'I suppose it must be hard to attract anybody of quality,' I taunted them, thinking of that poor fool from Across-the-Sea, 'when all they can expect by way of reward is a good stoning.'

The muscles in Malco's jaw tightened and twitched, while he gripped the table tighter still.

'Many of my own kind were killed too,' said Murgain, recalling the slaughter of innocents after last year's bout of the Yellow Death. 'Such things happen. When superstition replaces our faith in the Almighty.'

The monk was stumbling his way through a few lines about the Bright Island itself, though it was pure invention, claiming that the name *Seiriol* originated from some Christ-followers' holy martyr, rather than the Gathelic. Another imaginary monk too. Cybi. Nonsense about this Cybi's tanned face. Some people will swallow anything.

'I hope one day,' said Malco, wistfully, 'to have my tomb upon that blessed isle. Though not too soon, eh?' And he shook with laughter.

Well, I thought, *I shall be happy to oblige for the slightest reason.* The short blade strapped inside my tunic was tickling my ribs, anxious to be about its business at the first sign of treachery, and if it took no other's soul this night, it would certainly dispatch Malco Battle-Shield before all others.

Yet the feast came to a surprisingly peaceful end. Rather, it was killed stone-dead by the monk and his mournful music. So we were ushered outside again, cloaked once more, though there was little need. For, just beyond the gates, the twin bonfires of Summer's End Eve had been lit. Each twice the height of a man. Tomorrow, those beasts that could be spared, or which were too old, would go under the knife, the meat preserved for as much of the winter as might be possible. But the breeding stock for next season – sheep, goats, pigs and cattle – would now be run between the flames, all evil and wrong chance banished from them in a way no Christ-follower would ever understand.

'I am still waiting on your word, Ambros,' yelled Malco, as the drovers began the difficult task of forcing herd and flock to face the flames. 'Will you fulfil the client-oath? Stand with me. Or at least honour your position as my wife's daughter-husband.'

We were caught in something of a crowd. A ring of Malco's hearth-heroes just behind us. No sign of our own spear-hawks, the Skyhound's dog run off with its fellows. And, behind Malco's men, a second semi-circle. This time the guisers. Still masked, Grey Mare among them. Only now they stood silent. Grave and menacing.

'You want the truth, Great-Uncle?' Ambros asked him. 'Then I must tell you this. That you took the lands on all the farther side of the Narrow Strait by strength of arms. But not by any right granted you. Neither by your new god, nor any other. Such is the way of the world. We have what we hold until another comes along who may have a stronger arm, a sharper spear.'

It was not precisely the manner in which I had taught him to balance rhetoric with oratory. And I looked over my shoulder at the threatening faces, stared into the eyes of those who would soon kill us without mercy.

'And that's you, puppy?' Malco peered into the Skyhound's eyes, scarcely able to believe his ears. 'Glance around, boy. Tell me what you see. Nowhere to run. You're a prisoner, lad.' Rough hands grabbed my arms before I could reach the knife. I saw that Ambros was pinioned too. 'In a day, two at the most,' Malco went on, 'Rhun will come. Osla the Saeson too. And, when they get here, I will personally peel the skin from your living flesh. Inch by inch. While you watch. But I shall flay you only to the waist. Keep you alive so that Rhun can have the pleasure of pushing a pole up your arse. Plant you here like a tree. This worthless piece of shit at your side.' He jerked his head in my direction.

'You interrupted me,' said Ambros. He seemed perfectly calm. It disconcerted me even more than the prospect of a wicked death.

'Slay them both now, husband,' said Murgain. 'Wipe that smirk from his stupid face.'

'You presume far too much, woman,' Malco snarled at her. 'And I'm happy to hear the cockerel crow a while longer.'

'There's a second thing,' said Ambros. 'That, for all your excuses, I hold you responsible for the death of my father. And I was there when my mother died. I saw the agony of her passing, swore you would pay in kind for every pain she endured.'

Malco laughed then. But I saw something akin to fear pass across Murgain's face. Some inkling of other outcomes.

'Take them,' Malco shouted through his mirth, and his hearth-guards began to haul us away. Yet, at that moment, the silent guisers threw off their masks. One by one, the familiar faces were revealed. Gwri the Lost. Senent of Elios. Mabon Meleth's Son. Custyn Banon's Son. Anwas the Winged. Gareth Grim's Bane. Amron of Headland. Cai the Blood-Taster. And, finally, Grey Mare himself, bearded Birch Strong-Arm. Blades in their hands too. They cut. They hacked. They stabbed. They slashed. Until we were drenched in their victims' blood. I took one of our captors down myself, throttled him with my bare hands in the confusion, in which the revellers tried to decide whether or not they should intervene. But, by that time, Ambros was locked in a struggle with Malco, and the rest of our men had broken through to form a cordon around the skirmish.

Thus, they prevented Murgain's escape, held her. But she scratched and bit like some feral thing, cursing them in her own Gathelic tongue that made my blood run cold even though I could not understand the actual words.

At the same time, Malco had caught his opponent in a bear's grip, squeezing the lad's life away. He may have been a head shorter than Ambros, but he was more than twice the weight, broad beyond belief. So I found my knife, gripped the bone handle and moved in for the kill.

'No!' Ambros gasped. 'Stand down.' There was a trickle of blood running from his scalp, down into his eye and, with just one arm free, he was beating hard upon Malco's back and shoulders, or the top of the older man's head. Though this was serving little purpose, for Malco's skull must have been hard as iron, half-buried into the Skyhound's chest. I could almost hear the rib cage cracking.

'Let me finish this,' I yelled, but he shook his head violently.

'No!' It was barely a wheeze. Yet I saw his one free hand go to his own shoulder, struggle with the brooch that fastened his cloak. The same brooch Rigantona had gifted him at their wedding. The gold and jewel-encrusted scorpion. It was the pin, of course, he needed now. He gasped and groaned, for the pain must have been terrible. But he braced the brooch between his fingers, plunged the point into Malco's broad neck, right up to the clasp. Not a mortal blow, but enough. The big man's grip slackened, and Ambros kicked hard into his groin.

'Little bastard!' Malco cried, as he staggered back, Ambros holding him in turn now, following through by hammering his forehead hard against the bridge of the other man's nose. 'Fuck you, boy,' Malco whined. 'So what now? A moment of fame? But only until my son gets here. And then...'

'And then,' Ambros sneered at him, 'you'll not be around to see me kill him too.'

'You haven't got the stomach for this, puppy.' Malco looked around for help.

'Have I not?' Ambros replied, then turned to me. I began to shake my head, to find the words of good counsel that, I thought, he needed. But he had already stepped forward, gripping Malco's tunic, yet still staring straight into my eyes. 'I told you, Mentor,' he said, 'no going back now.' And he turned again to Malco Battle-Shield. He began to push him. The old bull roared his defiance. Ambros pushed him even faster. 'Just the Will of God,' he yelled into Malco's face. Then released him. Only at the last moment. So that his enemy tumbled into the flames of his own Summer's End Eve bonfire.

Chapter Twelve

Rhun did not come. Nor Osla Big-Knife. For the snows came in their stead. And folk took it as an omen. Well, they take most things as such. But an omen for good or ill? That is normally the question. Though this often depends on the side you take when trying to decide.

So, by the next morning, Summer's End itself, the first day of November and the New Year, an overnight blizzard had buried the bonfires in immaculate distraction, drifts of diversion piled high against the walls and palisades of the Fairwater Maw, heaped upon the thin memories of those within. The storm remained unabated too, and Ambros took full advantage. His loyal companions were dispatched, forcing a path to every dwelling that could be reached, summoning the occupants. Duty-holders, elders, craft-followers and all the oath-bound. Each unable to tell, through the swirling flurries, the blinding whiteness, precisely how the land now lay. No chance to exchange gossip, nor to rehearse response with any but the closest kin. A terrible sense of isolation. Shrouded stillness. Until they found themselves in Ambros Skyhound's presence, there in the gather-hall where Malco Battle-Shield had, only hours before, held sway.

Ambros must have repeated his performance twenty times that day, for the benefit of each small group brought before him. Each group the same. Cloak, hair and eyelashes heavy with crusted snowflakes that barely had time to thaw before they found themselves obliged to take the new client-oath, then dismissed, back out into the snowfall's squall, the lad's promises still ringing in their ears.

'Your former lord, Malco Battle-Shield,' he would tell them, 'is dead. Dead because he breached the laws of hospitality. Invited me to talk of settling disputes between us. And I came. Even though he had killed my father. My mother too. Yet, with the invitation, he plotted my murder. On Summer's End Eve, of all days.'

I was indignant for him too, almost had to force myself to recall that it was we who had brought the threat of war to Malco's gates.

'But he has paid the price of his perfidy,' Ambros would continue. 'Thus, I claim the lordship of Mona in his place. Rather, I present myself before you as though this were a Clearing. To accept your judgement. Tell me there was guilt in my slaying of Malco and, so soon as the snows permit, I shall stand aside. For Malco's own son, perhaps.' It was an easy point to score, for Rhun the Tall was hardly popular with these ordinary folk of the island. 'But if you find in my favour, I have to tell you that, as Lord of Mona, Overmon *and* Headland, I shall then also lay claim to all of the White-Wilds – *Venedoti*, in the Common Speech. Much else besides. And I shall tell you the reason.'

He did so. At length. Honeyed their ears with promises of a new world. Of the system he would introduce to ensure that no single part of his lands should any longer starve while another feasted to excess. Of the roads he would repair to strengthen trade. Of the words he would send to the rulers of Rome, Gallia, Across-the-Sea and a dozen more besides. Bargains to be struck, which would bring back the merchants, make the mines viable again. Freedom, to worship as one pleased. It was all received politely. There had never been any prospect of a different outcome, of course. In all that optimism, which always accompanies a New Year. Livestock about to be slaughtered. Crops freshly harvested – though even a cursory glance would show that there was nowhere near enough for any prolonged winter. And Ambros surrounded by his spear-hawks,

'You never thought to warn me,' I said to him in a lull between his orations, 'that you had arranged for Birch and the others to pull off our rescue last night.'

I tried to make light of it, and would have preferred to speak with him alone on the matter. It had stung me. But none of us had slept, keeping a tight defensive perimeter just inside the gather-hall in case of counter-attack from Malco's remaining faithful, with just a couple of men keeping close watch upon the unusually compliant White Lady Murgain.

'Ach,' Birch himself bawled at me, 'you'd have wanted to sit us down for a lesson about some bloody wordsmith or other. His use of deception on the stage.'

'And we had our own drama to perform,' laughed Ambros. 'To be honest, Mentor, I had no real idea myself. Not until near the end. I'd told Birch and Cai to make themselves scarce. Mingle a bit. And be ready for any trouble.'

'But the guisers thing,' said Cai, 'that was my idea. Brilliant, eh?'

I was still resentful that Ambros had not shared even his outline plan with me, but I was not his keeper. Not any more. And there was some backslapping, good-natured badinage, to mask our shredded emotions, as well as the insecurity of our position. But the next group gathering for an audience, included a fair number of Malco's own hall-guards who had survived the night and not fled, as a few had done. Our own men were cut and bruised, but we had lost only one of them, Senent of Elios. We still mourned his loss in our own way, though the speed with which these warriors of Fairwater Maw took the client-oath to Ambros did much to revive our spirits. We would remain wary of them, naturally. Not to be wholly trusted. But a good beginning. Their First Spear was an Incomer called Balor mac Neit, who even offered to stand with us from this very moment. Loyal to the White Lady, he said. Had been at her side since Laigin.

'I'll not speak ill of former loyalties,' he said, his black beard rimed with ice, 'but I would see that lady better used, Lord Ambros.'

'Then perhaps we should have the Lady Murgain herself come forward,' Ambros replied.

Anwas and Gareth Grim's Bane provided escort for her dignified procession from the rear of the hall to the front, where Ambros had set up Malco's oversized throne, complete with the dragonhead handholds. Her high cheekbones made Murgain aloof, haughty, as she stood before it. And the green cat-eyes seemed little affected, neither by a night without sleep nor the loss of a husband. It is the way of the beast, after all. One master dies and the feckless creatures will simply move on to find another. They will not mourn, as dogs are wont to do.

'You will treat his mortal remains with respect,' she began, before Ambros had even time to think of a suitable greeting.

We must all have lived the whole episode afresh as she spoke. The fury of sparks when Malco crashed backwards into the flames. The bonfire's collapse around him. The living torch that dragged itself from the blaze. That sickly sweet pig-stink again as his flesh crackled and spat his juices upon us. And if we expected any other sound from Malco himself, we were disappointed. His face was framed in a burning halo, at the sight of which each Christ-follower, Murgain included, had made their warding sign. His hair, all of it, had singed away, and I doubt those misted, agony-streaked eyes could still see. But he staggered there an age or more, confronting Ambros, his lipless mouth, the exposed fangs, wide in a silent scream. Until he tumbled back into the welcoming release of the inferno from which he had crawled.

It was a cruel sight for me, especially, whose mother had died by the flame also. Accidentally, perhaps, but a most vile of deaths, all the same.

'He has already been honoured with a funeral pyre, Lady,' Ambros replied.

Any frigid irony he may have intended, though, seemed lost on her.

'Then his ashes will go to *Inis Seiriol*,' she insisted. 'We shall build a martyr's tomb there for him.'

'You think he died for your Christos?'

'I know he did, Ambros Skyhound. And will you stop me, after all those words about freedom of faith? No amount of hollow promises to these poor people can save you from the Almighty's revenge.'

'Hollow?' said Ambros.

'Because,' she spat, 'you swear to heal their future hurts when you have not even begun to see the depth of those they already suffer. You take upon yourself the role of saviour, the right to rule, and do not even understand the nature of your inheritance.'

'I learn quickly, Lady,' he replied. 'And I have the best of mentors here to guide me.'

A mentor without contract, nor purse, I thought.

'And even if you begin to understand,' she said, 'do you think that word of this will not spread to the other Prefect Lords? You would take from one. Give to another. How long, do you think, before they close their holdfasts against you? Before they make sure this new sickness of yours should not spread to their own duty-holders? Before Malco's son comes to take your head, as he took your brother's?'

'There will be some who would stand against change, simply because that's their way,' said Ambros. 'But the others, those who have suffered most, like Cullough of Bright-Fields, or Bran of Romaland, they'll ride the flood with me. And by the time Rhun is able to gather his host, it will already be too late for him.'

He sounded confident. Another stratagem he had not shared, perhaps.

'And my second condition,' Murgain announced, as though she had not heard him. 'Once the remains of my lord and husband are safely enshrined on *Inis Seiriol*, you shall grant me safe passage to my daughter. Your wife,' she stressed.

'I had imagined no other future,' Ambros smiled, 'than one in which you enjoyed the protection of my own holdfasts, either at the Bear Fort or, if you prefer, at the Fortress of the Hammer-Fighters.'

'A choice of prisons, you mean?' she sneered.

'You are free, whenever the weather permits, wife-mother, to come or go, as it pleases you. And you shall have your own hawk-guard to give you comfort. Balor mac Neit as its First Spear.'

This was not the way I had taught him to negotiate.

He had secured no more than a worthless client-oath in exchange for her demands. And he had even thrown a free gift into the offering. That, regardless of the weather, we would deliver Malco's ashes to the Bright Island by no later than Mithras-Birth. Meanwhile, he worked like a demon. Stores organised. Messengers dispatched to those lords of the White-Wilds, closest and most accessible to him, both politically and geographically. Secret projects set in hand among the craft-worthy, so that each smith, carpenter, bone-carver and leather-master was taken into his confidence.

'No turning back, Mentor,' he would say, whenever I tried to fathom his mysteries.

But, by Midwinter's Sun Standing, with the crossings of the Narrow Straits defended against surprise incursion, sturdy ponies were harnessed to the six slider-carts, fashioned by the Maw's workshops in the manner of the tribole boards we used for threshing. In this manner we were able to set out on the journey through that desolate landscape from one side of Mona to the other. Across its widest edge.

We took with us the young hook-nosed monk who had sung so mournfully at Summer's End Eve, but who seemed less than anxious to rejoin his brothers. Indeed, he had picked up an entirely new style, his verse structure now owing much more to the music of Laigin –

I assumed under Balor's influence – and the words shockingly at heretical odds with his vows.

Summons the snow beast
when the passes need to close,
or tames the weather;
frees those taken at the feast.
Repays perfidy with fire.

Just a sample – a shameless praise-poem to Ambros Skyhound's godless gifts. But the whole had grown to epic proportion by the time we reached our destination, and even Murgain had given up trying to curb the monk's enthusiasm.

The *monasterios* stood on a rise of that sharp promontory – Mona's End – stabbing from the island's eastern extremity and lunging towards Bright Island on the far side of the Black Sound. A fine view of the white-capped ridges across the Narrow Strait. The Giant's Tomb. The Cairn of the Twenty. Snow-clad trees embraced the place, and the famished light made its bangor palisade seem a creation of the Fair Folk, one that would vanish forever at the first mortal word we uttered. Smoke from a hearth fire was the only sign of human occupation, though we could hear pigs grunting and snuffling within, and a brace of crows floated upwards around the smoke's curling pattern, carping an alert at our approach. The hermitage gate opened slightly and a shivering monk-brother peered through the gap, then dragged the thing as wide as he was able against the drifts when he saw the White Lady of Laigin before him like a very embodiment of the Winter Witch.

We slid into the narrow precinct before a clutch of wattle-walled buildings, climbed stiffly from the sliders, and were ushered into the chapel, while Custyn Banon's Son and Anwas the Winged took care of the ponies. Balor mac Neit remained also, to unload Malco's great funerary pot, while Bishop Deniol came blustering from behind a Christ-embroidered curtain at the opposite end, a dozen paces away, and tying a thick cord around the ample girth of his robes. His face was a mosaic of alternating images, welcome and surprise whenever his head turned in Murgain's direction, hatred and fear each time his vision was drawn back towards Ambros.

'The Lord be praised for your deliverance, Lady,' he cried.

'I should praise Him more fully for a welcoming hearth, Bishop,' she said.

'Bishop Deniol,' I suggested, 'is no more renowned for honest hospitality than was your dead husband.'

Balor struggled through the hurdled doorway, clutching the two-handled urn to his chest.

'Set him upon the altar,' Murgain told him, and Balor set his burden down upon the simple table, alongside a wooden chalice and fine silver Christ-cross. 'And then you can prove the Mentor wrong by showing us to the gather-hall.'

He studied her face, the yellowing bruise and swollen lip.

'They have used you badly, Lady,' he said. 'These Lord-burners.'

So, at least one of Malco's fugitive spear-hawks had made it this far. But further? Might they have passed over the Narrow Strait, carried word to Rhun before Ambros had closed the crossings?

'That's right, Bishop,' snarled Birch Strong-Arm. 'Man-burners. So perhaps wiser to have a care in the way you speak.'

'They have not harmed me, Bishop,' said Murgain. 'Though that hearth fire would be welcome. And a word with my elder daughter.'

'I will gladly share the meagre warmth of our gather-room with you, Lady,' Deniol replied. 'Though I doubt that my holy brothers – even your daughter – would willingly extend the same courtesy to this *Cuneglasus* and his oath-breakers. Usurpers have no credence in the eyes of God.'

'You should have a care, Bishop,' Murgain told him. 'For it seems this Skyhound also has some ambition to become a saviour. To release the folk of the White-Wilds from their sufferings.'

'Saviour?' he sneered. 'There is more, Lady. For I have word that your husband is not the only one to have met his fate in the flames at the hands of these heathens. A whole hermitage of Christ-brothers burned alive in the north, I am told. A holy war called down upon their heads by the Bishop of High-Pass. What say you to that, Red Slayer?'

How has this word come to him? I wondered. *From Morgose?*

'I say this, Bishop,' Ambros snarled at him. 'That I shall remove from you any dilemma of decision about sharing your hospitality with me. I have come only to ensure safe conduct of Malco Battle-Shield's remains. But with that task complete, I am happy to also enlighten your monk-brothers on the new ways in which your existence shall henceforward be ordered.'

'We obey God,' said Deniol. 'Not any mortal man.'

'And you shall do so as you please,' Ambros told him. 'As shall any other who chooses to worship differently. But you shall not benefit from any patronage of mine. The lands you have been gifted are now forfeit. They belong to the White-Wilds once more. You may reside here a while, or you may move on. But, if you stay, there are conditions. First, you will swear the client-oath. To me, Lord Bishop. And, second, you will accept that, in the event I may need your livestock – anything else for that matter – it will be delivered without question.'

'No man may lay a foundation,' the bishop objected, 'except that which is laid in the Christos.'

'You should consider yourself fortunate, Bishop,' Ambros snarled, 'that you are still able to spout this nonsense. For I swore an oath, not too long since, that I should make you suffer the same end as your Yesu for the fate your messenger monks forced upon my father and mother.'

'And you promised me a place under your roof, daughter-husband,' said Murgain. 'Why? So that you might make a martyr of me too? I should prefer to remain here, with the Christ-brothers, I think. If you banish our faith from your lands, Skyhound – the faith of so many now under your self-imposed rule – the Almighty shall unleash a terrible revenge upon your head.'

I had tried to tell him. Morgose had told him. Make use of the Christ-followers, we had said. Learn from them. But do not stir up the hornets' nest. And, as though their Yesu of Nazareth had given a foretaste of the danger, Custyn burst into the chapel.

'Ambros,' he cried, 'you must see this!'

From the hermitage gate, you could look east beyond the extremity of Mona's End, past the Bright Island, and see the outline of Draco's Head on the far side of the bay. Just to the right of that headland, the horizon seemed devoid of land entirely, for there lay the salt marshes we had traversed all those months earlier on our way to the Bear Fort, after we had dealt with the devastation at Twin Sisters. But if your gaze continued to sweep past the salt marsh, the ground rose in a series of ice-tipped hills, into which the channel wound south, disappeared towards Reed-Hold itself. And it was like living the moment again since, from the exact location of that holdfast, a pall of smoke arose, just as it had done when we returned with the plague-potion. Only this was blacker. Bigger. Much bigger.

Ambros strengthened his sparse garrison at Ridge-Mouth, assuming that Rhun had marched overland to torch Twin Sisters and would therefore arrive soon at the Narrow Strait. He was like a thing possessed: desperate to reach Reed-Hold itself, to see the damage done to the holdfast and his people; fretting about the fate of his own place at the Bear Fort; and anguished by the approach of Mithras-Birth – our inability to show the proper reverence, respect for the celebrations. Yet he was pinned here, gathering as many reluctant spears as he was able. For Rhun's force could not help but outnumber us. We were confident, though, in this place so simple to defend. We would trap them, whether they chose to use the rafting ferry to Dog Island and the causeway, or to swim one of the western routes.

Three days we waited there at the Strait's crossings, chilled and cheerless, using whatever protection the water's edge homesteads and fishermen's huts might provide. But there was no obligatory day of rest, nor feasting, nor exchange of tokens, nor holly boughs, nor sacrifice to the Invincible Sun on Mithras-Birth itself. In truth, Sol did not even bother to attend for its own celebrations that day but, instead, sent a morning of cold, wet fog, and from the fog came two ponies, labouring through the snow. One carried that same young monk. The other carried Morgose. We had seen no sign of her at the hermitage, such was our haste to leave and make preparations for Rhun's next move. But her name had been spoken often enough, bandied about, cursed, whenever we had succeeded in gathering for food. Yet here she was, bold as a brazier.

'Ambros Skyhound,' she cried, as their small mounts clambered down onto the shoreline, 'why tarry here when your foes are somewhere else?'

Ambros had been scouring his ring-mail coat with dried sand, and trying to settle some petty dispute between Cai and Birch Strong-Arm.

'And who do you serve today, Christ-bride?' Birch yelled at her. 'The fat bishop? Your mother? That false god you all share?'

'We've no patience for riddles today, Song-Sayer,' said Ambros. 'If you've news then share it.'

'Rhun the Tall is upon the water,' she told him, 'with many boats. He will not come to this place, but to the Blood Shore. I have seen it.'

'Or somebody has told you to spin this yarn for us,' said Cai. 'To lure us away while Rhun makes his crossing.'

'And seen it?' Birch laughed at her, the ice-cloud curling around his bushy face. 'Even with the eyes of an eagle there is nothing to be seen this day.'

'How did you see this thing?' Ambros demanded. 'A dream? A vision?'

'He rides the mist,' she recited, 'oar blades hushed; tall, son of death, weapons rushed, stands where Mona's dreams were crushed.'

'Sister Morgose woke me in the night,' said the monk, pulling the heavy hood back from his half-shaven skull. 'There were many verses. She bade me come with her.'

'You led her here, you mean,' said Cai.

'No,' said the monk. 'She led me. I had no idea how we might find you, Lord Ambros. But she did.'

'You do not fear to use my true name, monk?' Ambros snarled. 'What manner of Christ-follower are you?'

'One who thinks you may, indeed, be divine, Lord,' Morgose answered for the monk. 'Brother Owain has visions of his own. But, for now, you have a choice to make. Meet Rhun at the Blood Shore and you may not overcome. But if you stay here, he will take you in the flank and you will surely die.'

The place of which she spoke has many names. It is the bay on the southern side of Mona's End, close to the fortress of Gazing-Hold, below the *monasterios*, and cut into that wide stretch of shifting sands that gradually closes into the Narrow Strait itself, more than an hour's fast march east of where we now stood. It is variously called the Blood Shore. Or Long Battle Bay. For it is the killing ground of which Tacitus wrote so much. Where the Legions of Paulinus crossed to fight the island's folk, the warriors of Ganganio, in the year Eight Hundred and Thirteen, Rome Foundation Year – *Ab Urbe Condita.* And then the whole history repeated, fifteen years later, when the armies of Agricola returned to bring fire, sword and rapine in their wake. The Legions claimed both encounters as great victories, though our song-sayers tell a different tale.

Bright, bright, the Eagle shines, fills our eye. But Rome's blood freely spills, at Ganganio's battle skills.

'The Song-Sayer is right,' said Ambros, as though a shadow had been lifted from his own sight. And, suddenly, we all knew it too. A revelation. Epiphany. Even Birch and Cai affected. It all made sense. Rhun would not contest the crossings. He had no need. For there were the boats, which Malco sent forth from the Fairwater Maw when he had thought himself under attack by our meagre band. The boats intended to summon support – support that the blizzards had prevented from arriving. The boats that Rhun would have supplemented from along his own Slavehold coast and the Holy River. And, in this way, he caught us by surprise. Or almost.

You will have read the work of wordsmiths, or listened to the cadence of song-sayers, whose heroes are made to describe in detail their own part in the thick of a fight, at the very heart of battle. Every detail. The precise nature of the blows they struck. The way in which they stared into the eyes of foes before they clove their skulls apart. The words they exchanged with enemy and friend alike. Their recollections of how the fortunes of war shifted on one part of the field or another. Pig-shit! Let me tell you that, once it begins, you would be lucky to even remember your own name. You do not know what transpired within two paces, let alone elsewhere in the fray. Old men do not refuse to speak of their fights because the recollection is painful, but because it does not exist. The rest is simply chaos and red mist, good fortune or bad, and the only lingering memories are usually those of the smells that so permanently stained your nostrils.

And that day was no different. There were the opening verses, of course. The clumsy dash, war hounds bounding among us, back along the knee-deep track that wound and rolled over every rock-strewn outcrop, or through silent, shrouded trees. The arrival at the ooze-filled, tide-deserted bay. The doubts and accusations that we may, perhaps, have been deceived. The absence of all sign that Rhun was coming here at all. Then the careful splash of oars, hushed cries out upon the fog-banked waters of the channel, those who had lost their way, each separated from the rest. Finally, that mystic vision of the first boat's grounding, materialised from out of the mist before our very eyes, their crewmen mired in mud as they jumped ashore, and many taken down by slingshot or javelin or dogs' jaws long before we closed with them at spear-thrust. Mithras be praised, too, that they came in such a way, each currock separated from every other.

A series of cloying, desperate struggles from one part of the shrouded bay to another. Yet between? Nothing but the chaos of which I spoke. The red mist. The stench of foetid sludge. Seaweed. Piss and puke. The metal tang of blood upon my tongue.

Chapter Thirteen

By the time the red fury faded, as the fight finished, a crimson turning tide was tossing bodies up onto the strand, rolling them back and forth in tedious returning. Yet no sight nor sound of Rhun the Tall. Perhaps he had missed the landing point entirely. Or perhaps his own boat had come far enough into the bay for him to get some idea of that which awaited him should he step ashore. But he must surely have been able to hear the chanting that went up among us when our work there was done. It must have carried five thousand paces through that silent fog. Somebody began it with a simple *thump, thump, thump* of spear shaft on shield hide, and then began the refrains. Rhun's name bellowed out over the water. Hideous insults. About how he had left his balls on Mona's shore. Much more besides. And, as we sang, as we beat out the rhythm, on that day of *Sol Invictus*, the sun did indeed appear. Mithras shone upon our victory. And we felt that we, too, were now invincible.

We had lost warriors ourselves, including Gwri Powell's Son. Gwri who, like me, had fought the Yellow Death and lived to tell the tale. Gwri the Lost who was, in truth, now gone from us forever. But we had gained a fighter too, it seemed. That young monk, Owain. I had caught glimpses of him, his robes bound up about his waist, his own bollocks bare, and nothing but a mattock with which to carry forth the slaughter.

'Did they teach you to fight like that at the *monasterios*, Hawk-Beak?' Cai asked him when most of us finally sat, exhausted, on the shingle. There was not a single one of us without a wound, without every inch of our bodies and clothing caked in the mud of Long Battle Bay, without dark blood splattered upon that grey sludge. Even Morgose was similarly stained, but that was through the comfort she had carried to so many of the crippled. Blessings of our Oak Seers, or the Christos, whichever was appropriate. Or both, for good measure.

'They taught me to heal, Blood-Taster,' the monk snapped back at him, and continued to pass among the men. He had let his robes fall again and I realised that one reason, at least, for hitching them must have been to protect the satchel he carried. From its depths he had produced a large vial of vinegar, which he was using to purify wounds once he had washed them in sea water, before either stitching them closed or, where they gaped especially open, securing them with assorted *fibulae* – the arched medical variety, of course, rather than our brooch pins. Bandages were a particular problem, however, and he had soon organised those least damaged into forage parties, sent to gather as many clean linen strips as possible.

'We must do better than this,' he kept insisting, every time he passed Ambros, 'if there is to be any significant campaign.'

'It seems he has appointed himself *medicus* for your army,' I said.

'We'll certainly need one,' Ambros replied, but his eyes forever strayed across to the mainland, towards Twin Sisters. 'Can you still see smoke there, Mentor?'

'It was three days ago when we saw the smoke,' I said. 'It could not still be burning.'

'No, I suppose not. But when the fog lifted, earlier, I thought I saw some.'

I set my hand upon his shoulder.

'You'll get there soon enough,' I said. 'And then we'll see more clearly.'

He shrugged my hand away, turned to other business. Something had cooled between us, a guilty mind telling me the cause was one thing, but logic tugging me towards another, more opaque explanation.

'Birch,' he called, as he spotted Strong-Arm turning over some of Rhun's dead, gathering their valuables and weapons, 'any sign of the Saeson?'

Birch shook his ugly head.

'Nah,' he shouted back. 'And if Osla Big-Knife had been here, we'd have known about it. Slipped past, maybe?'

Ambros looked west, towards the start of the Narrow Strait. It was possible. We all knew it. That, while Morgose's vision of a landing here was plainly accurate, there was nothing to have stopped Rhun and some of his boats from continuing onwards, perhaps even as far as the Fairwater

Maw itself. In effect, a two-pronged attack on Mona. This eastern section of the claw a failure. But, further down the Strait? Nothing there to oppose him at all.

'Do not seek there for your foe,' Morgose told him, without turning from the writhing creature – one of Rhun's – she was trying to ease into the afterlife with her ministrations. 'You'll find him back in Slavehold.'

'We're supposed to take your word for that?' murmured Cai Blood-Taster. Birch nodded in agreement, though they were the only ones who seemed to even consider that she may be wrong, her prophecies perhaps sometimes flawed. Or remembered how she had apparently hastened to spread word of the monk-burning among those who would use the thing against us.

'And he'll be summoning more than just a few Saeson *foederati* to his side,' said Balor mac Neit. 'Those Slavehold holdfasts will be a tough nut to crack.' Like Owain, this Balor had shown his mettle here today. To me, at least, though Birch and Cai looked at him with a suspicion that, if anything, exceeded even their distaste for Morgose.

'We've trampled over Slavehold before,' Birch sneered. 'It was easy meat to chew.'

'Only because we were allowed to by-pass the Great Hurdle,' said Ambros. 'No resistance from the Slavehold folk themselves. It won't be the same this time. And if Rhun fortifies the City of the Legions against us, he'll have all the time in the world to bring together our enemies.'

Ambros could not be restrained more than a further week before insisting that we should cross the Strait and see the fate of Twin Sisters for ourselves – though, by that time, we already knew most of the details. Those of Rhun's wounded and abandoned spear-hawks capable of talking had either been put to the question with hot irons or had begged to switch allegiance in exchange for intelligence. And, from them, he learned the truth. Or, as we would soon discover, most of the truth. Then, in his fury, he had butchered each and every one of them with the Sword of Maximus. And we heard it sing indeed, in all its evil vengeance.

It was only stilled when, finally, a messenger arrived from the White Lady Murgain. News of the battle had reached her – through Morgose, I assumed – for she sent a curt though polite request that, when we marched, she should be accompanied at least so far as the crossings and then be escorted, by Balor mac Neit and just a few guards, to her younger daughter at the Fortress of the Hammer-Fighters. But she made no further mention of monk-burning and willingly picked up the mood of silent introspection that accompanied our column on its route to the Eleven, where we left her and plodded east, none of us truly wanting to reach our goal and my own head filled with shameful images of Rigantona. A longing for her.

Our ponies pressed on through further flurries of snow until we reached the Ridge-Mouth, overlooked by that hermitage to which Deniol had lured me like a rabbit and where, I assumed, they were still working on their copies of the Christians' *biblia sacra*, but we ignored the place and, instead, took a short stop at the holdfast Ambros had occupied below. Then, next morning, we were on the road once more, crossed the Reed and swung up the river's farther side, climbing the slopes to that place where we had previously dug the pits in which Owen White-Tooth and the Lady Uithera had been laid to rest, boulders and boards laid around them, then earth mounded above. Yet these temporary tombs were broken open now, and no immediate sign of the remains they had held.

We found them, though, within the holdfast itself, outside the charred ruin that had once been their pride. The great gather-hall of Twin Sisters was now turned entirely to torched timber ruin and, at its threshold, a pair of tall, sharpened stakes had been erected, each bearing a carefully impaled and corrupted corpse. Corrupted, yet after such a comparatively short time in the frigid tomb, still easily identifiable as the Skyhound's mother and father. Withered, naked, stripped of their burial shrouds, each still displaying the necrosis where the Black Hags had bitten. And facing them was a third, the gatekeeper, Braden, though the twisted limbs and contorted face showed that the old man had still been living when they spiked him. The dead and despoiled lay all around. Women and children, all ravaged regardless of age. And the men? These we found among fire-scorched remains of that tower upon the Second Sister, which was supposed to provide a refuge of last resort for defenders but, now, had been used to burn the menfolk alive. The Hill of the Dead, indeed.

'They came through the Yellow Death simply to die like this?'

Ambros murmured. He had insisted on visiting the corpse of each victim, making certain we recorded every name, before supervising their burial in a communal grave.

'You still intend to build afresh here?' said Morgose.

'I only planned to do so in their memory,' he replied. 'But nobody will ever live here again now. Not after this. I dreamed of ornate tombs for them. One on each side of the approach road. The same as I have seen beyond Legion-Hold and other places. And all those passing by would salute them. But none shall ever pass this place again without trembling. For those who died here. And for those who will perish in payment.'

I recalled that a glorious tomb for the Lady Uithera was supposed to serve a second purpose too, helping to free her soul from the mirror in which she had felt herself trapped. Yet Ambros must have determined that a more modest interment would now suffice since, while the new mound we raised for her was certainly larger than the first, it was plain that this would be her final resting place, and I held the torch for him in the narrow confines of the burial passage as he carefully laid her head upon a pillow of larks' wings, then set the silver *speculum* at her linen-wrapped breast. And I knew that, if this place was indeed now doomed to remain forever empty, it would have at least one visitor each year – so that, at Day of the Dead, old *Parentalia*, every Ides of Februarius, Ambros would be here, for so long as he may be able, and precisely as he had promised. To remember them.

From Twin Sisters we moved on to the Fortress of the Bear, relieved to find that Rhun had not chanced his arm there also. In many ways it was a different proposition entirely, its natural defences stronger, and its population boasting a higher percentage of able-bodied fighters, both men and women. A tough bunch, on the whole.

We paid our respects at Einion's Memory Stone and Ambros received a delegation of the local duty-holders, come to re-affirm their allegiance to him but also to discover what had happened at Reed-Hold. They had seen the smoke too, of course, but had made a collective decision that their responsibility lay in looking to their own boundary lines, holding those safe in the name of Ambros Skyhound. And none had ventured closer than the nearest beacon mount – from which it had at once been plain that there could be no survivors.

I suppose we would all tell our particular version of the facts over the next few days, but it was left for Morgose to recite some of the official account.

'Evil day, innocents crucified, lined the Legion's Way. Thousand slain – our price to pay. Leave them there, remember and revenge; shout the Oak Seers' prayer for souls now lost, once so fair.'

We fell into the exaggerations readily enough. And why not? A mere sample of a song-sayer's poetic prerogative. It mattered little that the folk of Reed-Hold had been hacked and raped, then burned, as opposed to nailed upon trees. In fact, crucifixion seemed positively benign compared to the deaths they had truly met. But it had that element of persecution that we so wanted to declaim – particularly the image of them crucified at the roadside. And, so far as the inflated numbers were concerned, it mattered not at all whether Rhun had butchered a thousand or a hundred. It was the nature of his crime that counted, rather than the scale.

It was the spreading word of that crime which brought some further pledges of allegiance – the first of the White-Wilds' other Lords Prefect to recognise Ambros Skyhound's claim. Bran of Romaland came to Bear Fort in the middle of Januarius, bringing with him a spell of modestly improved weather, the snows melting, and the rivers running full.

'They tell me,' said Bran, once the formalities were over, 'that this new breed of Christ-follower monk is taught to use young boys in place of women. That true d'you think?'

As yet there was not a single *monasterios* established in Romaland, for Bran had weighed his wagers before inviting the Christ-followers to build upon the lands he held.

'You can find out for yourself,' Ambros told him. 'We have a tame monk of our own now.' He thumped his pot of heather-beer on the gather-hall's table. 'Hey, Owain,' he yelled, 'come here!'

Hawk-Beak made his way through the crowd and perched himself at his new master's side.

'What is it, Lord?'

'When you were in the *monasterios*,' said Ambros, 'did you take pleasure with young boys? Our friend Bran, here, wants to know.'

'Personally not,' replied Owain. 'But you must remember that the Christ-followers' Law of Continence forbids those who have sworn their vows only from taking a wife and begetting children. The Council of Elvira reinforced this. The Council of Carthago too. But they remained entirely silent on the matter of conjugal relations with young boys. And so I should have to say that the practice is not uncommon. It is a cultural thing, of course, and I'm sure that Mentor Meridden could confirm the extent to which such pederasty has been publicly acceptable and widespread among the wealthier classes of both Roman and Greek society.'

As it happened, I had studied works by both Plato and Catullus on the very subject, though I felt that I was not truly required to expound at that moment. Otherwise, I should have told them that the custom seemed rampant among just about every other culture but our own.

'And those bastards want to condemn us for *our* beliefs!' said Bran.

'When they're done with the boys, of course,' Owain told him, 'they then cut their throats and drink their blood.'

'I'd heard that,' Bran snarled. 'I'd heard that damned same thing.'

I looked at Ambros, expecting that he might explain Owain's strange sense of humour. But he merely shrugged. Within a week, we all knew, Bran's own song-sayers would be inventing ever more lurid variations, which would spread like the most virulent of diseases from gather-hall to gather-hall, wherever the old faiths were still followed. More importantly, these pieces of nonsense seemed to seal some bargain. Bran now felt fortified in his wariness of the Christ-followers. His previously masked feelings about them could be expressed openly again. With Ambros as Lord of the White-Wilds, the traditional ways would be in the ascendancy once more. And, since the eastern edge of his own territories bordered a northerly section of Slavehold, he would watch and report on Rhun's activities, stand ready to join Ambros whenever he chose to take his revenge for Reed-Hold. But it was Cullough of Bright-Fields, they both agreed, upon whom success or failure may ultimately turn – for Bright-Fields filled most of the lands on the nearer side of Slavehold's western edge, the waters of the Hurdle's Flow serving as their mutual boundary line.

'Then tell Cullough,' said Ambros, 'that if he joins our cause, we will take Slavehold, divide it between you both.'

Cullough did not come to Bear Fort but, within a sennight, he had sent a clear message. A pledge of his allegiance. A promise of spears.

Horsemen too. And, with these promises, plans were laid. Our forces to gather on the border between Headland and Slavehold, at the Calends of Martius.

'What about the others?' said Birch. Bran had returned to Romaland and the wax tablet with Cullough's broken seal lay on the table between us at the counsel meeting. And the others? He meant Custain of Dunshome, of course. Mabon of New Laigin too. Kei of Meirionshore. Alios of Everfell.

'Custain,' Ambros replied, 'will sit upon his hands until he sees how we fare in Slavehold. About Meirionshore and Everfell, I am less certain. But they are both plagued by cattle raids each season – Meirionshore from Caradoc of Cerdeg's Edge, and Everfell from those Prosperity border-thieves. If they commit to no more than following Custain's example, to stay in their holdfasts until this thing with Rhun is settled, they shall have my protection from those ravages. But New Laigin is a different pot of fish. Mabon Modron's Son is thick with Christ-follower fleas. He won't come over easily. So we'll strip men from Fairwater Maw, reinforce Fort Overmon, make sure Mabon stays in his halls whether he likes it or not. That means a diplomatic mission to Dunshome and Everfell, of course.' He looked around the table, pretending to make a choice, although he would not have been Ambros had he not already decided. And I feared his decision would have fallen on me. It was a tough journey through those high passes while we were still in the grip of winter, thaw or no thaw. 'Birch. Cai. You can handle this?' he said.

They seemed insulted that Ambros had need to ask.

'And the rest of us?' I said, as soon as I had recovered from my relief.

'I have a wife waiting for me at the Fortress of the Hammer-Fighters,' Ambros replied. 'Did you forget about Rigantona so soon, Mentor?' His face was hard. Anger, perhaps, though I thought perhaps he was in pain. For he had begun, at times, to fold an arm across his stomach, gripping his side. But I saw Birch Strong-Arm too, puffing out his cheeks, the way folk sometimes do when they expect a storm to follow.

'Not just your bride, Skyhound,' said Morgose, 'but my mother too. It should be a wonderful family reunion for us all.'

It might have been bile-filled sarcasm but it was a welcome diversion – for me, at least. For Ambros seemed to forget about me entirely.

'Sadly, Song-Sayer,' Ambros told her, slapping his placatory hand over her own, 'you may have to wait a while before we all play at kin-kindness. I have a different task for you and my loyal Mentor.' His own irony almost matched that of Morgose, but I still breathed a sigh of relief that I would not have to face the inevitable quite so soon. 'Back to Mona with you both,' Ambros continued. 'I am loathe to leave Bishop Deniol at my back and with such a free hand. I need a clear answer from that bastard. Does he swear the client-oath? Has he stayed, or is he gone? And what of that holy war about which he spoke? You'll need some good men, Mentor. Men we can both trust. In case the answers you receive are not those we would wish. You understand?'

I understood perfectly. The prospect of my own reunion with Rigantona was the stuff of pure nightmare, and I would grasp at any excuse to avoid it. For I feared my own weakness.

'Have you asked what ails him?' Morgose said to me when we were upon the road, with Anwas, Gareth Grim's Bane and Amron of Headland some distance ahead of us, and in company with our new *medicus*, Owain Hawk-Beak, who had begged leave to join the mission.

'You seem much closer to him than me, these days,' I replied. 'I assumed you would tell me.'

'If you had wanted to retain his intimacy, perhaps you should have tended your duties to him more honourably. Not squandered his loyalty.'

'As you did, Song-Sayer, when you fell over yourself in the haste to tell Deniol about the monk-burning?'

'For a man of learning, Mentor, you show a sorry disregard for the checking of fact. Deniol received word from the Bishop of High-Pass long before we returned from Clud-Vale.'

'And you haven't told Ambros this?'

'Of course I told him. But he still doubts me. Cannot fully comprehend my attachment to both Oak Seer *and* Christ-follower. It must be even more difficult for you, who has no true belief in anything.'

'Only that which I can see with my own eyes.' It was an unfortunate thing to say, and I hastened to correct myself – even though a part of me hoped I had stung her. 'Or hear,' I went on. 'Or feel with my other senses.'

'And no different for me,' she said. 'I know, with every fibre of my being, that there is a power in the world, norms of existence, that we cannot understand. But I taste some essence of an answer in the lore of the Oak Seers. In the prayers of the Christ-followers. In the worship of Sol Invictus and Mithras. In the calculations of Claudius Ptolemy. They all have merit. Yet they are all wrong at the same time. But it doesn't matter. One day, they will all arrive at a single common point of understanding.'

'And Ambros?' I said. 'None of that explains why you swim in his wake. Nor how you think I might have tended my duties less than honourably.'

'I follow for the same reason as you, Mentor. Because we both love him. Because we each know that we have a part to play in helping him become the man he needs to be. And because these lands cannot survive without that man. For yourself? I think you know the answer to your question. Though it matters little. Ambros understands that before long he must set Rigantona aside. You may have helped him in that, though I sense that was not your intention when you bedded my sister.'

So Cai and Birch must have seen or heard more than I supposed, and I could feel my innards crawl at the thought that Ambros knew about my betrayal.

'He will set her aside,' I said, 'in whose favour, Morgose? As though I could not guess.' But she merely laughed at me. 'And you *have* asked what ails him, I suppose?'

'No, but I can hear the pain in his every breath, Mentor. I fear that Ambros Skyhound may have less time than he should like to build Greater Britannia for us all.'

Chapter Fourteen

We sought for Bishop Deniol at his most recent hermitage, that *monasterios* which stood on the rise above Ridge-Mouth. He was not present, and neither was he to be found at Mona's End. But there we received news that he had gone to Legion's Neck, to the monks' place where I had been so generously entertained by Brother Flavius. So I had plenty of time to consider Morgose's words as we crossed the island. I had no idea how I would face Ambros again, though with my usual ability to twist matters in my own favour, I soon built an alternative version of the truth, one in which Ambros had sent me to Rigantona deliberately. He had asked me to distract her, after all. Presumably while he ploughed his own furrow with the Song-Sayer. He had used me, and now wanted to pretend that somehow the fault was mine. Or so I told myself.

'Not like you to be so quiet, Mentor,' said Owain Hawk-Beak, as we rode the final stretch towards that island beyond the island, where we would have to await low water before we could cross.

'My previous visit here was hardly an occasion of great joy,' I replied.

'Yet you enjoyed your walks around the Cauldron, I recall.'

'You were here?'

He told me his story, by way of introduction to his answer. It turned out that he was some distant kin to Ambros, the youngest son to Caradoc of Cerdeg's Edge and, with not the slightest chance to inherit, fostered to the Christ-followers as a small boy and sent to Legion's Neck to take his vows.

'It was my duty to observe your movements,' he told me. 'I used to follow you up to the headland, then climb the Legions' watchtower.' He pointed to the squat structure, which sat high up on the skyline, and rising from the long-deserted holdfast. 'I could watch you more easily from there.'

'Is that still your duty?' I sneered. 'To keep account of my comings and goings. You still serve Deniol? Or some other spymaster now?'

'I now serve none but the Almighty and Ambros Skyhound, Mentor. And neither has asked me to undertake any such activity. How could you think so?'

'Just call me old-fashioned. Too much time spent in Gallia. It seemed to be the custom there. A small price to pay, though, for the quality of their society.'

'They say that you studied in the City of Clovis. They say it is a wondrous place and that the Frankoi have the gift of kinship shared across all their lands.'

'I was in Parisius, yes,' I replied. 'And that city is indeed a marvel. A city beyond anything in the Four Provinces of Britannia. Clovis is dead these thirty years past, of course, and his sons rule in his place, with other great cities at Aureliano, at Novioduno and at Remi. Yet those cities stand together in all things, despite the distance between them. They employ secret agents more diligent than Hadrian's *frumentarii* to keep a tight grip. The three long-haired Merovian kings who rule them are all of one mind – for the most part, at least.'

'The model upon which Ambros would build Greater Britannia,' Owain smiled.

'Perhaps not the secret agents,' I suggested. 'But yes, he was an excellent student of other cultures. Yet there is another distinct difference between the Skyhound's dream and the Frankoi reality. It is their faith. They are Christ-followers to the core.'

'There would be many more of us, I think, followers of Yesu the Christos, who would follow the Skyhound's vision if they did not think it threatened their faith.'

'Yet it doesn't trouble you, Hawk-Beak?'

'It was the vision that brought me to Ambros. A vision as certain as those of the Song-Sayer. The knowledge that, whatever happens, the Christian Church is here for all time. I pray each day that Ambros might succeed, that he may light our futures with a great unity of purpose, one of great learning, Mentor, as the Frankoi are doing. But should this not be possible, well, it could be that the only light available to us might be through Our Lord Yesu.'

'Perhaps,' I said, 'but for Mithra's sake, do not let him hear you say so.'

*

'The bishop took ship from here many days ago,' said Brother Flavius. 'He left me to act on his behalf.'

'And where has the good bishop gone?' I asked. He pretended not to have heard the question, feigning deafness. 'If you have trouble understanding me, brother,' I spoke more loudly, 'I shall ask my friend, Gareth Grim's Bane, to force a skewer though each of your ears.'

Gareth grinned at him. It was never a comforting experience, to be on the receiving end of that predatory smile.

'The Holy River, I think he said,' Flavius blurted out the information. 'Legion-Hold. Yes, Deva. I'm certain.'

That made sense, though Deniol must have been desperate to venture that crossing at this season when the seas around Mona were at their most cruel.

'And has he sworn the client-oath to my Lord Ambros?'

He hesitated, and Gareth fixed him with those yellowed fangs again.

'He said that he should rather quit his lands here in the White-Wilds forever than take an oath to one such as *Cuneglasus*. Those were his precise words.'

'He has no lands,' I reminded him. 'Not any more. And nor do any of you.'

'Yet I think, Mentor,' Morgose spoke at my side, 'that if Brother Flavius, standing now in Bishop Deniol's stead, should swear the oath, Lord Ambros would honour his offer and allow the holy brothers to stay at their devotions. It would not absolve the bishop himself, of course. But, for the rest...'

Flavius gladly agreed, then volunteered the additional news that Deniol, though bound initially for Legion-Hold, and Rhun's base there, was then intending to travel the Two, east to Yew Grove, where the Bishops of Sabrina-Rise, High-Pass, Elm-Wood, Fast-River's Run and the Land of Hosts were gathering under the watchful eye of the High Lord Lenocus.

'He received a message to that effect?' I asked. And it transpired that he had, indeed, for the original tablet, in which the Bishop of High-Pass, a fellow who signed himself as Sildag Stag-Shank, had spoken of the monk-burning and called down the wrath of God upon the head of this Red Slayer, this *Cuneglasus*, as he called him, was still here. Better, it seemed that Deniol had replied, even requiring the scriptorium to preserve a copy. And it took only a minimal amount of persuasion from Grim's Bane before Brother Flavius was able to find the parchment.

'A meeting in Yew Grove to plan the holy war that Deniol mentioned,' I said later, as we sat at a harbour pot-house just outside the Roman walls and overlooking the old harbour. There were tales about the Imperial Fleet that would once have been moored here, back in the day when the Incomers were still seen as a threat and Rome's *Classis Britannica* galleys patrolled the Hibernian Sea, sinking any Laigin vessels they could find.

'We should get back to Ambros with the news,' said Amron, and most of the others agreed. I searched for a plausible reason to remain, to avoid meeting him, or facing Rigantona, but it was Morgose, once more, who provided another reprieve.

'Tomorrow is Birth Cleansing Eve,' she said. 'We cannot get back to the Fortress of the Hammer-Fighters in time to celebrate the Cleansing itself, so it may be an option to observe the rites here. Ambros has his plans laid. And any news of the Yew Grove Council can't change those.'

They certainly could not. And, besides, another thought had struck me.

'I once had the misfortune to spend Mithras-Birth here,' I said. 'The Christ-followers are hardly great company at such times. But perhaps there's another reason to stay.' I reached into my satchel, pulled out the copy of Deniol's letter to this Sildag once more. For the most part it was relatively innocuous but, towards the bottom, he had included this sentence: "*Either a servant of the Almighty or perish in torment.*" It was intended as a condemnation of Ambros Skyhound's heathen ways. 'What if we had copies of this?' I said.

'To what purpose?' asked Morgose.

'I was thinking about Owain's words earlier,' I replied, 'about the Christ-followers who might support Ambros and his dream if they knew their faith is safe. But perhaps there's another way. Those who convert to the Christos do so because they are offered hope, the promise of eternal salvation. Yet it's not always that way. It may not be welcome news for Owain or yourself, but there is always a pattern to these things. New beliefs are persecuted by the older orders and then, when they become established, they persecute all others in their turn.

Festus and others say a great deal on the subject. The anti-pagan laws of Constantius and Theodosius. The accounts of the Empire's Christ-follower soldiers and Christos mobs burning the temples of the Vestals, the assembly houses of the Judaeans, the god-mansions of Aegyptus. Anybody they can class as non-believers.'

And so it was. Christ-followers, once treated so barbarically by Rome, had now become Christianised Rome's most feared zealots.

'It hasn't happened here,' Owain objected.

'Not yet,' I said. 'But it *will* do! That's my point. If we share copies of Deniol's missive with all those Lords Prefect who are newly converted to the Christos, or those even thinking of following such a path, Owain – men like your father – convince them that Deniol and other bishops are imposing this faith of yours by force, rather than through choice, perhaps they can be persuaded to turn their faces against any summons to holy war.'

At dawn on Birth Cleansing Morn, we stood, wrapped tight in our square-weave, silhouetted by the light from two more bonfires, this time with the flocks and herds driven from west to east, towards the gathering light of an almost invisible sun. Yet sun there was, indeed. Enough to raise a spark of hope. We had all survived another First Quarter, by legend the worst part of any Dark Half – though the gods knew that, often enough, it was the following three moons which brought most agony. But the days would start to lengthen now, and folk gathered here around the blaze on the headland above Legion's Neck counted themselves blessed they had survived another year of the Yellow Death, of tight bellies and even the loss of their Overlord. It seemed strange to think that we were only those few short months away from Bright Fire and Malco's death, but here we stood. And if only Brigida could be induced to spread her holy light upon the livestock and the farming land, perhaps she might make us bountiful once more. Perhaps this year the Endless Winter might truly be banished. The goddess must surely know how hard these people had tried. Beds of straw had been plaited for her on the previous night, at Birth Cleansing Eve, in every byre and storage barn, each bed adorned with snowdrop heads and the white birch wand they hoped she might use to dispense her blessings, with food and drink left alongside to succour her.

It had almost made me laugh, to see the desperation as family vied with family to appease this other deity, criticised their neighbours if they thought the offerings too meagre, the welcome bed insufficiently ornate. And even the monks were here to take their own share of the credit. For Holy Brigida, they claimed, had truly been a Christ-bride in Laigin, a miracle worker who cured lepers by a single touch, or dispelled disease with a single drop of blood from her finger, or brought forth magic waters from the living rock with just one tap of her staff. The Bishop of Laigin had declared her a saint, it seemed, after her death – a death that had occurred within living memory. Strange, then, that our people had been venerating the goddess for generations without number. But nobody seemed to mind. The monks' prayers could surely not harm.

'How long then?' I asked. 'For the copying.'

'Twenty copies?' said Owain, and he tapped his extended right thumb twice against the left in the old way. 'A few days. No more.'

I had hoped it might be longer. Extend my stay here. Delay the inevitable. But I should have known better. This young *medicus* had laboured in a scriptorium. So I spent the day praying for a miracle of my own. I even found myself intoning a personal litany as we all processed to Brigida's sacred well on the hills south of the settlement's Roman walls. Hopefully she would keep the waters pure for another year but, meantime, perhaps she might strike me down with a temporary lameness, or a fever just serious enough to keep me here a while.

'Will you help me with the steps, Mentor?' said Morgose, when our turn had come to climb down into the cistern and take our ritual taste of the waters within. Legion's Neck was fortunate to still have such a system in operation, its ducting pipes continuing to feed the settlement below, when those in many another city had long since failed. But I was thinking more about whether I should have preferred to push the song-sayer than guide her. I had come to frequently resent her closeness to Ambros, irrationally blamed her for my own distance from him.

'I suppose Ambros plans to restore all the water supplies, as well as the roads?' I sneered, as we negotiated the stone staircase down to the cistern's edge. 'Do you think?' I filled the silver cup, which the previous supplicant had hung back on its peg.

'Blessed Brigida, keep this, your bounty, pure,' she murmured, before putting the cup to her lips. 'That's what he told me,' she said. 'He dreams of a *ludus*, where young men may be schooled as *ingeniatore* again.'

'And the money?' I said. 'Where, in the gods' names, does he think it will come from?'

'He's been studying your Cicero. On taxation systems. The sinews of state, he says. Without it, no public works, no system for collective defence, no ability to defeat illness, no true education. Those territories falling within Greater Britannia will observe his new taxation system. Those without will pay in the old way.'

'An admirable ambition.' I hauled her back up the steps so the next worshippers could take their turn, and I noticed she had begun to let her hair grow again. 'But he knows my view on the training of *ingeniatore*,' I went on. 'They need a rounded education. As Vitavio recommended. Not simply calculating arts and natural philosophies, but history, law, geography, music and literature. So that those who build and create may not stand aloof from the broader context which their constructions must serve. Before we can train the *ingeniatore*, therefore, we need more mentors, and I fear the only way to acquire them will be to bring them from other lands.'

'You are too busy to begin the task yourself, Mentor?'

Well, it was a thought. I held no Chair of Eloquence, of course. But a new *ludus*? It was something to ponder, certainly if there was any chance that a new usefulness on my part might help to heal matters.

'Perhaps I might even receive honest payment again,' I said. 'I may discuss it with Ambros. But you've still not told me what you think ails him.'

'Likely it is nothing at all,' she replied, though her answer seemed evasive. It troubled me but, when we returned to Legion's Neck, a runner had arrived from Ambros himself. Brief but helpful. An instruction to meet him at Twin Sisters, in time for Day of the Dead, just over a sennight hence. I digested the message over our Birth Cleansing Feast, along with the onion and kale cakes, the dumplings filled with slake and cockle-meat, and some of the best sweet bread I had ever eaten. The culinary skills of Legion's Neck had certainly improved, and a reunion with Ambros at Twin Sisters was definitely preferable to the Fortress of the Hammer-Fighters and Rigantona. So we agreed that the runner should start the first stage back, on the following day, with word for Ambros that we had found a gift for him.

*

'This is welcome news, Mentor,' he told me, as I handed over the copies that Owain Hawk-Beak had already produced. 'Welcome, indeed.'

He had set up temporary shelters, goatskin campaign tents, against the charred stumps of the holdfast's palisade. It was a sad reflection on the fine place it had once been, and the ceremony of remembrance seemed also to be a mere shadow of the event he had intended. But Morgose had composed a new lay, emotive verses that told how Owen White-Tooth and his Lady Uithera would watch the road for all time, albeit a path that none would ever tread again. Ambros seemed to like it though.

I watched him carefully, seeking any sign that he might still be suffering. But there was nothing.

'How will it sit with your wife-mother?' I asked. 'This letter of Deniol's.' It was as close as I could come to an enquiry after Rigantona's own health.

'There's an uneasy truce in my halls,' Ambros replied. 'She barely mentions her dead husband by name. And the monk-burning? Well, not any more. But she is like a fire herself. The hearth embers kept just aglow all night and needing the thinnest kindling in the morn to fan its flames afresh.'

'You said she doesn't raise the monk-burning any more,' I said. 'So she has spoken of it.'

'Only once,' he laughed. 'But I told her – and Rigantona too – that better every monk of the Christos be burned than a single follower of Mithras harmed.'

Had he truly said that?

'I should hate to think that we gave Deniol's friends an excuse to say this holy war of theirs is simply a form of self-defence.'

'The White Lady of Laigin is no threat to us,' he said. 'But Rigantona? Unless I miss my guess, she's in contact with Rhun. Spying for him.'

'You have proof of that?'

I had not intended to leap so readily to her advocacy, and he stared at me a long time, his facial muscles tight, a nerve ticking in his cheek.

'If I had proof, Mentor,' he sneered, 'I should forcefully feed her, piece by piece, to that same dog that fucks her.'

I could feel my own self-justified anger rising in my gorge, confrontation building within me, a challenge around the fact that he had used me badly, sending me to Rigantona in the first place.

'Let me tell you, Ambros…' I began, almost snarling the name. But he held up an imperious hand, his features slackening.

'No, Mentor,' he said. 'I know how it is with Rigantona. And I know how it stands with those I love. The threat from Rhun will soon be dispelled. The gathering at Martius Equal Night, remember? We shall see then who stands with us and who does not. But, one way or the other, I can promise a spectacle that none will easily forget.'

Chapter Fifteen

Ambros was right. It was a sight to inspire the mythmakers.

His forces had gathered, as planned, from the Martius Equal Night onwards, at the last bridge over the Hurdle's Flow before it met the sea, and where the Eleven crossed from Slavehold into Headland. The place was named for the colour of the clay cliffs lining the river there, and upon which a formidable holdfast had once stood – until most of it was washed away in some long-forgotten flood. It was home now to no more than a small trading settlement, the bridge itself in a poor state of repair. But, small or otherwise, Ambros would leave a garrison here to protect our lines of communication and his home territories.

Beyond the bridge, in the estuary – where Ambros had been swimming, almost blue with cold, only an hour earlier – six currocks were hauled up above the tide line. For Elidyr of Clud-Vale had come. Nearly seventy spears. And the astonishing news that we were now almost kin, for his brother, Rhodri, had sent for my sister, Mirian, to be his wife. And even to adopt her son, Cador, as his own. A happy development, though at that moment I was more taken with the additional fifty spears brought by Bran of Romaland, ten of them mounted on stout war ponies. Cullough of Bright-Fields would meet us further south, as he had promised, in time to join us for the crossing of the Great Hurdle, since Ambros had determined that we would simply march around the most northerly of Slavehold's holdfasts and avoid the more obvious route along the Eleven. To this force, he could add his own men of Headland, forty from Bear Fort alone, many of them riders. And each party with its pack of loping battle-hounds. Yet it was the arrivals from Mona, from the Fairwater Maw, who provided the inspiration I have mentioned.

He must have worked hard to time the thing so well, for he chose the moment when all our war-band was ready for the advance, gathered in one place, with the bridge before us and a low ridge behind, over which the Eleven wound westward into a crow-haunted morning mist. There was a distant horn, to draw our attention that way. Then silence. Until the chanting could be heard. Coming closer. A marching song that announced them as the Men of Mona. Men of Ambros Skyhound. Come to stand with the Bear-Brothers, the brethren of the Bear Fort. Just thirty of them, emerging from the haze, but well-armed, carrying their campaign gear in the way of the Legions, strapped to a shoulder-pole. Thirty. Yet, at their head, a true wonder. A war-cart, precise replica of that upon which we had first seen Fingal of the Five Stallions. And you could almost taste the approval of our assembly. They may have had all manner of differences. But things that united them too. The Cousins' Tongue, of course, despite its various tribal and clan fluctuations. And their admiration for sheer flamboyance, especially among their leaders. By Mithras, how they loved the vainglorious. A lesson that Ambros was learning fast.

I saw him slip from his own pony at the roadside, wait for the *carrio* to come rattling along, striking sparks from its wheel rims, and then, without the thing even slowing, he caught one of the side arches and swung himself up behind the charioteer. This was Anwas the Winged, already a natural horse-tamer, but he had obviously taken time to master this new art. For he drove the yoked ponies now, weaving between the clusters of our column, and each group of us crying the Skyhound's Praise Names, the hounds all baying, while Ambros himself balanced against the filled spear rack, resplendent in his ring-mail coat, his red hair dragged back by the speed of their passage, and his cloak billowing behind.

Slavehold has a coastline of sand dunes and marshland, but it is defined by four other features running north to south. The first is the sinuous route of the Hurdle's Flow, Slavehold's western boundary line, and the course of which we were now broadly following upstream. Then the Great Hurdle itself, that range of hills which looks so deceptively innocuous and yet, on closer inspection, is steep-sided, with either a holdfast or beacon mound upon every peak, so that, effectively, it is a single, strung necklace stretching more than a dozen leagues, perhaps twenty *milia*. On the farther side of the Great Hurdle runs the Eleven, and that highway in turn sits in the winding shadow of a lower ridge, beyond which the lands drop to the edge of Slavehold's final prominence, the wide estuary of the Holy River, which narrows in the end towards the harbour at Legion-Hold, where fresh waters from the mountain meet the salt tides of the Hibernian Sea.

But we were still far from Legion-Hold, making progress down the lesser road of the interior, past dwellings abandoned at our approach, and already immersed in the familiar stink of the venture – acrid sweat, wet wool, old leather and damp dog. Our steps now constantly dogged by scouting parties of our enemy too.

'How many can they bring against us?' Owain Hawk-Face asked me, as we finally came in sight of the Red Fort, and the regular bridge crossing between Slavehold and Bright-Fields. It was here that Cullough and his men should have been waiting. But no sign of them. No trace that any large party had ever been here. And the homesteads all deserted here too, their inhabitants fled before us.

'If Cullough doesn't come,' I told him, 'it will all be somewhat academic.' I pointed at the ridge of rolling summits away to our left. 'We have to cross that. And we might as well piss into the wind unless we can muster more men. Those passes could be held by just a handful of determined slingers.'

We urged our mounts forward to where Ambros had halted the war-cart for a consultation with Elidyr and Bran of Romaland. Elidyr seemed even smaller in stature than usual, perched upon a borrowed pony that dwarfed him. Yet here was another whose pride and bearing made him larger than life. A diminutive giant. But he had brought his favourite harness, it seemed, for the bells tinkled and chimed merrily enough, with each movement of the beast.

'Your lords make a habit of this?' he was demanding of Ambros. 'Ignoring your summons?'

'He'll be here,' Bran snarled at him.

'In his own time, I suppose,' said Elidyr. 'You'll never hold on to the White-Wilds this way, Skyhound.'

'The White-Wilds and much more besides,' Ambros told him. 'But, meantime, we're going up there,' he pointed.

The flanks of the Great Hurdle were scarred at regular intervals by clefts which climbed towards the ridge. There they cut deep notches against the skyline. And here, east of the Red Fort, was the pass that seemed deepest of them all.

Elidyr fiddled with his eye patch, fingered the gems and enamel-work.

'That one?' he laughed. 'Steep slopes and trees on each of our flanks? You're a bloody fool to try it.'

'Yes,' said Ambros, 'but at least we can drive the chariot up there.'

The beginning was easy. But after an hour of sometimes difficult climbing up the drovers' track, we were all steaming, partly from sheer exertion, but mostly from disquiet about whatever lay ahead and above. I pitied the poor black cattle that must so often be forced up this narrow path, through the dripping vegetation just coming into bud on the branches above our heads. There was constant danger, too, of being plunged into the ravine and raucous stream that ran to our right. If we craned our necks to squint into the tree-shadow of the upper slopes, it was sometimes possible to see shapes flitting between the trunks. They may have simply been roe deer startled by our presence, but men began to talk of ambush. Or tell tales of the Dark Folk who, some said, still inhabited the high and secret places of our lands. And all this discussion shouted, to make ourselves heard above the chatter of the tumbling cascades. This was no stealthy advance, and Ambros seemed heedless of all danger, frequently having to jump from the war-cart and help free its wheels from one rutted obstacle after another, while his hound, Charger, did its best to hinder him, punishing its master for making it run alongside, rather than ride within.

We must have ascended halfway up the drove road when it suddenly levelled for perhaps a hundred paces. The place was little wider, however, and on our left flank the all-year vegetation – holly, juniper and yew – grew in deep green clumps. At the far side of this slight plateau, where the track began to climb and curve out of sight again, a shield-wall awaited us, spear-bristled. Difficult to say how dense, to tell how many stood against us there, but it seemed no more than sixty or seventy. And, to their fore, Rhun the Tall, with Osla Big-Knife at one side, a cross-bearing monk at the other. I searched their spear-hawks for other Saeson Outlanders, but I could see none, feared we may have walked straight into a trap.

'We missed you at Long Battle Bay, cousin,' Ambros called, as Anwas, his charioteer, came to a hasty halt. 'Worried for your health. So decided we'd better come check on your welfare.'

Behind him, our own press was forming, ponies sent to the rear, for they would be no use here.

'A simple twist of the tides,' Rhun shouted back, 'or I'd have saved you the trouble of the journey. You must find travel difficult if you need a carriage for your conveyance these days. And, so your wife tells me, you're not in the best of shape yourself.'

Now, that was a troubling remark, and I turned to see whether I could find Morgose among those behind us, then remembered that it would serve no purpose in any case. Yet I noticed some of the others – Mabon Meleth's Son, Birch Strong-Arm, Cai of the Nine Lives – whispering to each other. Urgent and angry whispering.

'Rigantona worries about me too much,' cried Ambros, and vaulted from the *carrio*, dragging a long shaft from the spear rack. The weapon bore a throwing loop, and I realised I had also seen its likeness elsewhere. 'As you see,' he yelled, throwing his arms wide, 'I am perfectly well.' Charger loped to his side, growling and fangs bared, while Ambros slipped the loop over his wrist, then let it fall down over his elbow. It was a single, fluid movement, almost too fast to be noticed. 'And I've brought you a gift. All the way from my good wife's homeland.' Ambros skipped forward, light on his feet, the dog dancing with him, and launched the spear. The range was short, and Rhun had plainly not expected the missile's speed of flight. He barely had time to dodge it, snarled and spun around to see the narrow blade shriek through a front rank shield, pierce its hide, skewer the warrior and cause chaos as he was hurled back into his fellows. 'They call that a *sleag*,' Ambros taunted his foes.

I had taken my place in our wall now, unslung my own shield and waited for the next move.

'I delivered a gift for you too, monk-burner,' Rhun snarled. 'Did you not find it? At Twin Sisters.'

'I do not burn monks,' Ambros called to the crook-toothed braggart, 'only serpents. The fathers of serpents. But yes, I saw the things you had left for me at Reed-Hold. They were my people. Not just my closest kin. All of them. It's the reason I'm here, naturally.'

'Then receive this blessing also,' Rhun roared, waved his arm in signal. And, from the heights above us, a storm was unleashed. Showers of slingshot and javelins. Our men, caught, looking in vain for those assaulting them. Falling. Limbs pierced. Faces gouged. Heads broken like shattered eggs. Too tightly packed for shields to be raised. Edging back. Screams. Curses. Ambros still out in the open, but calm, exhorting us to hold, selecting another spear from the war-cart's rack while Anwas the Winged tried to control the snorting ponies. And I was certain we would all perish there as we stumbled over the dead and dying.

'Bloody fool!' I heard Elidyr shout. He was away to my left, short and stocky, but solid as a rock, shoving men back into their positions.

Then a body came sliding and crashing through the undergrowth, slithered to a halt before us, a feathered shaft protruding from a Saeson slinger's back. A long shaft, weighted, like a legionary's dart. I had seen one of those recently too. A Laigin warrior's *gae*, or *birin*. Another body, this one falling from a bluff up to our right, and one more fletched javelin spiked through the man's neck. Cries, mayhem up on the heights. More and more of the ambushers being butchered by unseen allies.

Ambros was back on the war-cart now, barbed stabbing spear in his hand, and the driver turning his team, swinging the chariot in a tight circle, close to our front line.

'Bear-Brothers!' yelled the Skyhound. 'Bear-Brothers. Kill them now. Kill them all.'

The chariot was slewing away from us again, bouncing up the track, war-hound alongside, straight for Rhun and Osla Big-Knife. We yelled then, a great roar as we broke forward, running in the *carrio*'s wake. The red mist was filling my eyes but I remember the gap that opened in the enemy ranks to allow their leaders sanctuary – a gap which failed to close quickly enough, before the Skyhound's ponies were bowling men aside. Their combined weight, and the chariot's momentum, carried Ambros deep, deep within their midst. Stabbing, until the *craiseach* hooked into a man's belly and could not be freed. I caught a final glimpse of him as our shield-wall hit, rolled them back. He had drawn the Sword of Maximus, hacked and hacked. I thought I could hear it sing. And then I was stabbing too, thrusting my spear's point into faces – though I barely thought of those snarling teeth, snot-smeared beards or bloodshot eyes as human.

'Bear-Brothers!' I was screaming, and all those to my left and right were screaming too. Stabbing. Pushing. Heaving. Our battle hounds tearing at their throats. Until the bastards broke.

Rhun had escaped us once more. And so had Osla Big-Knife. But their men had paid dearly for the privilege, dying in droves as a rear-guard, though one that had cost us too. Twenty warriors either dead or too badly hurt to take any further part in our campaign. Almost a tenth part of our original force. A similar number with lesser wounds and presently being tended by Owain Hawk-Beak, using all the learning he had acquired from his monk-brothers and the Codes of Celsus. But our gravest hurt came from the news that Elidyr of Clud-Vale was among the more serious casualties.

He had rushed forward, with only a few of his hall-guards, when he had seen Ambros surrounded and badly outnumbered. They had pushed back our enemies with the savagery of their charge, and reached the *carrio*. But, after that, all was confusion. A dozen versions of the event. Yet the tale that had taken the tightest hold was the one which told how the Skyhound, in the wild depths of his battle-fury, unaware there were now friends at his back, had swung the Sword of Maximus wide in his fight with Rhun and, in doing so, had accidentally hacked into Elidyr's skull, slicing through bone and brain alike.

It was not entirely to the Skyhound's credit either that, until the fury finally faded, he was only able to bemoan Rhun's exploitation of the moment to get away, rather than lament the imminent death of the hero-lord who had braved the voyage from Clud-Vale to stand with him. But, once restored to himself, Ambros was riven by grief, tried to ensure that Elidyr should be borne, as comfortably as possible, up the final stretch to the high-pass and the holdfast dominating the ridge at that point. We had almost expected Rhun to have retreated there, to hold the peak, palisades and ditches against us. But he had continued to run, left the local duty-holders to their fate and they, seeing how the winds of change blew once more, threw open their gates at our approach. So Elidyr was carried to the gather-hall, with that gruesome flap, the crown of his head, flopping open at every jolt despite the temporary dressing Owain had applied.

A vigil was kept in the hall throughout the night, those of us huddled about his litter marvelling at Elidyr's grip on life despite the gravity of his injury. And, for myself, the added concern that my sister was not yet wed to Elidyr's brother, and here he was, dying at my side.

'It might have helped,' Elidyr scolded Ambros, his voice weak but steady, 'if you had bothered taking the rest of us into your confidence.'

'He's right,' said Bran of Romaland. 'And me, most of all. You made a fool of me, Skyhound. Sent me to enlist Cullough, then forged contact with him yourself to arrange that little drama.'

'I couldn't know for certain that Rhun would arrange the ambush there,' Ambros replied. 'Cullough's Bright-Fields men were just a security. On the off-chance. If we'd all known they were there, we may have inadvertently sprung the trap too early, not been able to take them.'

'But the darts,' murmured Elidyr. 'You had them made specially?'

'I thought they might be useful,' Ambros replied, and we all knew he must have laid this plan months before. There was only Morgose who showed no surprise at the revelation. Only Morgose, now, with whom Ambros shared his closest secrets.

'Well, they saved the day,' Elidyr grimaced through his pain. 'But not me, Ambros. They could not save Elidyr of Clud-Vale. And I'd not expected the need to name an heir so soon.'

'Your sons...' Ambros began. I had seen him shed no tear since Einion's death, but he was close to it just then.

'Too young,' Elidyr groaned. 'And too many others with greedy eyes fixed on my lands. So my brother Rhodri must hold it for them, Skyhound. Until they come of age. Let those gathered here bear witness to this. And, when I am gone, take me home to Clud's Rock. A final journey through the woodlands of Battle-Forest on the way.'

Elidyr died at dawn, but his remains accompanied us in our pursuit of Rhun, all the way to Legion-Hold. It was two years since we had been there and, at that time, we stood alongside Rhun, not against him, to put down the small insurrection when Cundruin had sought independence from the rest of the White-Wilds. And Cundruin had not been popular among his duty-holders, as you have seen, so that we had been comparatively welcomed back then. But Rhun had proved to be a harsh lord and, while his potential demise might be popular, the local folk were plainly not minded to see Ambros as their liberator this time. There was a sullen mood within each settlement we passed after descending from the Great Hurdle and picking up the Eleven again for our final march into the City of the Legions.

'As we may have expected,' said Ambros, when we stood in his campaign tent, near the bridge, 'Rhun has learned from the mistakes Cundruin made.' Owain had inked a rough map for him on an old hide that was spread now upon the floor. 'He's destroyed the ferry and made sure that every available boat is hauled up on the far side.' Ambros pointed with his toe at the harbour area of the mapped river. 'Which leaves us the bridge as our only viable crossing point. At least, without a very long haul upstream.'

But the bridge was strongly defended by the rest of Osla Big-Knife's Saesons.

'And no chance of turning the city folk?' said Bran of Romaland.

'I had somebody swim the river last night,' Cullough of Bright-Fields replied. Bran snorted. Sheer contempt. They had been close once, but Cullough's rising star – his perceived saving of the day during the ambush, his apparent favour in the Skyhound's eyes was creating jealousies. 'There was a lot of activity at the Arena over yonder.' Cullough pressed on, directing his report to Ambros alone. I remembered the old *circus* from our previous time in Legion-Hold. Partly ruined, but still an impressive structure, just outside the city's walls. A sad place, still haunted by the ghosts of all those who had died there. 'It seems,' Cullough continued, 'that Rhun rounded up everybody he didn't trust and turned them out of the gates. They're all packed inside the Arena itself now.'

'I dislike that place,' said Ambros. 'It stinks of ill-omen.'

He had taken against it upon learning that the officers of the Twentieth Legion had been put to death there after they supported old Carausio in his bid to become Overlord of the *Imperium Britanniarum*, as he had called it – his own version of Greater Britannia. It was ancient history now, but one that stuck in the Skyhound's mind like a presentiment of evil.

'All the same,' said Cullough, 'we may find those within the Arena walls willing to help us.'

'And when we take the place,' said Ambros, 'we shall give a reward to these honest Minerva worshippers. Build a temple to the goddess there, perhaps. In the *circus* itself. Help the souls of the Valiant and Victorious to rest at last.'

Valiant and Victorious, the Praise Name for the Twentieth, that same legion which had also lent its title to the highest peak of Overmon, the Cairn of the Twenty. And our camp filled the same village at the southern end of the bridge again, as we had done two years ago. That industrial home of smelters and copper-beaters who had now given Elidyr a temporary resting place within a disused furnace.

'I was also thinking,' I said, 'that Owain Hawk-Beak might be helpful to us here.'

It was coming up towards Pascha – the Passover Feast that fell, as all my disciples would have known, upon the first Sun's Day following the Martius Equal Night. The Christ-followers celebrated Pascha as the Last Supper of the Martyrs while, for Ambros and his fellow-worshippers, it marked the passing of Mithras into immortality, his ascent into Heaven. And even for the Saeson Outlanders, I was assured, it was a sacred point in the year also, upon which they showered offerings to their old goddess, Eostra.

'How so?' said Ambros.

'It occurred to me that neither Rhun nor Osla may know that Owain now rides with us,' I explained. 'If Deniol has already taken the road to Yew Grove, Owain might have little difficulty putting on his monk's robes again and infiltrating the city's defences. A pretence at having been left behind, perhaps. And, with Pascha upon us, one more Christ-followers' monk busy about his business will hardly attract much notice.'

'To what purpose?' said Cullough of Bright-Fields.

'To gather intelligence,' I said. 'Maybe more. Open a gate perhaps. Or, if he can get close enough, a potion into the heather-beer of one or the other. Both, even. Poison the two of them?'

'I'm no poisoner, Mentor,' Owain snarled.

'No,' said Ambros, 'you are not, Hawk-Beak. And too valuable to be sacrificed.' He glowered at me, then continued. 'But our Mentor has given me another idea.'

Though, naturally, he was not then inclined to share it.

There is a lay. Popular now among the song-sayers. Many versions. Many names. But the original was, of course, structured by Morgose. And she called it *Rhun's Reverie*, in honour of the Skyhound's artfulness.

In Legion-Hold, Rhun the Tall dreams, sleeping, drugged as death, it seems, while the Skyhound's Soul Sword gleams.

It is a long piece, entertaining when performed well. Full of bawdy jests. Rhun complaining about the paucity of Legion-Hold's hospitality, because of its whores and their lack of finesse – the filthy state of their bodies and their beds. His concerns about the battle to come, due to the lack of virility among the city's warriors. Rhun's relief that he has the Saeson Outlanders at his back, their hair yellow as ripe corn and their balls green with manly sap. His contempt for Ambros, and his plans for the order in which Maeve, the Lady Crow, would pick the Skyhound's bones clean. And then, of course, Rhun's rude awakening to find that time has passed him by and, while he has slept, the battle for Legion-Hold is already lost. Though it was not quite that way.

'You remember this place?' Ambros had summoned me to join him at the pot-house where we had shared a heather-beer once before.

'What did he mean?' I snapped at him. 'Rhun. Before the ambush. All that stuff about Rigantona telling him you're not in good shape.'

'Plainly she keeps in touch with him. But not with you, Mentor?' He turned to the pot-woman. 'Tell me,' he said to her, 'do you have a Throne-Sense board, sweet one?'

The old girl glowed for a moment, then produced a board and bag of playing pieces from a chest in the corner.

'You plan to play a game now?' I said, incredulous at his lack of concern about the siege.

'Think you can beat me?' He was already setting up the start. And the truth? I could always beat him. Or anybody else, for that matter. Except when I chose to lose. 'Attack or defend?' he said.

'Attack.' I was tired of defending. 'And I've heard nothing from Rigantona since I left the Fortress of the Hammer-Fighters,' I said, and he simply nodded, smiled. 'So,' I pressed on, 'your health, Skyhound?'

'You were angry.' He ignored the question, made a clever opening move with his king towards the board's edge. 'That I wouldn't share my plan for Owain Hawk-Beak.'

'Angry? Anger is for callow youth. No, Ambros, betrayal gets closer to the emotion I experienced. Disappointment. And not about Hawk-Beak. That one I understood. You *had* no plan. Not then. Needed time to work it through. No, for me, it was the same thing that's pissed Bran off so badly. That you'd been hatching that thing at the pass for so long. The darts. The messages to Cullough. But you only saw fit to share it with the Song-Sayer.'

'The woman knows how to brew a powerful potion. Did you know?'

'Poison?' I said. 'I think she has laid poison between you and me, Ambros.'

'You don't understand,' he told me. 'With Morgose, I have no fear of failure. The thing with Cullough was different. A trial of my new authority. If it had gone wrong, Cullough himself would probably have died in the attempt. The rest of you would have been little the wiser. It would not have diminished me, Mentor. Nor tarnished this image we're all trying so hard to build.'

I closed off his king's line of retreat.

'I understand,' I said. 'But Owain? If not poison, then...'

'A sleeping draught,' he smiled. 'If he can administer the thing, he'll at least be able to separate Osla from Rhun. Open a negotiation with the Saeson and no interruptions.'

'Negotiation? Poison's more effective.'

'The image again, Mentor. I've no scruples about poisoning that bastard but I have to win the White-Wilds in a way that builds reputation. Isn't that what you'd tell me?'

'I imagine it's what Morgose tells you. And you'll simply offer Osla Big-Knife more than Rhun is paying him. For what? So his men will abandon the bridge?'

'That,' he replied. 'Also to leave a couple of the gates open. And a pledge that he won't come back. For a while, at least.'

'You can't trust him,' I said, and moved my third successive piece into precisely the space I needed. This was one game that I did not intend to throw. 'You can't trust anyone. Not Morgose. Not Rigantona. Not me.'

He grimaced, saw that it was all done for his king, flicked it so that it fell sideways, but then gripped his side, bit upon his own lip.

'Mentor,' he forced a smile, 'I cannot even trust my own body. But I trust the gold and silver I have taken from the Christ-followers' churches to buy Osla Big-Knife for me. And Osla will deliver me the City of the Legions.'

Chapter Sixteen

Osla did indeed deliver Legion-Hold, as you will know from the lay I mentioned.

Ambros plays the Throne-Sense game, offers Osla gold and fame, Rhun's ambitions there to tame.

And he delivered more besides. He delivered Rhun the Tall himself.

The news arrived just after we had finished playing. Ambros had confided in me that he knew he was sick. The extent of that sickness, he claimed, he did not know. Yet he must have had his suspicions, even then. But, at that moment, Owain had returned, lathered in sweat. He had spun a convincing story to gain an audience with Rhun, and found him already in a heavy drinking session with the Saeson. Morgose's potion had been easy to administer – though hardly necessary – and, with Rhun apparently in a besotted stupor, our lapsed monk had been able to open a dialogue with Osla, persuaded him that he was sent by Bishop Deniol himself. Ambros had sent an urgent message, he claimed, wanted nothing but peace with the bishops and it was only the private feud between Ambros and Rhun which prevented a reconciliation with the Church – perhaps even a conversion. But destiny could not be denied, Owain had told him, and Osla must surely see, that Rhun had lost this campaign. In any case, Rhun would never accept a settlement with Ambros. And it was an evil thing Rhun had done, despoiling the corpses of the Skyhound's mother and father. The Christian thing, Owain had persuaded him, was to avert more bloodshed – and perhaps accept these few modest tokens also, as a reward from the Almighty.

So the Legion-Hold Bridge had been opened to us, and the Southgate too, three hundred paces uphill beyond.

There was a minimal amount of fighting against those of Rhun's spear-hawks who did not realise they were betrayed, or who shared some fanatical loyalty to their lord. But, one way or the other, we splashed their blood all the length of Praetorian Way and the lanes around, hunting them through the bathhouse ruins; around the trader stalls and whores' dens that now filled the old military hospital; and down into the empty granaries. Until we came, sweat-grimed and gore-smeared, to the centre, and the old legionary headquarters, now serving as gather-hall for the city.

'At least your brother had the balls to offer me the Champions' Challenge,' Rhun spat through the ruin of his already ugly mouth. His former friends had not used him well, and he was chained now between two stone columns, his arms spread wide. And Ambros seemed to be measuring the distance to those stretched sinews, tapping the tip of his Maximus sword into the open palm of his left hand.

'They tell me I would have to take my place in a queue,' Ambros replied. 'Isn't that so, Mentor?'

Well, my personal differences with Rhun the Tall seemed fairly insignificant compared to the Skyhound's own grievances, though I chose not to voice that observation.

'No need for a queue, boy,' said Rhun, his words still drunk-slurred. 'Let all come who think they have cause. Be it two or twenty, I'll take you all. I demand it, Ambros. The Champion Fight.'

Morgose pushed her way through the weary warriors gathered around us.

'You had no words so brave when you ran for your life from the Great Hurdle,' she cried.

'Will you strike the first blow then, blind one?' Rhun laughed. 'Though I thought you might consider yourself somewhat in my debt. For ridding you of that boy-shagger you married.' I saw Ambros tense, tighten his grip on the sword. 'And you, Skyhound. Osla tells me you've seen the light. Planning to convert. The True Faith, at last. And cut down Elidyr the Dwarf, Elidyr the Monk-Burner as a token for your redemption, they say. Well, you may have fooled the Outlanders, but you don't fool me, boy.'

It was a difficult moment, for many of Elidyr's men were present at our backs. And most of our warriors still devout followers of Mithras or Minerva. Or both. There was another thing too. That, while those who had seen Elidyr fall did not blame Ambros directly – we were all used to the frequency of friend-wounds in battle, for they had been a feature of close combat since the days of Thucydides – there were those who whispered about the blade, spoke of it being cursed.

'I knew that man only as Elidyr the Generous,' Ambros thundered. 'And there is none here that mourns his passing more than me. Those around me know the manner of his death. And the truth of the monk-burning too. But the rest is well enough. I would have peace with your Christ-follower Bishops. So long as the old faiths are left in peace. For we have greater problems. Little time left for the solving. The years turn, and we grow weaker with each that passes.'

'And you take cross.' It was Osla Big-Knife, stocky and pig-eyed, filthy flaxen hair, his grasp of the Cousins' Tongue still less than perfect, and trying his best to follow the exchange. 'You...promise. Sent to Bishop. Monk-brother told me.'

We had kept Owain Hawk-Beak well out of sight.

'They tricked you, Henga White-Stallion's Son,' Rhun laughed. 'And that bastard may have been a monk once, but now he's a running dog for this Skyhound. You can be sure of it. Who do you think drugged my beer? And that blind bitch brewed the potion, unless I'm much mistaken.'

Osla looked from Rhun to Ambros. Then back again.

'Our friend, Osla the Saeson,' Ambros snarled, 'has heard for himself the words I sent to Bishop Deniol. The monk who carried those words was one of the bishop's own. And you never needed drugs nor potions, so far as I recall, to put you in a stupor, Brother-Slayer, Defiler of the Dead.'

Ambros failed to mention the public insult to Einion's manhood, yet I could see that it was burning him. Then, suddenly, he shifted his weight, swung the Sword of Maximus back, but I caught his wrist, halted the blow that would have taken the first of Rhun's limbs. He glared at me, his eyes crazed with hatred, filled with a lust for revenge.

'No,' I hissed at him. 'There's no honour that way.'

'And your new friend, the Saeson,' Rhun sneered, 'took your gold and silver too, of course. Church gold and silver, is it not? The same Church from which you now claim redemption. Go on, Skyhound. Strike if you will not be a man and grant me the Champion Fight.

'You prove word, Skyhound?' said Osla Big-Knife. 'Simple thing. Free him. Take cross.'

'We don't need the Saeson any more,' Ambros whispered in my ear.

The Outlanders here in Legion-Hold were now outnumbered, of course. And they knew it. You could tell by their wary stance, hands never far from those wicked blades that, in their own speech, they call the *saex*, and gave them the name by which we knew them. Only Osla himself showed no sign of fear.

'And nor do you need his kinfolk seeking you out to settle a blood-debt,' I said.

Ambros shook his wrist from my grip.

'Very well,' he spat, through gritted teeth. 'Rhun shall live. But not within my sight. He may go where he will, though not within the boundaries of the Westerlands. If I ever find him within those boundaries again, his life shall be forfeit.'

'And I,' cried Morgose, 'place this doom upon him.' She used the Gathelic word, *geis*, the taboo that cannot be reversed, rather than the milder form of our Cousins' Tongue. I saw the colour drain from Rhun's face as he realised the strength of her curse. 'That he shall never bear arms again unless I should gift the weapon to him.'

Ambros did not take the cross. Not literally. But he gave leave to Osla and his Christ-follower Saesons so they might continue to worship at the chapel, which Christ-followers among the Legion and the city's population had dedicated to their Holy Peter, east of the forum. They would send for Brother Flavius, at some stage, to bless the place afresh. To provide a presbyter monk as well. And the Saesons, meanwhile, would settle some abandoned parcels of land beyond the city walls, with their families.

There was other work to be done too. Those same city walls in a worse state than we had imagined. Repairs to be undertaken. Bridges to be built with the local duty-holders. New oaths to be sworn. The Lordships of Slavehold, and their kinships with the duty-holders sealed, the trappings of tribal tradition maintained. A new but steady hand applied to Slavehold's administration. Taxes to be regulated. Protections put in place. Ploughing and planting contracts to be formalised – with those growing root crops commanding the best prices now that grains were so problematic. The Federation Council reformed. Judgements to be made. Magistrates elected from among the duty-holders. Disputes settled. Seeds to be sown, in practice and politically. Messages of support received and analysed. Acknowledgements of the Skyhound's new status. Lord of the White-Wilds. And, therefore, promises to be fulfilled. So that, with the arrival in Legion-Hold's broad harbour of those currocks which had brought the Clud-Vale warriors south to Ruddy Bank, Ambros was able to recover Elidyr's body and sail north for Clut's Rock.

For my own part, I chose to stay. You will remember that I have no great love for the whale-road. But, beyond this, Ambros had raised with me, again, the possibility of a *ludus*, in which we might begin to school his new breed of *ingeniatore*. And, before his departure for the north, we had visited almost the ideal site. Just behind the legionary headquarters building, the gather-hall, stood the forum and market and, somewhat to the west of the forum, that elegant building with a semi-circular apse at each end, giving the edifice an elliptical appearance. The *armaria* within showed that it had once been used for commercial administration and business purposes and perhaps even as a public library, though the racks were all empty now, many of them entirely missing, and the roof partly collapsed.

'You regret letting Rhun live?' I had asked him, as we huddled in a mostly dry cloister and watched rain bouncing upon a ruined serpent-pattern mosaic floor of the building's interior.

'There's always a price to be paid for reconstruction, Mentor,' he replied. 'How much to make this place sound again?'

'It must have been magnificent once.' I said. 'Modelled on the Ulpian basilica, I think. In Rome itself. Vitruvius wrote a great deal about its virtues. Much smaller scale, of course, this one. But, all the same...'

'It's a fair point,' said Ambros. 'Some things have a value that cannot be costed. And risks that cannot yet be seen. I met the carpenters' guild a few days ago. I'll ask them to work out an estimate. At least make the place dry again. Keep the sky from falling on our heads.'

The puddles from the downpour were rippling across the ancient marble, created an illusion that the viper living within its tiny fragments was slithering towards us.

'And Rhun?' I said.

'There will be a day, Mentor,' he murmured, 'when all debts must be settled. The Song-Sayer's doom is well enough, but I just pray to Mithras that your advice was sound, that we don't live to regret not killing the creature when we had the chance.'

*

Ambros was gone to Clud-Vale, and Morgose had sailed with him, while the rest of our company remained in Legion-Hold. A sense of being abandoned. Yet Pascha was behind us, and we were looking forward to the coming Light Half, preparation being made for Bright Fire. The weather seemed more benign than for any Aprilis I could remember. Folk could be seen almost visibly softening with every new moon that passed, relieved that there was no new word of the Black Hags from any corner of the lands.

'Your advice, Mentor?' Bran of Romaland asked me at the next council meeting. Ambros had granted him the joint prefecture of Legion-Hold, along with Cullough of Bright-Fields, since the Skyhound had not entirely decided the long-term future of this important city. But it was not an ideal situation.

'Just what we need,' cried Cullough. 'Another opinion.'

During the previous year's outbreak of the Yellow Death, the victims who perished had been burned within the cemetery, just beyond the Northgate. But the burning had been less than thorough and there were human remains still in evidence, among both the ancient Latin-inscribed tombs and also the more modern stones carved with the Common Speech. Even at Day of the Dead, it seemed, everybody now avoided the place, literally, like the plague.

'The *medicus*, Owain Hawk-Beak,' I said, 'advises that the sickness may still be lurking there, among the vapours of the cemetery. He says that great care should be taken. But the remains need to be properly burned, then buried.'

'So set the public slaves to the task and let them get on with it,' said Cullough. 'We've more important matters...' He was anxious, we all knew, because there was unrest in those parts of Slavehold now added to Bright-Fields as reward for his support. But the partition had been clumsy, split tribal boundaries, divided kinfolk.

'Forgive me,' I interrupted, 'but the *medicus* suggests that anybody employed on this work should, themselves, be confined to a quarantine area until we're certain they pose no risk.'

'Keep them in tents,' Cullough insisted. 'On site. And I've already offered a contingent of my own to help get the work done quickly.'

'Offered?' said Bran. 'Held us to ransom, more like.'

'You expect them as a gift?' Cullough sneered. 'The cost goes up every year. The Black Hags take almost the same toll of slaves as among our own. And the trade's all but dried up.' Well, it was a fact. I still remembered the days when you could rely on regular shipments brought from Hibernia, or from the lands of the Pictoi. But now? Rhun's defeat had provided only a few hands of a class that we could put into bondage. Hardly enough workers for all the tasks that faced us. And that included, of course, my own interest in the reconstruction of the *ludus*. I was still pondering the problem when I saw Osla Big-Knife stand from his bench. Ambros had agreed that the Outlander should be allowed to attend council meetings even though he had no official status there.

'We will work,' he said, simply. 'For right price.'

It turned out that the Saesons were demanding less silver than Cullough wanted to charge for the hire of his own *servi publici*. They were reliable too, those Outlanders. But Cullough did not see it that way, and the gather-hall was soon awash with waves of angry words, flushed faces burning in the gloom, so that I was only vaguely aware that the doors had been opened, a cloaked figure making its way down the length of the room, spear-hawks gathered close around. But when the new arrivals reached the high table, the square-weave hood thrown back, there was no mistaking the wild tangle of hair skeins it had previously concealed.

Rigantona had come to call.

'Is it true?' she asked me, as I stroked an anguished finger against her nipple, hard and tight as a drum. 'That my sister placed a doom upon him?'

'True,' I told her. 'And you're certain? Ambros has called this Grand Council together?'

I could scarce believe he would convene such a gathering, all the Lords of the White-Wilds, and not mention even a word to me.

'Why else should we be here?' Some measure of foolish hurt must have showed upon my face, and she laughed. The truth was that my heart had both leapt and sunk at the same time at the sight of her, and I had responded like a resentful but pliant slave when she summoned me. 'For you, Mentor? I told you already, any small pleasure I might derive from you is offset by the cost.' It was purest vanity that had persuaded me the cost must be emotional, a torment of her heart and affections. 'The cost of my confession.'

Rigantona had taken the house formerly occupied by Lord Prefect Cundruin before his demise, and since abandoned. Just opposite the old *principia*. Once home to a tribune of the garrison. And with its own latrines. Her mother was lodged in a similar dwelling, across Praetorian Way, but the daughter had chosen this *domus*, I think, more for the profusion of Christos symbolism still adorning its walls. She was staring at those signs of her faith as she spoke, and I pitied her. For she must be torn, not only by the Christ-follower teachings, but also by each of the other strictures against adultery, regardless of whether they appeared in the Incomers' Judex Laws, or the Oak Seers' Missives, or the Empire's Twelve Tables. They were all pertinent to us. And the prescribed punishments were harsh in them all. Harsh for us both.

'I can think of a dozen reasons that might bring you to Legion-Hold,' I said. 'But now? With me? It must be more than small pleasure to risk so much.'

She rolled from my side, reached for her cloak and wrapped away the nakedness, just as the curtain of hair enveloped the features of her face at the same time. For a moment, she gazed towards the door of the *cubiculum*.

'Did you hear something?' she said.

'Just the snoring of that damned deer-chaser,' I replied. The creature had accompanied her, of course, from the Fortress of the Hammer-Fighters, and we had left it sleeping alongside the atrium's hearth, Rigantona creeping softly from its side as though it were the hound she was betraying, rather than her husband. And I had crept with her, cowed beneath the storm that raged within me. Guilt, at my further disloyalty towards Ambros. Shame, at the weakness I could not, or would not, overcome. Fury, towards Ambros himself that he had left me here to face and fail this further temptation – deliberately, I decided. Disgust, when I dared imagine Rigantona's own weaknesses and proclivities. Pity, for the conflicts, which I knew played so heavily inside her exquisite head.

'Well, you sound less than certain, Master School-Builder,' she mocked. 'You like it here, I assume? I certainly hope so, since it seems to me your new duties will pin you in Legion-Hold for a long time. That's why Ambros no longer bothers to share his plans with you. Not so?'

My face must have betrayed me, for she continued to taunt. 'What? You still dream of being at his side when he becomes High King? Or helping him to win that power?' She laughed again, and the bitterness sliced through my ribs. Yet she used the same Gathelic term for High King that Morgose had often employed, *Arth Rhi* – so that my own mind played with the words and names, just as the Song-Sayer's tongue had once done. Ambros. Divine. Ambros the Skyhound. *Cuneglasus*. Ambros of *Dun Arth*. Ambros *Arth Rhi*.

'Whether I am at his side or not,' I snapped, camouflaging the putrid privy pool of my self-pity, 'Ambros will bring Greater Britannia together. There's no turning back from that now. Without a unity of purpose, we cannot survive more attacks of the Yellow Death. Nor the famines from the Years Without Summer. We will go down into the Dark. And all that we have learned, all that we are, will be lost.'

'That's a pretty speech, Mentor. But you think your salvation lies with somebody who's lost already?'

'What?' I said. 'This nonsense you shared with Rhun about Ambros being unwell. What fantasy did you feed him?'

'You see it within his eyes the same as I do, Mentor. It's not just ambition that eats him. Have you not observed his pain? And there is only one true power in this land now. The power of the Church. The power of the bishops. The power of the Almighty. You could be part of that. Ambros too, if he would only see the light. Accept the cross.'

My turn to laugh.

'Next, you'll be promising him loyalty,' I said.

'That I can leave to the other Lords of the White-Wilds,' she replied. 'Mabon Modron's Son. Bran and Cullough, if they can cease their squabbling. Kei of Meirionshore. Alios of Everfell. They'll all be here. For Bright Fire. But me? I owe allegiance only to the Almighty. Yet, if Ambros should indeed take the cross...'

But I never discovered the bargain she may have offered him for the Skyhound's conversion to the Christos. It was the deer-chaser that alerted us. Its wicked growl from the atrium. Then the deep-throated roar of its bark. Men shouting, yelling, as I grabbed for my clothes. Running feet. The piercing howl of pain from the beast, and its terminal scream of agony. Rigantona snatching at a dagger from the table close to her bed. The door flung open as I pulled up my breeks and she stood at bay against the wall, while Cai the Blood-Taster and Birch Strong-Arm burst upon us at the head of several others, spears all bloodied.

'Faithless creatures!' cried Birch.

PART THREE

The High Lord

The gods tire easily,
mankind's bane, to set contention free –
cause strife, destroy harmony.

Their battles split the skies,
fears in man. From Epona's hooves, earth flies.
Herne's arrow falls. Fate dies.

Mapon strums his cruth,
wakes melody, sings all Creation's truth –
deadly chords of endless youth.

Spears of Teutates blast
earth. Lightning bolts falling fast,
from fists of Taranis cast.

Where hoof or bolt cause strife,
arrow fall strikes or spear blades knife,
six more gods are given life.

Tugri Iron-Brow
Song of the Great Melody

Chapter Seventeen

Beneath the old *principia*, somewhere below the marble-slabbed floors of the gather-hall, lurked the living tomb of Legion-Hold's prison. Foetid. Rife with rodents. Only a deaf-mute gaoler for company. And there I was incarcerated for a lifetime, or so it seemed, with nothing upon which to chew but my confusion.

For a while, I railed against Birch Strong-Arm. We had never been close, but I had not realised the extent to which he despised me until I was being dragged down the steps into this pit of Hades. Cai at least had tried to persuade him that I should be housed somewhere more fitting to my rank as, I assumed, had happened with Rigantona. But Birch would have none of it and I was not entirely certain that he might care too much had I given him some provocation, the chance to mete out a summary justice of his own.

'Rank?' he had said. 'Just a bloody second-rate teacher. Thinks he's some god's gift to us. Treacherous bastard.'

But that was exactly how I felt about myself. Not about being second-rate, of course, though the accusation of treachery bit deep, if not quite deep enough. So my anger towards him was driven rather by a frustration that he seemed unable to analyse the situation more profoundly. We may not command the winds but we could certainly trim sails to weather the course of our lives. So the political union of Ambros and Rigantona might be an established fact, but that did not mean there was no scope for human emotion between those of us caught up around its fringes. It was Ambros who had engineered each of the periods I spent in Rigantona's company and it was clear to me that he had reason for doing so. He did not want her. That much was plain too. But what *did* he want? When I had tried to confess my transgression to him, he stopped me, yet called down damnation upon any hint of liaison between Rhun and his wife. 'I know how it is with Rigantona,' he had said. 'And I know how it stands with those I love.' But what did that mean? Was it supposed to give me some free licence in the matter? If not, why should he leave me here, knowing that Rigantona was coming to Legion-Hold?

At times, I slept. Though whether I slumbered for hours or mere moments I could not guess. There were dreams, of course. Usually, the same scene replayed in a variety of ways. But always the deer-chaser at the scene's core. The hound pierced by the spears of Birch and his followers, and Rigantona's wail of grief as we were hauled past the gore-pool in which it lay. And then, in one of the versions, a dark shadow was standing before me. Ambros, from the figure's stance.

'So,' he said, quietly, 'at least I no longer have the dog to worry about.'

I realised this was no apparition, hauled myself upright, enraged, and sprang at him.

'Mithras damn you!' I cried. 'You knew this would happen.'

He pushed me, hard, so that I fell back upon my arse.

'Calm yourself,' he yelled. 'I'm no longer one of your pupils, to be beaten whenever the frustration grips you. And I've come to get you out of here, whether you deserve your liberty or not.'

'You took your precious time,' I panted. 'The gods alone know how long I've been in this filthy hole.'

'You've been here no more than a day and a night, Mentor. And I came as soon as I landed, heard the news.'

'And now, what?' I said. 'Some public treason trial? A Clearing, so I may confess my calumny?'

'I owe you too much for that, Master. In any case, there are politics to be considered. I met your sister. She is already wed to Rhodri, so you are now kin to the Lord of Clud-Vale. Uncle to his adopted heir. No, I already told you. Liberty. You were not the fly I wished to web.'

I should have been pleased with my family's good fortune but I was still fearful. 'You mean me to simply walk out as though nothing has happened?'

'I suspect you might first prefer a visit to the latrine and bathhouse,' said Ambros. 'Then a change of clothes, while we fathom how to deal with the rest.'

'What about Rigantona?' I demanded, brusquely.

'For an intelligent man, Mentor,' he replied, 'you have a foolish heart. Don't you imagine she was using you too? She cares only to see me brought down, our goal thwarted, my allies and assets divided. But come.'

He helped me to my feet again, guided me through the open door.

'You judge her too harshly,' I said, stumbling up the steps past my silent custodian. 'If you would only embrace the Christ-followers within your scheme, she would work to your advantage.' He made no reply, but simply chuckled, slapped me on the shoulder. A little patronising, I thought. But as we emerged into the comparative light of the gather-hall, I saw that his copper-coloured curls were still crusted with salt from his voyage south. He had indeed come straight off whichever currock had brought him from Clud-Vale. Yet I saw, too, that the skin around his cheeks had an unhealthy grey-green tinge, as though it belonged to a much older man and, as Rigantona had suggested, there was something in his eyes that did not belong there. 'How have you been, Ambros?' I asked him.

'Longing for the bathhouse as well,' he smiled, and would be drawn no further.

My reunion with Birch Strong-Arm, some days later, was not a happy occasion. Ambros had sent him on a mission, back along the Great Hurdle, where there were still problems stemming from the clumsy partition of Slavehold. We were in council at the gather-hall of the *principia* when he returned, blustering into the meeting in his usual style, oblivious to everything but his own preoccupation.

'Ungrateful bastards!' he cried, flinging off his damp cloak and seizing the nearest horn of heather-beer. 'You need to watch them, Ambros, or you'll have an insurrection on your hands.'

'What?' said Cai. 'Thousands of them marching on Legion-Hold?'

The rest laughed, but I took care not to join their merriment. Those left of our close companions had accepted me back among them with a good enough grace – Mabon Meleth's Son, Custyn Banon's Son, Anwas the Winged, Gareth Grim's Bane, Owain Hawk-Beak and Amron of Headland – while Cai had been almost apologetic about his part in my imprisonment. But the relationship had lost something. Probably my own doing, for their generosity towards me rankled. I veered from one extreme to another, at times believing I deserved punishment for my action, at others that I was owed some compensation for the injustice I had suffered. And always there was Rigantona's image in the background to haunt me, particularly on the occasions when I must, as now, confront her sister, the Song-Sayer.

'I had to make an example of a few,' Birch snarled. 'Nailed some traitors to trees…'

His gaze fell upon me and he looked towards Ambros in disbelief.

'We were just discussing my wife,' Ambros told him. 'The part played by Mentor Meridden in uncovering her own treachery.' Birch spluttered something incomprehensible, glowered at me with unveiled animosity. 'A sore thing for me to confront,' said Ambros.

In truth, we had been discussing a boar hunt that the Skyhound planned for marking the meet of the White-Wilds' lords, which would take place within a matter of days. And it struck me how far he had come. That even the most recently added to our council meetings – Cullough of Bright-Fields, Bran of Romaland, sometimes also the Saeson Outlander, Osla Big-Knife, and Masul the Numidian, who had accompanied Ambros from Clud-Vale – did not gainsay him. Not even the blink of an eye, nor exchange of a quizzical glance. 'But as I swam the waters of the Holy River this morning,' Ambros continued, 'I realised that a public statement is necessary. Rigantona must be set aside. Formally and irrevocably. I have asked the good Mentor to prepare the process, given his early training as a lawyer, the breadth of his education.'

'Education!' Birch spat. 'Who needs it? The people want food. Yet you waste our precious resources on this stuff of schools and learning.'

Morgose unfolded herself from a step at the Skyhound's side.

'The people will always need learning too,' she said. 'Do you think, Birch Strong-Arm, there will ever be a generation that does not want its children to gather knowledge? And if you think the price of education is high, you should consider the cost carried by ignorance.'

It was news to me, of course, that I should be given the duty to legalise the annulment of the Skyhound's marriage. A part of my own Clearing, I supposed. No open declaration of my guilt but, rather, an official part in the prosecution of Rigantona's own.

'The only lesson I ever valued was about loyalty,' said Birch. 'We take our vows as duty-holders, then honour them.' His scorn-filled eyes turned to me once more. 'Those that break their oaths…'

'In this society of ours,' Ambros cut across him, 'there are those who have sworn oaths and must keep them, or pay the penalty, as my wife must do. And then there are those like Mentor Meridden, who owe duty to none but their calling. And, as my Lady Morgose reminds us, there is no higher vocation than the teaching of knowledge to others.'

At least he recognised that small fact, Well, he was always the brightest of my disciples.

'The Emperor Justinian is a great believer in the power of education too,' said Masul, the dark skin of his face plunged into still deeper shadows by the folds of black linen that fell about his features, held in place by tightly-woven red cords around his forehead. 'He is, after all, a beneficiary of such learning. Low-born, you will recall. Yet now the greatest patron of natural philosophies the world has ever known.'

'I hope that your master,' Ambros said to him, 'may be persuaded that a well-governed and settled Province – Britannia, let us say – may make a welcome addition to his Empire, even though we have a breadth of faiths followed here.' Masul the Numidian seemed uncertain, but made no comment. 'But there!' Ambros exclaimed. 'All settled. On Bright Fire Night I shall set Rigantona aside. Mentor Meridden shall prepare the *casus belli*.' He gave me his warmest smile and I was struck, not for the first time, that Ambros had a tendency towards narcissism. One of those charm-weavers, long on vision but sometimes short on the practical detail that we lesser folk are always expected to provide. A man not necessarily worthy of our affections from a distance, but always beguiling at close quarters. But at least I knew better than to ask him, in public, the grounds upon which I should prepare the case against her. So he waited, just long enough for me to grimace my acquiescence in return, then said, with finality, 'So, back to this business of Trwyd, King of Boars. And a-hunting of the brute!'

Birch Strong-Arm's features crumpled in confusion.

'Boar hunt?' he said.

Bright Fire Morn. The Calends of Maius. Legion-Hold's Bright Fire Bushes all hung about with yellow flowers, ribbon and painted shells. The black cattle from surrounding farmsteads all gathered, similarly adorned, then ceremoniously paraded towards the drove roads for the higher summer pastures. Not that there was much difference, these days, but tradition rules fools, as they say. And when all other duties had been observed, we set out for the great forest that spread eastwards across much of Lesser Gift-Given, the portion of Urien's domains which we still called Westwood.

I had tried to see Rigantona, but the guards outside the dwelling where she remained under house arrest made it clear that no such visit may be possible without a specific authority from Ambros himself. And I had decided that such a request would be foolish. But I missed her, and settled in the end on a curt report by which her mother, when we met in the market-place, assured me she was in good spirits. That was welcome news. Yet it did little to ease this tangential aspect of my guilt. The case against her was complete, though Ambros had at least realised that a judgement that day would no longer be possible. Postponed. No new date fixed.

The King of Boars, this legendary Trwyd, had been pursued many times in the past. For more than a hundred years, some claimed. And never a hunt lasting less than a sennight. Never one that had come even close to a satisfactory outcome. Nonsense, naturally, for everybody knew that even the strongest boar will not run far without turning to fight. And it was not truly the custom to hunt him so early in the year. The September Equal Night was the customary season's start, when he grubs the forest floor so voraciously for the nuts and acorns that will make him fat for the Dark Half. But Ambros had chosen to use the occasion for another purpose. It transpired that, for once, Birch Strong-Arm's news had been only marginally exaggerated. The folk of Slavehold were, indeed, on the point of insurrection. The partition of their land, the division of kinfolk, had caused great discontent and Ambros was keen to set the thing right, to unify Slavehold once more. But how to do so? Then Morgose had set a doom upon the whole expedition, declaring that whichever lord should kill the Boar King – bringing back, as proof, the sword-sharp tusks and bristled red crest of its shoulders, for both of which the creature was renowned – that hero should become the master of all Slavehold. Cullough of Bright-Fields and Bran of Romaland both readily agreed, each considering himself the better huntsman and feigning unconcern at the potential loss of land so recently acquired.

Easy won, easy lost, they taunted each other. And so, at length, we set out, numerically as strong as a significant war-band.

'Is the beast as savage as they say?' said Masul, when we wove a path through the dripping undergrowth, between oak and lime.

'An Elder, without doubt,' I replied. 'But whether it lives up to its reputation, that's something else.'

'How your people love a legend,' he laughed. 'But Lord Urien may not be so pleased if one of us slays the creature. He dined handsomely on tales of this Boar King when he visited Clud-Vale.'

'Elidyr was a sad loss to us all. Ambros still feels guilty for his death, I fear.'

The Numidian shrugged, and I caught a golden gleam in those pitch-dark eyes.

'I liked the man, despite myself,' he said. 'Despite his foolish hatred of my Christian faith. But his death must have been written. And whether for good or ill, we cannot yet discern. There are certainly some here who would not have followed Elidyr, yet may just give benefit of the doubt to Ambros. He is less strident in his discrimination. Not so?'

'Well, they all answered the call.' I looked along our line, as much of it as could be seen for the trees. Somewhere ahead of us were Ambros, Cullough, Bran, Osla the Saeson – who had promised to show us how the boar was hunted by true warriors, in his Outlander forests – and Balor mac Neit, taking time away from his duties as Murgain's bodyguard. Just ahead of us, sliding their ponies, their spear-hawks, their scent-dogs and kill-hounds down through midge-mire, marsh fern and white sedge towards a silver-slimed, stagnant lake, were Kei of Meirionshore and Alios of Everfell – each still waiting to see whether Ambros would help rid them of their cattle-raiders. But, somewhere behind, the less promising presence of Mabon Modron's Son, Lord of New Laigin, and Custain of Dunshome. Christ-followers, both of them. Clearly present under sufferance, yet knowing they must acknowledge Ambros as Lord of the White-Wilds, and keen to test whether he would truly show tolerance towards them. Yet each of us, regardless of our religious beliefs – with the exception of the Saeson, who did not believe in such nonsense, and the Numidian who still favoured his own headgear – wore his favourite hunting hood of good fortune, to assist us in the chase.

'They may recognise his claim to the White-Wilds,' said Masul, 'but as potential ruler of all *Britannia Magna*? We shall see.' It was another matter much debated in our time at Clud's Rock.

'And how long will you wait for the revelation?' I asked him. 'How long before you must return to Constantinopolis?'

'Most of my work here is done. Those trade deals that may be useful to the Empire are now rated. Clud-Vale and the White-Wilds were the last I needed to list. My own source of medicinal knowledge is improved, with the help of your Oak Seers. And I am pleased that the plague-potion helped you here, of course. But I am curious about this tale that the Song-Sayer and yourself seem to be weaving.'

'Tale?' I said. 'About?'

He laughed, and we splashed through the stinking edge of the lake, reeds brushing against our breeks and boots.

'What else would you call it?' said Masul. 'The making of a new legend. Like Trwyd the Boar King. Master of all it surveys. A new overlord for the whole of Greater Britannia. A king, perhaps. Everything in hope that the Emperor Justinian – Almighty Christos protect him – may take your islands under his wing. Well, I tell you, Mentor, Ambros shall not reach a satisfactory end to this story of yours unless there is accommodation with the holy bishops. But I'm in no hurry to discover the final act. It is a long journey back to Constantinopolis, and then to my own lands.'

'You think he makes a mistake in setting aside his wife?' I said, then wished I had left the subject alone.

'The mistake, I understand, may well have been your own.' There was no humour in his eyes any more. 'But at least the mother seems intent on staying within your Skyhound's entourage. Strange that she should wish to do so, regardless of Rigantona's fate. Don't you think? And she seems to have no closeness to Morgose either. But she is well connected to the bishops. Perhaps an asset.'

I tried to digest all this, turning the words around in my brain while, ahead of us, the scent-dogs had begun to howl. Men shouting. Those nearest to us straining to see better. All the clamour of a chase begun. And we kicked our ponies up through a stand of alder, out of the bog-veiled valley to the wilder woodlands beyond. Crashing through underbrush, hooves thumping, twigs snapping. Sweat, leather and crushed bracken in our nostrils, and snot dripping from them. The kill-hounds baying, echoing through the trees as the first relay was released.

*

Had this been a fantasy, the Boar King would have been an enchanted beast, leading a lone hero ever deeper into the forbidden woods and, finally, to his doom in some den of the Hollow Hills. And, in the aftermath, the Song-Sayer did her best to portray it so, fashioning the thing into a young warrior's quest for those same razor tusks and bristle comb, in order to gain blessings from the father of his heart's desire.

Fly, Skyhound's hunter fair! Chase your prey. Fly, find the Boar King's lair – White Trwyd – his soul yet bare.

Yet Trwyd, King of Boars, was not white. And it was not even Trwyd we pursued. Not then.

We had a quarry, that was certain, and we knew our trade well enough, fanning out to left and right of the hunt leaders, circling wide, the hounds given their head only by turns, so they should not tire too soon, nor chase false trails. And so, inside an hour, we found ourselves breaking around the edges of another clearing below us. More marsh lands. Two brackish pools. Clumps of dwarven shrub. Tangled bramble thorns. Thickly wooded hill in the centre. Riders and dogs on every surrounding ridge, looking down upon the brute. It was big. Tall as my hip. Ugly. But it did not fit the Boar King's description. Impressive still, and magical in its own right. A creature impervious to snake venom. Unchallenged by any other predator than ourselves. A beast that filled every legend from Odysseus and Heracles to these modern days. Yet it was not Trwyd.

But Ambros, Osla, Cullough, Bran and Balor, along with their hounds and handlers, had brought it to bay. The work of a hound-handler is never easy, for the dogs, by that time, were maddened at the prospect of blood, slavering, struggling to savage their prey, while the leash-slaves tried to hold them, wrestling to restrain them, beating them with their sticks, and risking vicious injuries themselves in the process. Even those hounds up on the surrounding rim were little better, and the noise was dreadful. Chaos. Yet the lore of the hunt required that the kill should be made by force of arms alone. So the five men must wait until some sort of order was restored. Easier said than done, and some time passed, with one hound after another scrabbling free and having to be restrained afresh, while Ambros and the others screamed their impatience, their own trepidation. And, all the while, the boar twitched its ears, sniffed and snuffled, tried to discern by sound, and taste, and smell, what manner of threat it faced from this tumult upon its territory. For it was all still too far distant from it, twenty paces, for the thing to sight anything clearly.

'You see?' yelled Masul, trying to keep his pony under control at my side. 'Here is the trade deal I still have to negotiate. The Empire has missed its supply of your wonderful hounds.'

I smiled.

'Claudian the Poet speaks of Britannia's hounds being able to break the backs of mighty bulls,' I said. 'I'm sure Ambros would make Justinian a fair offer. Yet I doubt the bishops could do so.'

He seemed to take the point seriously but, just then, the patience of Ambros exhausted itself and, still cursing the ineptitude of his own hearth-slaves, he began to move forward over the difficult ground, despite his own hound, Charger, and the other dogs not yet being fully subdued. Yet his companions followed, advanced upon the implacable boar which, like all its fellows, paid no real heed to threat or danger. Their spears were levelled – except for the Outlander, who seemed to think that his short *saex* blade was sufficient for the task. Stealth was impossible, and they stumbled often, over root and briar. The boar had its back to a wall of alder saplings, like the palisade of its own holdfast. And then, at fifteen paces, more certain of its foes, it charged – also in the manner of its brethren, standing start to full pelt fury in the blink of an eye.

'If we could breed men with such a reckless absence of fear,' said Masul, 'imagine the armies we could build.'

'The Saesons speak of men from far north of their homelands,' I told him, 'who have such a gift. One of the reasons so many of the Outlanders come here. To escape their torments.'

At the same time, Ambros was running his spear through the creature's tough flank, battle-frenzied, howling a war-cry over and over until he had pushed the squealing, snarling beast into the closest of the pools. There, it thrashed and bled for an impossible time, until it lay still. And the hounds, now scenting fresh blood, came up, plunging into the water too, tearing with their fangs at the carcass. A cheer went up from all who watched.

'Then let us hope those Northmen stay forever in their icy wastes,' Masul smiled, while Ambros struggled to dislodge the spear. For it was one of those *craiseachs* that had been fashioned for him, the blade barbed and now stuck fast in his quarry's innards. 'Shall we join them?' said Masul, as more hounds chased forward for their share of the kill, and other riders began to amble down from the higher ground.

I cannot recall who it was that shouted the warning but, suddenly, eyes were turned upon that wooded hillock beyond the pool where Ambros still heaved upon his spear shaft, hunting knife in hand so he could cut the barbs free. There was another boar, a sow, with seven small squealers, breaking from the trees and all making an appalling noise – those alarm calls of their young and females. *Ukh! Ukh!* They were in no danger, of course, though perhaps they did not fully understand the hunting lore.

And Trwyd certainly did not.

He sauntered from the trees, scars all over his rust-brown body, the bristles of his shoulders impossibly long and stiff, crimson red. But those tusks! Chipped and twisted, huge like sword blades. The beast shook its great head, stopped at a rock, and we must all have been mesmerised by it. Even the hounds had fallen silent. And we watched as this thing of legend flicked spittle froth upon its own tusks, then began to hone them, quite deliberately, against the sandstone outcrop. At the same time, it would occasionally pause to grub out some favoured plant, chew upon it, before returning to the sharpening.

'Have you ever seen the like?' Masul gasped. Well, I had not. 'What does it chew?'

'Some bog-myrtle, perhaps,' I said. 'To prepare it for battle. As the ancients are said to have done.'

'I've heard of such things, yet never thought to witness them,' he replied, as Cullough and Bran both broke the spell and began to run forward, though they were far beyond Trwyd's position, yet each hoping to gain advantage, a competitive edge, over the other. With Ambros already having made a kill, precedence now passed to one of them for the honour of slaying the Boar King – and winning Slavehold, of course. So we all held back once again.

Trwyd had his own ideas, however. Perhaps the Elder slain by Ambros was some kin and therefore a matter of honour to be settled. Perhaps the sow and her squealers were family too and required his protection. Or perhaps it was the hounds still ripping, rending and splashing in the waters, where Ambros still laboured to free the *craiseach*, ignorant of Trwyd's presence, and pushing back his hunting hood of right-chance so it would not hinder his efforts. But whatever its cause, the Boar King tossed its head in the air once and launched its enormous bulk down the slope.

Ambros heard it then, turned to see Death crashing down upon him, spittle still flying from those razor-edged tusks. The spear was forgotten. He turned to seek an escape route, but could see none. Some of us had already reacted by then. Kicked heels to ponies' flanks. Yet all too far away. And the only men close enough to help were those who owed him least allegiance. Osla Big-Knife and Balor mac Neit. Each fifty paces nearer to Ambros than Cullough or Bran.

There were more dogs racing at the Boar King, the Skyhound's own Charger among them, but each was slammed sideways or slashed open, without anything slowing the creature. Ambros had his knife in his hand, yelled his battle-cry again and sprang to meet it. But he was pushed from its path by Balor, who planted the heel of his spear shaft in the wet earth and levelled the tip to impale the colossal, bristling head with its crazed eyes.

Yet even Balor's hardened lance could not stop it. Trwyd swerved to its left, seemed deliberately to take the blade in its right flank, as though that were a shield, ripped the shaft from Balor's grasp and then, at the last moment, it struck. Those wicked tusks drove up through the Incomer's groin, and Balor screamed through his bushy black beard as the boar hefted him skywards, lifted him three feet from the ground and carried him onwards. Still did not stop. Ran on towards Ambros Skyhound, shaking the great neck until Balor was tossed away like a rag doll.

We were all riding hard now. But uselessly. Ambros still knee-deep in the pool, the knife in his hand woefully inadequate, the Boar King an instant away, with Balor's blood spraying from its nostrils – Trwyd's personal battle-mist. And there was Osla Big-Knife, the Saeson screeching in his own tongue, short and stocky, like Trwyd himself. Vaulting past Ambros. Something resembling the Dolphin Spin. *Saex* in one hand. He tackled the creature from the side, arms wrapped about its neck, head buried in the coarse bristles, one foot seeking a purchase on Balor's spear, still flapping from its hide. But it broke the boar's concentration. Prevented the tusks from seeking Ambros out, so that the combined bulk of boar and man simply smacked him back into the pool, all three of them going down in a gushing fountain of water.

The rest of us had arrived on the scene by now, leapt from our ponies and began splashing into the pool also, then halted, as one, when we saw the whole mere turned scarlet in thrashing waves and breakers. I shouted his name, I remember. Others did the same. But, as the violence subsided and we reached the place, I saw Osla rise in the shallows, heaving Ambros up, spluttering, coughing gore-stained water, but apparently unharmed. And Trwyd? He floated on his back, with throat sliced from ear to ear.

'See!' said Osla Big-Knife, brandishing the dripping *saex*. 'How hunting in land of my youth.'

Chapter Eighteen

We saved as much of Trwyd's blood as we were able, shared some of it, and used the rest to anoint Ambros as Overlord of the White-Wilds. There was no argument, not even from Kei or Alios, perhaps because they were somewhat encouraged by the Skyhound's adoption of one more Praise Name. Defender of the Faith, he now proclaimed himself – even though none of us had the least idea how that should be interpreted. But the Christ-followers among us seemed satisfied enough by the token. And, speaking of tokens, we took Trwyd's tusks too, naturally. That fine crest. The whole head, in fact. And as much meat as we could carry after the hounds had sated themselves – Ambros ensuring that Charger received its proper portion, relieved that the beast had suffered no lasting hurt.

Owain Hawk-Beak, meanwhile, did his best to make Balor more comfortable. He found herbs for the Incomer to chew – the same, we thought, that the Boar King itself had used – but the pain was too severe, the wound too terrible, for any medicine. And, in the end, he begged to be released. Ambros nodded his consent, and the young *medicus* began to sing some gentle verses in that sweet voice he had, verses about wandering forever among the stars. At the same time, Owain fished for his mercy blade, then stroked the black-bearded face as he carefully let the life pour from Balor's neck, and we saw peace slowly fall upon him once more.

But the death of that valiant man did nothing to quell a clamour for the Skyhound's judgement on Slavehold's future.

'We have no evidence that it was the Saeson's blade which killed the beast,' said Bran of Romaland. 'More likely it was Ambros who finished it.'

'And, if so,' insisted Cullough of Bright-Fields, 'he must surely decide that Slavehold should remain as it stands.'

'Ah, the *status quo* argument,' I smiled. 'Always a popular one.'

'Perhaps he will concede the kill,' suggested Masul the Numidian. 'Grant the lands of Slavehold to Osla Big-Knife.'

'Inconceivable!' roared Bran. 'Some damned Outlander?'

'That Outlander,' I said, trying to avoid all hint of irony, 'most likely saved the life of the White-Wilds' anointed lord.'

'Nonsense,' said Cullough. 'The Lord of the White-Wilds would need no such intercession to deal with a mere boar.'

'Not just any boar, Lord Cullough,' I reminded him. 'But the Boar King. Great Trwyd. The very stuff of legend.'

'And there is the small matter of this doom that the Song-Sayer set upon the hunt,' said Masul.

It was persuasive. None of us would have risked wrong chance by ignoring a doom so plainly cast. So it needed Ambros to make his decision. For, though Bran and Cullough could not help but be dissatisfied, regardless of the outcome, an open judgement by Ambros – driven, as he might claim, by the taboo could only be accepted as fate. Yet, in the end, he merely deferred the judgement and, in so doing, not only offended Osla Big-Knife, but insulted Bran and Cullough also by the appointment of Birch Strong-Arm – Birch of the Spirit-Lance, Birch who had now taken so strongly against me – to act as Warden of Slavehold, pending his decision.

Over the many months that followed, I began to take up my duties as magister of the new *ludus* we had proposed. Ambros took to the campaign trail for the remainder of that year's Light Half, heading south to first punish the cattle-raiders so troublesome to Kei of Meirionshore and Alios of Everfell. By this incisive action, he bound those two Lords Prefect more tightly to him and, though initially incurring their wrath by his incursions upon their lands, he eventually also won respect from Caradoc of Cerdeg's Edge – who was, in any case, distant kin to Ambros and also father to Owain Hawk-Beak – and from Prosperity's Brock of the Tusk, whose daughter, Cara White-Blossom, Ambros had wed when they were young. Brock still blamed Ambros for the daughter's death, but the happy portents here for the hunt, the connection between Praise Name and the slaying of Trwyd, were plain for all to see.

'Yet you must understand, Ambros,' Brock had apparently said to him, 'that these are young spear-hawks, difficult to control, who use the cattle-raid simply to make their way in the world. To earn wealth. Reputation. How else are they supposed to do so?'

And Ambros would have given his standard answer.

'How do you think the young hot-blood spear-hawks of the Frankoi do so? By investing their energies in trade. By using their blades only against those who threaten them, rather than against their own kin. By the best management of their farms and herds. After all, they have the same problems with the Endless Winter as ourselves. Yet they thrive, while we starve. And anyway,' he always reminded them with a sly smile, 'for some little while yet, at least, there could be plenty of work for their spears while we convert others to our particular persuasion.' In this way he recruited fresh warriors for his entourage, led them ever further afield on his keen-edged diplomatic offensive.

But before he left Legion-Hold, at the Midsummer Sun Standing, he had sent out messengers far and wide, announcing the establishment of this *universitas*, our community of masters and scholars. This would not compete with those few other academies still functioning at Moon's Glow and War-God's Fort – *Camulodunо* – but would essentially be a school for *ingeniatore*. I would take personal responsibility for the education of two or three disciples wishing, themselves, to become rhetors, though I held no Chair of Eloquence that qualified me to do so. Yet that seemed a minor detail to everybody else. In addition, I would provide a basic knowledge of literature, geography, law, history, natural philosophy and the calculating arts to those opting for indenture with the various Crafting Guilds. Masul the Numidian had offered to remain in Legion-Hold also, to help with these tasks. The music, of course, so vital to the understanding of the *arithmetica*, and some elements of the Oak Seers' lore, we could leave to Morgose the Song-Sayer.

And, to my astonishment, the students came. Sons of duty-holders still waiting to assume responsibilities of their own. All thirsting to know how stone, timber and plain dirt might be employed for the creation of small wonders. We had only a few texts, but Owain Hawk-Beak had helped us find a few monk-brothers willing to begin copying anything we could borrow from the Moon's Glow and War-God's Fort libraries. Better still, our new disciples brought silver with them for my payment, so that the small iron-bound coffer of my personal wealth began to rattle more healthily once more, so much so that I engaged some of the students to gain working experience by constructing for me a modest living space above the *ludus*.

Mostly, things went well. The guildsmen and our disciples were allocated a levy of slaves, as well as a few poorly-paid Outlanders, who were all soon busy in repairing sections of the Eleven; in learning road construction afresh; in draining and clearing the smaller local byways; in fortifying the worst damaged stretches of Legion-Hold's walls; in cleaning and re-commissioning the wells and cisterns beyond the Southgate; and, joy of joys, in refurbishing the most neglected rooms of the bathhouse. So that, before long, it was functioning fully again, even to the extent of attracting a fellow of Anatolian descent, who was soon making a good living from providing exquisite tonsorial services, singeing out our nasal hairs, or spoon-scooping our ear wax. Apart from this, the new activity generated fresh work in the stone quarries beyond the river bridge, or in the clay-fire kilns further afield, where they began to fashion pipes for water and sewerage projects once more, or roofing tiles.

On the downside, there were some problems. Birch, for example, applied his contentious duties with excessive zeal. Legion-Hold was still, you must remember, the administrative centre for Slavehold and, though Ambros would have had it otherwise, maintained the place in the old-fashioned way as a self-standing colony, Birch factually regarded Legion-Hold as part of his personal domain.

'Who gave authority for work to begin on your private palace?' he would demand, usually returning from some counter-productive attempt at pacifying the increasingly restless holdfasts of the Great Hurdle. 'You think it's easy to raise taxes from these tight-arses?'

'Two rooms only,' I repeated, each time the issue arose. 'And financed through my own purse.'

He generally responded with a stinging taunt about the small value added to society by my profession, or maybe a riposte about Rigantona's own two rooms – two more than she deserved, in his opinion, naturally. But, overall, he tried to interfere with almost everything, and I think we might have come to blows on more than one occasion without the regular intervention of Masul the Numidian. And it was Masul, too, who came to me with word of a second issue. About the White Lady of Laigin.

'A piece of gossip I gathered in the pot-house,' he told me. 'It seems

Balor's men blame Ambros for his death. But whether Murgain is fanning the flames, I can't tell. As the Skyhound's closest friend, perhaps you should investigate?'

Was I that thing? Had I ever been? Could I be so now, after all that had happened? I was never certain. But it was an easy temptation, a chance to find out how Rigantona was faring. So, after bathhouse that evening, I took the short steps down Three Horse Lane, across Salt Alley, down to Maingate Way and Murgain's dwelling house. There were hearth-hawks, Balor's Incomers, at the street door but they ushered me inside as though I were expected. As I was!

Murgain was waiting for me in the dimly lit reception room, reclining upon a couch, barely sparing me a glance from those feline eyes. In the gloom, her ash-pale flesh threw out almost as much light as the meagre oil lamps. A low table was set with a similarly parsimonious assortment of delicacies – a few offcuts of blood sausage, some finely chopped cheese, a small dish of nuts – and a flagon of wine, with three cups. On a second couch, Bishop Deniol.

'A simple invitation would have sufficed,' I said, seething inside but trying my best not to show it. 'That little pantomime with the Numidian was hardly necessary.' I sincerely wished that I did not like the fellow so much. Too easy to forget that he was, above all, Justinian's man.

'You would have come?' said the bishop. His bulk seemed uneasily balanced on that slender couch.

'Probably not alone,' I admitted.

'But then you could not so easily have made enquiry about my daughter, could you?' Murgain smiled.

'I came from concern about unrest among your hearth-guards,' I said.

'Did you so?' she laughed, picked at the blood sausage and waved me to the third couch, as though favouring me with the privilege. And no offer of wine, even then. So I chose to remain standing, turned my back upon them and pretended to study the wall paintings. Faded images of the Legion.

'And you, Bishop,' I said, over my shoulder, 'you've come back to swear your client-oath at last?'

'I am Bishop of the White-Wilds, with or without the grace of this *Cuneglasus*, this Red Slayer of yours. And I understand that Brother Flavius has observed the correct proprieties on behalf of my Church.'

'That will hardly satisfy my Lord Ambros,' I told him, then turned to the White Lady Murgain. 'Has anybody explained, Lady,' I said, even though she needed no such clarification, 'that in our Cousins' Tongue, my Lord's name also signifies *divine*? This seems to pose some problem for the Christ-followers. But you, Lord Bishop, he will pursue so far as Legion's Neck, if necessary. Or back to your friends in Yew Grove. To Rhun the Tall, I imagine. To Lord Lenocus, who gives him sanctuary there. Or this Bishop Sildag Stag-Shank, who still threatens holy war against us, I assume.'

'Ah, yes,' he said, 'you saw fit to read my private correspondence. Then shared copies with the world and his hounds.'

'I learned a valuable lesson from your scriptorium, Bishop. And it was a message worth sharing, don't you think? This nonsense of peace and love you preach when, in truth, you threaten non-believers with perishing in torment.'

'I'm impressed you understood the scriptorium's power,' said the bishop. 'It is the reason your *Cuneglasus* cannot win this particular hunt. But you understand that already, Mentor. Of course you do.'

'Why else should you keep such a grip on my daughter's skirts?' said Murgain, and I could feel her eyes burning into my back, forcing me to turn fully, to meet her gaze.

'Perhaps for the same reason, Lady, that you pretend protection behind the Skyhound's shield.'

It stung her for a moment, I believe – the thought that we might each be as duplicitous as the other. A game of spy and counter-spy. And I wished that this were the truth of the matter.

'Well,' said the bishop, 'he will be damned for his infamies. Including this attempt to set aside a wife taken under the eyes of the Almighty. Like others of his ilk. Fergna Urcol's Son, from your own South-End lands, for instance. That creature who rejected his wife in favour of their own daughter. And this burning alive by your *Cuneglasus* of those poor brothers at Three Peaks.'

I had heard many strange tales about Fergna, but never that one. But the incident at Three Peaks, it seemed, would forever come back to haunt us, even though we had been nothing but bystanders.

'What is it you both want?' I said.

'A simple matter, Master Mentor,' Murgain smiled. 'Rigantona does not wish to be set aside so easily as wife of this Ambros Skyhound. Like the bishop says, they were joined in the eyes of God, and she is a pious believer in the power of our faith.'

A woman who committed adultery not only with me but also with her hound, I reminded myself.

'When I was younger,' I told her, 'I was something of a gambler. But I liked nothing better than to weigh my wagers. It was the winning that mattered, you see, rather than the higher gain I might make from an outside chance. And this holy war you wish to pursue, you can't be certain of the result. Where would the influence of your Church lie in the advent that you lose?'

'Lose?' sneered the bishop. 'The Almighty steers our course for us, Mentor. You must understand that. And the bishops from the Land of Hosts, Fast-River's Run, Elm-Wood, High-Pass, the lords of those lands, and many more besides – none of us believe in any other outcome than that which I predicted to you once before. That in the face of those twin punishments, the Yellow Death and the Years Without Summer, which the Lord, Our God – Praise His Name Above All Things – has visited upon us as punishment for the deeds of men like Fergna Urcol's Son and *Cuneglasus*, only devotion to the Church can save us. Only the Church offers any hope for the continuity of civilisation. If there should, indeed, ever be a coming together of the Provinces here, it cannot be anything other than under the Church.'

'I still do not understand why I'm here,' I said. 'I have heard this fanaticism before, Bishop. What has this to do with Rigantona? With me?'

'You have prepared the case against my daughter,' said Murgain. 'Is that not correct?'

'Against one of your daughters, Lady,' I reminded her. 'Where does Morgose fit into your schemes?'

'Morgose is blind in more ways than you can imagine, Mentor,' Murgain replied. 'You need not concern yourself on her behalf.' Well, the truth was that I concerned myself very little with the Song-Sayer, barely gave her a thought. Why should I? That cosy little relationship between her and Ambros. Let them share their secrets. Let her fill her verses with his name and barely mention those others of us who stood also at his side. 'But Rigantona needs your assistance,' Murgain continued. 'You seem surprised?' she said. 'No need. It is by way of professional help that we seek. You see, we have an advocate of our own. A lawyer. In Yew Grove.'

'You wish a settlement to be negotiated?' I suggested. 'Under the Judex Laws?'

'No,' said the bishop. 'We want your carefully prepared case to fail.'

'Fail?' I stammered. 'I have bound our arguments together so tightly that they are unassailable. Under the Twelve Tables. Under the Brithem Rules. Anything you care to name.'

'But if another eminent advocate should be in possession of your case?' suggested Murgain. 'If an opposing and more powerful argument could be put to whatever council is chosen to hear rulings and pass judgement?'

'And where is there in all these lands,' I said, preening myself, 'an advocate with my own standing?'

'In Yew Grove,' she replied.

'His name?' I asked, though I suddenly feared I might already know the answer.

'Milos of Edessa,' said Deniol, as though he were giving the deathblow to a hunted stag. And that's the way it felt to me. A blade to my heart. My old master from Moon's Glow who did, indeed, hold a Chair of Eloquence. 'A follower of the Lord Christos now,' the bishop thrust harder. 'Unable, any longer, to follow the High-Born ways in that heathen land of Gift-Given.'

It was difficult to comprehend, though not impossible. The old fellow always had a tendency towards literal interpretation of Plato and would undoubtedly have seen the Christ-followers' philosophies as an enticing extension of Plato's own. He would have found a natural home with them. And he was a formidable advocate. The best.

'And why should I do this?' I demanded. 'Betray my professional codes.'

'Oh, let me count the ways,' murmured Murgain. 'First, if Milos of Edessa does not have any argument to the contrary, he will have no choice but to use Rigantona's own testimony. About how Ambros employed you to force yourself upon her. To create the grounds for a false adultery. There are risks in this, naturally, for Rigantona's own case too. But imagine the miasma of rumour that will build around your own name, Mentor. The stench. And there will be plenty on your own side only too willing to accept such a version. Persuasive fellows like Birch Strong-Arm.'

'Then, of course,' said Deniol, 'there are the wounds we could inflict upon *Cuneglasus* himself. Imagine also the impact if we passed word to Osla Big-Knife – already so unhappy, they tell me, that your Skyhound has not fulfilled his promise that the slayer of the Boar King should have Slavehold – that you tricked him into abandoning Rhun by that pretence of a letter from myself. Has he truly not already suspected that the monk-brother who carried it and Owain Hawk-Beak are one-and-the-same?'

'The Outlander, they tell me,' Murgain told him, 'was so drunk that he would hardly have recognised his own father.'

'It matters little,' Deniol continued. 'The Saesons will turn upon your people at the drop of a starter's stick.'

'And where will be his dreams of keeping Client Lords like Mabon and Custain on his side,' said Murgain, 'if I let slip his charming comment that it were better for every monk of the Christos to be burned than a single follower of Mithras harmed? You see, Mentor, we can all use the lesson you so cleverly learned at the scriptorium.'

I suspected they could have each continued in the same vein for some while. And I calculated my options; messages to Ambros; arguments and strategies to refute their claims and, possibly, by their very denial, strengthen them; a flawed version of my codex to buy time; and a variety of others. But there was always my fear of a false move damaging the Skyhound's future. Of corrupting the legend we were weaving. And, on the other hand, gods forgive me, always the prospect of some reward from a grateful Rigantona if I complied.

'So you want a copy of my case?' I said.

'And early information as soon as you know where and when the council will be convened,' said Murgain.

Chapter Nineteen

A message arrived with Cai the Blood-Taster soon afterwards. Ambros was at Uric's Hold by that time and seemed to be doing very well indeed. But I was instructed to join him and to escort Rigantona there also. Personally.

'He stressed that,' Cai explained, as we shared a heather-beer and a side of Throne-Sense near the river. 'There's a Grand Council meeting set for September Dead Moon Day. We're to be back just ahead of that. Does it give you a problem, Mentor?'

'The schedule?' I said. 'Or responsibility for Rigantona?'

'I don't understand any of these games.' He stroked the latest of his scars, a long one down his left cheek earned at Long Battle Bay. Throne-Sense was not one of his strengths but I guessed he meant something else. 'Why go to all this trouble just to set aside a wife? Before the whole world, too. Easier to just take another woman. Leave the wife to her own devices.'

'Or simply have her killed?' I suggested. 'As Malco did, so he could possess the Lady Murgain.'

'Well...' Cai began, then stopped himself. 'Ah, that's what you call irony, is it not?'

'Sometimes,' I said. 'Though it was indeed Malco who began all this. If he had followed the rule of law, as Ambros intends to do, our song may have fallen out in a very different way. And how is the new Lord of the White-Wilds anyway?'

A shadow passed across those grey eyes.

'Well enough, I suppose. Though he never rests. Eats like a sparrow. Suffers often from some gripe of the guts as a result, I think. I've told him. Needs to keep up his strength. But he still swims every day. The river there.'

'And Uric's Hold itself?''

'Every bit as wonderful as they say, Mentor. Not so big as Legion-Hold and I miss the mountains. We all do. But a beauty, all the same. At its heyday it must have been quite something. No walls, you know? And, even now, Lord Iago has been busy. New developments all over the place. Ambros has promised him that, as soon as your first batch of *ingeniatores* are trained, he can use them at Uric's Hold.'

'Then I'd better gather up Rigantona and go see it for myself,' I smiled.

'There's one more thing though,' Cai pulled at a straw-coloured hair braid. 'There's a Bishop of the Christ-followers there too.'

'Iago's no Christ-follower himself,' I said. 'But there's been a Bishop of Sabrina-Rise since his father's day. Old Morn thought it best to humour them, I think. But I thought the fellow would have scuttled off to Yew Grove with all the others who've been threatening Ambros with damnation.'

'That's just it,' said Cai. 'This bishop of theirs seems to have gone out of his way to let Ambros know that Deniol's been back here. Thought I'd better let you know.'

The road from Legion-Hold to Uric's Hold was easy enough. Following the Two, all the way. The Leftgate out of the city itself. Ten miles south to the border with Prosperity and that cattle-market town of Bovium, so familiar to the drovers of all the White-Wilds – the point at which we traded livestock with the outside world, whenever there was trade to be had. Eight more miles to the half-derelict *mansio* way-station where we would spend our first night, at Cai's recommendation, since he knew the route so well. Then, in the morning, out onto those rolling plains of Lower Prosperity itself, once such a bread-basket but now, like many of our lands, with large tracts of good soil returned to wilderness. In places, more enterprising folk had made modest fortunes by larger-scale cultivation of root vegetables – become kings of carrots, overlords of onion, princes of parsnips. And these were safer crops, anyway, for a time of strife. Not so easy to torch a turnip patch. But, overall, it was a scenery of farmsteads abandoned, and the once-prosperous brick-built houses of Mediolano – Midfield in our Cousins' Tongue – neglected and worn by woes. Twelve miles from the previous *mansio* to Midfield, so a reasonable place for our second night. An inn, flea-bitten, but serviceable. Our third day, twelve more miles, took us to the farther edge of Prosperity, at Rutinio, and another way-station, so that on the fourth we crossed the Old Ford into Sabrina-Rise and the final eleven-mile stretch to Uric's Hold.

These were short stages, by the standard of the legions, but sufficient considering we were not truly one party but several. Cai, for example, insisted on taking a couple of riders and scouting constantly ahead. For there were lawless and desperate men sometimes upon the road. Starvation and plague-loss loneliness had made them so. Some distance to the rear, there was a closed travelling *carrio*, with the White Lady Murgain of Laigin ensconced inside on the best cushions she could gather. She was jealously protected by those remaining men of Malco's original hearth-guards, previously commanded by Balor mac Neit as their First Spear but now, with his death, showing loyalty only to Murgain. And, in the centre, the main entourage – a pitiful gathering of the divided. Despite my protestations, and Cai's confirmation that it was my personal responsibility for delivering Rigantona to Uric's Hold, Birch Strong-Arm had made it clear that since she was under guard in Legion-Hold – Legion-Hold being part of his Slavehold command – it would be over his dead body that he would allow me and that "dog's bitch" out of his sight. So there he was, with spear-hawks of his own, yet never a word exchanged between us. At the tail of this central group, Masul the Numidian and Morgose the Song-Sayer, each of whom I had ignored so far as may be possible. But here, at the heart of it all, in more ways than one, the *carrio* which bore Rigantona herself. And, while I had initially arranged a decent pony for her, Birch had once again imposed his will, ordered that she should travel in a manner befitting her status as a prisoner – in the old cage-cart from Legion-Hold's prison, with nothing but a few handfuls of straw for her comfort. Well, at least it had rained little. But my hopes to spend some private time in her company were certainly dashed.

'Scribble, scribble,' she said to me, through the mask of her matted hair, on that final day of our journey. 'What is it that absorbs you so, Mentor?' She had barely spoken to me, in any case, since we left Legion-Hold.

'I dream that some day,' I said, without looking up from my tablet and stylus, 'we might need to repair this highway too. So, every time the holes are big enough to make you curse with the pain of their jolting, I note the location. More or less. It seems a reasonable way to prioritise the work.'

'There is no end to your illusion, is there?' she sneered. 'And me. Do you dream of me at night too? I wonder. How would that one go? The famous Meridden of Sea Fort. Eloquently sets out the case against his own disciple's wife that she is set aside. So grateful is she for the release, she falls into the arms of that worldly-wise Mentor instead.'

Birch had seen our exchange, and I watched him edge his pony closer, though the rattle and clatter of the cart's four wheels over the uneven flints and gravels, would make it impossible for him to hear us.

'No fraternising with the prisoner,' he bellowed, but we paid him no heed.

'It's a beautiful picture you paint,' I said to her, 'though it's lacking the obvious border frieze. The one which shows you going to all this trouble so you can keep the marriage alive.'

One of the wheels caught in a particularly deep rut, and Rigantona gripped the iron bars, hauled herself up, almost automatically, to avoid the worst of the jarring.

'Another one for your notes,' she said, though I could see the buffeting had pained her. 'And why should I wish to keep the marriage alive, after all this? But if I must endure your company, you might as well amuse me some more. Shall you not share with me the rhetorical arguments you will use to settle the annulment of my marriage? The style of oratory you may use to press them?'

Amusement value? I thought. *Yes, I suppose that's a fair summary.* But was this some new sport she had invented?

'If you want more details than those I've already given your mother, I shall have to disappoint you,' I said. 'This will make you laugh even more, but I decided that I needed to maintain at least a modicum of self-respect. Integrity, you might say. So I gave her only so much of the case as the rules of disclosure, one advocate to another, might demand. An outline only.'

I watched her turn this over.

'My mother has instructed an advocate on my behalf,' she said, more to herself than to me. 'So, her ardour has not cooled.'

I remembered the words of Ambros, his description of Murgain.

Something about embers that remained aglow throughout the night, waiting only to be kindled into flame again in the morning. And the Lady of Laigin, one more *Uindabhair*, another White Enchantress, had her own schemes, it seemed. So, whatever resentment I might feel about Ambros keeping his plans from me, it must be more bitter by far for Rigantona to be deceived or left in ignorance by her mother.

'I assumed you knew,' I told her while, from the rear, and despite the road noise, I heard her sister's voice begin the many verses of a marching song, one that had become popular among the Skyhound's war-band.

Bathe the Great Hurdle in blood. Ride to Legion-Hold where Rhun stood. Long Battle Bay and foes' flood. Ride on, Bear-Brothers!

'Who has she chosen as my advocate?' Rigantona asked.

'The best, naturally.'

'A choice made to hurt each of us equally, then. She perceives that Ambros will be at the centre of power. For a while, at least. So she would keep me there too. Tied to his side. So that when his time comes...'

'More nonsense about his health?' I said.

'I believe that Ambros may defeat most enemies that come against him,' said Rigantona. 'Yet not the foe which grows within him. None can outrun the Ravager.'

The word chilled my blood. A word that none should speak aloud.

'Is that the thing you have wished upon him?' I said.

'I would wish it upon none but my worst enemy. Like that one.' She pointed at Birch, who saw her do so and immediately made the sign of the horns to ward off whatever evil she may be conjuring. 'Him, and those who were with him.'

'The hound?' I asked, and it occurred to me that I had never heard her call the creature by name.

'Yet another reason I would see Ambros brought down too,' she replied, bracing herself against another jolt of the cart.

'And because you believe he has usurped the position that Rhun should have occupied, in your heart, and in the world,' I said, 'then why did you not simply resist the wedding?'

'My mother's ambitions, Mentor, naturally.' She parted twists of the hair that hid so much of her face, either to see me better or allow me to gaze at the sincerity in her eyes. 'Through me, she hoped to one day set a claim upon First-Province.'

'For Malco?' I said. 'But he already had his own dream of ruling the province.'

'A persuasive one too, in the beginning, when my mother allowed herself to be carried off by him. But she soon realised that her new husband was all bluster. Could never have delivered that for her. It is like I said. No end to your illusions.'

Rigantona was correct, I supposed. I was still clinging to some lunacy that I could possess her. But it had always been Rhun, had it not? One more score for me to settle with him. But I was not alone in my delusion. Our failure to observe that which was under our noses. That Murgain's lack of mourning for her dead husband was evidence that she wanted the Westerlands for somebody else. And there was only one other piece left on the board. It was all for Deniol, of course. For Deniol the man. For Deniol of the Christ-followers' Church.

Mensis Septembris Dark Moon Day. The sixteenth of that month. And the Great Council was finally gathered in the meeting chamber on the upper floor of a hall recently completed by Iago Morn's Son. Stone and timber. Impressive. Built, they said, on the site once occupied by Uric-Hold's Exercise Hall, on the south side of Market Street. The whole formed an administrative complex for the town – for all Sabrina-Rise, in fact – with the hall supporting a cluster of smaller annexes and, just across from its towered gate, the entrance to those sections of the bathhouse, which Iago had been able to preserve and maintain. Yet, even now, it was something to be admired, the solid outer wall of the bathhouse still as high as the hall itself. He had been busy elsewhere in the town too, though there were many projects only half-completed.

'And we have, each of us, undertaken similar initiatives,' said Iago, by now firmly immersed in his speech of welcome. He was prematurely grey, both hair and beard, but richly robed in greens and purples. 'The Lord Protector of South-End, for example,' he said, picking Fergna from the assembled Overlords and Lords Prefect gathered at the benches, 'has done much work to restore the gold mines north of Sea Fort. Aurelius Caninus has paved afresh great sections of the Thirteen and Fourteen around Corin-Mound, and tells me the wool trade flourishes there once more. Each of us engaged in our separate endeavours to develop these lands anew. To counter this Endless Winter. All the things which threaten us.'

'To be honest with you, Iago,' Gereint of Windstorm, Gereint Six-Fingers, interrupted him, 'I doubt there is any project more meaningful, more worthy of support, than that which we are pursuing around the iron mines of Aricon. The purest ore in all the land. And promise of new markets among the Frankoi.'

He was an oily character. Deeply scarred face. Terrible reputation for finding original and unpleasant deaths for his enemies. A reputation, too, for having set aside a comfortable fortune for himself, and without any benefit from a united First-Province.

'And these are all, indeed, heartening tales to hear,' said Ambros. He was the youngest lord here, by several years. 'But the purpose of our meeting is not, surely, to decide that one, more than any other, should receive our blessing, our investment, but rather to each support the other. A combination of our strengths, that we might prosper collectively.'

'I have heard Elidyr of Clud-Vale speak so on many occasions, Ambros,' Aurelius of Two-Tribes told him. 'He was my friend. And I always supported his vision. Just a pity he's not with us today.' The twist of his lips and the sideways turn of his eyes, as he resumed his seat, cast a powerful criticism in the Skyhound's direction. There were plenty, it seemed, who still blamed Ambros for Elidyr's death.

'A sad loss, Aurelius,' Iago told him. Oil on troubled water. 'But I believe you have word from Marcus Seahound. And Constantine of Horn-Head?'

'The journey is difficult for them both,' Aurelius replied, getting to his feet again. 'But each has said they support the concept of collective strength, so far as it may be practical. And they suggest that, should there be further gatherings of this council, perhaps we might meet at Corin-Mound, or further south again, to make their attendance more viable.'

But his suggestion lacked enthusiasm. These would be difficult territories to embrace. Wild lands, on the fringes, and beholden to none but themselves.

'There are more paths than one to collective strength and salvation.' Old Caradoc of Cerdeg's Edge hauled himself upright on his staff. 'The bishops are clear. And I, for one, believe them. That the Years Without Summer, the Yellow Death too, are sent by the One True God to punish us for our failure to follow Him, to worship His son, the Christos.'

'I will listen to none of this blasphemy,' shouted Fergna Urcol's Son.

'Mithras is our glory and our hope. And the Horned One's Pox on any that would try to persuade us otherwise.'

He had barely finished when Valor Bent-Back was on his own feet. Lord of the Glusio lands which bordered Fergna's self-styled Protectorate.

'The Horned One's Pox?' he said. 'More usually it is Fergna's raiders bringing fire and spear to any settlement of our Christ-followers within their reach. And such persecution is not confined to my own duty-holders alone. We hear tales of monk-burning. At the hands of the same Elidyr that my Lord Aurelius would have us venerate. And the bishops tell us that even Malco, whose lands Ambros Skyhound now claims as his own, was martyred for his belief in the Almighty.'

Ambros sprang up, his face flushed with anger.

'My Lords!' he cried.

'No, Ambros,' Iago told him. 'Be still a while, I beg you. For I know this tale of Malco as well as any other here. Perhaps better, since I heard it from the pony's mouth. It was a cruel end. But perhaps fitting. For Malco Battle-Shield had lured you, Ambros, to his holdfast with the purpose of murdering you.' Iago paused, looked around at the intent faces. 'And that same Malco was responsible, at least in part, for the death of the Skyhound's mother and father.'

'And how is this known to you?' asked Valor. 'From the lips of Ambros himself, I'm guessing.'

'No, my friend,' Iago smiled upon him. 'Rather, I questioned the wife of Malco in person, only this morning. It was the White Lady Murgain of Laigin, one of your Christ-followers herself. And this quibble between Mithras and Christos troubles me. For I do not believe the evils that plague us are God-given. There should be space enough within our federation for all beliefs. For tolerance. So let us face those evils as men must do. Shoulder to shoulder. Shield locked to shield.'

It was a language we all understood.

'And under whose generalship?' asked Valor of Glusio.

'My own vote goes to Lord Protector Fergna Urcol's Son,' shouted Aurelius Caninus. He had received considerable benefit from his old alliance with South-End. Time to repay the debt. 'And I believe I may speak for Horn-Head and Domna's Deep too.'

'You received word from Marcus and Constantine on this matter?' Iago demanded.

'Not precisely,' Aurelius replied, 'but...'

'Well I, for one, am content,' said Valor, 'to stand beside Ambros in this. He declares himself Defender of All Faith. And, if he will commit himself to defending our own beliefs, Glusio will support him.'

'Cerdeg's Edge too,' said Caradoc, quickly. Yet he sounded as lukewarm in his support as Valor, and it seemed clear to me that if there had been a Christ-follower with a strong enough force at his back, that is where their support would have gone. Ambros, to them, was simply a more benign option – they hoped – than Fergna.

'And Windstorm?' Iago looked to Gereint Six-Fingers for his input.

'Well,' said Six-Fingers, 'since none has seen fit to recognise my own suitability for this role...' He glanced around those lords who had not yet spoken, giving them time to take his prompt, but failing in the attempt. 'I suppose my own support must go to Fergna Urcol's Son.'

'Damned by faint praise, I think that's called,' snarled Fergna, while Iago invited the others to state their preference. Prosperity and Belthos for Ambros. Brychan and Aricon for Fergna. Hardly decisive.

'Looks like the choice rests with you, Iago,' said Six-Fingers. 'All our fates in your hands.'

'A difficult choice,' Iago replied. 'I can think of no two men I would trust more to lead us in battle. Yet there are other matters to consider here. And I think that our friend, Fergna, would be the first to recognise that at such a time as this, holding together all the interests of our lands – including those of the Christ-followers, of great lords like Caradoc and Valor – would not be easy for him. Of the two, my honest opinion is that Ambros may be the more likely to succeed, and I believe the support of Sabrina-Rise should therefore go to him.'

So it was that the Province was united again, after a fashion, for the first time in many generations. And, to less than universal acclaim, Ambros Owen's Son, Ambros Skyhound of the Bough-Gatherers' Bear-Brother Clan, Lord of the White-Wilds, became High Lord of the Prima Westerlands.

The lords gathered at Uric's Hold may have been grudging in their enthusiasms but among their duty-holders, kindred and spear-hawks, the news spread with greater joy. There were celebrations that night to match almost any I had ever seen. They spilled out from Iago's Council Hall and onto the streets beyond, and everywhere I went there were Song-Sayers. All the old tales. The Lay of Germanio. The Courtship of Olwen. The Death of Gereint Swift-Charger. The Giant's Spoils. The Four-Cornered Fortress. The Twin Serpents of Glusio. But there were new stories too. The Silver Cauldron. The Whale-Road. And, of course, the Slaying of Trwyd Boar King. Raucous chanting of our favourite anthems too, wherever a gaggle of revellers found themselves still capable of melody.

But, in the morning, with thick heads at the first Great Lords' Council over which Ambros presided as High Lord, there were some evident divisions. Now that the Province was established again, surely it would need regular governance. Under the old rights granted by the Empire, a province had been entitled to its own Provincial Council, with each territory sending two representatives, normally its elected magistrates, to protect its interests. But districts which saw themselves as independent of territorial rule – there were several of these within the borders of Glass-Isles and Rage-Rise – had also been granted representation rights and, argued Six-Fingers, would assuredly wish to have them once more. Then there was the issue of taxation. Each territory must obviously preserve the right to raise its own revenue. But how much should each territory contribute to provincial initiatives? How should their relative size and wealth be weighted? And those independent districts as against the larger lordships? Arguments that must have dogged politicians for all time. Federated region against independent district. They were fractious issues, few of them resolved by the time an impatient Ambros sought to introduce the issue of his own marital status onto the agenda, and I was called forth to set out the grounds by which our new High Lord wished to set aside his wife. But, before I could speak, Aurelius Caninus demanded to be heard.

'By the Horns,' he cried, 'what are we doing here? A Lords' Council is no place to be discussing our domestic affairs. For pity's sake, Ambros, if you want to get rid of the woman, just get on with it.'

'Yet I understand, my friends,' said Valor Bent-Back, 'that this marriage was blessed by the Church. That Bishop Deniol served as Auspex. The Theodosian Codes make it clear that such a union should not be set aside lightly.'

'And there is this, Lords,' Ambros told them. 'I made vows during that hand-binding and, should I simply ignore them, it would be too easy for my enemies to throw against me the charge of oath-breaker alongside the other things for which they falsely find me culpable.' He spat these last few words straight into Valor's lowered gaze. 'It was my marriage to Rigantona, also, which gave me the lands of Overmon – and therefore my claim to all the White-Wilds. If my title to the White-Wilds is questionable, I fear it would create a further weapon in the hands of those same enemies, which might be used to undermine my role here as your High Lord. I therefore wish this Lords' Council to hear the case against my wife, for it is one which bears upon our Province as a whole.'

There was considerable grumbling. Discomfort even. A precedent that many here would not wish to see set. Yet I was given leave to proceed, to introduce the parties. Rigantona, of course, who had been confined comfortably enough in the administrative quarter; the White Lady Murgain, who wished it known that she had served as Matron of Honour at the wedding; and, of course, my old master, Milos of Edessa. He had travelled here from Yew Grove with a small tail of monk-brothers and a veritable pack train of legal codices. He was old now. Still sharp-witted, the most intelligent man I had ever met. But old. Barely recognised me, either, for his eyes were so clouded by the shutter disease. Hence the need for so many assistants.

I had told Ambros, naturally. Not the whole of my conversation with Murgain and Deniol, but at least the essence of it. He had taken it all philosophically enough, perhaps saw some opportunity to trap Deniol in the event that the bishop might return again to Legion-Hold. And he even considered my decision to observe the etiquette between advocates, to disclose outline cases, as helpful. For it meant that we were prepared also. In any case, I had told him, there could be no difficulty for us since our key witness would be Rigantona herself. Whatever Murgain might have contrived, if the wife also consented to the divorce, under any of the laws we might use as reference, it was virtually secured.

So my carefully prepared case, for example, made no mention of adultery. How could it do so, since the main secondary party in such an action would be myself, the litigant's own advocate? Nor did we rely on the more frequently used grounds that the wife might be a preparer of poisons. Certainly no reference to bestiality. But it focused, rather, on the Skyhound's view that Rigantona had failed to properly administer his lands during his absence. Neglect of her duties as a wife. There was particular emphasis here on the fact that she had closed the Mithraeum at the Fortress of the Hammer-Fighters. A necklace of proofs that she had been profligate with his wealth. And, worse, evidence produced that she had betrayed him to his enemies – and particularly to Rhun the Tall. Therefore a treason against the White-Wilds and, by implication, against First-Province.

Milos responded brilliantly, of course. Murgain and Deniol must have briefed him well. The marriage vows first. Did promising her a first taste of his wine not imply that the husband's possessions were also those of the wife, to sup from as she pleased? What about that oath that the husband's lips should be sealed to strangers on all that may pass between the couple? Was this entire case not a breach of that pledge? The husband's body for the wife alone? Oh, how the implications of infidelity on the litigant's part were amassed, without a single direct allegation ever made. And the references quoted. Roman laws. Incomer Judex Codes. Portions of the Christ-followers' *biblia sacra*. Sufficient to drive many from their seats – men like Fergna Urcol's Son, who had set aside his own wife, you will remember, in favour of his daughter. Sufficient to dull the brains of others, to the point at which I knew, with certainty, that a vote on the matter would turn against Ambros.

Time, therefore, to play our best piece.

'My Lords,' I said, rising slowly and stroking some imaginary dust from my square-weave as though about to brush aside my opponent's arguments in one easy gesture, 'this is all very eloquent, but would it not help speed the proceedings if we heard from the Lady Rigantona herself?'

There was a collective outpouring of relief as I bade her stand. She had not spoken a word through that long afternoon, sat with bowed and humiliated head, those thick braids of hair hanging down about her face. And, as I framed the key question, she swept them aside, to expose the theatrical stage beyond. Tears on her cheeks as she answered me.

'But Mentor,' she sobbed, 'you, of all people, know how much I love my husband. Why should I wish such a divorce?'

Chapter Twenty

She had plucked me like those bass strings of the Song-Sayer's cruth. It had been a spirited and lengthy defence. Had she not always been faithful to her husband? Had she not given him her whole heart, when his own was still ruptured by the loss of his first young bride? Had she not closed the Mithraeum simply to protect the shrine in her husband's absence, knowing how devoutly he cherished his own faith? Had she not utilised his wealth simply in protection of the lands he loved so well?

'You forgot your Cicero, my friend,' said Milos as we plodded our way back north along the Two. His voice had lost nothing of its honey-and-herbs accent, though it now vibrated with the tremors of old age. '*Any man can make mistakes, but only a fool persists in his errors*. It was always destined to be your weakness.'

Perhaps he was right. I was still bitterly angry with myself for being fooled so easily. But I was not nearly so angry as Ambros had been. Angry with me. Angry with himself for being duped into believing that she would be happier set aside. Angry that she had twisted the very reasons for which she would see him destroyed as justification to remain at his side and see that destruction complete. To lay claim upon whatever might be left.

'How long will you stay in Legion-Hold?' I said to Milos, stinging from his analysis about my persistence in stupidity.

'Long enough to see this academy which may be your redemption. A few days. Then back to Yew Grove – *Eborac*, as we're now required to name it.'

'Common Speech or Cousins' Tongue,' I said, 'does it really make a difference? But nothing wrong with keeping the old names alive, I suppose.'

'In Eborac,' said Milos, 'it is some little way beyond that point.

Lenocus has decreed that the Common Speech should be more formally fostered. The Latin for celebration of our faith. But don't misunderstand me. Nothing wrong with that. Especially given the numbers of Outlanders east of the Spine. There are places over there where you could sometimes hear nothing but the Saesons' blather. Now they must learn to speak a more civilised language.'

'You'll be swamped by them before long,' I said. 'That's what we hear, anyway.'

'I doubt it,' Milos replied. 'Apart from the language, you can't tell one from another any more. Outlanders are just part of the landscape. But there are always those who'd use it as an excuse for mischief. Blame anything that happens on the Outlanders. That sort of thing.'

'Lord Lenocus?' I asked.

'His son. Gwrgi Hard-Spear. The Man-Dog.'

'I thought Lenocus had him locked away some place.' I recalled the strange stories I had once heard about this wolf-boy.

'When he was a child, maybe. But he's full-grown now. Or some parody of manhood, at least. And he's found a natural ally in your friend, Rhun. Thick as thieves, the two of them.'

'The stories about Gwrgi…' I began.

'Best not to ask,' said Milos. 'But, yes. True, I think.' They had not circulated for some time but, a few years earlier, there had been disturbing tales. The boy, Gwrgi, cursed with assuming a wolf's form at each Dead Moon and needing to feast on human entrails to quench his appetites. Pliny and Virgil speak of such things, of course, but those examples were surely not to be taken literally. 'The Numidian tells me,' Milos continued, 'he dealt with a couple of interesting cases, back in the East. Some form of madness, in which the sufferer truly believes himself afflicted by such a transformation. I'll ask him to cast an eye over Gwrgi. Discreetly, of course.'

'Masul is going back to Yew Grove with you?' I said. If so, I regretted it. Regretted the gulf I had allowed to grow between myself and the Numidian.

'He'll interview the bishops. On the Emperor's behalf. For a more complete picture of the faith here.'

'Is there a complete picture?' I asked. 'Things must look very different in Secunda than this side of the Spine.'

'The Emperor's unlikely to be overly discerning,' said Milos. 'Britannia will be all one to him.'

'It's the dream of Ambros to make it so,' I reminded him.

'Justinian's only concern will be whether it is all one in the eyes of God,' he said. 'You must see that? Storm clouds gather against your Skyhound's dream. Or his version of it. The bishops will not even speak the name of Ambros. And Lenocus sees himself already as High Lord of the North, would never see himself as subservient to some Greater Britannia unless he, himself, were its ruler. He will unleash the wrath of God upon Ambros should he try to make it otherwise. And the bishops will bless Lenocus at every step for doing so.'

'Your good and kindly Christ-followers,' I sneered.

'There is nothing wrong with the faith, my friend,' he replied. 'It allowed me to find myself. My true self. And you were once a great student and admirer of Plato. It is only a short walk from there to the Christos. I'm amazed you've not converted also.'

'You think it would help?' I said, though it was an absent-minded comment. For I was gazing ahead, up the road, to where Murgain's carriage rattled along a particularly straight stretch, though mist-shrouded woodland. Rigantona was riding alongside, hooded against the drizzle, and leaning over so she might converse with her mother through the open window.

'Perhaps to ease the pain in your soul?' he suggested. 'And do you think the women will remain in Legion-Hold?'

'Legion-Hold, or somewhere else in the White-Wilds,' I said. 'Rigantona is still the Skyhound's wife, after all. She will not give him the chance to bring a new charge, of desertion, against her. And they have each put too much effort into this. To keep their grip on these lands. For this precious Church of yours, I fear.'

There was, in those days, a pot-house near Legion-Hold's harbour wall. A place frequented by those who worked the storehouses and helped with cargo handling. Not that shipments to and from the port were frequent, but at least they were steady. And there were foreign vessels moored alongside that very night. A pair of currocks. Mother Clodia's, the locals called the place. A dingy dive with only two rooms. Low, arched ceilings. Curved alcoves set into the walls that held oaken casks of heather-beer, or an occasional long-jar of wine from the Middle Sea. Yet it had also gained a certain reputation as a gathering point for dissenters.

'Are you certain about this, Cai?' I asked him, as we stood on the wharf-side with the stink of river mud and rotten seaweed in our nostrils. 'There's no real evidence against them.'

'You think they'd meet in a hole like this unless they've something to hide?' he said. 'Ambros would not want us to simply leave them undisturbed about their plotting, whatever it is. Better this than have Birch blundering in. Then we'd have a real bloodbath on our hands – and still no evidence. Let's just see how they react.'

'And me?' I said. 'You've still not told me why I'm here.'

'A witness?' he replied. 'Somebody I can trust, who'll not set a match to the whole thing? Somebody with a brain, whose report Ambros would value?'

Personally, I doubted that Ambros would value anything associated with my name now, though I said nothing. He was skirmishing along Iago's eastern borders somewhere, punishing more cattle-raiders there. Imposing the new laws, as he would say. And he had sent Cai to keep him briefed on the home front. Birch may still be the notional warden of the White-Wilds, but it was Cai's network of watchers and spies upon which Ambros truly relied. There were several of them hidden now in the deeper waterfront shadows. Well-armed ruffians. Just in case. But we ducked through the doorway into the pot-house alone, huddled in our cloaks, trying to look as though we belonged there. Yet the wharf-men in the first room knew us almost at once, for Cai was a familiar figure around town. He was unmistakeable, in truth. Respected, though. Nods of greeting. And they soon went back to their conversations, left us to our heather-beer.

'The other one?' I said – an entirely redundant question since the men we sought were plainly not here and, guarding the entrance to the room beyond, there was a fellow who was far more out of place than either Cai or myself. He was trying to look casual, but he was tanned from too many years on the open seas. A Laigin man, perhaps. And there were others among the pot-house customers from the same part of the world. The currocks, of course. I was still counting heads when I realised Cai was no longer at my side.

'We're invited,' he was telling the Laigin sailor. He pronounced the words slowly but received only a stream of Gathelic invective in return. A restraining hand against his chest. That was a mistake, for nobody set hands upon Cai the Blood-Taster with impunity. And, in less than a heartbeat, he had gripped the extended wrist, spun sideways and wrapped his right fist around the sailor's elbow, pressing against it to make the forearm rigid. The man yelled, tried to reach for a blade at his belt, but Cai lifted his knee in one fluid motion, set it against the bones of the sailor's forearm, then pulled sharply with both hands, snapping the limb like a bundle of dried twigs. The scuffle, then the sailor's scream, brought the entire pot-room to its feet, folk on all sides seeking for anything that might pass as a weapon.

'Easy, boys!' I called out. 'You know us. Here on the Skyhound's business.'

I could not be sure whether that particular currency held any value, but it seemed to pacify most of the wharf-hands. Yet it meant little to the Gathelic-speakers of the currock crews scattered among them. And the fellow with the broken arm was obviously one of their own. A couple of them had rushed forward to intervene but, thankfully, some of the Legion-Hold lads stood in their way. More scuffles here and there while, from the second room, Osla Big-Knife came thundering out, cursing in a mixture of the Outlander Saeson and the Cousins' Tongue – until he saw who it was that had disturbed him, disrupted whatever was happening within.

'Friend Osla,' Cai beamed at him. 'Thank the gods. We thought we were alone among so many foes.' At his feet, the sailor was struggling to his knees, trying for that knife at his belt again, his left arm dangling, useless. Cai delivered a wicked blow to the side of the fellow's head, sent him sprawling, lifeless. 'And all we wanted, me and the Mentor,' Cai continued as though nothing had happened, 'was a quiet jug.' Osla took an uncertain glance over his shoulder. 'What?' Cai's eyes opened in mock wonder. 'More of our mates within?'

He began to push past the Outlander, while I turned to the local boys.

'Watch our backs?' I ventured, relieved to see at least half-hearted agreement and a cordon of wharf-hands forming between us and the Laigin crewmen. Then I followed Cai down into a room even smaller than the first.

'This is a private meeting,' cried Cullough of Bright-Fields, spilling wine all over the table and his breeks in his haste to rise.

'Well, if the Sea-God had cast his nets…' Cai laughed. It was exactly as he had been informed. They had met here the previous night, arranged to do so again this evening. Osla, Cullough and Bran of Romaland. A couple of their duty-holders too, that I vaguely recognised. And a sixth fellow. Skipper of the currock crews, I guessed from his features and his dress. Something familiar, though I could not quite place him.

'A commercial gathering,' said Bran, his usual, reasonable self. 'A gathering between Prefect Lords, Master Mentor.' He placed heavy stress upon *Prefect Lords*, carefully addressed himself to me, rather than to Cai. 'Is there good reason for this drunken interruption?'

'We've not touched a drop yet, my Lord,' Cai told him, lacing that final word with sarcasm as heavy as Bran's haughtiness. 'But, if you're offering!' There was a horn of wine still standing on the table, and he took a mighty swig, until the red liquid was dribbling down his chin.

'What you want here?' shouted Osla, coming back down the rough steps. 'More lie? More trick? More message from Bishop? I should have listen to friend Rhun.'

So, Murgain and Deniol had not kept their side of our little bargain. Or perhaps they thought that my only partial disclosure of the case against Rigantona was not sufficient to fulfil my own end of it. But they had won, had they not?

'It was a necessary deception,' I told him, trying to sound placatory. 'For the sake of peace. And your people have prospered from it, Osla. Have they not? Their own settlement beyond the walls. The right to worship at the chapel of Holy Peter.'

'That all I deserve?' Osla snarled. 'I save your Skyhound's life. Kill Boar King.' His hand went to the *saex* at his waist and I watched Cai prepare to butcher him if it was necessary. But the stocky Outlander simply smacked the leather sheath. 'And he break promise. Kill Boar King, win Slavehold. That's what he say. But nothing.'

'Well, to be fair,' said Bran, 'I've heard there's some dispute about whether it was your own knife, or that of Ambros himself, which finally slew the beast.' Osla began to protest, then took a moment to check that he had translated Bran's words correctly. 'But you can hardly blame young Osla,' Bran went on, 'for feeling a bit aggrieved. After all, Ambros hardly repays loyalty, does he? Look at my own case. First to recognise his claim as Lord of the White-Wilds. Last to share his plans.'

I had heard all this before. His carping about not being a party to the Skyhound's secret arrangement by which Cullough and the Bright-Fields men had sprung the trap for Rhun – and Osla too, as it happened – at the Great Hurdle.

'Is any of this relevant to our business here?' shouted Cullough himself.

'Hard to say,' replied Cai. 'Will you not introduce us?'

He extended the wine-horn towards the silent sailor at the table's end, and I wondered again whether our paths had somehow ever crossed before.

'The business is our own,' said Cullough. 'And perhaps I might answer to the Warden of Slavehold, or even to Lord Ambros himself, but never to the magister of a *ludus*, and certainly not to one of the Skyhound's hearth-hawks, regardless of his friendship with the High Lord himself.'

Well, that put us in our place. And there was no disguising the contempt behind his words. Contempt for Birch Strong-Arm. Contempt for Ambros. Contempt for Cai. Even contempt for myself, though I was unsure how I, personally, may have earned his animosity, except by association.

'A commercial deal?' I said, ignoring Cullough's protestation. 'With traders from Laigin?'

'Not Laigin,' Bran replied, before Cullough could protest. 'Traders from Ulaid.'

The currock captain nodded his head, repeated the word *Ulaid*. Well, we had spent a night at Firth's Head in that most northerly kingship of Hibernia. Not a particularly hospitable welcome, I recalled. But had I seen this fellow there?

'Yes, Ulaid,' said Cullough. 'And why not? New trade is healthy for the whole of the White-Wilds. We need it. By the gods, I thought I prospered badly under Malco's thumb but now I can't even hire out my public slaves any more, to earn me a meagre crust.' He tried to turn it into a jest, but I knew he resented my use of our own slaves and the Saeson workers, to carry out the road repairs and other projects of the *ingeniatore*. And he refused to be drawn any further on the nature of this strange business deal, which involved such unlikely bedfellows.

'Fair enough,' Cai said, at last. 'Yet I think Lord Ambros may have some further questions when he's back in Legion-Hold.' He started up the short stair again, glowered at Osla. Then he paused, as he was about to step over the sailor, who still sprawled there, groaning loudly, and he turned back towards the currock's master. 'Oh,' he said, 'and if anyone speaks the Gathelic, please apologise to the skipper. It seems he must sail short-handed – so to speak.'

And I finally remembered where I had seen the man. Not Ulaid at all. But sailing master to Fingal of the Five Stallions. The day we had sailed from Ferna on the *White Enchantress*. Not from Ulaid at all. Laigin men, as I had thought. He had bidden us clear the Black Pool quickly, reach Edar's Head at low slack, to aid our voyage back to Legion's Neck. Except that we were not heading east that day, but north, to Clud-Vale, in search of the plague-potion. We had lied about our destination. As Ambros had lied too, I recalled. A Kinfolk Oath sworn to Fingal – that we should return, and soon, to help Corpre mac Cormac destroy the Grandsons of Dunlain.

Ambros returned to Legion-Hold only in the middle of *mensis Novembris* and a driving snowstorm, his column strung out in a line of white spectres, coated by thick flakes, which the wind had whipped from benign softness to blinding severity. He took up his old quarters again in the gather-hall of the old *principia* building and, as I had feared might be the case, he did not send for me.

'So you were wrong?' I said to Cai, over a game of Throne-Sense and warmed by a decent fire at one of Legion-Hold's better-appointed pot-houses – one near that same Christ-followers' chapel of Holy Peter. 'About Ambros valuing my report?'

'He was more appreciative when I told him how you had remembered the face of Fingal's sailing master. I should have recognised him too, I suppose.'

'And what did he make of it?' I asked, sipping at my brew and wondering how long it would take before I found my way back into the Skyhound's good graces again.

'He's asked Owain to pen some missive to King Corpre. A personal apology. Assurance that he's not forgotten his oath to Fingal of the Five Stallions and is still committed to taking a war-band to Laigin, just so soon as the troubles along his own borders are settled. He's worried about the link between them all, though. So he'll give Cullough and Bran something else to worry about for a while.' He smiled, tapped the side of his nose with a knowing finger. 'And my boys will keep an eye on them. He's more worried about Osla. Which is where you come in, Mentor. You'll not like it.'

'You don't need to spell it out,' I said. 'I'm supposed to tell the Saeson that our bit of play-acting was all my idea? Nothing to do with Ambros?'

'Something like that. And, as a token of good faith, Osla Big-Knife receives his reward for killing the Boar King. Becomes Prefect Lord of Slavehold. There are conditions, of course.' Well, there would have to be. A Saeson Outlander as Lord of Slavehold, when he could barely use the Cousins' Tongue. There would be other claimants. A whole new set of conflicts to resolve. But at least Ambros had made sure that Osla's powers were limited, balanced finely with those of Slavehold's duty-holders. And, above all, those same duty-holders would be glad to see the back of Birch Strong-Arm, who was being sent north, to Urien of Gift-Given.

'The reports aren't good,' I said. And they were not. Lenocus of Yew Grove making his own bid to become High Lord of Secunda. Fighting along the borders between Gift-Given and Elm-Wood. 'But will Birch make them any better?'

'Mithras be thanked that he'll have no need of diplomacy up there,' Cai laughed. 'He can just concentrate on what he's good at. Breaking skulls.' I laughed too, found myself wishing that the gulf between myself and Birch had not become so deep. 'Don't worry,' Cai slapped my shoulder, reading my face perfectly, 'he'll come around. Just give him time.' Then he wagged a finger in my face. 'But stay away from the women, Mentor. They'll be your downfall.'

I hoped that he meant women in general, rather than Murgain and Rigantona though, in truth, I had seen little of either since our return from Uric's Hold. They were a frequent spectacle around town, of course. Flamboyant. Their own entourages. Almost a separate enclave around that junction of Praetorian Way and Maingate Street. But Cai had his spies within their households too and, so far, all seemed quiet. I had been too busy to worry about them anyway. The *ludus*. Progressing nicely. All the associated public works too, until the weather closed upon us, of course.

'You needn't worry about me,' I told him. 'But has Ambros inspected the sites yet?'

'There's not much to see, with all this bloody snow. And he's not here long. He plans to reach the Fortress of the Hammer-Fighters before the passes close properly. Winter there. Then Twin Sisters for Day of the Dead. He should be back in Legion-Hold soon after. Maybe things will have settled down by then.'

He meant between Ambros and myself, I guessed.

'And meanwhile?' I asked.

'Meanwhile, the High Lord of the Westerlands has another dream,' he smiled. 'One that you'll like, Mentor. Libraries, it seems, are his new passion. A place to set down all the stories of our people. An accurate account of our genealogies. Is that what you call them? Histories of those who speak the Cousins' Tongue. What d'you think?'

Chapter Twenty-One

In truth, I did not see Ambros again until the following Augustus. Lug's Day, which marks the beginning of the Light Half's second quarter – still technically summer though it was often hard to remember it in those times. And, besides, for me it was always a reminder that the Dark Half was looming nearer once more, the year's *clepsydra* time-thief dripping away the seasons and our lives. But none of that did anything to dampen the spirits of Legion-Hold's folk or, indeed, those of the lands for many miles around who had helped swell the city's population so greatly. For the whole area between Southgate – the old *Porta Praetoria* – and the river bridge, radiating outwards from the public wells and cisterns, had been transformed into one sprawling temporary encampment.

'How have your Christ-followers not stolen this one?' I shouted to Masul the Numidian, recently returned from Yew Grove and going out of his way to heal the wound between us – for which I needed little encouragement. We had taken up a position on a gallery of the main bathhouse, with a perfect view of the procession currently crawling up towards the town centre.

'Your Oak Seers seem to have too tight a grip,' he replied.

But there were devotees below us from just about every faith I could name. Oak Seers, yes. In great numbers. Carrying almost a walking forest of foliage. But Mithras worshippers too, with their makeshift wooden altars and miniature Mithraeums; Asclepians, bearing the famous staff with a symbolic snake wrapped about its length, or coloured flasks representing medicines and potions; Soterians, easily distinguished by their state of inebriation, even at this early hour; admirers of Priapus, displaying all manner of phallic symbolism, and dressed in the most outrageous costumes; strings of horses, decked with garland and ribbon in honour of Epona; the young women of Nymphae, daring in diaphanous blues, greens and reds; owl-masked followers of Minerva; and the wheels of chance that stood sacred to Fortuna. For this was the great annual festival of beliefs and clans for all those who shared the Cousins' Tongue. A sennight of celebration in each of the countless gathering places: all around the nearer margent of the Hibernian Sea; or north of that wild ocean, in the lands of Clud-Vale and the High-Born; south also, across the Southern Sea, among our blood-folk in Across-the-Sea; and all the way beyond the Bay of the Cantabri, to the coast of ancient Gallaecia, where the sun forever shines.

First Fruit offerings to be presented. Harvest Blessings to be received. Sacrifices made. The scent of aromatic herbs on crackling cook-fires. Singers and jugglers. Fools and strongmen. The squeal of beasts, knowing they were being dragged to slaughter. Auctioneers, each seeking to drown out the others in their bid to sell slaves, livestock, fresh fish or trade goods. Wager-takers calling the odds for each of the day's athletic events and music contests. Competition too among the official Matchmakers, given free rein to ply their trade openly on this one day of the year – a last chance to dispose of any difficult baggage who might otherwise remain on the shelf.

'But you see how dull it would be,' I said, when it seemed the procession was over, yet the crowds still howled for more, 'to forsake all this and convert to your Christos?'

'You considered my suggestion then.'

'I could hardly ignore the envoy of Justinian himself. But I doubt that one convert, here or there, will make any difference to the Emperor or his view of the Province.'

'You'd be surprised,' he shouted, almost impossible to hear over the baying blare of war horns somewhere beyond the gate. 'But look. Here comes your own great man.'

The war-cart had thundered into sight, spitting pebbles from its iron-shod wheels, the team's manes tossing in the spittle-flecked wind, Anwas his charioteer balancing upon the pole and lashing reins, while Ambros braced himself against the side arches. The burnished ring-mail shirt shone in the morning light, and his flame-red hair whipped often into his eyes so that his free hand switched constantly from clearing his vision to saluting the people, clenched fist punching the air in a gesture that was both defiant and, at the same time, disarmingly child-like. Yet I was struck by the sallow complexion of his cheeks, out of place in somebody who had spent so many months weathering the campaign trail.

'He should take better care of himself,' I muttered, hoping that Masul might take my bait.

'Rigantona had told me,' he replied, obligingly, yet looking around to check he was not overheard, 'that she believes him to be suffering some infirmity of the stomach.'

'She mentioned the Ravager,' I said, and could not avoid making the horn-sign as I spoke the word. The war-cart had halted, halfway up the street and, in its wake, marched a fine body of warriors, better equipped than those who had originally set out as the Skyhound's war-host. There were ring-riveted coats here and there among the ranks now, helmets of leather or iron too, shields often bearing a shared and painted image – a hound's head with open jaws, set upon a sky-blue ground. Sign of the Bear-Brothers.

'How old is he now?' Masul asked. 'Twenty-two summers?' I nodded. 'He is young to suffer that disease. Not impossible, of course. But without a thorough examination, difficult to say. Have you not spoken with him about this?'

'Some time ago,' I said.

The spear-hawks had split into two thinner columns, passing on each side of the *carrio* and then lining the route, forming a barrier between the crowds and the road itself. But Ambros still waited. And then the fanfare sounded anew, the trumpeters coming finally into sight through the gate, blowing upon those curved signal-horns, which the legions would once have used. Behind them came the horsemen, the Skyhound's cavalry, with my old companions at their head – Mabon Meleth's Son, Custyn Banon's Son, Gareth Grim's Bane, Amron of Headland, and Owain Hawk-Beak.

'And since he arrived back in Legion-Hold?' Masul asked.

'Oh, I've not had a chance for a private discussion just yet,' I told him. He said nothing in reply. For it was generally understood, I think, that Ambros had been closely ensconced with his inner counsellors at the gather-hall for the three days since his return. Yet I was no longer numbered among that select group. 'But that's a nice touch,' I went on, straining to sound indifferent, and pointing at the *carrio*. Ambros was down from it now, taking a leather pouch from the spear rack as a dozen men were ordered forth to receive a *phalera*, an inscribed medallion of bronze in the legionary style, which they might wear upon leather war harness as a mark of exceptional prowess in battle. It was a clever initiative – though another, of course, about which I had previously known absolutely nothing.

My summons into the Skyhound's presence, when it came, was not to the gather-hall, but the canopy under which he sheltered so that he might observe and sometimes pass judgement upon the afternoon's athletics. Perhaps the Arena might have been the obvious place to stage these but, as I have said earlier, the old *circus* was no longer a place of good omen and, besides, Osla Big-Knife had rather taken it for his own, heedless of its ghosts, and ordered the construction of an Outlander long-house for his palace, within the Arena's crumbling walls and banked terraces. So these games were being held in a makeshift stadium, cleared specifically for the purpose, close to the river.

'Mentor,' said Ambros, when he spotted me pushing through his private guard, 'it's good to see you. And well, I trust?'

'As you see, Lord,' I replied, and it was plain that I was here only to report on my progress, rather than renew old acquaintance. And a frosty reception too from both Birch Strong-Arm and the Song-Sayer, softened only slightly by the warmth of greeting from Cai and Owain Hawk-Beak.

'Cai tells me you very effectively pacified the Saeson,' said Ambros.

'It wasn't difficult in the circumstances and given my calling.'

'And the library here?' he asked.

'I may have exceeded my instructions somewhat.' And I went on to explain that, while the *ludus* – the Legion-Hold Academy, as it was becoming known – now boasted a fine accumulation of technical texts and natural philosophies, we had also made huge progress in cataloguing the contents for most other libraries of which I was aware. The small private collections like those at the Bear Fort, the Fortress of the Hammer-Fighters and countless others. But also the larger and more famous miscellanies housed at War-God's Fort, Moon's Glow, Bridge-Fort and elsewhere. 'And I'm sure the Lady Morgose,' I said, 'will have told you about progress with the histories.'

In truth, I had no idea how she fared with the task, since she had taken it for her own and rarely allowed me to see the work undertaken by her whole team of scribes in setting down for posterity an accurate story of our own people. But Ambros seemed at least to thaw a little at my reference to Morgose.

'You see?' he whispered in her direction. 'I told you Meridden would set great store by the work.' Had she told him I would not value it? How could she imagine such a thing? I would have appreciated some part in it, that was true. For it was a magnificent project. Almost religious in its significance, setting out the lineage of every lord and chieftain that had ever ruled in the lands, as they are remembered, passed orally and precisely by rote from generation to generation. The Oak Seers' lore in which Morgose was so schooled. Ambros smiled upon me for the first time in a long while. 'Birch,' he beamed, 'make room there and let the Mentor join our table. The first bout is ready to begin.'

Birch moved marginally along the bench, grumbled something in my general direction, to which I responded in kind. And I think that, if there had been a prize for petulance that day, I could not say which of us would have carried away the purse.

'Did you ever receive response from Corpre mac Cormac?' I asked. I knew the answer already from Cai, months earlier, but it seemed like a way to break the ice. Yet Ambros was already absorbed by the *pancratio* match, the fighters using fist and foot to inflict damage upon each other, and the Skyhound's limbs twitching involuntarily to match each move. His sentences blurted only in short jabs at each brief pause in the action.

'A letter found me at Corin-Mound,' he replied. 'Monk-written in the Latin. Greeted me simply as Lord Ambros. Bade me therefore fulfil my Kinfolk Oath. Take ship for Laigin by next Bright Fire's Eve. At latest, he says. Help him finally destroy the Grandsons of Dunlain.'

'Impossible,' Birch insisted. 'Our priority must be to aid Urien and the Horn-God folk.'

One of the boxers received a wicked kick to the bridge of his nose, went down in a welter of blood.

'I swore an oath,' said Ambros, relaxing after the exertion of spectating. He turned to Morgose, touched her shoulder gently. 'And how much wrong chance would fall upon the head of an oath-breaker?'

'You must write to him again, Lord,' said the Song-Sayer. 'It is overdue. Explain that your own lands are in peril. That you cannot help him until, perhaps, the following year.'

'Or send a token force in your name,' I suggested. 'As the Lady Morgose says, Corpre is bound to understand your position here. But a token force, enough to assist him...'

'And who, exactly,' snapped Morgose, 'would you send, Mentor?'

'Perhaps those hearth-hounds who guard your mother so jealously?' I said. 'Or Cullough and Bran? Emissaries on your behalf, Ambros. Maybe a couple of Cai's lads too. Keep and eye on them. Find out who's been pulling their levers.'

Cullough and Bran had indeed, meanwhile, found something to occupy them those past months. A cattle-raid upon the Bright-Field lord's personal herd, his prize bull killed. Allegations about who might be responsible. But the stolen stock found, of course, mixed with Bran's own cows, hidden in one of Romaland's high pasture valleys. Reprisals. A feud that still raged.

'We need to talk about those bastards anyway,' said Cai.

'They still insist on this story about trading deals with Laigin?' Ambros asked.

'They've even come up with the name of some merchant in Ruddy Bank who made the connection for them,' Cai explained. 'A real golden triangle. Slaves from Laigin to Bright-Fields. The slaves used to hack lead from Bright-Field's mines and traded with Romaland. Gold and silver from Romaland to Laigin. But I don't believe them. Somebody's making mischief for us.'

Ambros nodded.

'Too much of a coincidence,' he said. 'These demands from Corpre and those two mixed up with Fingal.'

'And if we thought there was a snake in our nest before,' said Cai, 'we've proof now.' He tossed onto the table a flat stick, perhaps a hand's span in length. Ambros reached for it, turned it in his fingers so the light might catch upon its edges.

The thing had his full attention, so that he paid not the slightest heed to the next match.

'Tree script,' he said. 'Can you read it, Mentor?'

I shook my head. They said that the first Christ-followers had developed the system for their own secret messages, but I had never studied any of its texts.

'I can read it,' said Morgose, and this surprised none of us. She took it from Ambros and ran her thumb along the edges. Then she smiled. 'You're right, Cai. These upper letters spell the word *Ambros*. Next, *Muster*. Then, *Legion-Hold*. Then dating numbers, I'm guessing. *Five*. *Twenty*.'

It was more than a guess. The fifth month of our year. Martius. And the twentieth day would be roughly Equal Night.

'Is that significant?' I asked, feeling I had missed something.

Those around the table exchanged glances, each with the other until Ambros gestured for Cai to tell me.

'We were in council,' he said. 'Two days ago. Ambros gave orders that the Bloody Spear of Mars Aeron should be sent out. We go to war against Elm-Wood. Lord Urien needs our help. A muster, here in Legion-Hold. And no time more appropriate that next Martius Equal Night. Yet it was supposed to remain secret. Until our preparations are made and the Bloody Spear goes forth.'

'When?' snarled Ambros. 'And who?'

'One of those Incomer spear-hawks of the Lady Murgain,' said Cai. 'Took him at first light, trying to get through the Leftgate.'

'Did he talk?' Ambros asked him.

'He had a vial of poison. My men didn't get to him in time.'

'Poison?' said Morgose.

'A quick one,' Cai told her.

Ambros contained his anger just long enough to award prizes. For the runners, the wrestlers, the flatstone-throwers, the *pancratio* fighters, and the Five Challenge contestants. But the thing gnawed at him, right the way through the evening's feast and judgements on the first of the bardic performances.

'That bastard, Six-Fingers!' he said. 'It must be.'

Something else gnawed at him too. He had grown pale with pain, clutched at his side. And we all contrived to notice nothing untoward.

'Using the Tree Script?' said Owain Hawk-Beak. 'That's a bit subtle for Gereint, isn't it?'

But we were thin on other potential traitors. Those present at the closed meeting in question had included only those now present – Ambros himself, the Song-Sayer, Cai, Birch and Owain – as well as Gereint of Windstorm, Caradoc of Cerdeg's Edge and Valor Bent-Back of Glusio.

And, fortunately, I was entirely above suspicion for obvious reasons.

'It's always possible,' said Cai, 'that the leak wasn't deliberate. Pillow-talk maybe. The bishops, or anybody else, could have agents anywhere among us. Including the city's whores. In which case, Six-Fingers would be an easy target.'

'A spy, all the same,' Birch snarled. 'But all this Tree Script nonsense. It stinks of the Christ-followers. You're right.'

Each of us had taken our turn, by now, to examine the message stick, the groups of flat and angled lines sliced into its edges. But also the tiny emblem it bore. A small circle, with six even more minute circles spaced around the outside.

'Which rules out Six-Fingers,' said Owain.

But not your father, I thought. *Not Caradoc. Not Valor, either.* Yet I said nothing. I had my own suspicions, though they were still shapeless.

'Gereint would sell himself to anybody who'd help him climb whatever ladder might tempt him,' said Ambros. 'So, back to the Lady Murgain. This messenger was one of hers, after all. Why should we look any further for the spy's master? Or mistress.'

'Perhaps I'm wrong,' Cai shrugged. 'But that was our first stop, as I've already said. We were there like a lead shot. And I think she was telling the truth. Thought the man was on duty. Still at his post. We had to show her the body before she believed us. Then went all the shades of boiled sheep shite when she realised the implication.'

'And my sister?' Morgose pressed him.

'Left for the Fortress of the Hammer-Fighters,' said Cai. 'The day before our meeting.'

The colour had returned to the Skyhound's face and he blew out softly, as though the ache had eased.

'Still,' he said, 'Murgain remains the obvious link.' He touched Morgose's hand. 'Time that we finally resolved this problem with your mother, I think.'

In truth, most of us wondered why he had not done so earlier. But Rigantona remained his wife, and the linked status of the wife-mother was still relatively sacred in our society. But Morgose had turned her sightless eyes to the canopy roof, ear cocked towards the performers.

'Listen,' she said, 'this is the lay that will spread your fame across the world.'

It had been agreed that Morgose herself would not enter the contest in person. But these new verses were her own composition, performed here by some song-sayer from Meirionshore who was currently making a name for himself on the bardic circuits.

Defender of Faiths, Red Spear of Law. Divine One, blood of Lir. Braving that which others fear.
Chariot-Slayer, great Seer and Lord. To victories will steer – shades of Breiddon, doubly dear.
No quarter given. Revere no foes. Elm-Wood's death song sounds clear, as Skyhound's legions draw near.

Forty more stanzas, with the epic form of Virgil, the bombast of Lucan, the satirical contortions of Juvenal. It would come back to haunt us more than once and, within days, it was said, it could be heard in every gather-hall for a hundred miles around. It left little to the imagination so far as the Skyhound's intentions were concerned towards Lenocus and Elm-Wood – though it stopped short, naturally, of naming the date, as the Tree Script message had done. But, in the end, it was the White Lady Murgain who stole the night in a different way entirely. She had seemingly sponsored a singer and cruth player of her own. Little more than a child. A young Christ-bride, born in New Laigin. Second generation Incomers' blood. Broke all the rules of structure and form, yet stole the judges' hearts with her words, and set ice into each of our own.

Myths, legends and lore
inspire our dreams, ambitions,
grant wings to heroes;
then turn, more potent than fact,
beguile us, mislead, betray.

Chapter Twenty-Two

When the muster finally came, it brought a morbid sky. Low cloud. Ominous. And from that drooping grey belly, deep blisters of black and darkest blue that roiled towards the northeast, our direction of march. For I was permitted to join the war-band. More. Ambros insisted that I should do so. His personal command. So that, when we reached our first camp, at salt-rich Confluence, old Condate, where the twin rivers meet, he sent for me.

'Birch tells me you've grown soft at Legion-Hold,' he said. 'Too soft for the war-trail, Mentor?'

'So soft,' I said, 'that, on top of the nine hours each day I spend trying to instil some knowledge into those feather-brained disciples you keep sending me, I must spend a further six up to my *testes* in mud or dust, hoping to put right the mistakes they make in your precious road repairs, pipe-laying, and a dozen other tasks besides. So soft that I've not yet cracked open the skull of Birch Strong-Arm for the daily insolence I must endure from him.'

'He sees the world as simply black or white,' Ambros smiled. 'And your dalliance with Rigantona set you, in his eyes, in the wrong half of his limited spectrum.'

'It might serve him better to recall that he remains within your puddle of possible traitors – while I do not.'

'Birch is above suspicion,' he said. 'You know that.'

'Do I? Then why am I here and he is not?'

'Can't I simply share a cup with an old friend any more?'

'You have not shared a cup with me, alone or otherwise, in a long while, Ambros – or should you prefer that I call you High Lord now? Therefore, I have to assume that you wish to speak without the presence of others. You would only do so if it concerned Rigantona or the spy in your camp. And we have already passed quickly over the subject of your wife.'

'Your tongue has grown acrid, Mentor. But you're correct. You're the only one who wasn't there when we made the decision to send out the Bloody Spear. The only one above suspicion. Congratulations. But please try to avoid a display of hubris. There are many paths to betrayal. And nothing more noble, nothing more venerable, than fidelity. Isn't that what you taught me? Cicero again, I think.'

I bit upon my words, longing to remind him that he had sent me into Rigantona's lair for a purpose. He had used me as much as she, herself, had done.

'At least,' I replied, 'if your spy is still among us, the pool of possibilities is reasonably shallow.'

'Reasonably,' he said. For the Bloody Spear of Mars Aeron – not truly a spear but simply a half-shaft dipped in Gallaecian vermiculus and a muster summons wrapped in oiled skin tied about the other end – had gone out at the Midwinter Sun Standing, the slave-runners braving some foul weather to cover the length and breadth of the Westerlands, all Prima. Both Valor Bent-Back and Caradoc of Cerdeg's Edge, each already knowing the muster date, of course, had sent private messages to Ambros, begging leave to be excused the gathering at Legion-Hold. Sickness had hit each of their territories. Not the Yellow Death but scourges almost as cruel. 'Although,' Ambros continued, 'Morgose suggested their absence might be evidence of guilt. What say you?'

'That it would be a poor spy who absented himself from the very thing he has been set to observe,' I said. 'That just leaves Six-Fingers, as you thought. And you're assuming that the message Cai intercepted wasn't a one-off. That Elm-Wood has known of our coming since long before the Spear went forth. But if Gereint is the traitor, where does that leave your wife-mother?'

'Is it so unlikely that Murgain has bought Six-Fingers too? But you're right. Deniol and Lenocus will be well aware of our muster. Our general intentions too. To some extent, they've dictated them. Their attacks on Gift-Given make no real sense except to draw us out. Much easier for the bishops and their holy war if we march upon them rather than the other way around.'

'And yet we go,' I said. 'Many students of military history might suggest that this is folly.'

To be fair, that folly was diminished substantially by the better-than-expected response to the muster summons. From his own the White-Wilds Prefect Lords, all but the most distant – New Laigin, Dunshome and Meirionshore – had sent contingents. Almost two hundred spears and twenty riders. Even Cullough of Bright-Fields and Bran of Romaland were there, their feud temporarily suspended, though Ambros kept a close watch on them still. Osla Big-Knife too, though at least he was present, with a mixed band of Saeson Outlanders and Slavehold men. From beyond the White-Wilds' borders, warriors from Windstorm, from Iago's Sabrina-Rise, Fergna's South-End Meta-Landers and, most surprising of all, from Constantine's Horn-Head warriors, two hundred more. All eager for cattle and plunder, to settle whatever old scores they might have with the Northlanders from east of the Spine.

'We're committed to helping Urien,' said Ambros. 'And it struck me we might turn some of this to our advantage. Alcibiades advised against ever using the same military strategy twice, but I think we might make an exception here. If you consider my plan workable, Mentor, naturally.'

'So, here it is,' Ambros told the Council of Warlords when we stopped for the second night. We had swung north onto roads that picked up the Ten and took us all the way to Coetio, the Wooded Place, which by then we had come to call Wicken. We were in the lands of Lesser Gift-Given now, in Westwood, and the local duty-holders greeted us enthusiastically, on Urien's behalf. Here, at least, they were well-warned of our coming. 'A change of plan,' Ambros explained. 'Lord Urien has sent word. Begged that we should ignore his earlier request to join him and, instead, to strike directly at Elm-Wood's heart. He says they have already seen the outposts of their enemies, probing towards Gift-Given's holdfasts along the Flower Basket Ridge.'

'Is it wise,' asked Morgose, 'to change our course at such short notice? When did Urien send this word?'

Council of Warlords this may be, but Ambros rarely held such meetings without his closest companions, and the Song-Sayer, at his side. Nor, indeed, without the presence of Masul the Numidian, who had almost demanded a place on the expedition in the name of the Emperor.

'Within the last hour,' Ambros replied. 'I was in discussion with Lord Iago about our supply lines. It was timely.'

Fergna was staring at the road-lists spread on the gather-hall's table.

'We could take them in the flank,' he said. 'Catch them between us and squash them like flies.'

'There's another possibility,' said Ambros. 'Lord Urien tells me he has enough spears available to hold the ridgeline. Good defences. And while Lenocus beats himself senseless trying to dislodge them, we take this road.' He pressed a fingertip against the next march-stop on our route, and we all craned our necks for a view.

'*Din Bremetenio*,' said Owain Hawk-Beak. 'The Holdfast of the Veterans?'

'The old legionary fortress,' I said, for I knew the place reasonably well.

'The Belisama Road,' said Ambros. And he followed the meandering line of the Belisama River eastwards. 'All the way to here?' He stabbed at the word *Eborac*. 'Catch them with their breeks around their ankles.'

There were questions, of course. Some minor problems raised. Concerns about heading so far into enemy territory. But Ambros assured them that, so long as we moved fast and light, we would always be a step ahead of Lenocus and would have taken Yew Grove – *Eborac*, he reminded us, most now called that city again – before he could catch us. And I could not help glancing at Gereint Six-Fingers, flicking his thumbnail thoughtfully against his front teeth.

Oh, I thought, *how I hope Ambros is right about him.* For the alternative was too terrible to contemplate. But there, the plan was set. Cai had been taken into our confidence. His Shadow-Watchers given the task of not allowing Six-Fingers from their sight even for a private moment. To observe and not apprehend. And, meanwhile, without even the knowledge of Cai, Ambros had sent a runner to Lord Urien, urging him to disengage as many horse as he could spare and scout for us along the Belisama Road – in the hope that, if the noble lord, Gereint of Windstorm, did indeed betray us, Gift-Given's cavalrymen would come to our aid, much as Cullough of Bright-Fields had done on the Great Hurdle.

*

Our enemies were waiting for us two mornings later. I had just finished stowing my bundle back on the Slavehold baggage cart, secured afresh the lead tag, which marked that particular bundle as my own, and I had strung those things I might need for the day's march on my shoulder-stick. I had no sooner hefted stick, spear and shield into place than I heard the horns. And there, from the tree line on the opposite side of the valley, poured the forces of Elm-Wood and her allies. Easily twice our number, and divided equally into two huge shield-walls, one on each side of the road.

Ambros was not far away, coming in my direction, a face like thunder. I had just observed him at the horse lines, fussing over his chariot team and checking that his stable-slaves had readied his riding mount – for he had been certain that, today, he would be marching with the column rather than charging into battle upon the *carrio*.

'Not Six-Fingers then,' he said, and there was defeat already in his eyes.

'Nothing is certain,' I told him. 'It's possible he may have caught wind of Cai's Watchers. Managed to get a message out, despite them.'

He shook his head.

'You've seen those skulkers go about their business, Mentor. Even a rat couldn't pass through without Cai's men knowing it. I just pray to Mithras that Urien got my message and has sent us help. We can't hold here forever. And I think Lenocus only shows us that part of his force he wants us to see. No cavalry, look.'

I looked, even though I was thinking about rats. About my unspoken fear. About the one person in our midst with the most connection to Bishop Deniol and the Christ-followers. About the one person with the closest possible link to Murgain and Rigantona. About the one person with the best reason for using Tree Script rather than a simple written message. So yes, I looked, but I found myself unable to speak or catch the Skyhound's eye.

They sang for our benefit. Almost a thousand voices, chanting spontaneous parodies of each lay ever invented in the Skyhound's honour. Terrible things that mocked the death of Owen White-Tooth and the Lady Uithera; that repeated the calumnies about his brother's sexual preferences; that named Ambros as *Cunnus Glasus* – which, of course, means something entirely different from Skyhound; that poured scorn on his manhood; that spoke of women who preferred dog-cock to the embrace of this Ambros Limp-Stick. Their words echoed in harmonies across the hillside while scores of white-robed priests and black-hooded bishops carried Christ symbols among them, bidding warriors to kiss the cross or bend to their blessings. And, for a while, it seemed, Ambros would take everything they could hurl at him.

'Anything that passes time,' he would say. 'Anything which allows Urien's horsemen to reach us.'

But those who had brought their war-bands here to fight under the Skyhound's banner saw the whole thing differently, wondered how any leader of men could stand and tolerate such insults.

'If you and the White-Wilds are afraid to fight, Ambros,' Fergna spat in his face, 'the Meta-Landers of South-End may show you how it's done.' He had never quite overcome his jealousy, I think, of losing the High Lordship of the Westerlands by such a slender margin.

'And do you not think, Lord Protector,' said Ambros, 'that they wouldn't welcome us offering ourselves to them piecemeal?'

'They are cockerels upon a dung-heap,' Birch Strong-Arm laughed. 'You think the bull is ever stung by their crowing.'

'I think the bull is full of shit,' Constantine snarled. 'If not, then lead us. Show us the *strategos* about whom we've heard so much.'

'Two-to-one?' Ambros asked them. 'On ground we've neither chosen nor prepared. And their own cavalry, perhaps even a reserve of spears, hidden from our eyes. There's no strategy in this. Only the waste of good men's lives. But if it will satisfy you, I will go down to the ford, offer the Champions' Challenge. See if any of them have the balls to accept. If I fall, let you choose another to lead you away from this place.'

'Lord Ambros,' said Cai the Blood-Taster. 'At least take your own companions with you.'

'You need somebody, at least,' Birch told him. 'To pass your spears.'

'A second?' said Ambros. 'Then you must not take offence, Birch Strong-Arm, if I choose Mentor Meridden.' If Birch was shocked by this choice, he could hardly have surpassed my own astonishment. But Ambros gripped my arm. 'Your own fault,' he said, 'for being so persuasive when I asked whether you'd grown soft.' Then he whispered in my ear. 'And for complaining to so many, in your cups, about no longer being in my confidence.' He looked around until he found Anwas the Winged among the gathered warlords and his closest friends. 'Anwas for my charioteer, of course,' he shouted. 'And Lord Protector Fergna Urcol's Son to form our own spear-press. Yet to hold here, unless they cross the stream and you have the advantage of a downhill charge.'

'That's work for old women,' Fergna snarled. 'But we'll hold the high ground, if you will hold the ford.'

And hold it we did. For a while.

Anwas brought up the team, and Ambros sprang onto the wood-woven bed of the *carrio* as though born to it. For myself, I had never ridden such a thing in all my life, and had barely fastened my shield to the side arches before it was bucking slant-wise down the rough moorland slope towards the road, through yellow furze and rust-brown bracken, larks and linnets scattering from our path, the morning smells of crushed grass spreading like a wake from our wheels, and the breek-clad arse of Anwas the Winged almost in my face as he balanced on the yoke-pole, laughing like a fool as he lashed the ponies onwards.

'Brace yourself against the arches and spear rack,' Ambros roared, and I tried to follow his example, even though the teeth rattled around my skull too much for me to make any response. In the end, I settled to a half-crouch, gripping the curved and carved side-pieces, trying to ride the movement as I might a horse. So I had only a shaking, bouncing, fragmentary image of the enemy's gradual advance, the increased clamour of their chanting, though the words were now entirely indistinguishable.

Yet, suddenly, we slithered to a halt, ponies lathered in sweat, upon a gravel-strewn beach at the stream's bank, bare of vegetation apart from some scattered alders, marking this place where the flow was wide and slow, shallow, allowing those travellers upon the Belisama Road to cross without need of a bridge.

'You don't know those scum,' I said, when I finally regained control of my jaw. 'How d'you know they'll honour the Challenge Lore?'

Ambros had jumped down, strolled to the water's edge and washed his face, as though that host of the enemy did not exist.

'How can we know, Mentor,' he said, 'without putting each mystery to the test? And fear of the future is worse than our present state of fortune.' Quintillianus again, but I was thinking more about Einion Iron-Anvil – his cruel death at Rhun's hand. And Ambros must have shared the moment. 'Yet I am not my brother.' He smiled up at me. 'Are you afraid, Mentor?'

'Not afraid. Simply out of practice.'

He laughed, splashed through the knee-deep waters until he stood on the farther margent and the foes fell silent on the rise above, where they had halted again, two hundred paces distant.

'You sing well, men of Elm-Wood,' he called. 'But tomorrow we will see how you laugh when I have nailed your own kinfolk to the Christ-crosses you love so much. All the long road from here to Yew Grove. We will see whether your women think our cocks are limp when our night's work with them is done.' And he went on, in much the same vein, for longer than I could keep count, each threat provoking howls of outrage from this crow-fodder that faced us, each insult causing the ranks to froth and foment as men were stung into coming down to us, to take out our tongues and worse, while their lords and duty-holders pressed and pushed them back into line. Until, finally, Ambros paused to draw breath. 'Or we could settle this here,' he yelled. 'By the Champion Fight. Send down whomsoever you choose. As many times as you wish. If I die, you will have that for which you came. And my Lord Fergna of South-End will lead our men home to the Westerlands.'

The silence was broken by a voice behind us, up among our own spear-press.

'And what if you kill them all, Ambros? What will be left for the rest of us?' I think it may have been Cai.

The clamour, in response from the men of Elm-Wood, was deafening, but their lords and their bishops had come together at their centre, upon the road, and I could see Rhun the Tall among them, armoured but without weapons, as the Song-Sayer's doom forced him to be. *A good piece of play-acting on her part,* I thought, my suspicions still festering inside, *though one which Rhun himself seems to have taken seriously enough.*

'Time to stir them up, I think,' cried Ambros as he waded back to the *carrio.*

'I thought you were trying to buy time,' I said, but Anwas had the measure of things.

'If we don't open the game soon,' he said, 'Fergna will lose patience and come blundering down like a lamb to the slaughter.'

I looked over my shoulder, and he was right. Fergna was already organising our line anew, bringing up our precious few horsemen and moving our slingers forward.

'You know what to do, Anwas,' the Skyhound told him, and jumped back aboard the *carrio*, which was already moving towards the stream. We sent up a magnificent spray on either side, up to our axle until we found the road's surface again and began to climb that eastern rise. It was a steadier ride on the paved surface but I was still jolted, formed only a fragmentary impression of confusion and chaos among their lords, of bishops being urged back to safer ground, of a bristling along their shield-walls, and of horsemen appearing somewhere up and away to our right. 'Well, at least we know where their horse was hidden,' yelled Ambros. 'That way, Anwas. That way.' Anwas swung his team to the right, churning over the open ground again, but now parallel with the Elm-Wood line. 'And *birin*,' cried the Skyhound, holding out his open right hand to me. I selected one of the fletched and weighted short spears from the rack, passed it to him. 'Good choice,' he shouted. 'Now, left, Anwas. Left. Take us close.' The charioteer spun us in a circle that felt tight as a shield's rim, though must have been wider, so that now we were running closer to the foe, and away from their cavalry, Ambros yelling his war-cry like some demon from the Halls of Death. 'Bear-Brothers! Bear-Brothers!' There were slingshots whistling around us, javelins thrown in our direction, even though we were beyond range of even the best. The best ordinary javelin, of course. But not for the *birin*. Ambros chose his mark carefully. A tall warrior in ring-mail, a duty-holder at the least, who sprang from the line to gain some advantage for his own spear, and died swallowing the Skyhound's barbed blade even as he opened his stupid mouth to shout some madness at us.

He was the first to die on that terrible day. But he would not be the last.

Chapter Twenty-Three

According to the lay you will have heard, Ambros made thirty passes with his chariot on that one morning. Yet I have to tell you it was only three. Though with each pass, he used another precious *birin* to good effect, even his worst cast embedding itself in a foeman's thigh. But, after the third, the ponies were exhausted and he gave Anwas the instruction to head back across the ford. I had not realised until we stopped how wild was the cheering from our own warriors. Cheering and singing. As though we, and not those of Elm-Wood, held the advantage, the upper hand. And none of our enemies formally accepted the challenge. Simply a lone warrior coming forth from among them, loping down the road. Leather war harness and iron-bound helm. Spears and a wicked little hand-axe. Yet he did not manage even to get his feet damp before Ambros skewered him with one of the longer javelins.

'Your duties as my second, Mentor?' said Ambros, and I set off immediately to retrieve the shaft, but also to collect the weapons of the slain challenger.

'Here's the next,' Anwas the Winged told him, as another began the descent. And, before long, there were a dozen dead, either in the water or along its edges. But, between each killing, Ambros himself would lean against the *carrio*, staring back up towards our own people, that same look of defeat and loss upon his face.

'Not Six-Fingers,' he muttered again, then turned as he heard the body of enemy horsemen coming slowly down to the ford.

A few well-armoured hearth-hawks with chain-shirts and shields; three bishops – one of them fat Deniol; squint-eyed Rhun the Tall, with his crooked teeth; six or seven Prefect Lords, none of them known to me; the man who seemed to lead them – Lenocus, I gathered, with a fine silk cloak of imperial purple, rare and costly, his tunic and breeks immaculately white, hair and moustaches stiff with lime, chinless, and the skin stretched so tight upon his cheeks that it was almost translucent; and, at his side, the son he had hidden away so long. If ever anybody deserved his Praise Name, it was this Man-Dog. A Praise Name indeed, for we valued our hounds above almost all else. In anybody else it would have been a title of huge respect, yet with Gwrgi it was difficult to see it as anything but a simple description. The nose and jaw bulged out from beneath brown-yellow eyes, like a snout. Gwrgi Hard-Spear – *Peredur*, as the Common Speech would have it.

'More innocent dead at your foul and heathen hand, Lord *Cuneglasus* – Skyhound,' said Deniol.

'I offered the Champions' Challenge,' Ambros sneered at him. 'And these warriors at least had the courage to come down and face me.' He kicked at the pile of weapons I had gathered. 'Though the tribute they brought was pitiful.'

'This was, as I recall,' Lenocus said, his voice reed-like, 'after you rode into my territory in this...' He gestured towards the war-cart. 'In your vanity. And attacked my men.'

'One of those you slew was my uncle,' said Gwrgi the Man-Dog. His voice was a low growl, deep in his throat. 'There is blood-price to be paid here.'

'Blood-price?' Ambros sneered. 'You block my road with your war-band, and expect me to tolerate the taunts with which they deride the sacred memory of my mother and my father?'

'It became your road, we assume,' said Deniol, 'when you decided to interfere in the business of these, our Northlands. To come as *foederati* in the pay of the oath-breaker, Urien of Gift-Given. Or was it when you announced to your rag-tag followers that you would follow the Belisama and put our beloved Eborac to the torch while the men of Elm-Wood... How did he put it again, my Lord?'

'While our breeks were about our ankles, I believe he said, Bishop,' Lenocus replied. I could not see the Skyhound's face but I saw him stiffen at the neck and shoulders, as he received the certain confirmation that one of our number had betrayed him.

'But it seems to be you, Skyhound,' shouted Rhun the Tall, 'who has his arse bared. Or would you kill me for that insult too? But, you see? No weapons. In binding of that doom your wife-sister set upon me.

Swings both ways, of course. Without weapons, I cannot be attacked in honour. So your little Song-Sayer helps protect me too. Now that she's free of that boy-shagger brother of yours.'

The double-thrust cut Ambros deeper than any blade could ever have done. I saw the blood drain from his cheeks, his brow furrow.

'You will understand, I hope,' Deniol said to him, 'that Lord Rhun has his own grievances. The loss of those lands which, by right, he should have inherited from his martyred father.'

'When Rhun the Tall is ready to claim those lands,' said Ambros, 'I am happy, as High Lord of the Westerlands, to hear his case. Once, of course, we have settled the small matter of the way he defiled the corpses of my father and mother, slaughtered the innocents of Twin Sisters. But, meanwhile, I stand at the borders of Elm-Wood since here are those bishops who, I understand, have declared a holy war against me. And I am not a man to leave the initiative, in such matters, to my enemies.'

'Holy War?' said another of those same bishops, this one a skeletal creature, already more dead than living. 'And this from the man,' he went on, 'whether he calls himself High Lord or not, who says it is better to burn all our monk-brothers than suffer any hurt to a single follower of Mithras. Holy War, you say. Yet who is there, among your own ranks, except those already guilty of unspeakable crimes against the Church? Fergna of South-End, himself a murderer of priests and now bedding his own daughter. Constantine of Horn-Head, who only recently raided around the Wectis Isle, killed the Frankoi priests there, then masqueraded in Holy Vestments so he could lure the Lord Prefect, Olaf the Yuti, along with all his family, and butcher them there.'

We had all heard the story, though Constantine claimed it was a blood-feud that had taken him to Wectis.

'The Lords of South-End and Horn-Head may speak for themselves,' said Ambros, 'if they are challenged in law to do so. For it is not against them that your holy war is declared – but against myself. If you will deny that such a state of war exists, Lord Bishop – and I am assuming I address Bishop Sildag?' The living skeleton nodded his acknowledgement. 'Then if you will confirm that there is no holy war, I can return to the territory of my friend and kinsman, Lord Urien of Gift-Given.'

'And there?' sneered Deniol. 'They say that you have ordered the building of pagan libraries. Great collections of ungodly texts. Those already proscribed by the Emperor in Constantinopolis and the Holy Father in Rome.'

I could hold my own tongue no longer.

'Proscribed,' I rolled the word around my tongue. 'Just as Theodosius ordered the burning of the Serapeum Library in Alexandria. Or the scrolls and codices of Nestorius were destroyed. You Christ-followers already have a long tradition as burners of books.'

'As High Lord of Northland, of Second-Province,' said Lenocus, 'I determine how the precious resources of my lands should be expended. And Moon's Glow, all of Gift-Given, sits within those lands. I gave no permission for such a library to be grown there. To become a breeding ground for those who deny the One True Faith.'

'And, by the Lord God,' barked Gwrgi Hard-Spear, 'do we truly owe these turds any explanation? Turn your men around, Skyhound, and chase your tail back to Legion-Hold. Or you will feel the blades of true Elm-Wood Champions plucking out your diseased guts.'

'Oh, godly Gwrgi,' Ambros laughed, though it was forced, his face still ashen – and I realised that it may be bodily pain he was suffering, rather than simply the agonies of betrayal. 'Is it true what they say?' he went on, now through gritted teeth. 'That, when your own sickness takes you, you must satisfy your inner wolf by ripping the throat from one person each day – except on your Lord's Day, of course. Too righteous to do such a thing on the Lord's Day. So you take two on Saturn's Day instead.'

It amused myself and Anwas, at least. But Gwrgi Hard-Spear was easily provoked, that was plain and, snarling, he kicked his pony forward to the attack. Yet, as he did so, I saw Ambros clutch at his own stomach, fall back against the *carrio*'s wheel and then drop to his knees in the shallows. Anwas, I think, must have believed his lord struck down, for he stared about him, wild-eyed, to see from whence the supposed blow had come while, at the same time, taking one of the remaining darts from the rack and launching the missile at Lenocus. It took the Lord of Elm-Wood straight through his unprotected heart – and all the chaos of Kernuno's Hounds was let loose.

'Get him out of here,' Anwas screamed at me, then lashed his team into action, drove the war-cart into the stream, separating Ambros from his enemies. 'False scum!' he yelled at them, and hefted a shield, launched the final *birin*, took down an Elm-Wood hearth-hawk with it.

I pulled Ambros out of the water, onto our own bank.

'Stop him,' he gasped. 'Stop Anwas. It's my illness. The Ravager. Not their treachery.'

But there was splashing close behind me, already a shadow looming over my shoulder, and I turned to see a horseman churning across the stream, his spear raised, both myself and Ambros defenceless. Yet Anwas the Winged stretched out a long and slender *sleag* from the *carrio*, towards our attacker, stabbed the pony's flank so that the beast screamed and reared, threw the rider – though it cost Anwas dear. For Gwrgi the Man-Dog had speared him in the back. He tumbled to the chariot's bed and the ponies, scenting blood, sensing an absence of control, seeking an escape from that place, plunged forward to scatter bishops, lords and warriors alike.

'May God damn you all,' shouted that bone-thin Sildag, as another rider heaved at his reins, pulled the bishop's mount from the war-cart's path and Gwrgi the Man-Dog stabbed again and again at the charioteer.

To my front, the hearth-hawk unhorsed by Anwas was still in the water, dazed but trying to regain his feet, while his spear had been washed away downstream. Yet he still had a blade at his belt and I was sure he would come for us again. So, while he shook the water from his eyes, and he stumbled about, I grabbed a fist-sized rock and fell upon him, beating out his brains until my face and fingers were dripping with them. Glimpses of the chariot now. But only glimpses, as it careered uphill and away from us. Anwas still being pursued, wounded again, feebly fighting back. More Elm-Wood horsemen galloping down upon us. Ambros at my side, hauling himself to his feet, pulling the Sword of Maximus from its scabbard, forcing a spear into my own hands.

'A good day to die, Mentor,' he managed.

Horses all around us now, our own as well as the enemy's. Then, that rage-red mist again. The senses even more confused. But I remember being slammed sideways, hit by a pony, I think, winded so that I could not breathe and my whole body crushed. Gripping the spear shaft and using it like a staff, parrying a thrust here, turning it to use the butt-end there, smashing bone and teeth. A man on top of me. Stink of his sweat. The iron taste of his blood as I bit deep into his neck. The yielding pressure and sickening plash as I gouged an eye. A glimpse of

Ambros, swinging his blade like a demon, hacking into horseflesh and warrior-harness alike. Mabon Meleth's Son trying to haul him clear, take Ambros up behind him, get him away from there – and taking a spear-point through the throat. Custyn Banon's Son, screaming the *Bear-Brothers* war-cry and crashing dead in the stream with his skull cloven in two. Gareth Grim's Bane and Amron of Headland, fighting back-to-back, seemingly invincible, taking down one foe after another. Madness. Endless madness. The whole valley floor seemingly packed so tight with men that they could barely swing or thrust a weapon. Tumbling over each other. Scratching flesh from each other's features. Screaming. Anything that might distinguish them for their friends, separate them from their foes. Just a piss-stink sewer mess that would not stop, which consumed men like fuel to a fire. Gareth Grim's Bane once more, cradled now in Amron's arms and Amron himself then speared through the spine. Warriors blown and bloodied. Only the strongest still able to stand. Ambros leaning on the Maximus Sword. Gwrgi the Man-Dog a hundred paces distant, propped upright by his spear shaft. Fergna of South-End sitting, spent, on a small death-mound of his own making. The rest of the living collapsed in small groups, or puking. And, just below the tree line opposite, the *carrio* still ran, the ponies beyond reason, almost lame, almost driven to death. And the corpse of Anwas the Winged dragging and bouncing behind, one ankle still tangled in the floor-weave, the shield still upon the charioteer's arm and flapping in cruel parody of his Praise Name.

In the end, the two armies had simply become a pair of mindless drunkards swinging pointless punches at each other, both so spent that they could no longer either feel or deliver a decisive blow, yet one of them just capable of crawling from the arena. And when Lord Urien Fair-Meadow of Gift-Given arrived at nightfall with his cavalry, he was too late to help us do anything but burn the dead.

'No help for any of them?' Ambros asked Cai. 'Anwas? Mabon? The rest of my companions?' There was a cold rage about him, so intense that his body shook, as though the battle-frenzy would not leave him.

'None, Lord,' Cai replied. He, too, was drenched in blood, mostly that of our enemies, though he had to support himself against the campaign tent's centre-pole, for a gaping wound still oozed red through the ripped wool of his breeks. 'They are all gone to the Halls of the Dead.'

Only myself, Cai and Birch Strong-Arm remained. Ambros gripped his side again. The Ravager, of course. For, apart from that, he had as usual taken not a single scratch throughout that whole wicked day. Yet Masul the Numidian had managed to administer a draught for him, eased his pain, despite himself, set him here, upon a cot.

'They gave their lives so we might have the victory, Ambros,' said Fergna.

Every bone and muscle in my body was bruised, aching, but I remembered my history, the campaigns of King Pyrrhus of Epirus, his absurdly costly victory against the Romans at Asculum.

'One more victory like that one, Lord Protector,' I said, trying to remember the precise quotation, 'and we shall be utterly ruined.'

'We drove them from the field,' Fergna replied. 'That's a victory in anybody's book.'

Personally, I do not recall that we drove anybody in either direction.

'We were betrayed,' said Six-Fingers, huddled in a corner, where Owain Hawk-Beak tried to staunch the many hurts he had taken. For, where the companions of Ambros had been the first to gather around him at the stream, given their lives to protect him, Gereint and his men of Windstorm had followed so quickly behind that, now, there were barely ten of his spear-hawks still living.

I exchanged a glance with Cai, the glance of conspirators who had set a trap to catch the spy in our midst and had failed so badly. But Ambros was watching us both, I saw, and caught that look of shared guilt.

'And it is the person who betrayed us that bears responsibility for all this,' he said. 'That, and a wicked twist of fate.'

Owain Hawk-Beak looked up quickly from his work with lint and vinegar, sponge, forceps and closing-pins.

'My Lord,' he said, 'the Lady Morgose was asking to see you again.'

The muscles of Ambros Skyhound's jaw became set, rigid with anger, a vein throbbing in his neck.

'Go to the Song-Sayer, Mentor,' he told me. 'Explain to her that we will not need her services again until my wife and her mother arrive from Legion-Hold.'

'You're bringing them here?' Birch Strong-Arm snarled.

'No, my friend,' Ambros told him. 'You will do that. Since you seem to be the only one of us still capable of sitting a horse. And when you fetch them, make sure to bring all the belongings they need. Be clear with them that they shall not be returning to Legion-Hold, nor to any part of the Westerlands. Not ever. And, before you ask, if any of her personal guards raise objection, you may kill any who cause you difficulty.'

I found Morgose the Song-Sayer – Morgose the Traitor – with the baggage carts, where those wounded still capable of treatment were being carried and succoured by those few who had received some training at Owain Hawk-Beak's side. A couple of former monk-brothers. The women who followed the war-band. And Morgose herself, of course.

'Am I to be chained then?' she sneered. 'Until my mother and sister are dragged here too? And then what? Burned alive? Left to drown in some rising tidal cove? That is the normal fate of a condemned enchantress, I think. And here you shall have three of us, Mentor Meridden.'

'Lord Ambros made no mention of chains, Lady. Simply that he would not have you in his sight until Rigantona and your mother are also brought before him.'

'Oh, what fortune. The ability to choose that which he can have within his sight, and that which he will not. And do you know, clever Mentor, the one prize for which I might have betrayed even Ambros?'

'This seems an inopportune moment for riddles, don't you think? Yet you will tell me it is your eyes, I suppose. The ability to see.'

She laughed. Cold and cheerless.

'I told him myself,' she said. 'Many times. I would give anything, even my love for Ambros, not for light and vision, but simply for darkness.'

'As I remember, you told us all. About the colours and shapes, which fill your head, even while you sleep. That night after we returned from Clud-Vale with the Numidian's potion. Yet here you betrayed him for much less.'

'The same night I spun the tale of Arth mac Conn and how he had banished the foul enchantress from his lands to heal its wounds. Though I never dreamed I should be that same *Uindabhair.* And yet, while you have never befriended me, Mentor, you know me for a truth-sayer. So, if I cannot win that one thing for which I might have betrayed him, where is the case against me?'

'Your mother and sister have both made it clear that they live for nothing more than to see Ambros brought down – to see the Westerlands under the control of Deniol and his Church.'

'I am neither my mother, nor my sister,' she said. 'Why should I share their false dreams?'

'Their flesh and their blood,' I told her. 'Yet you share their faith too. A Christ-bride, were you not? One of Deniol's own.'

'A lore-keeper and truth-sayer for the Oak Seers also. I am condemned for my beliefs?'

'Condemned, perhaps, for being the mouth-piece of Malco when we ventured to Hibernia.'

'Nobody despised my mother-husband more than myself – except perhaps Ambros.'

'Condemned then, Lady, for all this. The blood upon your hands. Give thanks you cannot see it. Oh, how we each are betrayed by our treacherous eyes. The seer who can already see nothing and wishes for still more darkness. And the visionary teacher who cannot observe the things under his very nose, and would prefer not to view any of this day's work in any case.'

'You think that, though eyeless, I can still not see this carnage with my nostrils, my ears, my fingertips, my heart. Many of those who died for Ambros today I counted as friends also. And as a lore-keeper of the Oak Seers, as a Christ-bride too, I am dedicated to life, peace and hope. Not this wanton destruction.'

'But the Tree Script,' I said, with finality. 'Why should a spy use such text when a simple message, plainly writ, would have sufficed for anybody else? Why else, except by one who cannot use the written word? Why else, except by one who can only make simple coded cuts on a wooden tile?'

'Can you truly not think of a reason, Mentor?' she said. 'Does Ambros think so little of me that I am the only object of his suspicions?' I had known Morgose in many situations, remembered her resilience during that storm-tossed crossing of the Hibernian Sea, or when we were forced to fight the Black Hags. But I had never previously seen her weep, regardless of the hardship. And then this weeping had the imprint of her own character upon it, for there were no racking sobs, no bawling, simply streams of tears that flowed steadily down her cheeks and would not stop. 'And you were with him,' she went on. 'When it all began. They say he was struck down by treachery. Yet they also say he has no mark or wound upon his body. Is that true? Is he unharmed?'

'You know well,' I reminded her, 'that no weapon may mark him. You have sung the lines often enough. And you once believed that these shapes and lights within your head might have meaning. That the gods may weave them together as pointers. Towards the secrets of the future. Do they not speak those secrets to you now?'

'Only this,' she said. 'That, without Ambros Skyhound at my side, the darkness that I now seek would simply be the darkness of oblivion. Will you not tell him that?'

I may have agreed to do so but, of course, I never did.

Chapter Twenty-Four

We reached Yew Grove, *Eborac*, three days after Urien of Gift-Given and Constantine of Horn-Head, following the butcher's trail of those they had slaughtered along the way – the straggling wounded of Elm-Wood's war-band which, itself, was now scattered with the wind. And not just the walking wounded, but the innocents of every farmstead, settlement and holdfast where they might have been given food and shelter. A pretext, naturally, though none was really needed. Spoils of war. The livestock driven off by each of those lords in competition with the other for the benefit of their respective economies. We found the remnants of the *carrio* at the roadside too, the ponies run to death in their traces, and the broken pulp of poor Anwas the Winged finally at rest.

We carried him with us until we reached a fortress city almost as magnificent as Legion-Hold. Though, here too, Urien and Constantine had wreaked havoc. They may have been few in number but they had swept through the gates alongside those they pursued, driven Gwrgi, Rhun and most of the bishops through the streets and out the other side. It was said that our foes had run all the way to the lands of Dark-Haven in Eastland. But nobody knew for certain. Ambros did not even seem to care. He was riddled with fury all the way through the cremation of his childhood friend and charioteer, a gigantic pyre lit upon the mound beyond the walls, which served as one of Yew Grove's cemeteries. And the reflection of that fire's ember-burn still shimmered, hours later, upon the ceiling of the gather-hall basilica, the reflections glowing through the windows set high in its upper walls. It was little different from the old *principia* in Legion-Hold, of course, except the extent to which the Christ-followers had made this their own, for even the old Mithraic shrine to the rear had been converted to one of their chapels.

'But rich pickings, Ambros,' said Fergna, sitting on the corner of the raised tribunal and admiring a richly adorned crucifix he had just found hidden in that church. 'I'd thought our friends would have gnawed the bones to dust by now.'

Ambros kicked aside the remains of a suckling pig, abandoned on the platform, and one of many that littered the entire floor, along with the debris of roasted kid and mutton scraps, mingled with the ashes of cooking fires, ale-horns and wine pots with which Urien and Constantine had celebrated their three-day feast.

'Have they truly eaten everything that cannot be driven away?' said Masul the Numidian. 'And how can so few have consumed so much?'

'They've been hiring *foederati*,' Cai told him. 'And drovers, of course.'

'They have so much gold?' Ambros asked.

'Now they do,' laughed Fergna. 'For they discovered the merchants' quarter. A Palmyran money-lender. Papias, a Judaean who makes the gold-glass. A batch of local silversmiths. Rich traders from Burdigala in the Frankoi lands of Vasconia, others from Across-the-Sea and even a fellow who fashions those Gallaecian gemstones. Constantine and Urien took what they wanted and now charge them protection dues so they may retain a portion of the little still left to them.'

'And you, Lord Protector?' said Ambros. 'No treasures left for you?'

'I have pens full of slaves that we took after the battle,' Fergna said. 'They will fetch a good price, if ever I can get them to market.'

'He's right,' said Six-Fingers. He was weak from loss of blood, barely able to rise from his litter. 'We're spread too thin here. Too far back to our own lands. Too few spear-hawks to fight our way from further attacks. Too deep in the territory of our enemies. And still open to betrayal.'

'We know the traitors in our midst now,' Ambros almost choked on the words. 'They will be silenced. The threat removed.'

'The Song-Sayer?' Owain Hawk-Beak asked. 'Hard to believe.'

'Burn the bitch!' Fergna snarled.

'She will face justice along with my wife and their mother.'

'Then we should strike while we're still able,' said Fergna. 'Urien is already among us, with all the Gift-Given lands, upper and lower. And now we hold Elm-Wood. Send to East-Haven, High-Pass and the Land of Forts. Tell them we have the greater part of Northland, of Secunda. Lenocus is dead. That makes you High Lord here too. Declare yourself

Lord of Battles, *Dux Bellorum*, for Greater Britannia.'

'And what would the Emperor in far Constantinopolis think of that, friend Masul?' asked Ambros. But the doors flew open before the Numidian could answer. The lords Constantine and Urien, Cullough and Bran, back from another hunting trip, prisoners dragged behind them.

'Look what we found, hiding in one of their little Christ-temples, just down the street from here,' said Urien. He had indeed changed since I first knew him. A famous family, descended directly from Coel the Great. It had been a privilege to serve them as rhetor in Moon's Glow. But then the Black Hags had taken his offspring one by one, so that his Praise Name, Fair-Meadow, had come to seem like a cruel irony. His wife, the Lady Feagh, had channelled her grief into the foundation of several learning-places across Gift-Given, and a library of some repute within her own holdfast at the Fortress of the Lark. But Urien himself had been made understandably cold, bitter. And he turned that bitterness now upon the beaten and bedraggled bishop who had ridden with Deniol and Sildag before the battle's beginning, kicked him in the arse and sent him sprawling before the Skyhound's platform.

'May the Lord God protect me,' murmured the bishop, crawling to his knees and pressing his hands together in prayer.

'From what, priest?' sneered Ambros. 'From my vengeance, perhaps. Since that field of blood, upon which you rode for your god, has cost me almost every friend I ever loved.'

'Your charioteer...' the bishop began.

'Defended me when he saw me struck down by treachery,' Ambros cut across him.

'Yet you are whole and unhurt,' said the bishop.

'A miracle,' Ambros snarled. 'You believe in miracles, don't you, priest? And for which part of these lands do you claim your title, by the way? Your bishopric. Isn't that what you call it?"

'One of the oldest in these islands. I am Mungo, Bishop of Elm-Wood.'

'And these others,' Ambros waved a hand towards the other prisoners, 'all from Elm-Wood too?'

'The monk-brothers are from our hermitage here at Eborac. These others are all Prefect Lords of Elm-Wood, each granted holy sanctuary.' He had stopped praying now, looked over his shoulder, then began to rise.

'Stay on your knees, priest,' Ambros snapped at him. 'We're not done with you yet. And I'm sure these lords can readily speak for themselves.' He invited them to do so, and though each of them nursed wounds, could scarcely stand, was mired with filth, they still answered defiantly enough. Prefect Lords of Loidis, Misson, Danum. Men oath-sworn to Lenocus but, with the High Lord now dead, and no desire to transfer their allegiance to Gwrgi the Man-Dog, willing enough to accept the Skyhound's supremacy, at least for now. And one of them, it transpired, was close kin to the Lords of East-Haven – those fiercely independent Sons of Soemil, the famous *foederati* commander who had rebelled against Eborac's rule two generations past, first separated East-Haven from Elm-Wood, just as Osla Big-Knife's father, Henga White-Stallion, had carved his own Land of Hosts from those of his paymaster, the Overlord Vitalis. So word was sent, as Fergna suggested – though somewhat short of a claim to all Greater Britannia. Simply the Skyhound's accession to the prefecture of Northland, in place of Lenocus, and pending a gathering of its lords collectively.

'And this Bishop Mungo, with his monk-brothers?' said Urien of Gift-Given. He was fingering the elaborate rectangular box of silver, bronze and gold, a Battle Ward, hanging at his throat and containing, by reputation, a sacred text written in the Gathelic language.

'Take them back to whence you found them,' said Ambros. 'Confine them within their Christ-temple.' He looked up at the final flickers of red and gold upon the ceiling, and he gripped his side in obvious pain. 'Until we manage to make a pyre,' he gasped, 'of this holy war also. And all the other evils, which afflict us.'

The same basilica gather-hall at the next Dead Moon, but packed now with those who had followed the news here. Good news and bad. Favourable responses from the Lords of Northland, though none of them would attend a Grand Council until the following Bright Fire, at the earliest. But word, too, that Gwrgi Hard-Spear, the Man-Dog, had been raiding back upon our communication lines, both along the Belisama Road towards *Din Bremetenio*, and also along the Two, around Mammary, that we sometimes also called Mamucio. Indeed, there had been a skirmish upon the latter route between some of Gwrgi's men and the column that Birch Strong-Arm had sensibly brought with him from Legion-Hold, both as escort for Rigantona and her mother, the

White Lady of Laigin, but also as some small relief for our own sparse garrison at Yew Grove.

'We knocked them aside quickly enough,' said Birch. 'But we nearly lost this precious cargo of yours in the process.'

Murgain stood before the tribunal, flanked by each of her daughters, and the three of them pressed around by the curious crowd of lords, duty-holders and common-folk.

'It would perhaps have spared us all considerable trouble,' said Six-Fingers, 'if you had simply surrendered them.'

'A less costly solution,' Ambros told him, 'though one that lacks both the seal of law and a proper sense of permanence.'

There was a commotion in the crowd, and I saw Milos of Edessa pushing his feeble way forward.

'My Lord Ambros,' he croaked, 'if there are legal matters to be considered here, I should remind you that the accused are entitled to an advocate.'

'These matters go beyond the niceties of the Twelve Tables or the Judex Codes,' said Ambros. 'You will step aside, old man, and allow these proceedings to continue.'

Milos made no further objection, though the man of middle years I had once known would certainly have done so, even at great risk to himself. And I saw fear in those cat-like eyes of Murgain for the first time that I could recall; Rigantona parting the curtain of her hair so that she could see her husband the better; but Morgose's dark brow remaining un-furrowed, her face calm, milky eyes turned towards a point above the Skyhound's voice.

'You already presented a case in law to set aside my daughter, your hand-bound wife,' said Murgain. 'And your case fell. What do you seek now, Ambros Skyhound, that justifies you dragging us like criminals all the way from Legion-Hold? What new falsehoods would you lay at Rigantona's hearth-stones?'

'Something that involves Morgose, I see,' said Rigantona. 'Did you tire of her so quickly?' She turned to the Song-Sayer. 'Or did he fail to satisfy you also, Sister? I hear the men of Elm-Wood made some fine songs about his manhood.'

'They sang well,' Morgose agreed, 'and they were paid handsomely for their performance. The crows feast on those songs now, I understand.'

Murgain smiled.

'Interesting,' she said. 'Still loyal to him, yet standing here as one of the Skyhound's prisoners. Accused of what, I wonder. What does he imagine you have done? Or is it enough now to simply share our blood? Did you feel our influence from afar, Skyhound, when you sought too late for peace with poor Lenocus, with the bishops of our faith, who you have offended so badly? Did you feel me twist at your innards and cause that fool Anwas to think you weapon-wounded?'

There were many who made the sign of the horns, but she was well informed, I had to admit. And maintaining the pretence of disassociation from Morgose was masterful.

'There was an issue that we did not press before the Grand Council at Uric's Hold, Lady,' said Ambros. 'Will you explain, Mentor?'

My moment of repentance, of course. A second chance. A reminder that the main case brought previously against Rigantona dealt with marital issues, and all those predicated on the belief that she would not defend herself against the charges. Yet her simple denial, her protestation of continued devotion to Ambros, had turned the hearts of the councillors. The marriage had stood. And those grounds, therefore, could not be revisited. But the additional charges, which the Grand Council had not explored, concerned the claim that Rigantona had betrayed Ambros to his enemies, to Rhun the Tall and, since this represented a treason against the White-Wilds, against First-Province as a whole. Thus, if further evidence of such crimes had now come to light, how much more profound the treason, when Ambros was also Prefect of Northland? Crimes against Greater Britannia itself.

I looked to catch the eye of Milos of Edessa. I had seen him only once before since our arrival in Yew Grove. A night on which he had come to find me. To check whether I was hurt. To ask whether I had thought any more about his suggestion that I should convert, become a Christ-follower. And I had thrown the thing back, told him he would not have asked such a foolish question if he had been with me, seen the things that men had done to each other in the name of God or some alternative loyalty, in that valley upon the Belisama Road that we now knew as the Valley of the Trees. Those who had survived already made light of the carnage, of course. Made verses about the alders that lined the stream; about shield, sword and spear; about the waves of others who arrived late to the fray, and the places from which they had come; about the Tree Script that had betrayed us; about the broom and meadowsweet we had crushed beneath our feet, and the meadowsweet wives whose husbands would never return to them; about my own part in the fight, the learned mentor who remained at the Skyhound's side through thick and thin; about the flood of our foemen and the Christ-crosses they bore against us; and about how none could stand against that Sword of Maximus. But the lay was one thing. The reality another. A reality that I had spat in the face of old Milos of Edessa. Yet he still cautioned me, reminded me that Urien of Gift-Given was not the man he had once been when Milos himself had held the Chair of Eloquence at Moon's Glow, or when I had returned there as Mentor. He warned me of the madness, even then. A madness still to come that would make the Battle in the Valley of Trees look like a child's game. And it was of madness that I thought now, as I caught his eye, saw him turn away, just as I began to set out the treason charges.

'I bear personal witness that, two years past' I said, 'at the Fortress of the Hammer-Fighters, in the land of Overmon, the wife of my Lord Ambros confessed to me that she had been in secret and conspiratorial contact with Rhun the Tall, a traitor and exile from those same lands, who still rides with our enemies, and rode with them at the Battle in the Valley of Trees.'

I could perhaps have mentioned that he rode there without weapons, due to the taboo that the Song-Sayer had set upon him. But I did not.

'And where is the proof of this conspiracy, Mentor?' said Murgain, and was then forced to shout the rest, for the crowd had been well schooled in their own part. This was not Uric's Hold, and the things they shouted at her were hardly polite debating points. 'Shall you tell them also how you tried to force my daughter too?' I could barely hear her, though she was now shouting as loudly as she was able. 'How it is bitterness at the rejection of your advances that cause you to bring these lies against her?' She had a protective arm about Rigantona's shoulders now, while her daughter sobbed, convincing yet almost unseen. But my instructions from Ambros were clear. I must press on with the charges regardless.

'I bear personal witness,' I continued, stressing my eloquent repetition of the phrase, 'that the Lady Murgain herself came to me, only last year in Legion-Hold. Attempted to bribe me in relation to the charges brought legally against her daughter by Lord Ambros.'

'There was nothing unlawful in my actions,' Murgain protested. 'What nonsense is this?' Her words were drowned once more.

'I bear personal witness…' I paused for effect, '…that the White Lady of Laigin was accompanied that day by Bishop Deniol of the White-Wilds – a Bishop of the Christos, admittedly, yet one who has unjustly declared a holy war against my Lord Ambros and all those allied with him. Another who rode with our foes in the Valley of Trees.'

A cry of rage from the gathering.

'There would have been no battle…' Murgain began, but those gathered around her howled the White Lady down.

'And I bear personal witness,' I roared, 'to the confession they each made to me that day, their seditious reasons for wanting to see my Lord Ambros and the whole of the Westerlands brought down.'

'Only this one man to bear witness against my family?' Murgain pointed at me. 'Let me tell you about that man…'

But she was given no chance to do so, naturally. Yet she had brought me to the place that I dreaded.

'Though the main witness in this case has still to be heard,' I said. And I called him. A Cerdeg's Edge man, a runner called Flavio, who had come to Cai after the battle with a confession in exchange for his life. He had been paid to carry a message stick when the war-band was halted at Wicken. 'Like this one? I said, and held up that which we had intercepted at Legion-Hold. And yes, he answered, a block embellished with Tree Script. 'And into whose hands did you deliver the stick?' I asked him.

'I was told to deliver the thing either to Lord Lenocus or the Bishop Deniol,' he replied.

'And who was it,' I said, slowly and regretfully, 'that paid you to deliver the message stick?'

He looked around, then stretched out his arm, and an accusing finger.

'That one,' he said. 'The Song-Sayer. The Lady Morgose.'

The gather-hall again, upon the following morning. The Council due to convene afresh to hear Ambros Skyhound's judgement and endorse it.

'Are you certain about this?' I said to Ambros, while the basilica was still filling. I had been awake all night, thinking about the likelihood that I would never see Rigantona again. But those waking nightmares mingled with images of the Song-Sayer too – the warning she had given us before the fight at Long Battle Bay, other occasions too when she had stood with us – and I prayed to Mithras that my resentment about the place she had stolen from me in the Skyhound's affections may not have coloured my judgement too badly.

'To be rid of Rigantona and her mother,' said Ambros, 'is worth almost any price. The Song-Sayer is another matter, Mentor. But the pool of treason, as you so recently reminded me, is shallow indeed. If not her, nor you and me, not Six Fingers either, there remain only these three,' he glanced at Birch Strong-Arm, Cai of the Nine Lives, and Owain Hawk-Beak, each of whom wore a version of the same expression. That form of reflected guilt shown always by the entirely innocent. 'And then there is the evidence from the man, Flavio. I'm not certain we should have spared his life, Cai, but his statement is conclusive, is it not?' Cai nodded his agreement.

I could not dispute that. Conclusive? Yes, it was certainly that. 'Yet it seems strange to me,' I murmured, 'that she did not even trouble to contest it.'

'And what could the witch say, exactly?' Birch thundered. 'I know you're fond of her, Ambros. But you cannot keep a serpent in your bed without the risk of being bit by venom.'

We all knew how close Ambros had come to her, and I could see the way he steeled himself now, as the three women were led back before him. He quickly brushed aside some attempt by Murgain to open their defence afresh, and hammered the arm of his chair for silence.

'My lords and duty-holders of First-Province and the Northland,' he said. 'You have heard the charges against these three women. Do you find them guilty or not guilty. And, if guilty, do you support my claim to set aside the Lady Rigantona as my wife?'

'Guilty!' they howled. 'Guilty.'

'Burn them,' some cried. Or, 'Crucifixion!'

But Ambros silenced them.

'My friends, I thank you for your judgement,' he told them, 'but you must remember the blood spilled so recently within the Vale of Trees. And while these women may well have been responsible for it, I would not add any further to that swamp of carnage. On those grounds, I have determined that they shall be exiled. Far enough away that they can pose no risk to the task that still lies before us. There are merchants in this town from distant Burdigala, in the deepest reaches of the Frankoi lands. And it is there they shall be transported as soon as a ship can be found.'

And whatever objections may have been made by Murgain or Rigantona, they could not be heard above the cries of either support or protest, which emanated from the gathering.

'There,' said Ambros to those of us upon the tribunal with him. 'It is done.' But the sorrow in his voice was shocking. 'And why,' he looked around at us, 'are so many of our number missing this morning, to hear the judgement?'

A good question. I knew that Urien, Constantine and a host of others had been feasting and drinking most of the night away, but it was strange that they had not returned for this session. But then the doors were thrown open, as they had been on that first night at Yew Grove. Only now it seemed to herald something new. For it was one of Cai's Shadow-Watchers who entered in so much haste. And a wind howled through the entrance at his heels. I saw that the courtyard beyond had grown dark, filled with smoke, it seemed. Men shouting in the distance, the whole town seemingly astir. And, in the smoke, threads of some substance I could not identify. But a fancy took me that they were remnants of those stanzas the Song-Sayer had so often composed for us. That they were blown apart, scattered on the wind, which blew now upon our faces as Cai's man spoke his words.

'Forgive me,' he panted, unsure whether to give his news to Ambros or to Cai, 'but I thought you would wish to know.' He glanced back at the dark clouds that had begun to drift among us, carrying an all-too-familiar stench. 'Lord Urien was not himself, I fear. Something about Trwyd the Boar King. His own beast to be hunted, he said. But he has fired the Christos-temple. The one in which Bishop Mungo and his monk-brothers were being held. He has burned them, Lord. All of them. Burned them alive.'

PART FOUR

A Failing Light

Elder gods, in war, brought
forth the new. Arawn and Brigid taught
gifts of crafting, metals wrought.

Hunting, farming, fire-bright
they gave you – Belenus, Lord of Light,
and Morrigan, Bride of Night.

Yet, see this story clear.
Remember, brave Danu, mighty Lir,
brought to you a gift more dear.

Children twins. Cousin Folk.
Danu's Kin, from sun lands, ice broke,
reaching homes of island oak.

While Lir's sons, from the dawn,
followed hard, found the second island, torn
from the sea, fair and forlorn.

Tugri Iron-Brow
Song of the Great Melody

Chapter Twenty-Five

The shards of misfortune cast upon the smoke of Bishop Mungo's martyrdom, those threads of misery borne upon the blackness, were sucked into the gather-hall of Yew Grove that night and fouled us all for the coming year and more. Something had shattered, and the wrong chance bottled within was released upon our world, cursed us with a doom, the words of which were not revealed to us. But we sensed them with every breath we drew, and I convinced myself that perhaps meaning might be found through the Song-Sayer, imprisoned during the winter months with her sister and mother, awaiting deportation at the old galley slave prison among the warehouses and wharves of the Isis Water. Their gaoler led me down steps as treacherous as Rigantona herself, lighting our way and muttering prayers to Arawn and Danu.

'Three curse-weavers in one cell,' he complained, and made the sign of the horns as he opened the worm-riddled, oaken door. 'Too much. Take care, Master.'

I promised him I should come to no harm and ducked beneath the lintel, allowed my eyes adjustment to the gloom.

'There,' laughed Rigantona, 'did I not tell you?'

There was a bench beneath the single, grilled window, a circular eye that cast down its segmented fingers of fleshy light upon the needlework, which occupied both Rigantona and her mother, each of them swathed in their square-weave.

'More likely,' Murgain told her, 'the good Mentor has brought news of our voyage.'

'It's common enough knowledge,' I told her. 'You sail for Burdigala tomorrow.'

'And you've come to bid me a tearful last farewell, have you not?' Rigantona simpered at me.

In truth? I felt as enslaved by her now, as I had always done. But she was not the main reason for my visit here, and it helped me focus that from the opposite corner I could hear the Song-Sayer's soft crooning. That familiar lay.

Chariot-Slayer, great Seer and Lord. To victories will steer – shades of Breiddon, doubly dear.
No quarter given. Revere no foes. Elm-Wood's death song sounds clear, as Skyhound's legions draw near.

'You hear that?' Murgain spat at me. 'Still spinning threads for him, despite all he has done. But we, who despise him, take heart from her words. No quarter given. That's the curse now come upon your Skyhound. Bishop Mungo's murder seals his soul within a speculum of fate – a looking-plate now shattered, the shards scattered wide. I set this doom upon him. Quarter he may not give, but neither shall he receive.'

It chilled me even more than the cell's cheerless interior and I made the horn-sign myself, behind my back.

'Ambros is beyond your nonsense, Lady,' I told her. 'Risen above your reach.'

'The usurper has no standing in the eyes of God,' said Rigantona. 'And if the Church or his foes do not bring him down, the Ravager shall certainly do so.'

That chilled me too. For, whatever ailed Ambros, it seemed lately to have eaten into him with renewed vigour. His cheeks had begun to sink into his skull, his eyes permanently set in dark shadow.

'Bishop Deniol once told me something similar,' I replied. 'And where is that skulking priest now?'

I made my way across to the corner of darkness occupied by Morgose.

'Does he still sicken?' she whispered.

'I cannot tell whether it is the illness,' I said, 'or the want of your company, Lady.'

'I thought he might have sent me back to the *monasterios*, to rejoin the Christ-brides. Or perhaps placed me in the custody of the Oak Seers. But Burdigala...'

It was a perilous journey. Nine or ten days, depending upon wind and tide, down to the Land of Hosts, the First Corner of Britannia's

Southland. Then across the Frankoi Channel, eight days along their northern shores, to the border with *Armorica*. Ten or more to negotiate Across-the-Sea's treacherous cliffs, reefs and islets. Four final but easier passages to Burdigala. The winds and tides now more favourable, with the coming of the Dark Half's Second Quarter.

'The Oak Seers sent a delegation to him on your behalf,' I said. 'Urged him to do exactly that. But his heart is set.'

'So simple for men,' Morgose replied. 'To open and close their hearts at will.'

'Treason is hardly an offence within the scope of normal emotions. And, as High Lord, he must set his heart against all traitors.'

I spoke the words loudly, harsh, for the benefit of Rigantona and Murgain, though I paid no heed to their retort.

'Yet now you doubt my guilt, Mentor,' Morgose murmured. 'Is that it?'

'You could have defended yourself against the charge,' I said.

'It is usually impossible to testify to your own innocence,' she replied. 'Don't you find? To prove that you've not done a thing? I fear that Ambros has to find his own way through the treachery that surrounds him.'

I knew this, but I shut my mind to the implications. If not Morgose, then who? And how?

'Not just the treachery,' I told her. 'Constantine has brought some sort of doom upon us. I can almost taste it.'

'And you came to find out whether a Song-Sayer can put it right.' She laughed quietly. 'To make your world safe again. But you've left it too late, Mentor. Ambros loves the land, but he must see the impossibility of facing a united enemy with divided friends.'

'It's for that reason I seek to understand this blackness,' I said. 'He strives for the dream that the Emperor will see value in his endeavours.'

She laughed again.

'And who,' she hissed, 'does he think will convey that good opinion? Masul, the Emperor's emissary? If so, you should ask the Numidian to share with you the messages my mother carries for him to Burdigala and beyond. If you're looking for an answer to the web you perceive, you will need to understand that Masul is the spider at its centre.'

I pressed her to say more, but she turned her face to the wall, began to sing a lament.

Curse and doom have laid me bare, stolen heart and senses fair, left me with no deeper care.

They had sailed away, and the darkness grew ever more profound. The ash and ember of misfortune blotted the sun with even greater vengeance than usual, so that crops were blighted in all our lands. The failed crops, in turn, fuelled rift upon rift within Ambros Skyhound's already fragile alliances, and we became familiar travellers on the Two as we chased back and forth between Yew Grove and Legion-Hold to deal with them.

'We were promised a sharing of wealth,' said Fergna Urcol's Son, as we toured the grain pits that should have fed all of Slavehold, but would now barely keep the wolves from Legion-Hold's gates. 'But all we have here is a pooling of our fleas.'

It could have become an anthem for all our territories, so familiar was the refrain.

'They say you have plenty grain,' Osla Big-Knife snarled at him. 'Plenty to share with others.' He added something else too. Something guttural in the Saeson tongue.

'You think I'd have come all the way here,' Fergna told him, 'if we had enough even for ourselves. Three rebellions already since Bright Fire. Fools stoked up by these bloody monks that are suddenly all over the place.'

It had begun much earlier in the year. Travelling Christ-follower priests like a swarm. Reports from this place and that. A miracle here. A tale of non-believers and their fate there. Usually some nonsense about how they had committed heathen sacrilege – and dropped dead on the spot. Or the appearance of murdered Bishop Mungo's wraith, appearing in a fiery cloud upon one hill or another.

'They speak true,' said Osla. 'Bad grain because God is angry.'

'Your god, Osla,' said Ambros, his voice weary, as it was so often in those days, 'seems equally angry with those lands where he is most worshipped.' He turned to Fergna. 'And the rebellions, Lord Protector, how have you handled them?'

'Caught the treacherous bastards and nailed them all to trees,' Fergna replied. 'What else? It's what Maximus would have done. Followed the example of Cyrus. And Romulus. Eh, Mentor?' He slapped my shoulder.

'Strength of arms, that's what we need. You put down the disaffected. Reward the tepid. Frighten shit out of the doubters. We share his blood, Ambros Skyhound. Yet you are High Lord and I am merely Lord Protector of South-End. So use the Sword of Maximus, High Lord. Destroy our enemies. Take from them what we need to feed our faithful – or else pass the sword to one who would put it to better purpose.'

It was an interminable argument, and made worse when, at the next Dead Moon, word reached us that a new evil had struck. The Cattle Pest. By coincidence – though by way of divine punishment in most folk's eyes – it had struck particularly hard in the lands of both Constantine and Urien, each of whom had retired, with slave-captives and plunder, to their respective holdfasts, almost immediately after the Yew Grove Council, and lucky that Ambros, in his fury against them, did not have them put to death for their brutal stupidity. Yet now it seemed that everywhere we went there were emaciated cows, staggering around or already dead, haemorrhaged blood or necrosis caked about their lips, their nostrils, their genitalia. And no hope of a cure, it seemed. I had found a copy of Columella's *Res Rustica* in a collection within the old legionary fortress outside Mammary, that suitably maternal, untroubled holdfast at the Two's mid-point between Yew Grove and Legion-Hold, at the confluence of the White Spring and Swift Deer rivers, and for which we still often use the Common Speech name, *Mamucio*. And, in Yew Grove, we found Masul the Numidian poring over a codex edition of the Vegetius tome, *Mulomedicina*, in consultation with the local Oak Seers' representatives – mostly the Spirit-Speakers who commune so easily with the wraiths of the dead, animal and human alike, but also some of their herb-healers, lore-keepers and women of great wisdom.

'The advice is all the same,' Masul said. 'Keep the herds divided, separated, into small groups. Move them to new pastures. Kill the diseased beasts. Burn the carcasses.'

I had wondered often about the Song-Sayer's words, though I had not yet challenged him on that issue of messages sent with Murgain to Burdigala. Harmless, perhaps. The Numidian obviously trusted her, and the messages were presumably dispatches for onward delivery to Constantinopolis. But Murgain, rather than the ship's captain?

'It sounds like the Black Hags,' said Ambros. 'Is there no silver cauldron cure for this too?'

'It will be Summer End very soon,' one of the Oak Seers told him, a Spirit-Speaker from his animal skins, the patterns etched into his face. 'Only by running the herds between the fires can we be rid of this illness. We have seen this before.'

'If that would suffice,' said Masul, 'we could have simply lit the bonfires already and been rid of it. No, Lord Ambros, you are correct. There are real similarities between this and the Yellow Pestilence.'

'The Three-in-One will only hear us if the healing fires are lit at Summer End's Eve,' the Spirit-Speaker protested. 'By Epona, Kernuno and Lug...' he began to intone, but Ambros drowned his prayers.

'We will send out word, as though it were the Bloody Spear,' he decreed, though with little enthusiasm, his face ashen and grave. 'The only intelligent thing to do. Every farmstead, drovers' guild and market to isolate any sign of the disease and slaughter the affected cattle. Burn the corpses. The whole herd where it seems especially widespread.'

'And who, Lord,' said an elder, a duty-holder who seemed to invite himself to many such councils, 'do you think will obey this edict? Nobody but a fool, faced with empty bellies for the whole Dark Half, will readily burn his livestock for no good reason.'

'Have faith, Bona,' Ambros told him, 'that we shall require each client lord, each duty-holder, each elder to keep account of every family's cattle lost to them, and when we come out from this darkness, we will find some way to recompense them, at least in part.' But I do not think he noticed the dismissive way in which his promise was received, for he was seized by an attack of pain that bent him double.

Ambros Skyhound's quarters in Yew Grove were modest as a Spartan's eating plate, and he lay upon a simple campaign cot, with a cold sweat glistening his brow.

'Lord Ambros,' Masul whispered, 'shall you allow me to examine your hurt?'

Ambros had relied on Birch and Cai to disperse the Oak Seers and most others who had been present during his attack, sent them away with encouraging words, assurances that the High Lord was simply exhausted after his travels. But then the two companions had helped him back here to his bed. And he had not objected when Masul the Numidian and Owain Hawk-Beak had followed close behind.

'By Mithras,' Ambros snarled, 'can you not leave me in peace? And when did you become a *medicus* among all your other talents?'

Yet, despite his words, he reached down and fumbled with the hem of his tunic, pulled it up towards his chest to reveal the hollowed pit of his belly. Hollow, except for the angry lump at his waist.

'You did not ask me that question,' said Masul, 'when you came seeking a weapon with which to beat the Black Hags.' And he probed around the lump. 'You know what this is?'

'The Ravager, is it not?' Ambros replied. 'The thing that a *medicus* would call the Crab.'

'A *karkinos*, yes,' Masul told him, and I think each of the rest of us gasped, felt ourselves choked, despite ourselves.

'You cannot be sure of that!' Birch Strong-Arm grasped him by the shoulder.

'As sure as it is possible to be,' said Masul. 'You have had the bloating, the gut pain, the loss of appetite, and the difficulty swallowing?' he asked Ambros.

'As Owain will have told you,' Ambros groaned. 'He has been dosing me with his potions long enough.'

'Potions?' I said. Something else he had kept from me. 'What potions?'

'For the pain,' said Hawk-Beak, 'a mixture of mandragora and papaver juice. To help him rest, a draught of henbane and belladonna.'

'Belladonna is a poison.' I must have sounded like a fool, simply to say so.

'Not when administered in the correct dosage,' said Masul. 'And the symptoms are exactly those described by Archigenes. By Galen and Leonides of Alexandria too. Any blood in your vomit or your shit?'

'No,' said Ambros. 'And the treatment?'

'When did you first sense its presence?' Owain asked him, and Ambros laughed.

'You remember, Mentor,' he said, 'the day I told Malco that his Church of the Christos was like the Ravager, devouring all that is healthy in the world.'

'I remember it well,' I replied. 'Four years ago?'

'Yes,' said Ambros. 'Four years ago.'

'You had this thing even then?' Masul was aghast.

'Not then, but soon afterwards. You see? The Christ-followers' curse. I brought it upon myself. Just by speaking its name. And the treatment?'

'It is a long time, Lord Ambros,' said the Numidian. 'Archigenes believed that, in its early stages, a *karkinos* could be treated by medicaments. But, in its later stages, only excision would serve. Galen believed in excision alone. Yet Leonides believed that the body should be left closed, the Ravager contained. A diet with little or no flesh, a high content of seeds, seasonal berries, hazel nuts – almonds too if we can find them.'

'And the medicaments?' I said.

'The sap of liliacum,' Owain replied. 'Garlic. And absinthium. But after all this time...'

'Where would we find them?' I ignored his pessimism.

'There are traders and storekeepers,' said Masul. 'Here in Eborac. Though the liliacum sap is more potent when fresh. Excision would still be the preferred treatment, I think.'

'There will be no excision,' Ambros insisted. 'Storekeepers we may possess, but not a surgeon capable of internal procedures. Those that we have might be dependable enough with a saw on bones, but I would trust none of them to open my guts.'

'Well,' I said, 'this Ravager is one more traitor in our midst, it seems. And perhaps, friend Masul, the next time you are dispatching messages to Burdigala or beyond, you might think to order some fresh sap of liliacum.'

Something flashed behind those dark eyes, and he could not help but cast a quick glance in Owain's direction. I caught that glance, held it tight, but I noticed that Hawk-Beak remained impassive, as though he had not noticed the fleeting look that passed between them.

'Yes,' said Masul. 'Yes, you're right. But, for now, we should start with what we have.'

'And how long, do you think,' Ambros asked him, 'might these medicaments keep me alive?'

'My lord,' Masul told him, with great care, 'you have already suffered with this *karkinos* for three years. Or four. I have never heard of anybody surviving the Ravager more than five.'

*

The hours that followed were among the most difficult of my life. Masul left us to find the necessary potion ingredients and to consult with a physician of his acquaintance, another of the town's Judaeans. And Birch, Cai and myself were left to take part in one of those conversations, which pretend at normality when all the content is, by definition, beyond even the extraordinary. The Skyhound's living testament almost. Plans made in the event that Masul's prognosis might be optimistic, his remaining days shorter than we all hoped. Cai almost incapable of participating, such was his palpable grief. But Birch was, as always, our rock.

'And these draughts, these potions of yours,' he said to Owain Hawk-Beak. 'I take it, Master *Medicus*, that none shall be administered unless you have imbibed them yourself?'

'Of course,' Owain replied, and it seemed to me that his response was just too ready. For myself, I would have been enraged at the suggestion implied in Birch Strong-Arm's question.

In the end, however, I made my apologies, determined that tomorrow I should return to Legion-Hold, check on the Academy, resume the studies of my disciples, try to regain some regularity in my own life, within this chaotic world. Yet, in the morning, there was a message from Ambros, telling me that there was news. Grave news. And I found him alone at his writing-table, message tablets, scrolls and an itinerary spread before him.

'Well, Mentor,' he said, 'you remember the water-clock, the *clepsydra*, which we took upon our voyage?'

'You can hear its dripping?'

'Even in my sleep. And that sleep chilled too by a fear that never ends.'

I asked if he wished to speak about his fears, about the illness itself, but he simply shook his head. 'No,' he said. 'But Cai tells me you went to see the curse-weavers before they left for Burdigala.'

That had been many months earlier, of course, and he had never before made mention of it.

'I went only to see the Song-Sayer,' I told him. 'I thought she might be able to make some sense of this darkness that eats us all.' His face was set hard. Questions that he could not ask. About her well-being. About her guilt. Yet I could find no medicament for that particular infirmity except to tell him that she seemed strong in both body and mind.

'Well, for me,' he said, 'time is short, it seems. Though I sense that the bishops have all the time in the world at their disposal. And I had not fully understood the danger from these Christ-followers until now.'

'Each new faith tries to displace that which came before,' I said. 'We've had that conversation many times.'

'The religion is one thing, Mentor. But a runner arrived in the night. With this.' He picked up a scroll. 'A detailed report from Aurelius of Two-Tribes. It seems that Gwrgi Hard-Spear has a new army. Hired men mostly. *Foederati.* Mercenaries. But the bishops with them too. And Rhun the Tall. They attacked the guild-gather at Corin-Mound, captured all the Oak Seers there. Speeches were made, it seems, to all the local duty-holders and elders. The old message again. That those who would not become servants of the Almighty were less than the beasts of the field. Without a place in this modern world. Their traditions and history an affront to God.'

'I remember,' I said, 'being accused by Deniol that we have been building pagan libraries. Collections of ungodly texts, he said. Texts proscribed by their Holy Father, as well as the Emperor.'

Ambros nodded.

'But then,' he said, 'Gwrgi had each of the Oak Seers impaled. Men and women alike. Yet he made sure to leave each of them alive long enough so that his men could flay them, peel the skin from their living flesh.'

'The bishops observed all this?' I was hardly able to credit the tale. 'And where was Aurelius while all this took place?'

'Defending the town itself, though with no great success. For the bishops had taken another war-band within the walls. They burned down his gather-hall. Revenge, it seems, for the fact that Corin-Mound once had its own bishop – though Aurelius expelled him, many years ago. But what you've said about Deniol makes sense. For they took great care to burn the library too. Every codex. Every record. Our traditions and our history, Mentor. They seek to expunge each detail of our existence.'

Chapter Twenty-Six

They make a desert and call it peace, Tacitus had written. About his own people, of course. About the cruelties so often committed by the Legions. Though it could have applied equally to those Christ-follower bishops and that horde of *foederati*, which their gold had financed.

We took our collective identities for granted, since they were woven into the fabric of our very existence. Our lore and our history, whether oral or written, or bequeathed in our music, rooted in the land itself. Indelible, we imagined. Passed from age to age in whatever form of learning may be appropriate to us. For there has never been a generation, in any land upon the earth, that had not valued the accrual of knowledge in one form or another. It was the blessing of my life – to have been part of that process, that wonder, that growing, that continuum. A rich one, there in the lands to which Empire attached the name Britannia, its earliest writers calling us *Pretani*, the Painted Ones. Not the Pictoi alone, but all of us. Yet, while we might share the Cousins' Tongue, customs and legends, a way of life, beyond that we had a hundred different entities, united only rarely in a variety of shifting and temporary alliances. To the song-sayers, we might be the Isles of Fair Presence. Or the Mountain Lands. It was Britannia that we had become, however. The only word in the Cousins' Tongue that implied any lasting connection between us. The Empire's word. And we had been part of that Empire for longer than we had ever been collectively otherwise.

Yet Tacitus and many others recorded the occasions when the Empire ranged up against peoples who would not, or could not, be assimilated within its provinces. And then, in almost every case, those peoples disappeared, every trace of them scoured from the earth. Only those beyond the edge of Empire – like the Pictoi, down across the Severanus Wall – could survive untouched. And the Christ-followers were the heirs of

Empire. So why should they not apply the Empire's logic, its proven practices? I had seen for myself how, in the Frankoi lands, when they had come up with the older faiths, they had overwhelmed them quickly, absorbed them, melded with them. But here, in so many territories, the differences were intractable and, following the Empire's lead, those territories must obviously be turned to a cultural desert, stripped bare. If we let them, we would simply disappear – only tantalising fragments left to tease folk in some distant future, to merely hint at our existence, our names, our lives. And even those hints fogged and warped by the Christ-followers' own re-telling of our tale.

Thus you will find no monk-brother account of Gwrgi's atrocities – a well-timed raid as well, too late in the season for any idea of retaliation, so we all fretted through the famished snow-months and the most miserable Mithras-Birth I ever knew. Yet, at last, the Bloody Spear of Mars Aeron went forth once more. An initial muster at Legion-Hold and a second at Corin-Mound, an impossibly small garrison left behind at Yew Grove in the hope that we might keep the Two open behind us.

Yet, at that time of year, raiders would have been lucky to even find the highway, and particularly those stretches that climbed over the cruel uplands of the Spine. It was the Calends of Februarius once more, and Ambros was determined on his annual pilgrimage to Twin Sisters in time for Day of the Dead, though we lost our way many times, floundering in snow that iced our ponies' bellies, and often shrouded in freezing fogs through which we heard the siren songs from the Hollow Hills. We imagined ourselves lured away by the small dark folk, bewitched to sharing their food, their lodging in the Mystic Mounds, then waking in some distant morning to find five hundred years had passed and all we had known now turned to dust. But the reality was worse for, as we struggled through that journey westwards, found our path once more, it took us through one settlement after another where there was no succour to be gained, a seemingly endless repetition of the same scene – dead infants being borne by emaciated parents to their burial places, the sound of keening where once we had imagined we heard the Sithian-singing.

And we must have looked like the living dead too, as we passed quietly, unchallenged, almost unobserved through Legion-Hold and onwards, to the Eleven, Ambros being much affected by the starvation that we found in Slavehold too, and then throughout Headland itself.

But we paid our respects at the tombs of Owen White-Tooth and the Lady Uithera, before retracing our deep hoof-prints in time for the first of the gatherings – a bitter disappointment.

'Fifty spears,' said Ambros, when we sat in the old Legion-Hold *principia* building once more. 'Fifty spears!'

'Too many mourning the death of their young ones,' said Birch Strong-Arm.

'Or hiding their herds from the Cattle Pest,' Cai told him, though both their comments were self-evident. And neither of them dared mention that countless more were simply sitting upon their land, holding it against the lawless raiders whose numbers grew in direct proportion to the rising levels of food shortage.

'Do you not wish we were back in the mountains once more?' Ambros asked us. 'In the old hunting grounds of my people. The horse-runs. You remember? Perhaps it had been better to have left well alone. Kept alive all those we have lost. Brave Anwas. Mabon. Custyn. All the others of our companions.'

It was rare for Ambros to lose his optimism, even when the pains of his illness gripped him, as they did now.

'But all was not well,' I said. 'Do you not remember Deniol's words, all those years ago. He was right – the world already changing, yet we had failed to notice the fact. And he made it clear, even then, that he believed it a dangerous thing for our Oak Seers, our Song-Sayers, our Mentors, to have the power to shape the minds of our young people. For Deniol, and those like him, nothing will satisfy until only the Christ-followers have control of our learning. And neither Anwas, nor Mabon Modron's Son, nor yet any of our friends, would have begrudged their lives to keep us free from the Christ-followers' enslavement.'

'Well, he's right about that, at least,' said Birch. 'And I keep them all alive here.' In anybody else, the thumping of fist against his heart would have seemed purely theatrical but, in Birch Strong-Arm, it was simply a side-effect of the drug that fed him. The inebriation of battle. 'The gods will guide us to new victories, Ambros. Drive the Christ-followers into the sea. Total war. Nothing less. Forget all this nonsense about learning or, before we know it, they'll have offered some deal about leaving your precious libraries alone – and they'll settle for simply burning our souls instead.'

'I'm no great one for learning either,' Cai told him. 'But new victories? It seems to me that our victories have simply added to the butcher's bill for our people. Perhaps a deal, a compromise, is exactly what we need. For how will these bishops control any learning at all when they permit and encourage the burning of books?'

'Because,' Ambros told him, 'as our Master Mentor has already said, the Christ-followers fear the learning we already possess. Most are only interested in imparting the half-starved knowledge that supports their faith. And despite my maudlin words, it's this that makes our war-trail against them so unavoidable. For now, Cai. And Fergna has sent word that he will join us at Uric's Hold. There must be no mistakes about this. Gwrgi and his rabble of butchers must be caught and brought to justice. So there is work for each of you. Birch to Sea Fort. Make sure Fergna meets us no later than the Martius Dead Moon at Uric's Hold. Cai and your Shadow-Watchers to form a screen from there eastwards, then probe south – find the Man-Dog and his pack, keep them in sight until we can come up with them.'

'And me, Lord Ambros?' I asked, and he no longer even remarked upon my use of the formality when I addressed him. It was his due now, after all.

'I fear,' he said, 'that Cai may be right. Time to begin considering other solutions if we cannot simply drive our foes into the sea, as Birch would prefer. I sense a need for the bitter scent of compromise to waft swiftly across the land. But I will not negotiate except from a position of strength – in the eyes of Justinian as well as these bishops. And, as things stand, there are too many uncertainties.'

'You are High Lord of the Westerlands,' Birch protested. 'Lord Warden of the Northland. Who else has such a claim to be Lord of Battles for all Britannia?'

'High-Pass is barely one-third of the Walls-Land,' said Ambros. 'The biggest portion is held by Morgan Thunderbolt of High-Pass and this Bishop Sildag. And you know well, Birch Strong-Arm, how those lands run up across the Wall to cover all the territories of Northland over which we have no control whatsoever. And our Westerlands? I dread to think how long we would hold the province together if the bishops' gold finds its way into the wrong hands. You know the danger as well as I do. And then there is the small matter of my own water-clock, the time left to our purpose.'

'I see you've not lost your sense of humour,' I said. 'Is there no bad news then?'

'Only for you, Master Mentor,' he grimaced. 'For we need to test the other provinces. The Flavia. And the Upper-Lands of the south.'

'You want me to go there?' He nodded. 'But I know little of them,' I said. 'Less than I should.'

'Then your travels will add to our learning,' he replied. 'And when you return, you may write a codex that will have pride of place in our libraries. And you shall not go unassisted, for your friend, the Numidian, has agreed to go with you.'

'You no longer entirely trust me, I sense,' said Masul. He kicked his pony, urged the beast down the slope and into the wind, which had finally slackened but still watered my eyes. The snows were receding, even upon the high moorland passes through the Spine, as we began this seventh day's march from Legion-Hold. Seven days during which an early-Martius storm had barely abated, made communication almost impossible upon the road while, at night, we had stayed in one *mansio* or another, forced to huddle too closely among our small escort to permit any private discourse. Yet, despite the storm, we had successfully found the place – almost as far as Yew Grove – where we left the Two and headed south-east on the Five, into Flavia and towards Dark-Pool, our first destination.

'I am simply surprised that you've not yet returned to your own lands,' I replied.

'My work is not entirely finished, I find,' he said. 'My reports to the Emperor still incomplete.'

'Perhaps I should trust you better if I knew the conclusions you might be reaching. If I did not believe that your conclusions shall only be precisely those that the Christ-follower Bishops desire. Or even if I understood the content of the messages you sent to Burdigala with Murgain and Rigantona.'

'Ah,' he smiled, 'so that is the source of your suspicions. Yet you did not include the Lady Morgose among my list of supposed spies.'

'Should I have done so?' I asked, but he simply shrugged aside my question.

'I assume it was the Song-Sayer who told you? About the messages.'

'Perhaps it was Rigantona.'

'I think not. And you faithfully reported the conversation to your Lord Skyhound, I imagine.'

'He was more concerned with the Song-Sayer's state of health. Ironic, is it not? Besides, he seems to think that Justinian's Emissary must sometimes move in his own mysterious ways. In any case, he still feels in your debt for the plague-potion.'

Masul lifted a quizzical eyebrow.

'He does? Well, it would hardly be a Christian act to possess such meagre knowledge and not use it. Just a pity that the Almighty had not made that message clear to the Laigin bishops. And your Skyhound is right, my friend. The messages were simple updates on my progress. The Lady Murgain nothing but a convenient carrier to make sure they reached Burdigala safely. The courier services from there to Constantinopolis are well-established. The Imperial Post. The *Cursus Publicus*. A matter of some pride to us all that the dispatch riders can make the journey between Rome and Constantinopolis in under twenty days. This modern world, Master Mentor,' he sighed. 'Oh, this modern world, which God has gifted us.'

'Remarkable,' I said, though I was thinking about the mention I had made of the messages when we were all together in the Skyhound's company, the discussion about his illness. But when I had spoken of them in the context of other traitors in our midst, there had been that concealed yet conspiratorial glance which passed between Masul and Owain Hawk-Beak. Could simple updates about the Numidian's progress truly have inspired such a glance? 'And Dark-Pool?' I asked. 'We'll reach it on the morrow, will we not?'

We were already well within the Flavia, and specifically that territory which shares its name with the city serving as its main holdfast, the domain of Edel Broad-Blade. The lands were well-titled for, even here, the road ran along the brackish, evil-smelling waters of extensive salt marshes. Settlements were numerous, however, and the folk we passed seemed generally in better health than any others I had seen on our travels. Outlanders though, almost all of them, who stopped their work to stare in wonder at the Numidian's ebon features – while they, by contrast, shared the typically fair complexion of the Saeson. I commented upon the fact. Nothing but broad Saeson faces, wherever I looked.

'Not Saesons, my friend,' said Masul. 'Not here. These are Engloi.

From Engeln-Land, which sits to the north of the Saeson homelands. They tell me that Lord Edel has married his daughter, Alwen, to one of the most important Engloi chieftains here.'

'Christ-followers?' I asked.

'Dark-Pool has a very fine church. Just behind the old forum. Lord Edel is very proud of it. Rightly so.'

'And will he stand alongside Lord Ambros?'

'Well,' said Masul the Numidian, 'that remains to be seen.'

'So many wasted days,' I fumed, when we were finally free of the place and travelling up the Six, the road-list showing five further night stops we must make before reaching Benin's Cross, the junction of the Six, the Two, and the Eight.

'Things change,' said Masul. 'And you see how the land lies here.' I knew he was not referring to the topography – even more expansive salt marshes to the south of Dark-Pool.

'How complicated can it be?' I said. 'A simple opinion on whether the Flavia would wish to present itself to the Emperor as part of a single, united province.'

'It was an honest enough response. Not Lord Edel's decision to make alone. A great credit to him that he retains the lordship when, as you've seen, the majority of his duty-holders are those you call Outlanders. Engloi. And not just here, of course.'

Lord Edel had been at some pains to describe the fragility of his borders to the west, where territories that centred upon Three Bridges were like shifting sands. There, I already knew, lived the last of the Isa-River Folk, those who had once fought the legions under the Queen of Victories – *Boudica* in the Common Speech. A once-proud people, pushed steadily here from their original homelands, and now living cheek-by-jowl with yet more of the Engloi tribes, the whole held loosely together by Cenba Ocel's Son, himself one of the Outlanders.

'And were you not familiar with all that, before we came?' I said.

'When I was last here,' he replied, 'matters were less confused elsewhere in your lands. Lord Skyhound's declaration of himself as Defender of All Faiths does not sit well with places where so many already follow the Cross of Christ. And then, of course, there is the monk-burning.'

'For pity's sake,' I snapped, 'to hear Edel's song-sayers, you'd think it had become a daily ritual. I could see the disbelief in their eyes when I tried to tell them the truth of it. And not a scrap of interest in the atrocities committed by Gwrgi the Man-Dog in the name of your Christ-followers.'

'Gwrgi no more acts for the Christ-followers than you do, Master Mentor,' he said. 'A zealot only for his own warped desires. The bishops need his forces. Not the man himself. And only because they have no choice. Truth is in the eye of the beholder. And every lay, in every land, now sings of the Skyhound's war upon the Christians. But at least Lord Edel has agreed to give the matter further consideration. And perhaps you will enjoy a better reception at Fast-River's Run. Or their Saeson neighbours in the *Lundenwic*.

They fell upon us while we still slept. According to the road-list, we were at Solon's Hill, one march south of Broad-Hand, and only one west of our final destination at Fast-River's Run. No *mansio* here, however. Simply the tumbled ruin of an old staging fort, overgrown with bramble and ivy. It provided little protection from the weather – and none from attack.

In the fog of my fitful dreaming, I thought I heard water babbling over rocks. Then my slumber split by a scream. Curses. Shouting. And I was awake, rolling away from the noise and threat by simple animal instinct, before I was even aware of doing so. No light. For we had set no fire. So that, in the darkness, somebody stumbled over my threshing legs. He swore. The rich tones of the Numidian.

'It's me,' I shouted, shielding my face with my arms in case he should strike out blindly. Yes, blindly. For we were both as sightless as Morgose would have been, though I think she would have fared better in the circumstances.

'Where's your spear?' he yelled, and I sensed him thrust at somebody with his own. He grunted with the effort. The smack of wood upon wood as he knocked aside an incoming shaft. The smell of leather and blood.

'Just my dagger,' I hissed. He stepped over me and I sprang up, drew the blade, slashed out at some phantom noise to my right. 'And I can't see a bloody thing.'

Well, that was another of my life's bigger mistakes. Whether the attackers' eyes were better adjusted to the gloom than our own, or whether my words provided target enough, I shall never know. But the blow that smashed into the side of my head, that knocked me senseless, was certainly well aimed. And it was a strange thing that, upon beginning to regain consciousness after such a blow, the pounding in my brain, the disorientation, the blurred vision, the inability to find my feet, the numbness, were all welcome. So too was the fact that although I could only have been senseless for a few minutes, I had awoken at all. For I had seen enough battles to know that those knocked hard upon the head, and dead to the world for more than a fleeting while, usually remained dead to the world forever. Yet there had obviously been time enough for some sweat-stinking oaf to be sitting on my back, pressing me into the stones, beginning to tie my hands with rope. And time, besides, to subdue the Numidian. I could hear him struggling still, but his cries of outrage muffled now. Yet at least they had not killed him – if, indeed, that was any blessing.

For myself, I was past caring, dealing with the waves of nausea, the stabbing pains in my skull, and the loss of feeling in my limbs partly the result of the blow, part to the binding of my wrists. And, as I swam back and forth between oblivion and bodily woes, I could hear the night-vultures searching and scattering our possessions, laughing, sharing their easy victory, but arguing too in the strangely accented dialect of the Cousins' Tongue, which they favoured in these parts. I had rather hoped they might turn out to be Outlanders, but they were not. And why should they have been?

Eventually, there were streaks of pale grey in the sky, the merest hint of first light, but enough to allow me some image of the scene, whenever my vision cleared sufficiently for the purpose. They were a ragged band, naturally. Wiry as weasels. Predatory faces, and one of the gang was holding up my silver neck-ring, which I had not even realised was taken from me. At my side, one of our three spear-hawk escorts lay sprawled, his throat cut from ear to ear, a dark pool surrounding his head, the stream of his life's blood all babbled out now. And the other two not far away, both dead also. Yet Masul and myself the bandits seemed to have deliberately kept alive.

'They must have been following us for a while,' whispered the Numidian, and I managed to turn onto my other side, so I might peer up at him. 'How do you feel, my friend?' he asked.

Always such a useless question, it did not merit a reply.

'Only six of the bastards,' I said. 'It felt like a whole war-host.'

'It seems,' he said, 'that they intend to ransom us. If I have understood them correctly. They have assumed, from the colour of my skin and the quality of our clothing, that we must have a value.'

'And who, do they hope, would be stupid enough to pay such a ransom?'

The night-hawks were building a fire at last, one of them also dragging aside the pony I had been riding, slicing the beast's neck when it was sufficiently distant from the rest of our mounts, while the other thieves began scattering the contents of our saddle-packs.

'They seem to have no true sense of value,' murmured the Numidian. 'That pony alive would have been worth far more to them.'

'In times of famine,' I replied, 'the dead pig has more value than its weight in gold. They are hungry. And hungry men think no further than their bellies.'

'Then we must hope that Lord Cabul Grey-Wolf remembers me and thinks the Emperor's favours might be worth the ransom price.'

And soon, I hoped. For the thieves' arguments had become more heated in direct proportion to their disappointment. Only a fool would have carried great wealth upon the roads, and my neck-ring had so many lumps cut out of it that it was now worth little more than a handful of silver numbers. Forty maybe. A purse. A *follis*. And Masul's own pack had presented them with only a similar reward. Everything else they simply cast aside, so that they spared only a passing glance for those possessions of the Numidian, which gripped me more than I could possibly have imagined. Worthless? Yes. But significant? Oh, certainly. Since, in that fleeting moment, I saw them hold up, then throw away, a handful of flat wooden sticks – exactly the same as the one carved with the Tree Script that we had taken outside Legion-Hold.

Chapter Twenty-Seven

'It was you,' I spat at him, struggling like an eel in an effort to sit upright. But the nausea overcame me once more and I spewed bile onto my breeks.

'Me?' he said. 'What? I carry message sticks. Of course I do. You know well that the blessed ancients, the earliest Christ-followers, developed the Tree Script. Is it so strange that we should still use them when the need arises?'

'The need to betray us?'

'Is it possible to betray that to which you do not belong?' he said.

'You have lived with us, broken bread and shared our wine.'

'I received no more than an Emissary of the Emperor may be due.'

The night-vultures had almost come to blows now. Over both the method of splitting their loot, as well as its paucity. And, for a while, I harboured the foolish illusion that they might slay each other. But such things are simply devices for weavers of tales, and there was far more chance they would vent their anger upon our bodies. Beyond mere chance, in truth, for one of them came swaggering across, his meagre share brandished in a clenched fist, and he kicked the Numidian in the side of his face. Not a hard kick, but enough to topple Masul onto his side.

'You bastards better pray that somebody values your skin,' the man screamed, 'or that's exactly what your rich friends will get as a gift.' His hare-lip quivered with rage, while his companions laughed at him, yelled abuse or encouragement, broke the tension somewhat, so that the fellow finally rejoined them.

'You sat in council with us,' I said, deliberately ignoring Masul's discomfort – savouring it, in fact, 'while we tore ourselves apart about the traitor's identity.'

The Numidian groaned softly, shook his head to clear it, but stayed where he had fallen.

'You think I should have confessed?' he hissed. 'To what? Doing my duty?'

I remembered the Cerdeg's Edge man, Flavia the runner, who had bought his life with a confession that he had been paid to deliver the Tree Script message to our foes, the message that had resulted directly in the slaughter at the Valley of the Trees – the message Flavia swore that Morgose had paid him to deliver.

'But the messages,' I said. 'The messages that warned our enemies of our movements. They were yours.'

'It would have been a betrayal of my own faith had I not warned the Bishops of the Skyhound's change of plan.'

'And you persuaded the man, Flavia, to point a false finger at Morgose?'

'You think it so unlikely that all those around your Skyhound should be true to him? The message may have been mine, but I did not carve the Tree Script marks. You have much to learn, Master Mentor. I like you, yet there are moments when I doubt your suitability for the posts you have held. Elsewhere in the Empire, *rhetors* hold a certain reputation for cynicism.'

'So Morgose did betray him?'

I was almost relieved, but he laughed, managed to sit upright again, then shouted at the man who had kicked him.

'Lord Cabul Grey-Wolf at Fast-River's Run will certainly value us,' he cried. 'Though he'll pay you nothing for damaged goods and will hunt you down like pigs if we're harmed. Tell him that you hold Masul the Numidian and I believe he will arrange fair trade for us.'

'More bishop's gold?' I asked him, as the thieves debated their next move.

'No bishop any longer in Lord Cabul's land,' said Masul, 'but he himself is still a devout believer. Given the nature of his duty-holders though, he does not profess his faith too openly just now. But that faith is at least enough to keep his trade routes open with the Christian lands of the Frankoi.

'And me?' I said. 'He may be prepared to pay for your life. But mine?'

'I like you, Master Mentor,' he repeated. 'Despite everything. So I shall try to keep you alive. At least until we reach Fast-River's Run. After that…'

He hesitated, looked to the east.

'After that,' I said, 'you will hope for a gazelle moored in the river. You will consider your work done. And you will return to Justinian with word that Britannia is not worthy to be included as a province within his Empire.'

The Numidian smiled.

'Greater Britannia, my friend,' he said, 'is a concept whose time has not yet come. I had to ensure that the Church here would see that.'

Yes, I thought, *and you have been careful, even in adversity, to neither admit nor deny that the Song-Sayer is guilty of the charges brought against her. That I brought against her.* And why would he not do so? Some strange reluctance to tell a deliberate lie, perhaps? A doom placed upon him by his faith? But more likely because he knew that I would now be left to carry word back to Ambros that Morgose was, indeed, guilty of treachery – while the real traitor, Masul's associate, remained hidden among us.

We were released a sennight later, some deal obviously having been reached only after days of back and forth negotiations between the night-vultures and, we assumed, Lord Cabul himself. But I could bring myself to say little to the Numidian and passed the time, to my surprise, growing closer to our captors. Some of them, anyway. Yet never close enough for them to share any news about the way in which their ransom demands had been received. We could only measure the progress of their negotiations by the moods, fair or foul, that fell upon them. And, on the fifth day, they plainly felt the need for emphasis, for raising our commodity value, by hacking the head from the corpse of one of the spear-hawks they had previously slain and dumped beyond the ruin – and the wretch responsible for the bargaining leapt onto a pony's back and with the dead warrior's top-knot gripped between his fingers, galloped away towards Fast-River's Run, whooping and brandishing his trophy aloft.

But we were finally assured that our release was imminent and forced to march eastwards, our wrists still bound, rope leashes about our necks like slave-bonds. Thus we attracted troubled glances at the homesteads we passed: the scattered farms of Saeson Outlanders, which grew steadily more numerous as the wide river came more often into view through the trees, or from higher ground. Until, just below, on our right, there was a settlement of such size nestled against the nearer bank that it could almost have been a small city, though without the ordered close-knit streets of any city I had ever known.

'Look,' said one of the night-vultures, the same hare-lipped man who, back on the night of the ambush, had kicked the Numidian's face. 'The bastards. Head down there, friend, and see how long it takes to find anybody you can understand. Take our lands. Take our women. More of the pricks arriving every year. I was born down there. Family was there. When I had a bloody family.'

'The Black Hags?' I asked him.

'Black Hags be arsed,' he spat. 'Those bastards came. Thick as fleas on a dog's bollocks before you knew it. Wife and kids ran off with one of them. Lost everything.'

I suspected there was more to the story.

'And is that the town they call Lundenwic?'

Yes, they did, he confirmed. Just as the legions had named it *Londinium*, each of them hearing our own name 'Fast-River' and twisting it to suit their foreign tongues.

'And you've got it right too,' he went on. 'About the Black Hags. How come those bastards never catch it, eh? But one day we'll take it all back. They say there's a new warlord in the west. A proper fighter who's happy to burn Christ-followers and Outlanders alike. A warrior who rides a golden war-cart into battle and never takes hurt from any weapon of his enemies. A great man who'll drive these land-grabbers back into the sea. You must know of him. You're from the north, aren't you? The song-sayers are always going on about him. The Bear-King, they call him.'

From the battle-cry, of course.

'Yes,' shouted Masul the Numidian. 'We know him. This man is his closest friend. And all this time you've been holding him prisoner.'

'This true?' asked hare-lip, and I saw the fear in his eyes, the axe of retribution swaying above his head. I recalled, too, the story of the Empire's first Caesar: how he had been captured by sea-raiders; how, upon his release, he had sworn an oath to hunt them down; and how, many years later, he had fulfilled his vow and watched them all crucified.

'True,' I said, as the fellow hurriedly began to slip the rope from my neck. 'Ambros Skyhound is my friend. But you have nothing to fear from him if we are treated well.'

'Ambros Skyhound?' the man looked at me as though I had lost my wits, then thought twice and left the neck-rope in place. 'Who's that then? I was talking about the Bear-King of the West.'

'You see?' the Numidian said to me. 'How could I, in all faith, propose to the Empire that it should align itself to an ally who's no more than a song-sayer's myth?'

I watched his ship sail with the Fast-River's ebbing waters. As he had predicted, there were trading ships there at the rat-infested wharves, just beyond the longest bridge I had ever seen. A huge affair of broad timbers driven deep into the mud, long ages past, by the Empire's *ingeniatore* and, somehow, still withstanding the twice-daily struggle against those vicious tides. It carried the road south to the Muddy Estuary, the legions' *Ritupis*, Red-Tops, and north through the lower gate of Fast-River's Run, right into its heart, to the basilica and forum beyond the Roman walls of the city to which Lord Cabul's forefathers had fled following the legendary Battle of River's-Bend Ford many years before, against the Outlanders. Yet, now, the Saesons were their neighbours, just along the river in that Lundenwic. And it was almost impossible, they said, to distinguish between Cousins' Kin and Outlander anywhere across the Great Forest, the Saeson Shore or the Land of Hosts, from whence Osla Big-Knife had come to us.

'It's been an uneasy peace,' said Imris Cabul's Son, as the gazelle's oars carried the vessel out of sight around the river's meander. 'But at least it's peace.'

'You are fortunate,' I said, 'to have not known war.'

'I've bathed my blade in blood many times,' he told me with a young man's indignation.

'Of course,' I replied. 'But I was thinking more of the horrors these lands must have faced during the Fifty Years War. We were spared much of that, away in the north and west. Our own problems, of course. With the Incomers. Raids by the Painted Folk. But nothing like the devastation up here. Long before you were born though, lad.' And

I slapped him on the shoulder. Yet we had not been spared. For war had caught up with us now, not against the Saesons this time, but against the Christ-followers. Against our own. As if fighting the Cattle Pest, the Yellow Death and the Years Without Summer were not enough.

A rat scampered across my feet and I kicked it into the water. It brought back to me that theory which Masul the Numidian had expounded when we were at Clud-Vale, about how it may be the rats that carried the pestilence. Foolish. Yet I knew I would miss him, despite his duplicity.

'The war in the west,' said Imris, 'must be a glorious thing. I would give anything to join the spear-press of the Bear-King.'

There it was again. That nonsense about the Bear-King. *And glorious?* I thought, and remembered those slopes littered with slain and dying after the battle at the Valley of the Trees.

'And what would your father think of that?' I asked.

'Because he has taken the Cross?' he laughed. 'There are few Christ-followers here. A small hermitage by the river. A few monk-brothers who keep to themselves, Mithras be praised! But the church they had built on the White Mound is burned down now. The bishop gone off to seek easier converts along the Saeson Shore.'

I had seen the ruin of that church. It must once have been impressive but, like so much of Fast-River's Run, it was no longer thus. The town did not even possess a decent bathhouse, simply a crumbled ghost of that which had gone before. A place that had never been glorious, even under the legions. And I was certain it would never be so in the future either.

'And if the Bear-King should seek to bring all these lands together,' I said, 'to create a single province, Greater Britannia, would he have support?'

'To the last drop of our blood,' the young man replied.

And I thought about all this as I rode out of the Flood's Gate a few days later, in company with Imris and his spear-hawks. About the fractured and insular territories of Flavia, the Easterlands. About the divisions and conflicts which had riven Second-Province, the Northland. About the fragile jealousies in Ambros Skyhound's own province. About the fervour of Imris Cabul's Son – the fervour that was bringing no more than twenty wild but beardless boys to our ranks. About Masul the

Numidian's derision concerning the Emperor's disinterest in our plight. I thought it all as I passed through the Fast-River Hold's western burial grounds, at the start of our seventeen-day journey back to Legion-Hold. And I knew that we were living an impossible lie.

Beyond the burial grounds, we followed the Two northwards, from its junction with the Seven. We could have taken that other route as an alternative, heading for River-Port in Rage-Rise, then taking the Thirteen to Bright-Place, and thence through Corin-Mound and Uric's Hold. I was more likely to pick up news of Ambros and his campaign in that way but, on the other hand, there was also the possibility that we could run straight into Gwrgi Hard-Spear, Gwrgi the Man-Dog. In any case, I was keen to visit Solon's Hill once more – where we stopped to give decent burial to the three warriors slain by the night-vultures. And not just burial. For two of those warriors, I was certain, had wives and children back in the White-Wilds. Mithras knows, there was precious little of any value left upon their bodies, even their tunics and breeks having been stripped from them. But there was a simple cloak-pin belonging to one of the men and I took the thing with me, even though I knew it would provide no real solace to his family.

'Are you sure you want to find them?' Imris asked me.

'Yes, of course,' I said. 'If it's possible. Apart from anything else, we should try and recover the silver that your father invested in our ransom.' It had not been the fortune for which the night-vultures had hoped, a few purses each, and each purse, or *follis*, worth no more than forty silver numbers. But twenty *folli* could have fed a whole family for a couple of years – at least, before the Years Without Summer struck and the price of grain leapt like a serpent-bitten sheep. So I hoped that, in the unlikely event we ever found the thieves, Imris might forget his father's claim upon the coins and allow me to gift them to those same bereaved wives and children. 'Besides,' I went on, remembering that first Caesar again, 'we should never allow such creatures to go unpunished.'

'Yet you told me you grew to feel sympathy for them.'

'I can feel sympathy for a man's actions yet still expect him to face justice when he breaches Judex Law, or Oak Seers' Missive, or the Empire's Twelve Tables – whichever happens to apply in your father's lands. They could be anywhere, of course. But I suspect the rogues must have followed us here from Broad-Hand. Maybe even further. But Broad-Hand seems like a good place to start. If we can't find them in a few days though, we'll be forced to give up the chase. Ambros wouldn't thank me for not bringing him the news I have to bear.'

Yet I was not entirely sure what that news might be. The Numidian gone back to his master, of course, and all chance lost that Justinian may come to our aid, gift us the beneficence of his Empire. The ruptured politics of the Easterlands of Flavia, and the even greater uncertainties of these southern territories. Yes. But Morgose? What might I tell him of the Song-Sayer? That Masul had admitted the existence of some conspirator within our faction? Certainly. That he would neither confirm nor deny whether our case against Morgose was valid? Absolutely. That I had made assumption, therefore, of her innocence? Problematic. And the usual conundrum. If not Morgose, then who?

'Perhaps it might be best that we should not all appear at Broad-Hand looking like a war-host,' Imris suggested, 'else we'll never flush them out.'

'True,' I said. 'But here's a better plan. Another investment. There was a *mansio* at Broad-Hand, now serving as a pot-house too. We broke our journey in the place and I think it likely they picked up our trail there too. So two of you, perhaps. Finest cloaks. Splash some silver numbers around. Keep yourselves safe but leave before first light. The rest of us will stay out of the way but somebody will keep watch, check to see if you're followed, then bring on the rest if our quarry's on the move.'

A decent plan, though a wasted effort, for there was no sign of the thieves and all but two of us had spent a miserable night in the rain for nothing. So, the next day, we gave up the chase and trudged onwards to Ridgeway's Gap. The Numidian and myself had changed ponies there on the way south, since some enterprising Outlander had reopened the old staging post, and a small but mixed settlement seemed to be surviving happily around the crossroads where the Two cut the much older Ridgeway itself. The Ridgeway that runs all the long miles across Southlands, from its western boundary with Domna's Deep, to Bridge-Fort in the far eastern Marsh-Mire. There were a couple of long-houses, not so large as others I had seen, but in the normal style of the Saesons – a few kin-families living together with their beasts, and usually hospitality for the occasional traveller with silver to pay for the comfort. But, since it was not yet dark, we aimed first for the fenced enclosure, a few hundred tree-shrouded paces or so beyond the settlement itself, where we might gain fresh mounts once more. We had fallen into silence, and the road was muddy, masking our approach so that, as we rounded the bend, we came upon the night-vultures without them having any warning. In any case, they were so engrossed in haggling with the Outlander over something or other, I doubt they would have heard us even had we been singing a bawdy lay.

We took four of them with the least of struggles and despite protestations, and the other two after an annoying chase through the woodland. Useless, really, for most of the silver was predictably spent. And I had intended that a couple of Imris Cabul Son's lads might drag the bastards, trussed and tethered, back to Fast-River's Run so that Lord Cabul himself might deal with them. I was tempted, naturally, to follow the example of the First Caesar, and have them crucified as an example. But Imris determined that, with life so cheap at every turn, crucifixion might not be a sufficient deterrent. And thus, against my feeble protestations, he set about the task, with his youthful fanatics, of removing the ears, nose and fingers of each thief. Their cries haunt me still, and especially those of hare-lip.

'May the Bear-King of the West take all your souls,' he screamed, until the blood gushing down from his nasal cavities turned his words to incomprehensible spluttering.

Chapter Twenty-Eight

'You brought wine,' said Ambros, back in the gather-hall at Legion-Hold. 'I suppose I should be thankful for small mercies.'

His sunken cheeks and stretched brow seemed permanently creased by pain now, and his left hand rarely relaxed its grip on his midriff.

'A gift from Lord Cabul of Fast-River's Run,' I told him. 'And here is another, a true token of his good faith.' I introduced Imris Cabul's Son and his spear-friends, then told him almost all that had transpired on my journey, though I spared him the details of the way we had mutilated the road-thieves.

'Twenty?' he said, his disappointment thinly disguised. As thinly as the progress of his illness, for I had never seen him in worse condition. His hair lacked much of its fiery lustre and his cheeks and eye-sockets showed dark shadows.

'Not just wine either, Lord Ambros,' Imris smiled at him, 'but olive oil, fish paste and pepper too. All from the Frankoi ships so recently arrived at our wharves.'

'The same vessels that carried away Justinian's Emissary, I suppose,' Ambros sneered, 'and all our hopes for the Empire's succour. But pepper, you say? A small mercy, at least. And perhaps an omen. For, on the road south, we rested near the ruins of a house that must once have been very grand indeed. Mosaics just beneath the dust and rubble. On the walls too. And when some of the men were digging shit-holes outside the camp, they dug up a small chest. A handsome catch of silver numbers. Even a couple of gold solids. And this.' He reached inside the folds of his cloak and took out the leather pouch, which normally hung from his breek-ties. 'You see?' he said, holding up a thumb-sized and exquisite silver pot. A pepper pot. 'Inscribed with the names of Quintus Teleus. And his wife, d'you think? Julia Placidia. The whole thing decorated with symbols of the Christ-followers. How long, Master Mentor, since they buried their treasure? And to what purpose?' He allowed the light to reflect upon the decorated silver, spoke as though he were dreaming, seeing another time, another place. 'What happened to them, we shall never know. But Christ-followers, even then. It made me think again about our campaign. This seemingly cursed campaign.'

'Cursed, Lord Ambros?' said Imris. 'How cursed?'

But Ambros collected himself, made some weak apology for his reveries. Yet he would not be drawn any further on the matter until Imris and his companions had been led away by the house-slaves and shown to their quarters.

'I tried to find news of you,' I said, when we were alone. 'But the only words spoken told of some new warrior-king sprung up in Westerlands – the Bear-King, they call him.'

'I've heard the stories,' he snapped. 'But the truth lies somewhere else. We marched south to Uric's Hold and waited there until three days past the Martius Dead Moon. Fergna never appeared, and neither did Birch. So we went on without them. Pitiful in numbers, but Cai's Shadow-Watchers strung out in a screen to make sure we should have word of Gwrgi Man-Dog if he tried to slip past our flanks. Yet when we reached Corin-Mound, for the second muster, we found precious few willing to take the war-trail and Aurelius himself wounded from another skirmish with Gwrgi's hired men.'

'They were still in Two-Tribes then?' I asked, though it seemed obvious from the disappointment etched into those gaunt features that Gwrgi had slipped the net again.

'No, they were not,' he said. 'And would you believe it? They'd found the one place in Cai's line where his lads were spread too thin to be much use. The bastards marched straight past us unseen and escaped back into the north. Then Birch showed up. At last. Said he'd been taken with a fever before he managed to meet up with Fergna. A fever! Can you believe it? The man must take me for a fool.'

'You cannot believe that he lied. Birch Strong-Arm and myself have no bond of friendship, but there is no man more loyal to you than he, Lord.'

'You told me yourself, Mentor. The Numidian confessed to a having a confederate within our ranks. And why should he not point the finger directly at Morgose if she were, indeed, guilty?'

'To sow confusion, perhaps,' I said. 'He made it plain enough that he saw it as his duty to see your vision confounded.'

'That hardly explains,' he sneered, 'the wrong chance we've suffered since I sent her away. It just happens, by coincidence, I suppose, that Gwrgi knew exactly the point at which to slip through our lines? A coincidence that Birch failed to bring Fergna to the muster, on the very day we might have caught the Man-Dog and those bloody bishops? No, I was wrong to send Morgose away. And who do I have to thank for that, Master Mentor?'

I thought to remind him that I had prepared the case against the Song-Sayer at his own insistence, but his mood was too foul to risk logic or rhetoric.

'An advocate presents the facts as they are known to him at the time, Lord,' I said. 'The facts need to be checked – as we did in this case – but that is not always a guarantee of their veracity. And it was a wise judgement you made. To simply exile the Lady Morgose. A decision that can be reversed if you are satisfied an injustice has been done. And Birch?' I asked. 'What of him?'

'Gone, of course,' he spat. 'Run, like the traitor I now see him to be. Back to his own kin in the Headlands, I imagine.' I could barely imagine the scene. Ambros confronting that most loyal yet most stubborn of warriors with accusations of treachery. An insult that Birch Strong-Arm would not, could not forgive.

'Have many gone with him?' I ventured to ask.

'Why? Do you have desires to follow after him? Will I find a whole coterie of traitors waiting for me in my homeland when I return there?' The words burned my soul and I felt something akin to battle-fury begin to prick the hairs of my neck. Yet he thrust again before I had even a chance to parry the blow. 'What, Mentor?' he yelled. 'Have I chosen the wrong phrase for this occasion? Then how would you correct me? Were your days with Rigantona not betrayal too? And your false case against Morgose? Your friendship with the self-confessed Numidian deceiver? Oh, how you must each have shared your jests at my expense. And now, when I trusted you with forging alliances between myself and the Easterlands, or with those in the south, what do you bring me? Is all of that worthy of any other description than treachery?'

My anger turned to cold rage, yet I controlled it stoically.

'Then if you will forgive me, Lord Ambros,' I said, 'I shall take myself back to duties perhaps more fitting to my station in life.'

'Yes, back to your books, teacher,' he cried. 'While you still may. Before those damned bishops burn them all. And find that bloody pedlar of potions on your way out, will you?'

'Hawk-Beak?' I asked. 'He still doses you?'

I recalled the various medicaments that Masul the Numidian had prescribed to deal with the Ravager: for the pain, a mixture of mandragora and papaver juice; to help ensure rest, a draught of henbane and belladonna – the latter administered in precise dosage; and, to depress the *karkinos* itself, the sap of liliacum, blended with garlic and absinthium.

'And forces upon me a diet of seeds, nuts and berries. By Kernuno's Horns, I would give my weight in silver for a decent dish of suckling pig.'

'But the belladonna,' I said. 'That dosage is carefully watched, I trust?'

'If Owain Hawk-Beak had wanted to poison me, you fool,' he cried, 'he could have done so many times over. No, Master Mentor, of all of you, Hawk-Beak is the only one who does not let me down. Now, get you gone to your books.'

I decided to take Ambros at his word. Literally. For, while he had plainly intended to banish me simply to the Academy at Legion-Hold, some days later I set out to travel the roads westward until I reached the Fortress of the Hammer-Fighters. To be honest, I needed to get away. To be so openly decried and insulted is intolerable, even though I was perfectly capable of finding a dozen excuses for the way in which he had spoken to me. And, despite all that, I stopped first, naturally, at Twin Sisters, so that I might pay my respects at the tombs of Owen White-Tooth and the Lady Uithera, and also reflect further upon their son's condition. I recalled all those happier days when he had been my disciple and we had explored these lands together – lands that had been his schoolroom just as much as the small *ludus* within the holdfast itself or, later, at the Bear Fort. And then, as I swung south into the forests and mountain passes of Overmon, in the ridge-shadow of the Giant's Tomb and Cairn of the Twenty, I remembered words he had spoken to me on one of our first forays here – a reckless deer-chase that had taken us both, and our hounds, far beyond his own borders.

'I am bewitched,' he had said, 'by those days when I hunt alone in the mountain forests. Those when the trees are shrouded in low cloud and dripping with freshly fallen rain. When the birds are made silent by the mists and there is nothing to hear but the wind's sighing through the branches, and the beating of my own heart to remind me I still have life.'

He had been little more than a boy, wearing his favourite hunting hood, which he swore brought him fortune as well as masking his red thatch, yet I could see the ambitions struggling within him and I had been struck by the maturity that gave this youth such a vivid sense of his own mortality. And here he was now, in no more than his twenty-third year, staring death in the face. Though from how many directions? The *karkinos* was bad enough. But I could not rid myself of those concerns about Owain Hawk-Beak and his belladonna. Yet I shook the worry away. It was foolish, for belladonna, in anything other than its mildest dosage, is quickly fatal. Still, it was plain that Masul the Numidian had used an accomplice, a treacherous confederate. And I could not believe that this traitor could be either Birch Strong-Arm or Cai of the Nine Lives.

It still perplexed me when, on Bright Fire's Morn, the Calends of Maius, I finally sat my pony before the Fortress of the Hammer-Fighters. There was little need to call upon the portal-keepers and watchman to grant me entrance since the great gates were thrown open, decked with ribbon and flower to match the Bright Fire Bushes lining the approach roads. And though the folk were still pinched with hunger, there was an air of optimism about this particular Bright Fire that I had not seen for some years. Not just the cattle-drovers, garlanded as brightly as the furze clumps, but traders' stalls set up between the palisades in great variety. Vendors of skin, furs, cheeses and those clever Saeson jewellery imitations, all silver cell work, coloured glass instead of Anatolian bloodstones – without which, it seemed, none of our women could now survive. Hagglers of timber, leather and linens. Auctioneers of goats, hawks, ponies, hounds and slaves. Workers of tin and copper, wax, flannel, glass, shale and jet. Pedlars of pots and tiny figurine images for the gods: Taranis and Herne; Epona and Kernunos; Danu and Arawn;

Lugos and Brigida; Senuna, Mithras and Yesu the Christos.

'Another Light Half already begun, my friend,' I shouted to Severo, the duty-holder and elder Ambros had entrusted with stewardship of the holdfast.

'And Mithras grant us a better one than the last,' he replied.

'The Cattle Pest?' I said.

'Half the livestock gone. But we did our duty. Burned every affected beast. Yet it seems to have passed.'

As he spoke, a colourful procession from one of the outlying settlements came driving their black shorthorns down the Silver Willow road for the gathering – one of the most renowned Bright Fire festivities in all those lands.

'I see you opened the Mithraeum again.'

'Lord Ambros sent word that I must do so,' Severo replied, scratching into his thick grey beard. 'But I should have done it anyway.'

'Yet we may have to close it again, I fear,' I told him, and explained – a pack of lies, of course – that Lord Ambros wanted each of his holdfasts to be put in readiness against the eventuality of attack by Gwrgi the Man-Dog, his people to be prepared, kept safe. And, here at the Fortress of the Hammer-Fighters, for the treasures of knowledge and learning, his library, to be hidden from harm's way.

So, while the cattle were led ceremoniously to the high pastures, and the reveries continued long into the night, I was free to continue the task I had set myself. It was perfect for my purpose since, with the gather-hall and living quarters almost empty, Severo had taken seriously my insistence on secrecy and put his two most trusted body-slaves at my disposal. He trusted them, I suppose, because they had no tongues with which to speak. They were brothers, once sea-raiders from Manu's Isle. And taken when their currock had failed to negotiate the Narrow Strait after an attack on Fort Overmon ten summers past, allowing their capture. Their toes had been removed to impede their escape but they had tried it anyway – and lost their tongues by way of reward, with clear and dire warnings about any subsequent attempts at flight. But, Severo insisted, they had later been purchased to serve here, at the Fortress of the Hammer-Fighters, and had finally settled to their new condition.

I fussed around as they loaded carry-baskets with scrolls and codices, covered them carefully with oiled skin wrappings against the drizzle.

Then they staggered on still-clumsy feet, head-straps straining with the loads, as they covered the five hundred paces to the Mithraeum. The painted tiles around the entrance arch showed the damage from the rocks that Rigantona's men had used to seal the place, and which still lay heaped just beyond, but at least it was open once more, and it must have taken thirty trips before the entire library was relocated within. The *armaria* were assembled afresh inside the cavern, and the filled frames draped with some of the heavy hangings, which had once adorned Rigantona's bedchamber. They brought back memories, of course. And those images. Queen Maeve. The Lady Crow. A shimmer of gauze-weave. The sheer black veil through which I had first seen the delights of her body.

But, with the light failing, I put thoughts of Rigantona aside and peered beneath the hangings one last time, trusting they would adequately protect the precious books from the damp. It was cool in the temple-cave, but perfectly dry. Ideal, I thought, as I said farewell – temporarily, I hoped – to Homer, to Augustine of Hippo, to Vegetius, and to Cicero. To Priscus, Ammianus Marcellinus, Martius of Mamucio, and to that wicked Book Nine of the Apuleius *Metamorphoses*, of course. There was a particularly fond reunion and then further sad parting with the *Anthology of Northern Song-Sayers* which, you may recall, I was proud to have penned in person. But I had brought back my copy of Quintillianus's *Instituto Oratoria* to keep them company, too, as well as my old copy of the *Geographia.* And there were also those codices upon which Ambros himself had worked with his slave scribes, during his time here. Many were unfinished, but one stood out among the drafts – a *Genealogy of First-Province Lords and Prefects.* He must have consulted widely with the Oak Seers' word-weavers and lore-keepers to compile such comprehensive lists. It was a magnificent piece of work and, involuntarily, I found myself muttering a prayer to Mithras for the protection both of the book and its author. And, since the Oak Seers were so closely in my mind, I also spared a few moments to hope that, should Ambros be taken by the Ravager – which seemed inevitable now – Belos would convey his soul to the afterlife and, eventually, allow his re-birth in a new and stronger body. So I thought that a final supplication to the Triple Godhead – to the Great Mare, Epona; to the Horned One, Kernunos; and to Lug Long-Arm – might not go amiss either. I had no great faith in any of them, you understand, but I knew Ambros would have appreciated the gesture.

So it was full dark by the time the slave-brothers had sealed the entrance again with those convenient rocks and boulders, and masked the arch with branches. And even though I had physically done little myself, my muscles still ached. Age, I suppose. Yet it caused me to decline Severo's invitation to join the Bright Fire feasting. Instead, I collapsed upon the bed once shared with Rigantona and spent the night haunted by dreams of the woman – though never once imagining that I would meet her again on the very next morning.

The war-band arrived barely an hour after dawn. A horn's blast by the gate-wardens sent us all running for our weapons and out to the palisades.

'So soon,' Severo said to me when I joined him on the watchtower. 'Your arrival was timely, Mentor. With the feasting last night, and without your warning, they'd have caught us with our breeks down. Mithras be praised that Lord Ambros had the presence to send you.'

Well, it surprised me too. I sometimes fear that I was cursed, that the lies I made possessed that strange habit of coming to pass in reality.

'You know who they are?' I asked, for their behaviour was unusual. Warriors, plainly, some horsemen among them, but they were coming up the track from the south, rather than any direction from which I might have expected Gwrgi Hard-Spear's hirelings to fall upon us. And they had halted, at the edge of those oak and elm groves which sat below the holdfast.

'Our scouts brought word of them,' said Severo. 'Forty men, they counted. A dozen of them mounted. Not enough to pose any real threat since we were so forewarned.'

I pulled my cloak over my head to shield it from the rain, and watched as five riders came splashing up the road.

'Well,' I said, 'there's no mistaking that creature.'

The leader dwarfed his pony, toes almost dangling in the dirt and puddles. Rhun the Tall, without mistake. Without any weapon, so far as I could see, and I wondered whether he still thought himself bound by that old curse of the Song-Sayer. Yet he dwarfed the man at his side – in height, at least, if not in girth. The bishop, Deniol. But Rhun dwarfed his other three companions too. Lightly built, they did not possess the characteristics of horse-warriors. Cloaked and hooded, it was impossible to discern their features, certainly at that distance, but as they began to climb the twisting approach road through the maze of outer ditches, I saw one of them throw back the square-weave in a familiar gesture, part a veil of hair, and stare up at my position with a look of such venom that it almost froze my heart. Rigantona. And not alone, for I could see now that, at her side, were both her mother and the Song-Sayer, Morgose.

Chapter Twenty-Nine

Quintillianus had once written: "*A Woman who is generous with her money is to be praised; not so, if she is generous with her person.*" But, in Rigantona's case, I found neither attribute particularly admirable.

'Is it true she tossed you a coin for your troubles?' Cai laughed, though he did not look at me, keeping his eyes instead always on the heights and thick forest that rose on either side of us. We were still several days from Mona's Isle but this pass, the Hurdle's Ravine, had so often been a site of ambush that it was mentioned in more lays than I could fully remember.

'Well, you should never gainsay a gold *solidus*,' I replied, my own gaze fixed upon the rock-faces and trees also. 'But yes, it's true. Paid me like any humble runner, to carry their message back to Ambros.'

And I had done so, driving my pony with the news like there was no tomorrow, reaching Legion-Hold in less than two days. Though I then wondered why I had bothered. Ambros took the news from me as though I were somehow its author, rather than simply its bearer. He had clearly never heard the admonition against executing messengers. But the delivery took little time, thankfully, for the content was short. The women had seemingly returned from Burdigala in the very vessel upon which Masul the Numidian had later sailed away. Rigantona thought it amusing that my "friend" had kept their presence secret, warned them that I was also in Fast-River's Run. He arranged for them to remain hidden until my departure, and before saying his own final farewell to Britannia's shores. But he had also given them a fair idea where they might find Gwrgi Hard-Spear, Rhun and the bishops, then raiding and making converts at spear-point in the Glass-Isles. Masul assisted them with couriers and they had effected a reunion at a Christ-follower church in that region. And they would be welcome there, since their ship had also brought gold in response to Masul's earlier messages, conveyed abroad by Murgain herself. Gold to hire more *foederati*, I assumed.

'And you believed Rhun?' said Cai. 'About his break from the Man-Dog?'

'I can't see why he would lie,' I replied, as a pair of crows came swooping through the narrow defile towards us, their raucous outrage bouncing from cliff to cliff. 'He's not given to admitting any weakness of stomach, but he owned he would have no more of Gwrgi's barbarity. It was strange to hear that word on the lips of a man like Rhun.'

'Ambros believes it's simply a ruse,' said Cai. 'To lure us away from Legion-Hold. Leave the way open for Gwrgi to take the Northland again.'

'He could be right. But he'd never be able to resist Rhun's taunt. Their threat to reclaim Mona's Isle in the name of his clan is real enough. He might not have much of a war-host but it will suffice. Nobody's tried to stop them thus far. The people all too tired, sick and hungry to care very much about their comings and goings. There'll be plenty in Fairwater Maw willing to hear the bishop's promises of bread tomorrow. And if it's true they've sent word to Laigin for Fingal to come and settle that broken Kinfolk Oath, we may be marching straight into a fight we can't win.'

'Better an honest battle with blade and blood,' Cai told me, 'than this daily skirmish with suspicion and mistrust. Ambros would face anything now to be reunited with the Song-Sayer again. A lust for trust.'

'He blames me for causing him to set her aside,' I said. And I resented Ambros for it. Sometimes despised him. Sometimes pitied.

'He blames us all for one thing or another. Me, for allowing the Man-Dog to slip our lines at Corin-Mound. And Birch for failing to bring Fergna to the gathering.'

Behind us were the spear-hawks, running at their fast march and, beyond them, at the column's rear, Ambros with Owain Hawk-Beak and a dozen horsemen. 'And oh, Master Meridden,' Cai sighed, 'how I wish we had that braggart Birch Strong-Arm beside us now.' But Ambros would not even have Strong-Arm's name mentioned in his presence. Cai glanced over his shoulder to check that the line was not overly stretched. 'That just leaves the *medicus* in favour,' he said. 'Ambros claims he'd be dead now, if not for Hawk-Beak.'

Well, perhaps Ambros was correct in his belief. But me? I had my doubts.

*

A muster had been arranged to take place at Ruddy Bank, that neglected holdfast on the Hurdle's Flow that sits so neatly near the juncture of Headlands, Slavehold and Romaland. And, by the appointed gathering date at the Maius Dead Moon, many lords of the White-Wilds and beyond had assembled in the Skyhound's campaign tent – though it seemed to me there were almost as many war-masters here as spear-wielders. And confronting Rhun the Tall seemed to be the last thing on their minds.

'This Outlander has freed every slave within the lands you entrusted to him,' spat Cullough of Bright-Fields, his arm outstretched in Osla Big-Knife's direction. 'Does he not know it's called Slavehold for a reason?'

'My people need no slave,' the Saeson bristled back at him. 'Each family have one-plough land. Pay *feorm* to lord. All are free.'

'What sort of lunacy is that?' said Bran of Romaland. 'Such nonsense will spread faster than the Yellow Death.'

'The problem isn't whether we keep slaves,' Gereint Six-Fingers told them, 'but whether lands like this, so much nearer the main trade routes, and therefore relatively so much richer, should not be paying more in taxes to the province than the smaller and more remote lands like Windstorm. I don't speak for Windstorm alone, of course. But for Everfell too. Dunshome. Meirionshore.'

'Everfell speaks for itself here,' cried its lord, Alios. 'Though I suspect there are those who would wish it otherwise. My own people, and those of Meirionshore, remember well how my Lord Ambros rid us of the raiders who troubled our borders so long. We may be few in number, but we will play our part.'

'And, my Lord Gereint,' argued the Oak Seer Lore-Master, Utha White-Staff, 'if we do not seek justice for the slaughter of our herb-healers, spirit-speakers and song-sayers of Two-Tribes, the gods will damn us all, and these quarrels will not amount to a handful of seeds.'

Valor Bent-Back of Glusio's Land jumped to his feet.

'Yet we were promised help after the Cattle Pest,' he shouted. 'Where is it? That's what I need to know.'

'The Lore-Master's correct,' Ambros finally cried. 'There are demands on all sides, and no resources to meet them. Two foes to face as well now, it seems. Rhun in the west, in our own lands. Gwrgi Hard-Spear and his tame bishops to the north and east. They even have a name, I'm told. This Phalanx, as the bishops call themselves. And spin my name again. Red Slayer, they style me. While the Man-Dog rapes and burns at his leisure with his hired killers. We received word from Gift-Given this morning that even the Painted People ride with them. And where are the spear-hawks I was promised to deal with these threats?'

'We brought all that could be spared, Lord,' protested Valor. 'But at least we came. Yet where are the others? Where is Fergna Urcol's Son, my good neighbour? Fergna, who is too busy poking his own daughter to ride with us now. Fergna who so likes to raid the lands of my own Christ-followers. If he hates the bishops so much, why is he not here?'

'My Lord Ambros has told you why, old man,' spat Cullough. 'Those who would normally come in hope of reward know there is none to be had. Those who would come through duty to their fathers are too occupied with scraping a living from their own lands.' Then he turned upon Osla Big-Knife again. 'And slave-blades who might be here seeking freedom,' he yelled, 'know they only need to wait for even more Outlanders to arrive in our midst and they can get it for nothing.'

I remembered the meeting, of course, in the pot-house at Legion-Hold that myself and Cai had broken up. Cullough, Bran and Osla, plotting mischief with Fingal's sailing master, rather than a trade deal, as they had claimed. And I smiled now to see them each divided, one against the other, yet with a common enemy at least.

'There are many others who have missed the muster,' said Ambros, and winced with the pains in his gut. He glanced accusingly at Owain Hawk-Beak so that I thought, for a moment, he blamed the potions for failing to deal with his illness, but I then realised that Owain's father, Caradoc of Cerdeg's Edge, was also absent from the gathering. Another Christ-follower who would not ride against the bishops and this so-called Phalanx, I guessed. Or who had taken their gold. 'But the gods be praised,' Ambros continued, 'that we still have loyal friends to the south, at least. Aurelius of Two-Tribes. Iago of Sabrina-Rise. Brock of the Tusk and a contingent from Ogfran's Ring. All responded to the Red Spear. Gathering men as we speak to go north with us from Mammary as soon as we deal with this upstart, Rhun.'

Gereint Six-Fingers, Cullough and Bran leapt to their feet almost in unison, each with the same word on his lips.

'Mammary?' said Six-Fingers. 'We were told only that we needed to march as far as Mona's Isle!'

'And so you shall,' Ambros told them. 'Those others I've mentioned will be sufficient to deal with Gwrgi. 'And Aurelius promises men even from Domna's Deep, though we shan't rely on that. Yet there are others. Urien's Gift-Given spear-hawks from Westwood, Abundance, Glitter-Water and White-Havens. With both the Man-Dog and the Painted People at their borders, we shall not want for spears. There will be a reckoning now with all our foes.' He fell silent a moment, then seemed to remember some lesson of diplomacy. 'And, of course,' he concluded, nodding vaguely in the young man's direction, 'we are blessed to have Imris Cabul's Son among our host. All the way from Fast-River's Run. As soon as we are finished with Rhun, the rest of you may return to tending your lands. With my thanks, and with as much reward as we may gather along the way. Cai Blood-Taster will take his Shadow-Watchers, travel fast to Mammary itself and let Urien know I'm coming.'

It seemed strange to me that Ambros would so willingly split his meagre forces. But perhaps he understood that he was best to do so rather than have them simply drift away – a habit to which our war-hosts were always prone, even at the best of times. Or perhaps he still did not entirely trust some of them. And then, in addition, of course, as usual I had no idea of the plan that was actually in his mind.

We stood once more upon the Blood Shore, the sands firm beneath our feet, though this time the sickly sun was in our eyes and we faced across Long Battle Bay, as the invading legions of Paulinus and Agricola must once have done, from the Overmon side. There was this other difference too, of course, that Osla Big-Knife now stood with us, rather than against us, leading his mixed shield-press of Outlanders and local Slavehold men.

It was Third-Quarter-Moon Low Water, the channel barely awash and certainly no barrier to closing with our foes, whose numbers were almost evenly matched by our own. Eighty we had brought from Ruddy Bank, and facing us were thirty or so who had ridden with Rhun when I saw him at the Fortress of the Hammer-Fighters; a score of his old friends from Fairwater Maw, including some that I recognised as Malco's former spear-hawks; and a final few dozen clustered behind Fingal of the Five Stallions – come, indeed, it seemed, to settle the broken Kinfolk

Oath. These were men with the distinctive garb of the Laigin warriors with whom we had once spent time. Many of these sported the simply belted amber-dyed tunic, or stood almost naked except for the pigment-point marks adorning their limbs, chests and faces. Others wore boiled leather, similar to our own, and a couple followed Fingal's fashion, with stitch-plate vests. But all the Laigin fighters wore their hair long and dark, and each carried a stud-patterned shield much smaller than those we favoured this side of the Hibernian Sea.

'Mithras be praised,' I heard Bran grumble, 'we had so few problems of our own that Lord Ambros did us the courtesy of also bringing the Laigin folk down upon our heads.'

'I suppose,' replied Six-Fingers, 'you might say the same for those Laigin scum too. Have they truly not enough to worry about at home?' Then he turned to me. 'And that is the legendary Fingal of the Five Stallions, I gather. Will he fight, Master Meridden?'

'He lives for nothing else,' I smiled. 'Though I've never seen him do so without his war-cart.'

'But at least he was able to bring his weapons with him,' Bran laughed. 'Is he asking Rhun, do you think, why a warlord should come to battle without even a knife to his name? And will Lord Ambros be polite enough to let them finish their debate? If we wait much longer, the flow will make it impossible to reach them.'

It felt to me, also, that we had stood there beyond all logic, with the seaweed stink masking all other smells, and gulls screeching above our heads. But I thought I understood the Skyhound's reluctance. Two reasons. First, he seemed naturally disturbed by the spectators we could see at some little distance, outlined against the sky near the Mona's End hermitage – four riders and, without doubt, we knew their identities. Fat Bishop Deniol and the three women. The Song-Sayer was there. Near to him. Yet at such a distance too. And, second, Fingal had archers within his ranks. Far more than we ourselves possessed. Our slingers would be no match for them once we were struggling thigh-deep in the channel. If Ambros had been less afflicted by the Ravager, I believed, he would have launched us across the water much earlier. But, even so, here he came, trotting and prancing his pony down the line, the hem of his ring-mail coat jouncing and jingling against his knee, thinning red thatch blowing about his face, a fringed and beaded spear-cover sparkling as it rattled, slapped upon the pony's flanks.

Ambros was shouting his war cries, each in turn. For his Bear Clan of the Bough-Gatherer folk. For his own lands of the White-Wilds. For the whole of Westerlands Province. So that we began to beat our weapons upon shield-rims in response – and caused our foemen to do the same. The Skyhound's voice may have lost some of its strength but it still had the power to whip our battle-frenzy, to quell the shit-churn in our stomachs, to steady our shaking knees and, when he judged us wound sufficiently taut, he drew the Sword of Maximus, waved it once, scribing a full circle in the air, then reared his mount and urged it forward to the water's edge with his hound, Charger, bounding alongside.

Yet, on the farther bank, none moved. None except Fingal of the Five Stallions with a single companion, both of them striding down the strand towards our attack. And, of course, Fingal's advance halted our own, with only Ambros continuing, holding his pony mid-stream, brine eddying gently around its knees. Fingal splashed into the water as well, hefted one of his shafts and began a lengthy and passionate oration in his Gathelic. And it may have been impolite to break his concentration but that, I think, was precisely the Skyhound's intention.

'Wait!' Ambros yelled to the third man, plainly brought forth as an interpreter, for he was also an Incomer, though now living in Fairwater Maw. I remembered him. And he translated as Ambros continued. 'Please beg Lord Fingal,' he went on, 'to forgive this interruption, for I have no time to waste on such preliminaries. But if he has come here to issue the Champion's Challenge, you may tell him I accept it gladly. On three conditions. One, that should the outcome favour his cause, and that of his ally, Rhun the Tall, there should be no retribution against those who ride here at my side. And, two, that I should be buried on this northern shore of the Narrow Strait, where my spirit may forever gaze upon the forests of my childhood, upon the resting place of my kinfolk at Twin Sisters, and upon the snow-lipped ridges of the Giant's Tomb.'

'He expects to lose this fight?' Bran looked around him, confused, more than a little afraid, I think.

'A mere piece of theatrical rhetoric, perhaps,' I said, as Fingal turned to Rhun for guidance, and I saw the big man shrug, knowing that any such agreement would hold no water in the event of Ambros Skyhound's defeat.

'My Lord Fingal agrees,' cried the translator. 'But he asks for your third condition.'

'Simply this,' said Ambros. 'That if the outcome falls in my own favour, Rhun the Tall should surrender himself to my justice without the need for more blood to be shed here.' And it was a surprise to some of our number that Rhun should have agreed so readily. But then Rhun the Tall had no doubts about the likely outcome. Yet he had also not banked on the possibility that Ambros might not choose to fight in person, as was his right under the Champion Combat Lore. It was unusual, and the decision was greeted with some derision by our enemies, so that we heard again those same sorts of taunt, first hurled against us at the Valley of the Trees. Ambros *Cunnus Glasus*. Ambros Limp-Stick. Several others in a similar vein, while our own men fell silent and their ardour for battle was quenched. But it seemed that this, too, may all have been premeditated by Ambros for, in the instant that Rhun had accepted the last of his conditions, and without any word of command or debate, without Ambros even once having to turn his head, Osla Big-Knife stepped forward and swaggered to his side. 'Then know this also, Fingal of the Five Stallions,' Ambros cried. 'Fingal, whom I once counted a friend, and still do so to this day. Know that I swore a Kinfolk Oath to you in good faith. To return and help great Corpre mac Cormac in his struggle with the *Ui Dunlainge*. I even made the Christ-followers' cross-sign to seal the bargain. But no fault of mine that I could not yet fulfil that promise, and I remain happy to do so once the wounds to my own lands are healed. So you may still go in peace, if you choose, and no loss of honour upon your house. Though, should you decide to maintain your challenge, know also that the Kinfolk Oath makes it impossible for me to fight you in person, since that would simply leave a further blood-feud to be settled with your family. For this reason, should you insist on battle, it will be this man who shall act in my stead. A worthy man. He is the Saeson Lord of Slavehold. Osla by name, Henga White-Stallion's Son, from the lands which his people call Cantia.'

I heard Bran mutter under his breath, doubtless some remaining bitterness that it was Osla, and not himself or Cullough of Bright-Fields, who ruled the territory in question. But it was hard to hear his exact words, for the thing that started as a murmur in our ranks, the merest whisper of approval for Ambros Skyhound's pragmatism, began to grow in volume until the whole war-host was chanting Osla's name and the rhythmic thumping of weapons on shields rose to a thunderous crescendo. And I almost regretted that it so plainly left Fingal with no real choice in the matter. No more words were exchanged, and he simply dismissed his interpreter, turning his attention to the spear bundle he carried – one of each from the three styles he favoured, and which Ambros had subsequently also adopted. Osla carried spears too, though he seemed uncomfortable with them and, as Ambros trotted away from him, back to our lines, the Saeson clumsily launched a javelin in Fingal's direction. Not a bad cast, though it fell wide of its mark. Fingal, on the other hand, used his own twin-fletched dart, the *birin*, with great skill, moving quickly from side to side, feinting with the thing to distract Osla's guard until, at last, he perceived an opening. He hurled the shaft with such power that Osla was lucky to catch it on his shield. But the barbed blade pierced the hide easily, penetrated one of the cross-planks too, almost as far as the Saeson's chest. It made the shield so unwieldy that it had to be cast aside, leaving Osla only with his heavier spear and the long blade of his *saex*.

Fingal's second throw, with the slender *sleag*, whispered through the air, almost caught Osla unawares and, indeed, lanced a blood-spray slice from the top of his left shoulder, forcing a bellow of rage from the Saeson's lips. He staggered, turned to see where the spear quivered like a withy marker behind him, then leapt forward, with Fingal wading deeper to meet his charge. And there they struggled for the next punishing hour, exchanging blow for bruising blow, each gashed and gouged, while the waters slowly rose and roiled about them. Past their thighs and buttocks. To their waists and above. Until they were chest-deep in the flooding tide, their spears lost and floating downstream. The two men fought with their respective blades now, locked together, but barely able to strike without losing their footing. And Fingal was struggling to sustain the contest, the weight of his stitch-plate vest, the small oblong scales of iron dragging him down, forcing him to edge back, seeking the shallows. But he did not find them. Instead, he lost his balance, stumbled back, so that his head almost disappeared beneath the zealous waves. A simple second or two. Yet enough for Osla's sword-hand to free itself. The light glittered upon the *saex* blade as it fell, hacked into Fingal's face. Then again. Splash. Splash. And the sea turned to scarlet.

On the farther shore, a cry of despair rose among our enemies' ranks. Fingal's men started to follow the channel's flow, to dive into the waters, hoping at least to retrieve their warlord's corpse. At the same time, Rhun was shouting orders to the rest of his fragmenting band, ignoring the promise to surrender himself and urging his force westwards, back towards the Fairwater Maw.

'After them!' shouted Six-Fingers and began to force his spear-hawks to strip anything which might hamper them, to cross the channel in pursuit. 'They must not escape,' he yelled. Others began to follow, but Ambros seemed unconcerned. He certainly pressed his pony into the tide, belly-deep so that he could grasp Osla's wrist, help him back to the sandbank.

'Well done, my brother,' I heard him say to the Saeson and then, away to our left, a war-horn sounded. Rhun's warriors stopped short as, from the trees before them, a line of horsemen appeared. And, even from this distance, I could make out the features of Cai Blood-Taster, Cai of the Nine Lives, leading his Shadow-Watchers to cut off Rhun's retreat. Ambros had not sent them to Mammary after all, had used them instead in this covert operation. A secret shared with none but Cai himself. And Rhun the Tall may have escaped from Long Battle Bay once – but he would not do so a second time.

Chapter Thirty

Fairwater Maw and its dunes, I found, held too many memories for me. My first visit, dragged there by Deniol's monk-brothers so that I could be ransomed against Owen White-Tooth's duty oath to Malco. My first sight of Rigantona. My return there, after the mission upon which Malco had sent me to test the loyalty of Fergna Urcol's Son. The place where the Black Hags had tried to take me. The madness in the place after the Yellow Death had struck and folk there had stoned the latest Laigin Incomers, blaming them for the pestilence. And, of course, the death of Malco Battle-Shield at Ambros Skyhound's hands, in the fires of retribution. Yet, otherwise, it remained strangely unchanged. The holdfast still stood, surrounded by thickets of silver birch upon its promontory, protected physically by that double wall of timbers and sheer ditches and, spiritually, by the fabulously painted Memory Stone. And, below, the abandoned and depleted stones of the old legion fort, just above the harbour. The bathhouse remained in decent repair, however, and we had taken advantage of its facilities to rest and clean ourselves before assembling once more in the Great Hall. The long-benches were filled afresh with a mixture of anticipation from those who supported Ambros Skyhound, and resentment from duty-holders who did not.

'What is to be done with you, Cousin?' said Ambros, sprawling with exhaustion across the raised gallery's throne once occupied by Rhun's father. 'I told you at Legion-Hold, did I not, that if I ever found you within the boundaries of Westerlands, your life should be forfeit.'

Rhun was roped about his neck, the noose-end running down his back, binding his wrists. His men had been herded into slave-pens near the harbour. All except the Laigin men who had finally discovered Fingal's body, washed ashore at the narrowest part of the Strait – the same place where Cai and his Shadow-Watchers had crossed, it transpired –

and been allowed to sail home with it under their own Kinfolk Oath never to return. Whether they would honour that pledge remained to be seen, though I had no doubt that if they ever claimed a blood-debt, Ambros would no longer be there for them to seek revenge.

'Forfeit at whose hands, Skyhound?' Rhun snarled, trying to lift his head high enough to look Ambros in the eye, but hampered by his bonds. 'You look barely capable of doing it yourself.' It was a fair observation, though I knew that, even in his present condition, Ambros had still swum that morning in the Fairwater's cold shallows. 'And when the Ravager finally takes you,' Rhun went on, 'who will be left to rule here? What manner of warlord is it that leaves no heir to his lands?'

The question tightened a tension already palpable around the hearth pit. For each of the Prefect Lords gathered in the hall saw himself as standing on the verge of mastery over the White-Wilds at least, or the whole of First-Province at best. And I simply had no idea of the Skyhound's own possible solution to the problem.

'There are those here who could claim more right to your head than I,' Ambros replied, ignoring the point about inheritance. 'But not many. The Oak Seers alone may seek your sacrifice as blood-debt for those you butchered at Corin-Mound. And how many have you put to the skinning knife or the impaling pole since then, creature of the Man-Dog?'

The Lore-Master of the Mona's Isle Oak Seer guild nodded his approval, banged his staff upon the earth-pressed floor in agreement.

'Believe what you want, Limp-Stick,' said Rhun. 'Yet I had no part in that. And nor will I have any further part of Gwrgi Hard-Spear. He is no more a true follower of the Christos than you are.'

'I can attest to that,' cried fat Bishop Deniol. He was trussed in a similar way. Though a little apart, where Murgain and Rigantona were also bound, though to one of the hall's exquisitely etched upright ribbing crooks, rags stuffed into their mouths to gag them. I understood the necessity, for they had each, at the opening of proceedings, screamed down endless imprecations and curses on Ambros and all who rode with him. Yet I would have given anything to free Rigantona from here, to take her away with me. Despite everything.

'Well, Bishop,' Ambros sneered, 'you might be inclined to so swear, given your own part in those same atrocities. But who, here, might be foolish enough to believe you? And I, for one, have seen Rhun's own handiwork against my own kin. Against the defenceless folk of Twin Sisters who cry out for justice.'

'I would believe him, Lord,' said the Song-Sayer, stepping out from among the Oak Seer herb-healers and spirit-speakers, the word-weavers and matchmakers, the judgement-jurors and loss-layers. 'For our guilds have all heard the news. *Hard-Spear, Man-Dog, scourge of Two-Tribe lands,* she began to intone. *Sacred Three-Bridge slain too at his hands. Bane of oaken-law and holy strands.*'

'He has taken Three Bridges?' Ambros demanded.

'Not simply taken it,' said Deniol, keen to show himself also a bearer of valuable tidings. 'Slaughtered every Oak Seer he could find. And Ridge-End too. All through the Flavia. Committing acts of which I can barely speak. Burning all in his path.'

'Not all,' said Morgose. 'For he favours putting two things in particular to the fire. First, our sisters and brothers of the Oak Seer guilds. Or those from the older faiths.'

'And second,' I said, 'our own blessed books? Our libraries? But you, Bishop, would have no concern about that, I suppose. Anything which gainsays your Christos-god. Anything which glorifies the days before we were cursed by his presence. Do you deny it?'

'Why should I?' snapped the bishop. 'Though now this Gwrgi Hard-Spear seems incapable of distinguishing one codex from another. Even those upon which our monk-brothers have been working for many years are going to the torch. The Almighty has spoken to me, Lord Skyhound *Cuneglasus*. He has bidden me to follow a fresh path.'

'You should believe that too, Lord,' said Morgose. 'For, as we speak, the Man-Dog's war-host must be probing the borders of Gift-Given. Those other bishops see only a vision of the martyr, Mungo, before their eyes, and will not rest until Lord Urien and all his people have paid for that death. They have gold a-plenty. They purchase hired spears as they go. And my song-sayer brethren speak of another force for evil, sweeping south from the Pictoi lands towards the wall, and across it into lower High-Pass.'

Ambros turned to the Prefect Lords and duty-holders assembled in the Great Hall.

'You all know,' he said, 'they will not stop there. They will not rest until all our beliefs are destroyed. They are incapable of understanding what they demand of us. And that goes for this Bishop Deniol too. They suppose that everything we have ever believed, all that lore which has guided our steps for a thousand generations, which provides our roots to the land, our place within the pattern of life, can now be set aside at their whim. Yet you also know,' he went on, 'that I am dying. That I will soon no longer be able to bind you. And I had promised that, once we defeated Rhun and Fingal of the Five Stallions, you might all return to your lands. To continue the task of caring for our people. But, for my own part, I must journey north again. One last time, I fear. This Man-Dog must be destroyed. Other lords of Westerlands have pledged to join me at Mammary. Yet how many I do not know. So I must leave it to you, my friends. Return to your lands. Or join me. The choice is yours.'

He began to ease from the chair.

'And what about Lord Rhun?' said Valor Bent-Back. 'It would be a Christian act to absolve the punishment you promised. Perhaps give him into my secure custody?'

He never gives up, I thought. *Always hoping that Ambros will somehow see the light, convert to the Cross.*

'Rhun is a faith-breaker,' cried Bran of Romaland. 'Not to be trusted. And you think he will honour Valor simply because the old man is a Christ-follower? Banish him again and the serpent will simply pounce once more when he is ready.'

'And the witches,' said Gereint Six-Fingers. 'They were banished too. You must name their punishment also, Lord Ambros.'

I almost stepped forward, ready to advocate on Rigantona's behalf. But I saw that Ambros had seated himself afresh. His hand clawed at his stomach, but his voice was steady.

'Very well,' he said. 'You want judgements? Then these are my words. About Rhun Malco's Son, I say this. I can think of few men that I would rather slay. But I ask him now, this once, to consider the needs of our Kinfolk Clans. We face great threats, and we're too few to meet them all. And so, if he will accept this thing, I would offer him the guardianship of Mona's Isle and Overmon. What he does with them, before or after my death, is his own affair. I simply ask him to muster his war-band and march with me to defeat Gwrgi Hard-Spear if, as he says, he wishes to prove himself distanced from the Man-Dog. Not a Christian act, but a logical one. A correct one.'

'Is that punishment?' said Six Fingers. 'Most would say it was more akin to reward.'

'Sometimes punishment must be tempered by intelligence,' said Ambros. 'I think we need each other. For a while, at least.' He looked to Rhun the Tall for response, and I heard the fellow grunt, almost a laugh.

'Why should I not accept?' said Rhun. 'And I'll be at your side, Skyhound, until the end. If, for no other reason, than to savour the moment when the Ravager finally chews upon your soul. Yet I can serve you little without a weapon.'

The Song-Sayer's doom, of course, was still upon him and I realised that, Christ-follower though he might now be, the old ways still coursed through Rhun's blood too. And if they ran so thick within the veins of a creature like Rhun, perhaps there was more hope for our way of life than I had always thought. Perhaps some possibility that the Christ-followers might not have quite the grip they hoped upon our futures. And I was so wrapped in those thoughts that I hardly noticed Morgose slip to Osla's side.

'Might I borrow your blade, Champion?' I heard her voice sing, and Osla carefully placed his *saex* in her extended hands. For a moment, I wondered at her intentions. Revenge for the death of Einion Iron-Anvil? I thought not. But by then she had felt her way across the gather-hall until she touched the back of Rhun's head, fingered the noose and the rope that ran from it. Rhun held himself straight, upon his knees still, but his face grim with pride. And she sliced quickly with the blade, severed the ties that bound him, then helped him remove the hempen cords from his wrists, raised him to his feet. 'I place this weapon in your hands,' she said, laid the *saex* across his palms, 'and, in doing so, I release you from your *geis*.'

The hall erupted in consternation, and I thought I saw temptation flash a moment within Rhun's eyes as he held Ambros Skyhound's gaze.

'And punishment?' Ambros shouted above the clamour of divided opinion. 'What of this? For my Lord Gereint of Glusio has properly drawn attention to these others that I banished also. So, more judgements. First, that the Lady Morgose is absolved of all crimes previously laid at her feet. Second, that her sister, the Lady Rigantona...' He paused, looked at me briefly, long enough to spark some foolish expectation. Then dash it.

'That the Lady Rigantona shall be bound in marriage to Rhun Malco's Son, now Lord of Mona's Isle and Overmon.' He made no mention of Murgain, of course, though I doubt I could have heard him even had he done so. For I think I hated him more at that moment than at any other of our association. Yet he had still not finished. 'For a union with the Lady Rigantona,' he said, 'is a punishment I would hesitate to inflict even on the most bitter of my enemies.'

Cold flurries of debate and argument had blown around the Great Hall, and even kettles of Four Brothers Broth could not bring comfort to the protagonists. Yet, while the gathering supped on the root vegetable stew, Ambros had slipped away, assisted by Cai and the Song-Sayer, then beckoned me to follow almost as an afterthought, so that we crowded now within one of the small sleeping rooms. He was in pain, but not to the extent that he was prepared to let my own sullen mood go unremarked.

'For me, Master Mentor,' he bellowed, 'there is nothing I despise more than ingratitude. How many times must I make allowance for you? You come back from your mission empty-handed. With no new allies when I need them most. And now, what? You still lust after Rigantona, though she would chew your life to shreds and spit them out upon the straw.'

I seethed with possible responses, though it was Cai who interjected.

'There are many others out there, Lord,' said Cai, 'who will see the union of Rhun and Rigantona as a marriage of evils, a deadly alliance. A mistake.'

'They will likely be more deadly to each other than to our cause, my friend,' Ambros sighed. 'If we have any cause left, that is. Yet I heard just as many concerns about my concession to Deniol.'

'You have gifted him everything he ever wanted,' I said, glad of the chance to move conversation away from the subject of Rigantona. 'To make him Bishop of Westerlands, all First-Province. And gratitude? You think Deniol shall give you even a word of credit for your beneficence? The only thing I ever lusted after was to share your dream of a Greater Britannia. Yet where is that dream now if even you have lost faith in it?'

I could feel salt tears running down my cheeks as I spoke. Tears of frustration. That Rigantona was now even less attainable than she had ever been. That Ambros should have dismissed her significance to me so readily. That he should have been so correct about the fecklessness of my continuing desire for her. That his own life and dreams were slipping away and we could collectively do nothing to stop them.

'Dreams?' he gasped, convulsing as his agonies gripped him, and Morgose mopped his brow. 'Let me tell you about dreams, Master. There's a day I remember when I swam in the Ridge River. The water was clear and placid, the sand below me rippled in endless slender dunes. The sun shone more often in those times and cast my shadow upon the sand-bed bottom, though the shadow was not my own. It belonged to some other creature, a thing of the deep, a great fluid turtle edged all around with fine halos of golden light, its flippers like grasping claws, and themselves emitting rays of shimmering glow, which flashed across the river's floor. I imagined myself then as one of the spirit-speakers, those of the Oak Seers who commune with all the beasts of the seas and skies and lands. A wonderful illusion, Master. As much an illusion as those with which I've filled my life these past years.'

'There was never foolishness in your vision, Ambros,' I said, though I almost choked upon my words. 'And Deniol is – for the present, at least – separated from those other bishops still riding with the Man-Dog.'

'We give up then?' said Cai. 'Leave Gwrgi to his devices?'

'No,' said Ambros, 'but we must adapt. I no longer believe we can drive out the Christ-followers forever. But we can still slow their incursion. Use the time to preserve the best of our own values. Morgose has the thing by the tail.' He reached up and squeezed her hand. 'Much of the Christ-follower teachings have value. But I never needed their monk-brothers to lecture me on those things the Oak Seers have always known.'

'Then we must protect the Oak Seers from further harm,' said Morgose. 'They are, and must remain, the counter-weight to the Christ-following. The moon and stars to the Christ-followers' sun.'

'Sun?' said Ambros. 'I fear you give them too much credit. Have you heard the nonsense they spout about the creation? No Great Melody for the Christ-followers, my love. Denial of our fundamental belief that the threads of creation have no beginning and no end. Yet, to protect the Oak Seers and the spirit of our being, we must all play our parts.'

And he allocated new duties. Cai to ride with his Shadow-Watchers to Mammary, as originally planned. But now he would go in truth, to rouse and muster our friends, hold them together against our coming.

For himself, Ambros would remain in the White-Wilds a short while. There were places, he said, that he must visit once more, to briefly walk again the forests and ridges of his youth, though I doubted he still possessed the strength for any great exertion. In any case, I expected that his decision to remain was governed more by the need to make sure Deniol's scope for mischief was at least reasonably constrained.

'And might your wanderings take you, perhaps,' said Cai, 'towards the Bear Fort? That Vale of Wood-Temple where Birch Strong-Arm glowers in splendid isolation while our world falls apart.'

'We face challenges,' Ambros replied. 'Deniol must be made to see that we shall defend all faiths. Not his alone. The Man-Dog must be defeated, and our centres of lore and learning protected. And we need to further bind our lords and duty-holders to our purpose. You think any of this can be achieved with traitors like Birch in my camp?'

'Birch Strong-Arm may be many things,' I said. 'But no traitor, Lord.'

'No,' he groaned. 'Your own failings I can attribute to other causes, Mentor. Including those false allegations against the Lady Morgose.' He squeezed her hand again while, I recall, I began to stammer out some foolish protest, though he waved it aside. 'Yet Birch, I see now,' he went on, 'must have deliberately ignored his orders to bring Fergna to our aid. And who else was in a position to help the Man-Dog slip through our net? He has long bristled over my decision to place Slavehold in Osla's hands. And a thousand other grievances seethe within him.'

There seemed no point in pressing this any further, though I still harboured my own suspicions about treachery.

'And me, Lord?' I asked. 'Are my own failings so heinous that I'm not to be entrusted with anything further?'

'For now, Master Meridden,' he said, 'your road lies east. To Legion-Hold. Take a small escort and make sure the Lady Morgose arrives there safely. Tell Hawk-Beak he should gather his potions. Prepare batches of my medicaments. The rituals of the spirit-speakers and herb-healers are well enough, but it shall be Hawk-Beak's poisons, I think, that might fortify me on the road north.'

Chapter Thirty-One

I shared my fears with Morgose as we travelled the Eleven once again, in company with much of the war-band, and it surprised me somewhat that she neither retained any resentment from my advocacy against her, nor showed much surprise at my conclusions on the subject of potential traitors. And so we agreed that I should act as the Skyhound's eyes in Legion-Hold, and she his ears. Though, when we arrived at that city, our senses were assailed by more than we had anticipated. A series of events and tragedies, which had kept Cai, contrary to his orders, from advancing on Mammary.

First, news from the south, where Osla's father, Henga White-Stallion, had died and been succeeded by the elder son, Octan Oxen-Strong. He had instantly pronounced himself Lord of Cantia, declared that Land of Hosts to be Saeson territory, with the new Saeson name, born again as a Christian kingdom, from which all other faiths were proscribed.

'Lord Cabul therefore insists you return to Fast-River's Run,' the messenger told young Imris.

'To what purpose?' Imris demanded. 'Why should matters in the Land of Hosts, in Cantia, trouble my father? Is there more?'

The weary messenger, still caked with the mud-splashed evidence of his journey, stared around our hastily convened gather-hall assembly, but cast his glance downwards when he set eyes upon Osla Big-Knife.

'You ride long way,' said the Saeson, 'to say little. Speak, man. More news? My brother? You need no fear. Only small love lost between Osla and Octan.' In truth, there also seemed to have been little love lost between Osla and Henga either, the Saeson accepting word of his father's passing with barely more than a nod of the head. 'Speak!' he demanded.

'Very well, Lord,' the messenger replied, though he was shaking with fear. 'But the news is grim,' he stammered. 'Still without verification. Yet Lord Cabul received word that your brother has recalled Bishop Elbios from the Phalanx Council, allied himself with others from the Fenlands to launch a new holy war to the east and north of Fast-River's Run. The great libraries at Bridge-Fort and War-God's Fort are gone, burned to ashes, and all members of the Oak Seer guilds killed along their route too.'

I felt myself stagger at the enormity of the man's claim, my mind unhinged a little, I think. All that knowledge. The collected wisdom. And the room stilled, stunned into silence.

'And my father fears they will turn on Fast-River's Run?' said Imris. 'Yet why should they? He's a Christ-follower himself, is he not? Perhaps he even welcomes these barbarisms. But I do not, and nor shall I return there. My place is here, at the side of Ambros Skyhound and all others who resist this curse. The big question, my lords, is whether we may trust the presence of Octan Oxen-Strong's brother here among our number. Can brothers truly be so different?'

Osla may have been short and stocky but, as you have seen, he could move with all the speed of the forest boar he so resembled. So that, almost before we had realised it, he had sprung from his seat and flung himself the twenty paces between, to grip Imris Cabul Son's throat and heave him bodily up one of the hall's wooden columns, spitting imprecations in his Outlander tongue.

Cai and some of the others leapt to separate the two men before blood was shed. Turmoil now replaced the silence, Prefect Lords screaming into each other's faces, and duty-holders almost coming to blows. Christ-follower divided against Mithras-worshipper or Oak Seer-faithful. Friends of the Saeson against those who still resented his power. Loyal supporters of Ambros against those with grudge and grievance. Yet I noticed that Owain Hawk-Beak held himself aloof from the affray, remained upon his bench, the ghost of amusement upon his lips. But, above the noise, one voice spoke clearer than all the rest. It was Morgose singing the Lay of Lir in cadences that resonated around the rafters.

Sweet water, I gave you, banished thirst. Children of the Lake Sea, your father set you free.

Mountains of rock I made to guard you, hold back the lake I laid. Walls of ebon and jade.
Yet no buttress can guard against fate, nor jealousies so great as Danu's sister-hate.
Such hate may breach the wall, flood your world. So you must save it all, Deolu, straight and tall.
Deolu, favoured son, build the craft, complete the task undone, before the floods to run.
Carry all beasts aboard, start anew. Two by two shall reward the cautious husband's hoard.
Twelve moons will wax and wane, voyage long, before land appears again. Great peaks arise through rain.
Isles of Fair Presence find. Name them so. Protect them for your kind. Leave jealousies behind.
Children of Lir, stand true. Never fail, nor falter in this view. Fair Presence lives through you.

The words resonated through each of us too. All of us who spoke the Cousins' Tongue. All who had been raised with the creation tales of the Oak Seers. All who were rooted in the endless whorls and patterns of the Great Melody. She shamed us into silence and, when I looked again, Owain Hawk-Beak had vanished from the assembly.

The second storm of malevolent news broke around us upon the Calends of Octubres. It was getting uncomfortably close to the end of the campaigning season and Cai had still not been able to extricate himself from Legion-Hold's fractious divisions. But he was about to finally leave for Mammary when travelling merchants brought word that the Yellow Death had struck Fast-River's Run once more. The population, they said, was being devastated, all through the south and, as usual, it was the more crowded settlements, towns and holdfasts of our Kinfolk Clans that suffered most, while the Black Hags seemed blind to those more scattered homesteads of the Outlanders. But one thing was certain. The Black Hags were running abroad like stampeding beasts. And panic fled before them through our streets, fear that the merchants might have brought more with them than simple trade goods and intelligence. Two of them were stoned to death before Osla could restore order but, beyond that, there was nothing to do but wait. Wait and see whether the pestilence had journeyed so far north. Yet, for once, fortune seemed to favour us and, a half-moon passing with no symptoms, Cai finally set out upon the road.

'A hard winter ahead of us,' he said, and glanced at the iron-forged clouds pressing down upon Legion-Hold's Leftgate, where his riders were saying their farewells to wives, lovers and children. Though I knew he was worried about far more than the weather.

'And, when the winter's done, an even worse new-growth,' I replied. 'Famine in the south, riding right behind the Black Hags. Nowhere for folk to go but down here. Or over the Southern Channel to Across-the-Sea.'

'Here?' said Cai, and waved for his Shadow-Watchers to mount. 'Will any of us still be alive to celebrate Bright Fire, d'you think?'

I patted his pony's neck as he vaulted into the saddle-fur. A dark ember settled in my throat, for we all now saw our own fates linked directly to that of Ambros.

'He grows weaker with each moon that passes, Cai. You know that. I'm only surprised he's survived the Ravager so long. We'll be lucky if he's able to lead us through this war-trail into the north. But it must surely be his last. Yet not yours, nor mine, I think.'

'Then he must name the man who will lead us when he's gone. And where is Ambros now, anyway? The people need him, Mentor. Can you imagine how it will be without him?'

Oh, I could imagine. Certainly. I could see it as plain as day. The roads, clearing of snow, but clogging with starved survivors from the south. Our Kinfolk Clans in the north struggling to accommodate the influx, while our Prefect Lords fought for their individual supremacies. Our Isles of Fair Presence crying out for repair and revitalisation, yet the wisdoms that may have helped us provide such development now burned to ashes. People desperately in need of spiritual fortitude, the certainty of their roots, but having the foundations of their beliefs and hopes shaken by the Christ-followers – blamed for the disasters that befell them, encouraged to meekly accept their fate, go down into the dark, on the promise of milk and honey in the afterlife. And no Ambros to inspire our responses, our dreams.

'The Song-Sayer,' I told him, 'has a view that the greater the dread, the better will be the outcome. We may not have Ambros with us next year, but perhaps the gods will grant us a new leader who can carry his vision into reality. So, meanwhile, I prefer to imagine you and me at the pot-house, supping heather-beer and arguing over a game of Throne-Sense about what a pair of old women we've become.'

He laughed then, tugged on one of his straw-coloured hair-braids.

'I'll hold you to that game whatever happens, Master Meridden,' he shouted, kicking his pony towards the open gates, 'when we meet in Mammary.'

'Then you'd better get some practice, my friend. For you've never beaten me yet.'

He was away, his men following him out onto the Two, and I almost ran after him. Cursed myself. I had meant to ask him how much of the Skyhound's revised plans he may have shared with Owain Hawk-Beak. Yet I had forgotten to do so.

'Gone then?' Owain looked over his shoulder at me, though his hands continued to work independently at the bench, like a gorse-spider spinning its web.

'The Shadow-Watchers?' I explored the scrolls stacked within his *armaria*. 'Yes. Gone. We'll be following them to the muster, of course. As soon as Ambros is back. But you know that, I suppose. From Cai?'

The fish-oil lamps cast only a feeble glow across the small chamber, which served as Owain's dispensary. Shelves and bottles. Spirit crucible and mixing jugs. Mortar and pestle. Measuring spoons and bronze scales. Cabinets and storage chests.

'I know as much as anybody else in Legion-Hold, Master Mentor. I just hope that Lord Skyhound's supply of medicaments has been sufficient. I did not expect him to be gone so long.'

'What fortune that your potions help keep him alive.' I tried to follow his work, observe the secret of his concoctions but, as usual, he guarded his prescriptions jealously, throwing a cloth over his ingredients before turning to face me.

'We all play our part, Mentor. Osla Big-Knife and his wardenship of Slavehold. The Song-Sayer and her dream-spinning. Yourself and the Academy. Such wonders your *ingeniatore* have worked upon the roads. The water supplies too. A true blessing. Me too, I suppose. A humble gift for palliative care.'

'And Cai,' I said. 'Where should we be without his Watchers?'

His lips parted in something resembling a grin.

'What is it you want with me, Master Mentor?'

'Your father must have been disappointed when you abandoned your vows as a monk-brother. Such a devout Christ-follower. Does it not anger him that you gave up the Church in favour of becoming the Skyhound's *medicus*?'

'It was the Church that first introduced me to the skills of Celsus. Why should my father regret my use of the healing, which Almighty God placed within my hands?'

'Lord Caradoc makes no secret of his preference for a Christ-follower to be High Lord. Yet here you are. A Christ-follower yourself. And helping to keep alive the very antithesis of your father's vision. Your own vision too, perhaps. And how fortuitous that you had the Numidian, Masul the Emissary, to supplement your education for so long.'

'You speak in riddles, Mentor. I fail to see the link.'

'Perhaps there is none,' I said, though I remembered the Numidian's words. His confession of an associate within the Skyhound's inner circle. His refusal to either admit or deny that Morgose had been guilty of the charges against her. The obvious fact that, with Morgose still in exile, and the Numidian sailed away, the treachery had continued. Was I supposed to believe that it was Birch Strong-Arm? And I was just wondering whether I should simply put the thing to him direct, as I had debated with the Song-Sayer, when I heard the knocking at the street door – the knocking that I had contrived with Morgose as a distraction, as an alternative way of testing our fears, but which I had given up hope of hearing. 'Shall you not answer?' I asked him.

He stared at me a moment, chewed upon his lip, then gave me that crooked smile again before a final glance at his covered bench. Then he was out into the small atrium, his steps loud upon the slabs as he made for the entrance corridor.

Not a moment to lose, and I made a mental note of the way he had draped the cloth, lifted it to see what he had been doing. Jars of dried powders. Roots. Vials of liquid. His mixing bowl. The small measuring balance.

I quickly checked off the ingredients, as I remembered them. For relief of pain, mandragora and papaver juice. For a sleeping draught, henbane and that tincture of belladonna, the Death-Berry. And, to help combat the Ravager itself – the *karkinos* – a bottle of precious liliacum, almost empty now, and certainly far from fresh, as well as garlic and absinthium. They were all there, as they should have been. Yet I noticed one more small jar, its lid still set to one side. A fine, white powder. Arsenicum. It had many uses, of course. But none that I could associate with treatment of the Ravager. And then there were those symptoms displayed more frequently of late by Ambros. His loss of strength. The tendency towards confusion. Those bouts of paralysis. Was I wrong about this? Had I not read a text of Dioscorides, which described those things as the effects from a slow application of arsenicum? It chilled me to the bone. Just the slim possibility that this might be something more than simple betrayal.

I listened, satisfied myself that Owain was still in conversation at the street door. The voice of Morgose too, her words indistinguishable. Yet I knew she would use her skills to hold him there a while longer. So I set the arsenicum back in its place. Carefully. Then draped the cloth across the table in as close an imitation as I was able to the way Hawk-Beak had left it.

What else? I could hardly accuse him on the basis of the arsenicum alone – a substance I could have found in the stock of any apothecary. But on the same table as Owain's preparation for the medicaments? It filled me with dread, though I knew there was no time to dwell on its implications just then, and I continued my search. Nothing out of place on the shelves. A hasty and nervous exploration of one cabinet, then another. Little to attract my attention. A quick lifting of a chest lid. Only Hawk-Beak's clothes inside, so far as I could tell. But the second chest was locked, and I remembered seeing a bunch of keys hanging in the larger cabinet.

I peered out into the open space of the atrium, saw that Owain was still at the far end of the corridor on the opposite side, still holding the door ajar. I could not see Morgose herself from here, but Hawk-Beak's voice was raised now. Angry. I heard him say the word "traitor" and then, with no warning, he quickly turned his head, looked in my direction. I ducked back inside the room, thought that he could not possibly have seen me in the gloom and when I was satisfied that they were still in conversation, I ran to the cabinet, found the keys and returned to the locked chest. The mechanism was stiff, noisy when I finally shifted the thing, and the damned lid squealed like a stuck pig when I lifted it. Owain's campaign kit. The pieces of his shoulder-pole. A couple of wool blankets. Hooded cloak. Cooking pan and duck-handled spoon. Red-clay drinking cup. His sword, swaddled in fleece, pampered, precious. The netting bag with his lamp, writing tablet, dice pot and a leather coin pouch. And one of those broad cowhide satchels in which we all carried our most personal possessions.

I was drawn to the satchel, eased it from the chest, then fumbled with the fastening. In the silence, I lifted the flap, plunged my hand inside. There was a cloth-wrapped Christ-cross, wrought in iron. A winter tunic. Helmet liner. New sponge-stick. A couple of ancient bronze coins, bearing the Greek letters *Chi* and *Rho*. A thumb-sized ceramic fish, also Greek lettering forming the familiar acrostic that the Christ-followers valued. And, at the bottom, a small bundle. Message sticks. Blanks. No Tree Script yet notched upon them. But the familiar symbol on each one. That small circle, six smaller marks etched around the outside, the upper one larger than the other five. It nagged at me, as it had done when I first saw it. Yet now, in the stillness, it came to me. Something to do with the proximity of those Christ-follower icons. A turtle. Symbol of the legionary god, Mercury.

In that quiet gloom, the hairs pricked upon the nape of my neck.

Quiet.

The realisation. I could no longer hear voices. The shiver up my spine. The knowledge that I was no longer alone.

He hit me hard. Two-fisted, I think. Sent me sprawling but, mercifully, not senseless. Not quite. Yet before I could move, he was on my back. Bigger than me. Younger. Stronger. His weight pressed me into tiles still smelling of the kiln, and his arm was around my neck, the crook squeezing my throat and his other hand pushing my head down, into the strangulation. Burning in my chest as I fought for breath. Vision reduced to mere pinpoints of light. Hearing almost gone except for an empty echo in my ears. I tried to reach behind me. To grip any part of him upon which I might inflict pain. And I kicked backwards. But all feeble. Impossible.

'You could not leave well alone, could you, Mentor?' I heard Hawk-Beak snarl, though from some point in the far distance.

The pinpoints of light faded to nothing. Yet I still tasted blood in my mouth. And the image which kept bringing me back was the memory of my first encounter with Deniol. The *monasterios* above Ridge River. Something he had said. Though it would not come to me through Owain Hawk-Beak's grunting, which I felt rather than heard. His arm was tightening again, insane pressure behind my eyes as though they might burst from their sockets.

Slipping away. I could feel myself slipping away.

And when the pressure finally relaxed, I thought it must be over. For there was the strange sensation that I was buried. No arm around my neck. But a huge weight upon my head, darkness all around me, and my face pressing down through the tiled floor. Then the heaviness shifted, writhed and groaned, finally rolled from me so that, when my eyes cleared, I was looking into those of Owain Hawk-Beak. There was pleading in them, and the arm with which he had so recently tried to choke me was now reaching over his own shoulder, seeking for something I could not see. But I managed to roll away from him, saw Morgose behind us, one hand upon the workbench, the other stretched in front of her, tickling the empty air and her head cocked to one side.

'Mentor?'

'Still here,' I croaked.

'My powers of persuasion weren't sufficient to give you more time, I fear,' she said.

Owain was still writhing on the floor.

'Take it out,' he cried, and I crawled to his side, saw the thing that his fingers sought. The grip of a small dagger, up to its guard in the upper portion of his spine.

'Your blade, Song-Sayer?' I gasped.

'Only a fool would be abroad these days without one.'

I was tempted to make some comment about my good fortune that she had struck in the right place, but I chose instead to simply oblige Owain Hawk-Beak and ease the knife from his back, tossed it across the room.

'My legs,' he moaned, and I saw that his lower body held that unnatural inertia which marked those paralysed in battle.

'I found these,' I said, picking up the message sticks and placing them in the Song-Sayer's right hand.

'The symbol...' Morgose ran a fingertip over the inscription. 'We never identified it.'

'Turtle, I think. Mercury's turtle. We had it wrong. All the time I swallowed the Numidian's story about being an emissary for Justinian. He was lying. Or not telling us the whole truth at least.' She urged me to explain. So I did. That first conversation with Deniol. The new Father of their Church in Rome, who had chosen the name Yohannes Secundus. Because his true name was Mercurius. Mercury. 'Masul is an emissary of their Papa,' I said. 'And this was his creature.' I kicked Owain's legs, though there was no reflex in them.

'My duty to the Lord Yesu and God Almighty,' he groaned.

'To poison the Skyhound?' I said. But I knew his motive, remembered when he had first come to us. Before the fight at the Blood Shore, at Long Battle Bay. He had conveniently been waiting at the hermitage. Waiting to see the light. To join Ambros Skyhound's cause. Deniol's weapon. And we should have expected it.

'To hasten the fate to which God had already sentenced him. To speed the work of the *karkinos*.'

'Poison?' whispered Morgose. 'But it was me who sought him out. At the *monasterios*. I asked him to lead me to Ambros.'

And me, I thought, *who first suggested he might turn his skills to poisoning. Against Rhun and Osla Big-Knife. All that long time past, when we had them holed up in Legion-Hold.*

'He was waiting to be sought, I think.' I told her. 'He would have come to us in one guise or another. And yes, poison. Arsenicum in his potions. Not enough to raise suspicions, naturally. That would not have served their purpose. Just sufficient to shorten his poor life still further. So the bishops could claim his death as punishment for his want of faith.'

She wept then. Short, racking sobs of sheer anguish.

'My cross,' Owain whispered. 'Let me kiss it. Hold it.'

I wished I could feel anger against him. But I did not. Just numb. Thankful to still be alive. So I went back to the satchel and found the cloth-wrapped crucifix again. I unwrapped it, touched it to his lips. But when he reached for it, I snatched it from his grasping fingers, gripped the upper portion as though it were a dagger, and this its handle. I wondered for a moment whether I should feel whatever power it wielded for those Christ-followers. But it was just a length of cold iron. So I set the foot of the crucifix against his eye, and rammed it down into his brain with every ounce of strength I still possessed.

Chapter Thirty-Two

The muster at Mammary was a strange affair, marked by those who obeyed the summons – and those who did not. Octubres Dead Moon, and Ambros made his grand entrance in the new war-cart which had been the reason for his delay in joining us at Legion-Hold. It had a second purpose now, of course, since he could barely stand without assistance and I doubt he would have stayed on a mount even had his fading life depended upon it. Yet the *carrio* had been fashioned with care, a bench between the side arches upon which he could rest during the journey. The wood-woven floor platform was especially well-sprung, with the goat-willow suspension ropes, upon which it sat, braided to make the travelling more comfortable, while a half-moon canopy kept out the worst of the weather. The canopy had been taken down, of course, for the occasion, but its frame still provided a useful support against which Ambros could lean with some semblance of normality – though his condition must have been a shock to those who had not seen him for some time. Still, his eyes remained sharp as he surveyed his forces: those who had marched north with us. Imris Cabul's Son; Osla Big-Knife; Gereint Six-Fingers of Windstorm; Bran of Romaland; Cullough of Bright-Fields; Rhun the Tall – though his recent adhesion to the Skyhound's cause was still shrouded with suspicion; and Valor Bent-Back of Glusio. Those also who had awaited us in Mammary's holdfast. Iago Morn's Son of Sabrina-Rise. Aurelius of Two-Tribes. Prosperity's Brock of the Tusk. And it was upon Brock that the Skyhound's smile lingered before he spoke.

'Wife-father,' he said, 'it's good to see you at our side again.'

I wondered whether it was the confusion of his illness. Perhaps the arsenicum. Or maybe Cara White-Blossom stood beside him just then, to remind him of the bond that had once united her kinfolk with his own. That loved, lost and nameless child of their youthful union.

'And, in my daughter's name,' Brock replied, 'I stand once more in your service, Lord Ambros.' He stressed the title, as though he needed to do so, any previous animosity between them set aside.

Ambros smiled.

'Never fear,' he said. 'There is fight in me yet, as you shall see. And the traitor-serpent is now driven from our camp, finally. So wrong chance banished from it also.'

'Is it true, Lord?' said Valor. 'What they say about poison?' It must have been difficult for him. A Christ-follower himself, yet now those rumours abroad that the assassin may have been acting in the name of the very Church to which he had been converted.

'Somebody once told me,' cried Six-Fingers, 'you should always beware if one of those charlatans tells you to trust him because he's a *medicus*.'

'Good advice,' said Ambros, 'though a little late in the day. And I hold no grievance against your faith, Lord Valor. Only against those who hide behind it for their own ambitions. Yet even those are honest enemies.' He had no need to spell out the corollary. That the worse foes were those who feigned allegiance but failed the final test. Fergna Urcol's Son, the self-styled Lord Protector, the *Vorteporigas*, of South-End. And now Hawk-Beak's father, Caradoc of Cerdeg. 'But we will face them soon,' Ambros continued. 'A good beginning.' He made a sweeping gesture with his arm, open hand embracing the three hundred who already stood around him. 'Yet at Moon's Glow, Urien of Gift-Given awaits us. Let's hope he does something now to atone for the mayhem he heaped upon us with Mungo's murder. But, that aside, according to his runners, a war-band also in the charge of Cador Pale-Meadow too, the adopted son to Rhodri of Clud's Vale. Master Meridden's nephew.'

He had grown to manhood since I saw him last.

'And how is she, sister-son? Your mother?' I asked Cador when we finally tracked him to his camp. The Clud's Vale men had lost no time upon their arrival in pursuing a group of raiders who had already laid waste to entire swathes of northern Abundance and southern Glitter-Water.

'Her husband treats her like a simpleton,' he snapped. 'Did you not know the manner of the man before you settled the match?'

'Yet he trusts you with his war-host,' I said, knowing it for a limp-weed response.

'Thirty horsemen,' he laughed. 'That's all he would trust to me. And we crossed the trail of the Painted Folk three times on our way here. They're out there somewhere. Thrice our number, Uncle. Maybe more.'

Then those rumours were true also. That the Pictoi had allied themselves with the Man-Dog. They might have no love for the Christ-followers, but they always knew an opportunity for plunder and slaves when they saw one.

'You can have faith in Lord Ambros,' I told him. 'He is a great warlord.'

'Truly?' said Cador. 'My spear-hawks thought him a wraith when they first saw him. Believed him one of the Deathless. He cannot even stand unaided, it seems. The war-cart is impressive but it fools nobody. And he is surrounded by men who would plainly just as soon see him slain. That creature, Rhun. And the one who calls himself Six-Fingers. Is there good news in any of this?'

And there was none. Three days later came word that the second of Urien's great holdfasts, at Peak Fort, upon the Wall, had been destroyed by those same raiders. Worse, Lord Urien had only recently built a new hall there and – for better safety, as he had believed – relocated the Great Library of Moon's Glow within its timber walls. It had been a true wonder, they said. Yet now it was gone. The only blessing? That the Pictoi had spared the Oak Seers. But that was little consolation for the horror still awaiting us.

The enormity of the library's loss continued to haunt me. It had been a repository for so much of our collective memory. Lord Urien had many faults, among them his abhorrence for the continued use of the Common Speech, so that he had shunned everything but the accumulation of codex, scroll and calfskin parchment upon which the Cousins' Tongue was inscribed. So there, at Peak Fort, you could find the entire works of our greatest song-sayer, the recently deceased Tugri Iron-Brow. Or the *Five Eagles* of Talon Muse-Maker. Dozens of other composers of praise-poems. But Urien had insisted too on maintaining the practice of his Oak

Seer judgement-jurors in recording, also in the Cousins' Tongue, each and every verdict determined in land disputes, matrimonial claims, civil misdemeanours and blood-price settlements. And not the Cousins' Tongue alone but copies of holy texts in Gathelic too. A version of that sacred scroll they called the *Battle Ward*, the written Hymn of the Great Melody, which Urien was wont to wear about his neck for the gods' protection.

All gone. And I wept for it.

But that morning I had helped Ambros bathe himself in the Rushing River, along which our forces were spread. It was too cold to even touch, let alone for immersion, and he was soon blue with the chill, joked that at least it gave him some colour. Yet he insisted that the swimming was his main line of defence against the Ravager. That and his diet. Nuts and berries mostly, depending upon the season. In truth, of course, he could no longer swim at all, but the self-deception of plunging into the waters was perhaps sufficient to achieve the same effect within his mind. And he seemed at least somewhat stronger, now that we had halted the accrual of arsenicum within his system. Less frequent confusions. His limbs less prone to paralysis.

'Still dreaming of Rigantona, Master?' His teeth chattered so much that the sentence came out like the beat of a silversmith's hammer.

'I never understood why, if she hated you so much, she did not simply resist the marriage.'

'Her mother's influence, I think,' said Ambros. 'Another thread in the fabric she wove.'

'And Hawk-Beak?'

'Better not to mention his name, my friend.'

There it was again. "Friend." I was not certain I understood the meaning of that word. Something I associated with almost none except Cai of the Nine Lives. And I was still pondering this strange game of relationships when we had wrapped Ambros in his heaviest check-weave, helped him on the paths back to his tent. But the sense of doom touched us all, long before we arrived there. A quiet broken only by the mocking cacophony of a rookery. A mist, which wove through the woods like a legion of the lost with its banners flying. The spear-hawks who could not look us in the eye, and fell back in shame at our approach. The duty-holders and clan lords gathered in a knot, but alarmingly and uniquely silent.

I had been thinking of Cai, so perhaps it helped me identify him. For, the gods knew, when the gathering parted there was little enough about the sight that greeted us to recall the man I had last seen a sennight earlier, when he had set out with his scouts to find Gwrgi's army.

My brain screamed, and an iron lump filled my guts. For the charred and blistered, headless remains of that brave man had been lashed to his pony, and the terrified beast still bucked and skittered, eyes wild with a madness which, I think, I had already begun to share.

The animal had been led back to us by one of Cai's Shadow-Watchers – a warrior I recognised. Just about. They had spared him so that he could deliver Cai. A message for us. But they had not released the poor bastard until they had gouged out one of his eyes, sliced the ears from his head, and amputated each of his fingers so that he was almost senseless from blood loss. Still, he was just strong enough to tell us the story when the herb-healers had done all they were able for him.

Gwrgi the Man-Dog, of course. He had trapped Cai and most of his men. Held a great ceremony to celebrate. Bishops there to bear witness and bless their rituals.

'They spitted him,' wept the Shadow-Watcher. 'Like a pig. But carefully. So he should not die. Revived him before they set the spit above a fire. Seared him. Until his flesh bubbled. And each time he lost consciousness, they revived him again. Nine times. One for each life of his Praise Name. For three days and nights they tested him. Songs for his valour. For he would not scream out. Even though, each time, they cut parts from his body as my Lord Cai was made to watch. The Man-Dog…' The Shadow-Watcher faltered. 'Before he took his head. He feasted upon him – while he still lived.'

The lament that Morgose made for him still sings in my memory. It cuts most often through the crazed drooling which so often now afflicts me. And we sang it, all together, that morning, when we finally faced Gwrgi across the brook they called the Burning Stream. Another irony. For it ran no more than a day's march from Peak Fort where the Great Library had so recently been torched. And it was, too, within a few spear-casts of the place where our enemies had roasted brave and loyal Cai to his cruel death. Yet it had always borne that name. Something to do with the illusion it created. Fire and flame within the waters from the ore-rocks over which they tumbled.

The Burning Stream. And the only warmth of that place, its name. A cold November day, when we should all have been huddled at our hearth-pits rather than shivering here in our wet woollen wrappings, smelling like damp dog's fur.

We were few in horsemen, while Gwrgi's ponies were plentiful, almost as numerous as our entire force. For we did not face one war-host but three, spiked across the ground below a holdfast – Long-Rock, I think it was named – on the ridge opposite our own. From my place in the shield-press, I could see each of them plainly enough, for they had formed on that higher land above the low-lying fog which presently obscured the stream and fording place between our positions.

To the left, Gwrgi and his raiders, many on raven-black mounts, gathered about a gruesome standard – Cai's head upon a spear, brandished aloft in mockery each time we chanted his praise names and stamped our feet on the frost-hard turf to the rhythm of the Song-Sayer's lay.

Against our front, a mixed force of spear-hawks, those warriors hired by the bishops' gold, and as many Outlanders there as Gwrgi's own duty-holders from Craven-Peak and High-Pass.

To the right, another cavalry – the Painted Folk of the Pictoi lands on their shaggy horses while, behind them, the bishops with their crosses, their entourage of monk-brothers. They sang some Christ-praise hymn in the Latin, barely audible over the cries of our deep-throated callers and our own less-than-harmonious responses, but still strangely haunting, almost beautiful, soaring and swooping through that vale, otherwise only disturbed by an occasional buzzard's shriek.

Ambros had chosen our terrain carefully, the Burning Stream across our front and our left protected by quagmire, which spread all the way to the Rushing River itself, somewhere beyond our vision. At the edge of this swamp, on the nearest firm slope, a small body of our horsemen – brought north by Brock of the Tusk, Iago Morn's Son and Aurelius of Two-Tribes.

Away to my right, and at some distance, our remaining horses held a position on the open plain, below a rocky and forested outcrop protecting our rear. From that position, Imris Cabul's Son and my sister-son, Cador Pale-Meadow, would guard us, we prayed, from any attempt by the Pictoi to use the next eastward crossing-place and turn or crush our flank.

And, in the centre, straddling the road, which ran behind us, southeastwards, to Peak Fort and the Wall, he had planted our main hope – all our slingers and spears, myself included, formed in a hollow square. Lord Urien commanded here, with his own Gift-Given warriors forming the square's sides, and the rest of us – the war-bands of Rhun, Osla, Valor, Gereint Six-Fingers, Bran and Cullough – ranked along the front and rear. But all under clear instruction that we hold this formation at all cost, so that, hopefully, from the opposite rise we might appear more numerous than the three hundred we were in reality.

Neither was this our only ruse, for Ambros had asked the Song-Sayer to perform that skill with which she had once falsely been accused – carving Hawk-Beak's message sticks, using the Tree Script, and trusting that Gwrgi had not already learned of Owain the Traitor's demise. The warning was simple. Conveyed by a willing volunteer, a survivor of Cai's Shadow-Watchers, who would claim to be in Hawk-Beak's employ. Word that our main force lay hidden behind the low hills to our rear. A trap, waiting to be sprung. It might help to make the enemy cautious. To attack piecemeal, test our defences, enable us to whittle down the absurd odds against us. A ruse, yet how I wished it were true. For the actual result was an interminable wait. Impossible to build and hold a battle-frenzy despite our discordant singing.

My left arm throbbed from holding the shield so long in place, since Ambros had insisted that we form a two-deep wall to the square's front, keep it erect to help mask our weakness in numbers. And Ambros himself? He was in that place where a war-chieftain ought to be, upon his *carrio*, wedged against spear case and side arch, lashed upright to the empty tent frame, and thundering across our front, summoning every sinew to scream his battle-cry, to taunt the enemy, to swear revenge for Cai's death, and to offer the Champions' Challenge, while the hound, Charger, snapped at the war-cart's wheels.

'And who will he choose to stand for him today,' Rhun shouted at me, 'if the Man-Dog is fool enough to accept?'

He stood just a few shoulders away from me, towering above us all, and fearsome with those snarling, crooked fangs, his hog-spawn animal eyes.

'He knows they won't accept,' I said. 'They want our blood. All our blood. To wash this valley in it.'

'Do you not wish to bathe in my blood too, Mentor? Rigantona tells me you harbour grudges. Do I need to watch my back today, as well as my front?'

'In my wildest dreams,' I told him, 'I never imagined standing at your side in battle. A more relevant question might be whether Ambros can trust you to watch his own back, Rhun Malco's Son.'

'And I never thought to stand in a spear-press under the command of a priest-burner like Urien of Gift-Given.' He glanced around, to the place where Lord Urien was surrounded by his hearth-guards, protecting the standards that marked our centre – Ambros Skyhound's own banner, the hound's head with open jaws, set upon a sky-blue ground, alongside Urien's smaller dragon emblem, suspended from a crosstree, rippling in the light breeze and surmounted by a cluster of bleached skulls. But the old wolf paced up and down, restless, and his hand strayed often to the place where he would normally have worn his Battle Ward. 'Bad enough as it is,' Rhun went on, 'without having to fight under a man who thinks the battle already lost.

They attacked at noon, the waiting game ended, and Gwrgi seemingly satisfied that he could probe us without danger. A great cry went up from his horsemen as they broke forward in a trot, angling down to the ford, through the clinging mist, splashing and screaming through the water, then dividing so that one section could charge against Brock, Iago and Aurelius, while the rest surged at the broken slope towards our shield-wall. I had time to see our square open long enough for Ambros, his war-cart and his dog to enter, but then my vision narrowed only to the equine savagery thundering up the hill before me. The ponies' gnashing teeth. Flying hooves. Snorting, flared nostrils. Spittle flecking like the sea-foam substance of the Earth Mother, Senuna, herself. Crazed, blazing eyes. Manes and tails flying. Riders towering above them, screeching, hair flowing behind, and spears reaching for us even at fifty paces distant. I could not see the lead shots released by our rear-rank slingers, but I heard them. They whistled through the air, brought down a few ponies, and those fallen men and beasts brought down more. Yet they were pebbles in the ocean.

'Spears!' shouted Rhun, and we braced already weary muscles to firm the wall while, at the same time, our shafts were levelled into the notches formed where shield-rims met, so that we became a thicket of bristling spear-points. We were all trained from boys, of course, to know that no horse was stupid enough to impale itself on such a defence. But, sadly, as a student of history, I could recall just too many recorded occasions where the logic had not held. In battle, I knew, the impossible happens all too often. But we stabbed. Stabbed into the air before us. And there they were. Halted just short of our line. Rearing, hooves lashing. Snot-spraying. Riders' spears spiking in towards us. To make gaps. To breach our barricade. All the usual blood, piss and shit. Weeping. Moans. Cousins' Tongue curses. The drumming of wood upon wood. The maddened, rebellious protests of the ponies.

Yet we held. Three times they came. And three times we drove them back, though our numbers were thinning. Cullough of Bright-Fields was down, carried from the field, and most of his men gone with him. And Lord Urien had joined us in the front ranks.

'We are a rock,' he screamed. 'A Horn-God rock upon which their waters may foam and rage yet cannot conquer.'

But even the hardest rock might eventually be washed away, I thought, as our two sides parted and Gwrgi led his depleted horsemen back to the lower ground. Depleted, though still outnumbering us and, as we panted and gasped for water, throats and mouths parched dry, I could see that, to our left, we were no longer protected. The horsemen of Brock, Aurelius and Iago had disappeared entirely, presumably destroyed.

Over to the right, the ponies of the Painted People were making for the eastern ford and I knew that, while Imris and my sister-son would try to hold them, the effort was useless. The Pictoi would come crashing against our right and, with the square caught between them and Gwrgi's dark riders, the enemy spearmen would come forth. To finish us.

It is the worst thing. To watch your certain fate approach and still have to stand your ground. And yet we watched, as Gwrgi Hard-Spear's horsemen circled below our left, picking over the remnants of Brock's host, pissing upon the wounded, mutilating them and only occasionally slaying them with some degree of mercy. We watched, trying to hold back those maddened by the sight, who wanted only to break ranks and throw away their own lives in a useless attempt to stop the slaughter. We watched as the foemen's spears began their inexorable march towards our margent of the Burning Stream. We watched as Imris and Cador swung their pitifully inadequate fifty in an equally vain attempt to hold the Pictoi at the farther ford. And we watched as, mere minutes later, they came sweeping back towards us in full flight, with the Painted People upon their tails.

Beyond that, I have these images. Gwrgi and his men, tired of their distractions, shaking the ground, assaulting our ears with their howls, and hurling themselves onto the square's corner, some of them breaking through. Then our line having to open once more, as Imris, Cador and their survivors pleaded for sanctuary but, when allowed inside, were followed into the square's centre by a dozen of the Pictoi, some pulled to the ground, others striking out wildly in all directions. Others of the Painted people too, horse archers, staying beyond reach of our spears but picking off Rhun's men one by one. Rhun himself pierced by arrows, but still on his feet, taking down one enemy after another. Yet the beginning of the end.

Another image. Being pushed back by one of the Painted Folk. A big man, reeking of sour sweat and onions. The shield ripped from my grip. Our spear shafts crossed, one against the other, like practice staves, but my own efforts against him ineffectual, weak. So that I found myself pressed against the Skyhound's *carrio* wheel, and the Pictoi's fingers about my throat. But then Ambros was above and behind me, driving the barbed *craiseach* down into the warrior's skull.

I gasped for breath, turned and saw Ambros draw the Sword of Maximus, hack down into those of his foes now almost falling over themselves to reach him. And there, just beyond his line of vision, Gwrgi Hard-Spear on his pitch-black stallion, spear poised to throw. Yet he did not do so, for he was staring back across the stream. I parried a couple of thrusts as we formed a hasty last stand around the war-cart. Rhun was still on his feet. And so was Lord Urien, though both were slashed and battered. Osla Big-Knife as well, bleeding heavily from wounds to his head, arms and legs. Yet no sign of Valor, nor Six-Fingers, nor Bran of Romaland. And when I finally managed to discern the thing that drew Gwrgi's attention, I could not be certain my eyes did not deceive me.

A new body of horsemen had appeared. But not engaged in the battle. Rather, they were making for the position from which those damned bishops were observing the struggle. Safe from harm, they may have thought. With them, the baggage carts. And those carts must have carried more than mere tents and equipment, since the Pictoi, also spotting the newcomers, immediately began to break off from the fight. Ones and twos at first. Then dozens at a time.

It looked, for all the world, as though they were in flight – even though it was greed, I thought, that drove them. Yet it looked like flight to their allies too, those spear-hawks who, moments before, had been marching to our doom, but who now broke and began swarming towards their rear.

A running rout – through none of our doing – and only Gwrgi's men left facing us. But, even so, they were certainly more plentiful than our own tattered remnants. The battle still raged. Of course it did. How could it not in that death struggle? Ambros still holding off his attackers. The war-hound, Charger, tearing out throats. Our surviving Prefect Lords and commanders rallying their men, keeping each other upright, matted with gore. And Gwrgi Hard-Spear, now wild with rage, kicking his pony towards the *carrio*. Imris Cabul's Son already dead among a cluster of his young companions. My sister-son, Cador, assailed on three sides by enemy warriors.

My hand found the war-cart's spear case, fingers wrapping themselves around the slender shaft of a *birin*.

I hear men speak of choices, decisions, they have made in the thick of a fight. Yet I think they must be liars. Unless they mean those decisions which our instincts, our unconscious mind, might make for us. Because I have no memory of any calculation. Ambros Skyhound's life was all but over in any event. And how better might he have wished to die? Yet everybody knew his legend. Never taken harm from any weapon. And there he was, still lashed to the *carrio*'s tent frame, not a scratch upon him. While Cador? Almost my only surviving kin.

But instinct intervened. I only recall the javelin-dart leaving my hand. Straight and true. It pierced Gwrgi Hard-Spear's neck and protruded a forearm's length through the other side. He clutched the shaft in both hands, then toppled backwards. As he did so, Ambros turned, finally saw his danger. He was hollow-eyed, utterly exhausted, and slid down the frame while, just beyond reach, Cador Pale-Meadow – who might otherwise have inherited Clud-Vale eventually – died under the spears of our foes.

Chapter Thirty-Three

'Better to have granted me a warrior's death, Mentor,' Ambros groaned as we trundled south again, the floor of his war-cart piled high with sheep-fleece to make his journey more comfortable, 'than this slow misery.'

He was too weak to stand unassisted now and, to his rage, he had virtually lost control of his bowels.

'And given victory to the Man-Dog?' I said. 'What would it all have been for? Besides, I owed you for my own life.'

'No chance to make your peace with Birch Strong-Arm either,' murmured the Song-Sayer, cradling his fevered head in her lap. For it was Birch who had saved the day. Guilt had finally set him upon the road when he learned that Ambros was going north. So he had mustered his hearth-companions and determined to follow. But he had taken the wrong route from Peak Fort, arriving at the Burning Stream with the battle raging, almost lost, away to the west.

'Thought it was all over,' Birch shouted, as he rode alongside, 'so decided we might at least relieve those bloody bishops of some loot. Maybe pick up a few slaves from the camp followers. Salvage something from the mess you'd made.' In truth, he had been lucky to escape, running off with enough of their baggage wagons to have the Pictoi pursue him for many miles – then left them and doubled back to help us mop up the stubborn remnants of Gwrgi's force. And to retrieve Cai's head from the foe. 'But I knew,' said Birch. 'About Cai. A dream maybe. Something like that. When I was on the road.'

'I dream of him too,' said Ambros, 'and all those others who now wander with him in the Four-Cornered Fortress. I see them.' He stretched out his hand, as though he might touch the spirits of his visions. 'Imris Cabul's Son. Valor Bent-Back. Cullough of Bright-Fields. Iago Morn's

Son. Aurelius of Two-Tribes. Brock of the Tusk – my wife-father. Did I tell you that, Mentor? How shall I face her again in the Dark Halls? Cara White-Blossom. And our son.'

'Many have gone there, Lord,' said Morgose.

'Many,' he replied. And he began to list them as they walked before his pain-glazed eyes. Those who had sailed with us on *The White Enchantress*. Elidyr of Clud-Vale. All the others. Though he did not mention Cador Pale-Meadow and, for a moment, I was jolted by a false hope that my sister-son still lived. Perhaps among the wounded that we carried back with us into the south – Bran, Urien, Osla, Gereint Six-Fingers. But I knew that Cador was not upon the carts. I had seen him buried in the pit along with those warriors of the Stag-Son Blood who had ridden with him. And I had burned with the guilt of his death ever since. I had written a hasty note to Mirian, simply to say that her boy had died for our shared cause at the Burning Stream, and promising that I would come to her so soon as I was able. But I doubted I would ever do so. How could I explain to my sister, after all, that I had not lifted a finger to save him. The thought served to unhinge me, I believe. That, and my continuing grief at Cai's loss.'

'And much has gone with them,' I murmured.

'The lore shall live, Mentor,' said Morgose, 'while there is a song-sayer left in the world. The loss of so much knowledge and wisdom is a grievous thing. Yet we can build anew, perhaps.'

I brightened at her words. For I knew of one library, at least, which had survived the Christ-followers' book-purge.

It ended where it had also begun. Near that fording place on the Ridge River. Another fall of snow to mark the Midwinter Sun Standing, just days before we should have celebrated the Invincible Sun on the day of Mithras-Birth itself. *Sol Invictus*. And the anniversary of our old fight at Long Battle Bay. Yet there would be no celebration this year.

We had left Lord Urien in good hands at Moon's Glow. He would survive, at least. Unlike Osla Big-Knife, who died only hours after our return to Legion-Hold, his death almost immediately prompting a flurry of demands from competing families of the Hammer-Fighter folk for Ambros to name one or the other as Lords of Slavehold and thus eradicate the guilt and stigma of Cundruin's betrayal of Malco, which had taken those lands from their traditional care in the first place. But Ambros was too weakened now to judge such claims and, while we summoned a new physician – that well-recommended Judaean from Yew Grove, an acquaintance of Masul the Numidian, though no friend of his, apparently – the potions needed to ease his pain were so strong in papaver juice that the Skyhound was barely conscious most of the time.

But he always seemed aware of developments, even in his drug-induced slumbering. And, on the day before he died, Ambros opened his eyes and took my hand. We had already made offerings for him at the Bear Fort, where Cai had also been buried by his family with great honours bestowed upon him. Then we had moved on to Twin Sisters, though Ambros was determined to reach that old Auxiliary Camp, which he had made his own first holdfast alongside the Ridge Estuary. He had not eaten for many days, telling us that he had no desire for food – that it was the way our bodies tell us it is almost the end. And his old war-hound, Charger, knew it too, also refused to eat, refused to leave its master's side.

'But Mentor,' Ambros whispered, the skin of his face now stretched across cheekbones like parchment on a drying frame, 'one of them must summon a muster. Decide a new High Lord for Westerlands. Settle these disputes before we pull ourselves apart altogether. Slavehold. Bright-Fields.'

I wondered how he knew about the latter. For word had only arrived about the internecine strife also breaking out in Bright-Fields – following Cullough's death – while Ambros slept. But it made little difference.

'Fergna Urcol's Son has already laid claim to the title,' I told him. 'And to the Sword of Maximus also. He says it is a natural choice. Obvious, given his existing position as *Vorteporigas*.'

'Self-styled *Vorteporigas*,' said Ambros, 'and the bishops will never accept him.'

'Do you care?'

'It seems I cannot escape their Christ-god, Mentor.'

'You will take the Cross?'

'Is this sacrifice of my life not enough? For I know now, there can be no peace while still I live. And it will be worse with Fergna.'

Sacrifice? I wondered at his choice of words, yet I supposed he might be right.

'If not Fergna, then who?' I said.

'New stars must fill the sky, my friend. For Westerlands, Constantine of Horn-Head. The gods damn him for whatever part he played in the martyrdom of Bishop Mungo, but he can justly lay a claim to be my heir through our blood-ties. His own World-God Folk and my mother's *Fir Domnann*. And for the White-Wilds, perhaps Mabon Modron's Son of New Laigin – a man with one foot in the old faiths, one in the new. You must go to Deniol, Mentor. Tell him my will in this thing. Seek an understanding with him, his confederacy. And I would have you do one last thing for me. I wish you to go to Ogfran's Ring. To the Memory Stone of Cara White-Blossom. The boy should not remain nameless. It is wrong. So have them carve one for him. Call him Arth. Let it stand for the seeds from which I am sprung – the Bear Folk of the Bough-Gatherer Blood – and let it stand also for memory itself. That night when Morgose spun the tale of Arth mac Conn for us. Remember? Will you do it, Mentor? Good. Then go fetch the Song-Sayer. There is a darkness falling upon me. And I know fear now.'

I was afraid too, yet when I returned with her to his chamber, he was asleep again – both the Sword of Maximus and the dog, Charger, beside him, as they had been ever since our return there. He raved a little that night, his breath rasping in his chest, and his body shook often as he fought his last battles, locked in struggle with the Ravager. And I hoped, beyond hope, that the *craiseach* was in his hand. That he stood braced against the side arch of his war-cart. That he would strike one final victory blow against that worst of all his enemies. And, to be sure, just after daybreak, Mithras-Birth Morn, he awoke almost clear-eyed. His flesh once more showed that sheen it had known in his youth, although his breathing was still difficult.

'The Invincible Sun, my love.' He smiled up at Morgose, despite the heaving of his chest. For the beams were bright that day, motes of dust floating in the brilliance, which filled his doorway. 'This year, the crops will grow high again. But I would feel its warmth. Outside, perhaps?' I sent for Birch. A couple of others too. And we carried his litter to the threshold of the gather-hall, accompanied of course by the war-hound. There was snow, as usual, at the summit of the Giant's Tomb, and the bare-branch forests showed sharply against the green of the lower slopes. 'Is there anything more beautiful?' he said.

'You shall always be with me,' Birch murmured, 'when I take the Goose Hawks hunting. Or when I swim in the waters of the Ridge River.'

'Spare me those tears, Strong-Arm,' Ambros told him, 'for you have more important tasks to perform.' And he took up the Sword of Maximus, though with great difficulty. 'I fear that Fergna will lay claim to this blade and use it for ill purpose. It is already cursed. I could feel the evil within it, both when it slew Elidyr, and then again in that slaughter after the fight at Long Battle Bay. We need no more wrong chance from it. So you must rid us of this thing.'

'Plenty of time to worry about such trifles,' cried Birch. 'We have to beat this Ravager first. Fresh colour in your cheeks today, lad.'

But Ambros reached for Morgose, struggling for breath, as though he was drowning in his own fluids.

'I go down gladly into the darkness now,' he gasped. 'To make our world whole again, and to quit this pain. Yet I would bear the pain through all eternity of the Dark Halls, for just one more moon spent in your company, sweet Song-Sayer.'

'Close your eyes, my love,' Morgose told him. 'These good men will cherish your lands now. You and I shall share that darkness a while, and we may talk more when next you wake.'

Ambros closed his eyes as she bade him and, after mere moments, his breathing stilled, a final rattle, and then stopped.

Humanity's curse – that we, alone, of all the creatures set upon this earth, may comprehend the true nature of death and therefore invent so many myths for the attempted avoidance of its finality. Yet I understood then the sublime gift that one human being can give to another: to ease their fear in the moment of passing into oblivion's unknown.

Though perhaps we are not quite alone in that understanding for, at the precise moment of its master's death, the war-hound, Charger, lifted its great head to the distant mountains and let out a howl of despair, such that it gave voice to all our collective grief.

We stood upon the point at the Bright Isle and watched the currocks carry him towards us. A fleet of boats with white sails, and the Oak Seers within them all robed in white too. Banners flew from their masts as they took the tide ebbing eastwards from the Narrow Strait, bringing with it a favourable wind, though one which chopped the sea on this first day of favourable weather since Ambros had passed over. A cold, late Januarius day, but the sun shining. A day filled with good portents.

I turned to look at the site prepared for his arrival, pleased that there had been sufficient time since Mithras Day to make the place worthy of him. The pit was lined with stone and, within, we had set the war-cart to receive his mortal remains – preserved by the winter's cold through the weeks between. Around the pit's edge, all else stood ready. The crowd of mourners gathered, having made the overland journey to reach the island. And the Memory Stone painted, carved with his name.

Ambros Skyhound, Lord of Battles and Greater Britannia, Owen's Son, Bear Clan of the Bough-Gatherer Blood, Kin to the World-God Folk of Laigin and Horn-Head.

Morgose had insisted that the thing should not only be written in the Cousins' Tongue, using the lettering of the Common Speech, but that the edges of the stone also be etched with the same inscription using the Tree Script.

I could see her plainly now, standing in the prow of the second currock, that which bore the Skyhound's body. And the westerly wind carried her singing to us, even above the sea's churning and the waves breaking below me on the seal rocks. Endless verses. *The Song of the Great Melody.* Though not the modern version made famous by Tugri Iron-Brow. This was an older lay. As old as time itself, the verses alternating between our Cousins' Tongue and the Gathelic of their shared ancestry.

For this would be a ceremony of many faiths and many traditions.

'Yet he will not rest easy with that Christ-follower Bishop and his heresies here,' growled Birch, as the boats passed below us and made for the landing place.

'I think he would have it no other way,' I said. 'He bade me speak with Deniol. To suggest some compromise. The Christ-followers to pursue that faith among their own. Others, of the older truth, like yourself, to be left in peace. The people given time to build afresh. Recover from the famine and the Black Hags.'

'And you think he will honour that?'

'Of course not,' I smiled. 'But it may buy you some time. That was all Lord Ambros wanted, after all. To buy time. Yet what that time will bring, we cannot say. You must simply fulfil the work he set upon you.

Warden of Headlands until its future's decided. The bloodline is ended there, now Ambros has gone.'

'And the Sword of Maximus?'

'Destroy it, as he bade you.'

The procession of Oak Seers was climbing the path, their voices raised to the skies and joined by those of us who were not Christ-followers. They, of course, were clustered about Deniol and his monk-brothers, while the small *monasterios* they had built overlooked us from the island's highest point. There were many in Deniol's group too. Among the Prefect Lords, Caradoc of Cerdeg's Edge – Hawk-Beak's father. Mabon Modron's Son of New Laigin. The others too. Those who had paid lip-service loyalty to Ambros but rarely given him practical support, and plainly become converts somewhere along the way. Kei of Meirionshore. Custain of Dunshome. Alios of Everfell. And Rhun the Tall, naturally, with Rigantona at his side, as well as her mother, the White Lady Murgain.

'They outnumber us,' said Birch. 'The Christ-followers.'

'Perhaps they always did,' I replied. And I saw the future then, as the Oak Seers arrived before the stone-lined ditch, still open to the heavens, which led into the burial pit. They carried the corpse upon a litter, Ambros resplendent in burnished mail-shirt and gold neck-ring, befitting his warlord's status, his red hair whispering in the wind. He was laid out upon the *carrio*, his prized spears alongside him, and a wealth of precious goods for him to carry into the Dark Halls. Silver spoons, plates and goblet. Coins clutched in each of his hands.

The priest who had once officiated in the Mithraeum at the Fortress of the Hammer-Fighters intoned the Mystery of the Seven Circles, while the Christ-followers grumbled, crossed themselves, spat upon the ground. But at least there was no funeral tower for him to bless. No ritual of leaving Ambros Skyhound's body to be devoured by crow and raven. And, when the priest had finished, Deniol himself was given the opportunity, as we had agreed, to speak some words from their *biblia sacra*. It was the thirtieth day of the month, so auspicious, the Christ-followers said, for a burial, but we had still refused to allow them their custom of draping the body in a black pall. Yet that did not prevent Deniol from chanting in the Latin, close enough to the Common Speech for us to understand it.

'The cords of death entangled me,' he said. 'And the anguish of the grave overcame me. I was overcome by distress and sorrow. Then I called on the name of the Lord. Lord, save me!'

'Lord, save me!' sang the monk-brothers.

'Does anybody believe that nonsense?' Birch snarled. But I made no answer since Rhun the Tall had come to join us. Rigantona too. And a new deer-hound, I saw. Another huge beast, almost a small pony.

'The words offer us hope, Mentor,' Rigantona said. 'You remember hope, don't you?' I saw that her belly was swollen. Too recent to be any seed of mine, but there stood the hound at her side and, for a moment, I wondered...

'It will be a boy,' said Rhun, noticing the direction of my gaze and interrupting my sinful imaginings. 'We shall call him Malco. For my father.'

'There have been many errors made,' I told him, 'these past years. On all sides.'

I heard Birch Strong-Arm mutter something under his breath, and it might have been a betrayal of the Skyhound's actions, but I felt it worthwhile to try and appease Rhun somewhat. But he simply snorted like a pig, spittle gathering around the crooked chaos of his teeth.

'At least your Skyhound was a better man by far than his boy-shagging brother,' he said. 'And Gwrgi Hard-Spear was an evil that could not be permitted to continue. Yet being the enemy of my foes did not make my father's murderer a friend.'

I had no doubt, then, that their breed would soon rule the White-Wilds once more. It would never be as Ambros had intended – a peaceful transition to a lordship by Mabon Modron's Son. *And no place here for me, when that happens*, I thought.

'And where shall you go, Mentor?' Rigantona was always able to read my mind.

'North, I think.' It seemed bizarre that we should be having this banal discussion and I struggled both with my emotions and a host of images that I should rather have lain hidden. 'My sister is wed to Rhodri of Clud-Vale. Her son fought with us at the Burning Stream. It seems fitting that I should visit her. And Lord Rhodri, I'm told, has a wish to restore a library. At Clut's Rock.'

I saw her smile. That evil grin I had observed so many times. I wondered at the source of her amusement but, by then, their rituals were all done and slaves, the un-free, were called upon to begin the sealing ceremony, to close over the entrance ditch, to lever the roofing slabs over Ambros and his war-cart, then to bank the earth once more, creating the mound on which his Memory Stone would stand. It might take many days, of course, dependant upon the weather, and tonight there would be feasting in many halls to remember him. Yet, for now, there was one more service to perform: the offering of the Maximus Sword, flung by Birch Strong-Arm from the cliff tops into the waiting surf of the Sea-Foam Goddess, Senuna.

'A waste of a good blade,' said Rigantona, still close at hand.

She was correct, of course. All swords were precious. A rare commodity. And yet the whole point of sacrifice was to make the offering sufficiently valuable.

'No,' said her new husband. 'It stands for too much that is past and gone. We balance on the edge of a new age. And you, Master Mentor,' Rhun asked me, 'when do you leave for the North?'

'I imagine,' Rigantona laughed, parting the hair so that I could better observe the malice in her eyes, 'the Mentor believes he has treasures to collect. Is that not so, Master Meridden?'

She could barely contain herself, and I knew then, with dread certainty, that even the precious volumes I had hidden in the old Mithraeum, at the Fortress of the Hammer-Fighters – that even those were now lost to us. And Rhun's new age? A place of darkness and ignorance.

Then let this stand as our epilogue. For I did, indeed, travel north, though almost empty-handed, to Clud-Vale.

But first I carried out the Skyhound's bidding, went by way of Ogfran's Ring and found a sculptor who would, at last, give his son a name. Morgose journeyed with me, as did the old war-hound, Charger, though it did not survive Ambros by many months. Morgose is with me still, however, here in Lug's Ditch. Nothing between us except the hollow void left by Ambros Skyhound's absence.

Yet it was there, at Cara White-Blossom's tomb, that I first heard the Song-Sayer sing the lament, which has since made the legend so strong. Ambros slaying tyrants in the pursuit of love. Battling giants for possession of a cauldron with great powers. Defeating the Black Hags. Hunting the Boar King through his magical kingdoms. Braving passage through the Dream Lands to confront and bring down the Ravage-Reivers. All for love of his lands.

But, once arrived in Clud-Vale, we were received with cool indifference by my sister and her husband. Mirian blamed me, somehow, for the loss of her son, and Lord Rhodri seemed to see in us the shadow of Ambros, still held culpable for Elidyr's death. Yet he granted me some lowly position, contracting with me to act as a Grammarian – though not at Clut's Rock but away to the south, on the edges of Battle-Forest, in Lug's Ditch, and not far from the Burning Stream.

In the intervening years, I have heard the words of Morgose's lament spun in a thousand ways. Sometimes with heroic grandeur. Sometimes as though the song-sayer in question had swallowed far too many pots of heather-beer.

'You remember what he said?' I asked her one night. 'About the crops. How they would grow high again?'

'Sometimes,' she replied, 'the land requires a great offering. An offering of blood. To heal its hurts. And it has never received any offering of blood so noble as that of Ambros Skyhound.'

The Years Without Summer had passed. The wheat grew once more and the land became fat. Yet, by then, folk were so thin upon the ground that it became almost impossible to farm efficiently, with the Outlanders and their new ways – their release of the un-free wherever they went – steadily filling the void we had left behind. And welcome too, for the most part. For the strife among our people had ceased a while. Nobody now talked about the civil war on either side. And nothing written except that copied in the Christ-followers' scriptoriums, and only then words to support their own narrow beliefs. The worst of their scribbling, I heard, was written by a priest styling himself as Gildas. Wretched nonsense in which he damned Ambros – *Cuneglasus*, he called him, as Deniol had done so often – as well as others of the warlords who stood against those rabid bishops, and it took me some time to realise that this must surely be the same Sildag Stag-Shank of High-Pass who had led their so-called Phalanx. And Deniol himself? He married the White Lady Murgain, I understand, and is still Bishop of the White-Wilds.

But at least the Yellow Pestilence seemed banished forever also – though I often thought about Masul the Numidian, his theory of the plague spread by rats and the irony, if true, that those rats may have brought the pestilence on those same ships of Justinian's Empire that we hoped might bring us succour. It is the thing that Fergna Urcol's Son suspected when I played the game of Throne-Sense with him at Sea Fort. And it is one of the things that fuels my moments of madness. Those when I can barely remember my own name and I find myself drooling from the spoon with which Morgose attempts to feed me. Along with the news. Fighting broken out again. This time between the Saesons and our Cousin-Kin. Along the Ridgeway, it seems. At Corin-Mound and Sulis Wells too, in each of which, they say, you will now find nothing but the Outlander tongue spoken, so that the people of Domna's Deep and Horn-Head talk of themselves as an island, cut off from the rest of our folk by foreign lands. Rhun is dead too, she tells me. And Rigantona. While their son, Beli, presently rules over the White-Wilds.

'Was he mistaken?' I say to her. 'Not to simply accept the Christ-followers? Were the songs we spun not the thing which brought down their wrath upon him?'

She searches my face with her fingers, seeking to fathom whether I ramble or whether it may be worth a considered response.

'Sometimes,' she says, 'our intentions may be right but our actions wrong. Yet often, when that happens, we may still leave behind us the essence of that for which we stood. And that essence can be a light, one which may survive the darkness, become a symbol for those who struggle against great odds. All great ideas have their day, Mentor, as you know. The best of them arrive a little ahead of their time, appear initially somewhat absurd. But when their time comes at last, the world wonders why nobody thought of them earlier. The vision of Ambros Skyhound will be one of those. The vision of a Greater Britannia.'

Her logic is impeccable. But then my mind becomes confused once more. The authors of all those lost works scream at me and I run naked in the forest to escape them, pursued by the knowledge and wisdoms they once possessed. The Song-Sayer may be right. Ambros Skyhound's torch may guide us through this gloom of ignorance, yet it can never recover all that has now gone forever. The foundations. All that we ever believed, turned to nonsense by the Christ-followers, not through rational debate or proper persuasion, but by the simple expedient of burning the alternative. And it is little consolation to me that, by the same token, their own superstitions will one day become ash in their turn.

But, for now, the curtains of madness part a while, allow me to see him clearly. A boy. They call him Arth. A name suddenly popular for no better reason than its frequent use among the Incomers. Not that the Incomers are so thick upon the ground here in Lug's Ditch. Simply a fashion. So that, whenever I venture from the protection of the forest, every third child seems to be a Conor. Or Deidre. Or Eithne. Or Arth. Thus, he is not the lad you imagine him to be. And though I am certain that this boy is also destined for a significant future, you must not confuse him with the warrior of legend. For that man, that hero, carried a different name entirely. And, as a certain song-sayer from New Laigin once told us,

Myths, legends and lore
inspire our dreams, ambitions,
grant wings to heroes;
then turn, more potent than fact,
beguile us, mislead, betray.

The End

Historical Note

Normally, in this section at the end of my novels, I explain that most of the story is based on generally accepted history and then I come clean about those details where I may have veered away from the known facts for the sake of the plot. If there are previously untold elements to the story, I explain them, and then I try to answer some of those questions that readers are bound to have about what happened next. But, as I said in the Preface, in the case of sixth-century Britain, this is difficult so that, with *The Song-Sayer's Lament*, these notes will almost be the opposite of my normal process – for the things that are known facts here will be the exception, not the rule.

I paid my first visit to sixth-century Britain almost fifty years ago. It was Rosemary Sutcliff's fault, since it was through the pages of *A Sword at Sunset* that I first began to realise my school-text image of the so-called Dark Ages might not be entirely accurate. So I picked up histories like Laing's *Celtic Britain* and *The Celtic Realms* by Myles Dillon and Nora Chadwick, to find out more. Astonishment. It seemed that those beautiful Celtic manuscript illuminations may not, after all, have been the original invention of some highly creative solitary monk on Iona, but borrowed from a much earlier indigenous literacy; that Romano-Britons probably did know one end of a stylus from the other, and had not simply committed to prodigious memory all of their accounts, land-holdings, legal judgements, histories, philosophies and a million other things, in some exaggerated "oral tradition"; that the Dark Ages may be so-named due to Romano-British documentation being lost to us, rather than never having existed; and that "Arthur" may be no more than the imaginative product of some medieval Tolkien.

So I spent chunks of my twenties working through the early sagas I found in *Ancient Irish Tales* (edited by Tom Peete Cross and Clark Harris

Slover), the *Irish Sagas and Folk-Tales*, as told by Eileen O'Faoláin, and *Saga and Myth in Ancient Ireland* by Gerald Murphy. Lots more besides. Wonderful stories, cogently written tales, so that I thought I must be leaving the best until last when I eventually turned to "Welsh" mythology and began reading the *Mabinogion*. And was disappointed. The stories have a huge following but, personally, to me, they generally feel as though somebody has taken random paragraphs, snippets, from a hundred tales, sagas and poems, then re-assembled them in an equally random order. For me, they work best when adapted as stories for children – as in the recent *Four Branches of the Mabinogi* (available in English and Welsh), by Siân Lewis. But surely they must once have been so much more. And I wondered how it was possible for two blocks of mythology, separated only by fifty miles of the Irish Sea, to be so wildly different. I wondered, too, whether there might just be some link between the abysmal state of our sixth century historical knowledge and the examples of our non-Irish story-telling from that period.

It continued to trouble me, on and off, over the intervening years but I did little about it until, looking for a theme for this fifth novel, I chose to set *The Song-Sayer's Lament* roughly between the years that we would now call 540–550 AD – although it's worth noting at the outset that even the *Anno Domini* system was not then functional, so we cannot even be certain how post-Roman Britons themselves calculated the time in which they lived. Most of Britain had been occupied by the Roman Empire for a period of roughly 400 years. The first half of that occupation saw several insurrections against the occupying forces but, for around two hundred years, the two societies, Roman colonial and British, had steadily come together, with the Legions pulling out to deal with problems nearer home over a timescale from perhaps 410 AD until 430 AD. So, roughly a hundred years before the events in *The Song-Sayer's Lament*. By the time they left, the territory known to the Romans as Britannia was administered as several different Provinces – most likely called Britannia Prima, Britannia Secunda, Flavia Caesariensis, Maxima Caesariensis and Valentia – though there's still debate even about where these might have actually been. How much of this administrative culture survived, and how much broke down through local warlords carving out their own domains? We don't know. And how much did people continue to live as they had done under Roman rule? We don't know that either but, contrary to some of the "old" history, we can now see, archaeologically, that towns like Canterbury, Cirencester, Chester, Gloucester, Winchester, Wroxeter – and presumably many more – continued to be developed, with new-build taking place, well into the sixth century and beyond.

Meanwhile, we can be reasonably certain that, from the third century onwards, there had been increasing numbers of continental migrants settling mainly in the south and east of Britannia. We speculate that some of these may simply have been auxiliaries in the Roman army – since the Legions were, of course, filled with soldiers recruited to fill the ranks from all over the Empire. Or that they were mercenaries, *foederati*, employed to fight in the various conflicts that beset the period. Or that they were simply economic migrants – Angles, Saxons and Jutes. This is often portrayed as an "invasion", but there's little hard evidence for this. Battles are cited. Dates given. Yet all the sources are questionable, to say the least.

The documents normally taken as "primary sources" for this period are: the *De Excidio et Conquestu Britanniae* of Saint Gildas, originally written, we think, in the early sixth century; Saint Bede's *Historia Ecclesiastica* (*The Ecclesiastical History of the English People*), written about two hundred years later; the *Historia Brittonum*, compiled by some anonymous editor we now know as "Nennius", also allegedly from the ninth century, though the actual manuscripts are much later; the so-called *Harleian Genealogies*, the British Library's Manuscript 3859, purporting to detail lineages for Welsh princely families, back to the calculated birth of Christ, but itself dating from the twelfth century; the *Annales Cambriae* (*The Annals of Wales*), a complex of chronicles setting out a history of early Wales, Cornwall, Ireland and Scotland – but, once again, the earliest copy of the Annals dates from the twelfth century; and such Irish documents as the *Annals of Tigernach*. That sounds like plenty of resources, yet there are very few who would be brave enough to claim these as providing the same level of "evidence" as we might expect for almost any other period of history. Only the *De Excidio* is contemporary and, after that, we have maybe five or six documents, scattered over the next 600 years and subject to all manner of copying errors, fashion and culture changes, political and religious tampering, literary adaptation, or simple grapevine misinterpretation.

And then there are those even later literary manuscripts – those that are now frequently described as The Four Ancient Books of Wales. The documents are written in a form of Welsh and date from the Thirteenth to Fifteenth Centuries, but contain copies and versions of texts that may have been set down originally in the Sixth or Seventh Centuries. But that means an even longer gap, 200 years longer, which makes *The Black Book of Camarthen, The Book of Aneirin, The Red Book of Hergest* and *The Book of Taliesin* priceless as historical artefacts but entirely unreliable as historical sources for the period. As that excellent author, Richard Denning, has put it: "Yes, they are mostly poems and semi-myth. Indeed they are confusing and difficult to read, but for the historian and for the historical fiction writer of the post-Roman period, for whom the expression *beggars can't be choosers* might have been invented, they give us something to get our teeth into and extract something approaching a history."

I agree – at least in part. For those writing about the early Anglo-Saxon era of the late sixth century onwards, all of the manuscripts detailed above may indeed provide something upon which to bite. But for those writing about the hundred preceding years, and about the very uncertain fate of the Romano-British population, they hold little of real value. And here's just one example of the difficulty. For those interested in the "Arthur" issue, it's worth noting that there is no contemporary reference to a person of that name. The most commonly cited evidence for his existence comes from *Y Gododdin*, a medieval Welsh poem, which may have been written at the start of the seventh century by a northern poet-prince called Aneirin, and contains the tantalising Old Welsh half line *bei ef arthur*, previously translated as "he was an Arthur". Clear enough, except that subsequent linguistic scholars argue that it actually means, "he was no Arthur"; or, "he blamed Arthur"; or, even one assertion that the word *arthur* is not a name at all but, rather, an obscure noun. In truth, the earliest manuscript version of *Y Gododdin* dates from the thirteenth century so that, added to the problems brought by perhaps 600 years of errors and tampering, we can now add the uncertainties arising from disputed translation of Old Welsh and Middle Welsh.

So, from where did I draw the inspiration and "historical evidence" for the story's roots?

Like almost everything else relating to sixth-century Britain, the extent to which the country was affected by the "Extreme Weather

Event" of *circa* 535 AD is disputed. David Keys in his 1999 book, *Catastrophe: A Quest for the Origins of the Modern World*, provides evidence for volcanic eruptions, possibly in the Far East, which caused a "volcanic winter" across many parts of the world, including northern Europe, and led directly to more intense levels of migration than usual. Much of that evidence is refuted by British archaeologist, Ken Dark, although later tree-ring analysis by the University of Belfast bears out legendary tales (*Annals of Ulster*) of crop-failure, in Ireland and elsewhere, at that time. Research by Columbia University attributed the global weather disaster to multiple comet impacts, but with largely the same result. I was satisfied, however, that such a natural catastrophe had actually taken place and therefore chose to set *The Song-Sayer's Lament* against the background of that Endless Winter, and the famine it must have brought in its wake.

Similarly, I was satisfied that it was within the boundaries of possibility that Britain was struck by an outbreak of bubonic plague during the period in which the novel is set. Most of us think of the bubonic plague striking much later in our history, in the Middle Ages, but Procopius and other contemporaries record the plague as devastating Constantinople in 542 AD and then spreading both east and west. Gildas refers to the pestilence in Britain in the same era, though without dating the attack. The documents now known as *Annales Cambriae* (Latin for *The Annals of Wales*) record that Maelgwyn Gwynedd (my Malco) died of the plague in 547 AD – though this is hardly reliable, since it was written hundreds of years later. And the *Annals of Tigernach* (also much later) record "a great mortality" – believed to be the same plague – hitting Ireland at this time.

The third uncertainty I faced was the extent to which Rome's occupation of Britain had left a legacy that still endured more than a hundred years after the Legions had marched away. The archaeological evidence shows that sites like Wroxeter, Chester and Birdoswald were not only still occupied as towns in the mid-sixth century but were also subject to the new-build developments I mentioned earlier. But it was the road system that intrigued me. We all know that the Romans built a sophisticated network of highways and byways across Britain, as they did everywhere within the Empire. So I concluded that the roads in question were likely to have still been very much in use, though I had to use my imagination in calculating how they may have been known. We are blessed that history has left us the Antonine Itinerary, which describes the Empire's roads in great detail, including their lengths and distances between way-stations, or *mansios*. The *Iter Britanniarum* covers Britain's section of the network, with a different itinerary for each of fifteen major routes. So, Itinerary XII, for example, covers the journey from Carmarthen to Wroxeter – and it seemed reasonable to me that this road may have been known, both to the Romans and to the post-Roman Britons as "the Twelve".

So far as the language is concerned, I wrote this story, in its original form, in modern English – and English therefore stands for the Brythonic language, variations of which would have been spoken in sixth-century Britain by all those disparate but related clans, which most certainly did not think of themselves as "British" or "Welsh" or "Celtic", but as separate peoples, tribes, linked (or possibly divided) by a common speech – the Cousins' Tongue, as I have called it. And, because English substitutes here for that Cousins' Tongue, it was important for me to make sure that place names, nicknames and individuals' titles should convey in English those images that their original Brythonic names might have conjured up. In other words, I specifically chose not to use some form of pseudo-Welsh, for example, in place names. Welsh is a beautiful, lyrical but highly descriptive language, the rich simplicity of which would be totally lost for English-only readers who simply found themselves coming across locations like *Gwynedd* or *Dinerth* without knowing that these words convey something like the *White-Wilds* or *Bear Fort* respectively.

In truth, we have no real idea what most locations were called at all in sixth-century Britain. We can speculate, using those names the Romans adopted from what they thought the locals called them, or by looking back retrospectively from accounts and stories written down only hundreds of years later. But there can be no certainty about any of this without some major new archaeological discovery and research. Still, it seemed reasonable to assume that the language of the Romans, which had been so prevalent in much of Britain for four hundred years, might still have some currency even a century after the Legions had left these shores. Not high Latin, but that form known as the *sermo vulgaris*, the Common Speech. And I have therefore taken the liberty of pretending that some places may have retained corrupted Cousins' Tongue forms of the Roman (Common Speech) names, which the Legions would have borrowed and warped, in the first place, from the original Brythonic – and it is those names that appear in the glossary and fictional maps at the front of the book.

Similarly, we know almost nothing about individuals who lived in Britain during the sixth century. The same accounts and stories written down hundreds of years later leave us a patchwork of "names" that, on closer inspection, turn out to be, far more likely, titles or praise names, simple shadows, which may never have been anything more, in the first place, than folk-tale characters – in the same way that Little Red Riding Hood or Snow White or even Robin Hood have now assumed far more than simple fictional and legendary status. My favourite, of course, is *Gwenhwyfar* – the character we all know as Guenivere. But even a cursory examination will show us that *Gwenhwyfar* may not originally have been a name at all, but a title, or description. It means *White Enchantress*, or similar, and explains why there are so many apparently confusing legends with multiple characters all called *Gwenhwyfar*. Similarly, there are characters like *Peredur* (*Hard-Spear*), *Vortigern* (*High Lord*), *Vortepor* (*Lord Protector*) and scores of others. So, wherever I came across a "name" that I thought to be suspect, I have used an English approximation of the meaning to signify an appropriate title, nickname or Praise Name.

And, still on language, I remained intrigued by the lack of primary sources for the period from a "Celtic" viewpoint, and the old myth that indigenous Britons must have only kept their lore, traditions and genealogies orally. Yet there are literally hundreds of inscriptions, revealed by archaeology, dating from around 500 BC onwards, in their own Celtic languages, though using Etruscan, Greek or Latin alphabets. These include entire poems, such as that found in 1887 at Deux-Sèvres – a hymn to the goddess Epona. So, highly literate Celtic Britons, who then lived alongside the literacy of the Mediterranean world for 400 years, and it seemed entirely inconsistent to me that Romano-Britons should have written no texts on their own history, philosophy and beliefs. And is it pure coincidence that the only fragments of Celtic language texts from the sixth century are Christian documents, such as the famous *An Cathach*, attributed to St Columba? Peter Berresford Ellis, in his excellent study, *A Brief History of the Celts*, provides an entire chapter on Celtic literacy, and cites the references which imply that Saint Patrick, "in his missionary zeal", burned hundreds of non-Christian texts. If true, then how widespread was the practice of Christians burning "pagan" texts?

Romano-Britons and Irish of the period were, of course, also familiar with another form of writing – the Ogam script. Inscriptions using its dash-and-slash letters have been found widely across Ireland and western Britain, all dating from the fourth century onwards. There are many theories about its origins, the two most common being, first, that it was created by Druids (my Oak Seers) as a code to help resistance against the Romans – or perhaps even earlier – and, second, that it was the invention of early Christians in Ireland seeking a unique alphabet to convey simple messages or inscriptions. Readers will note that I have rather embroidered upon this latter theory and given Ogam the working title of Tree Script.

So far as the final battle is concerned – the event generally known as the Battle of Arfderydd – this is mainly recorded in the *Annales Cambriae*. But the earliest copy of these chronicles date from the twelfth century, and this is thought to be a copy of a tenth century original. In other words, this "source" was written, at least, four hundred years after the battle was supposed to have occurred. So I felt no great urge to slavishly follow the details, and used the text only as a broad canvas. The *Annales Cambriae* seem to indicate that Arfderydd was fought between warring "Britons" – the brothers Gurci and Peredur on one side, and somebody called Gwenddolau ap Ceidio on the other. The protagonists are listed in the so-called *Harleian Genealogies*, another series of manuscripts written no earlier than the tenth century. And there are references to Arfderydd (or somewhere with a similar name) in the documents we now call the *Red Book of Hengest* (*Welsh Triads*) and a couple of poems about Merlin (or Myrddin) in the *Black Book of Camarthen*, which also link another character, Rhydderch, to the tale. These are even later and often contradictory. So I chose to see Peredur as a Praise Name (Hard-Spear) and to composite this with Gurci's character to make him Gwrgi Hard-Spear. Similarly, Gwenddolau means something like Pale-Meadow, so he became Cador Pale-Meadow – and I made him Rhodri's (Rhydderch's) son, and Myrddin's (Meridden's) nephew.

All of which brings me back to the only potentially primary written source for those studying fifth and early sixth-century Britain – certainly the only one that can claim to be contemporary. This is the text by Gildas called *De Excidio et Conquestu Britanniae*. Gildas, a Welsh-Breton priest and saint, apparently wrote one hundred and ten historical chapters and admonitions, upon which Bede drew heavily almost two hundred years later – although the oldest actual manuscript of the *De Excidio* dates from the eleventh century. For students of the Dark Ages it's still invaluable – well, it's actually all we've got from early sixth century Britain itself – although, over the last hundred years, a growing body of academics and researchers have questioned the authenticity of the work and, at times, whether Gildas was even the author's real name. It is certainly strange that Gildas should have such an enigmatic name, not obviously Celtic or Saxon, and neither could I find any record of Gildas as a Latin name – and, because of the way *De Excidio* applies puns to the names of contemporary British warlords, some have suggested that Gildas may simply be an anagram for Sildag – a concept upon which I have readily seized. In truth, I came to view the admonitions in my translated copy of *De Excidio* as a sixth century version of articles in the British satirical magazine, *Private Eye*!

My conclusion, of course, is that the period between 500 AD and 600 AD is effectively a "lost century" in British history. But at least we know with more certainty what happened next. *The Anglo-Saxon Chronicles* and other sources confirm the way in which Angles, Saxons and Jutes consolidated territory into the Kingdoms of Northumbria (most of what we now know as northern England), Mercia, Anglia, Wessex, Essex, Sussex and Kent, with the more specifically "Celtic" folk confined to the Southwest, Wales, Cumbria and the lands north of Hadrian's Wall. According to the Chronicles, there were one or two more battles in the period, like that at Deorham around 577 AD. But all of the foregoing contrived to give me the premises for *The Song-Sayer's Lament*. What if the Black Hags appearing so often in Celtic mythology were actually the outward symptoms of plague and pestilence? What if post-Roman Britons were also devastated by the effects of the Extreme Weather Event (535 AD)? What if the "invasions" by Angles, Saxons and Jutes were no more than economic migrations by which those folk, for the most part, at least, simply "filled a void" – the sixth century's answer to labour and skills shortage? What if most of what we've been taught about the period comes down to us simply from propaganda aimed essentially at boosting the development of Christianity in Britain?

What if (the corollary), for the same reason, the true record of Romano-British culture and philosophy had to be deliberately expunged? What if some of those early Christians were as rabid and destructive as fanatical Jihadists? And what if the impact of these things was eerily similar to the effects of Jesuit priests and migrant settlers upon the First Nation Americans?

But, in the end, as I said at the outset, *The Song-Sayer's Lament* is simply a work of fiction, a story – and I hope readers enjoy it on that basis.

Acknowledgements

I owe a huge debt of gratitude to the UK Society for Co-operative Studies who, in October 2013, invited me to their conference at Gilsland Spa in Cumbria so that I could speak about my second novel, *The Assassin's Mark*. As it happens, the hotel sits almost alongside Hadrian's Wall and just a stone's throw from the Roman fortress of Birdoswald. Curiosity led me to research Birdoswald, its post-Roman development and a possible link with the nearby Battle of Arthuret, or Arfderydd. And this set me on the trail that would eventually lead me to *The Song-Sayer's Lament*. Not an easy trail either, as I began to understand how few reliable sources existed to help with the research and background.

So far as online resources are concerned, I am indebted to the following. For farming as part of the sixth-century economy, Michelle Ziegler's www.hefenfeith.wordpress.com (Heavenfield: Exploring Medieval Landscapes) site on *Post-Roman Reforestation of Britain*. For my invention of place names and characters' given names, or praise names, I used a mass of different websites that provide possible etymologies. Too many to name them all but those to which I turned most frequently were www.roman-britain.org (also for details of the Romano-British road networks listed in the Antonine Itinerary) and www.historyfiles.co.uk (Britain section and Celtic Kingdoms of the British Isles). Similarly, for my inadequate attempts to mimic some of the cadences that my song-sayers may have used, I went to the www.kernewegva site (A Guide to Welsh, Cornish and Breton Verse) and, while I'm not aware of any actual "Welsh" creation story surviving, I borrowed heavily from those Celtic tales told variously at www.historyarchive.whitetree.ca (Celtic Creation Story) and www.educationscotland.gov.uk (Celtic Creation Myth). For Meridden's skills as a Mentor and rhetor, I turned to the www.artofmanliness.com site (Classical Rhetoric). For an insight into a wide range of relevant cultural issues, to www.bepress.com (Selected Works of Kirsten Jarrett) for the 2010 paper on *Ethnic, Social and Cultural Identity in Roman to post-Roman Southwest Britain.* For Ancient Greek and Roman treatments of cancer, I went to the *Annals of Surgical Oncology* site for the views of physicians like Archigenes, Galen, Leonides of Alexandria and Paulus Aegineta while, for contemporary and natural treatments of bubonic plague, I went to sites like the online version of Joseph Patrick Byrne's *Daily Life During The Black Death*, www.naturalnews.com and www.faculty.virginia.edu on the use of silver in medicine – but please don't try any of the book's "remedies" at home! And for the Justinian Plague generally, I referred frequently to the Cambridge Catalogues paper by Lester K. Little, *Life and Afterlife of the First Plague Pandemic.*

It was principally online resources that I used, also, for establishing some shape to my characters' years. As I've said elsewhere, there was no single calendar system in place at the time to which my story relates. The *Anno Domini* of the Julian and Gregorian calendars with which we are now familiar did not come into common use until much later, in the eighth century (although probably invented initially in the sixth century) while, at the time, the Empire was still using the *Ab Urbe Condita* (AUC) system – basically, Rome Foundation Year (although the Emperors played with that, to suit their own propaganda needs) – or simply the regnal year of the Emperors themselves. So, depending on the source, 540 AD could have been known, even in official circles, variously as 1293 AUC, or simply Year 18 (Emperor Justinian's regnal year) or, for Christians, the Third Year of Pope Vigilius. And locally? Possibly just the year number from which your local warlord might have seized power. Or from some other significant event. Yet I have a nagging suspicion that the British Celts, with such a rich lore (oral or otherwise) might have enjoyed their own Foundation Year notion for their lands. Well, we may never know. But can we be a bit more certain about how each year was actually structured? I turned to sites such as Dolores Whelan's blogsite, www.doloreswhelan.ie (Celtic Year) and the www.transceltic.com pages for a broad idea and cross-checked the details against some of the source books listed below – and then, of course, attempted to use my etymological resources to put the names of festivals into my Cousins' Tongue.

But I must also make special mention here of Carla Nayland – the pen name of a wonderful historical fiction novelist with a scientific background and a keen interest in the history of Britain between the fifth and tenth centuries. Carla's website, www.carlanayland.org (Essays), is filled with excellent blogs on Anglo-Saxon England and Early Medieval Britain, which are a true delight. As a scientist, her articles take a look at any modern evidence we may have (in relation to place names or people, for example); then examine any primary source references (in the *Historia Brittonum* or *Annales Cambriae*, etc); finally, supply notes on any archaeological findings; and, next, provide a forensic interpretation of the evidence, plus some conclusions – which Carla is always careful to note as being simply her own considered opinion. So, for example, her blog, *Chronology on the Kings of Gwynedd* in the Sixth and Seventh Centuries, strips away all the assumptions I had read elsewhere and simply leaves us with the tiny fragments that may be factual – though even these details still contain some conjecture: that Gwynedd was ruled by a man called Maelgwyn (Malco) until his death around 547 AD; that he was succeeded by his son, Rhun, until Rhun's own death around 565 AD. Rhun had a son, Beli (died around 585 AD). And Beli had a son too (died around 613 AD). Yet, in addition to her blog, Carla also found time in a very busy schedule to engage in e-mail correspondence exchanges, which allowed me to chew over many of the problems I faced – particularly concerning the Romano-Britons' sense of their own time and place in the world. It is unlikely that they thought of themselves as being "in Britannia", for example. But did those in the west still consider that they lived in the Roman administrative area of Britannia Prima (First-Province)? Had they reverted to the old tribal names? Of course, we don't know that either. But Carla's insights helped me to make some "balance of probability" decisions about how I should shape my own fiction.

Besides the online resources, of course, there were the books. Aside from those I've already mentioned, there were a few that inspired me, in one way or another: Peter Berresford Ellis's *A Brief History of the Celts*; Flint F. Johnson's *Hengest. Gwrtheyrn and the Chronology of Post-Roman Britain*; *Wales and the Britons, 350–1064* by T.M. Charles-Edwards; Stuart Laycock's *Warlords, the Struggle for Power in Post-Roman Britain*; the British Museum and National Museum of Scotland catalogue, *Celts: Art and Identity*; and *The Celts: Origins, Myths, Inventions*, by John Collis.

Finally, of course, many thanks to the post-writing team that's helped bring the story to publication and life. My wife and "ideal reader", Ann, of course; an additional beta reader for this one, too – Dylan Hughes, my Welsh expert, and Head of Wrexham's Library Services; my writing friend and colleague, Alison Morton (*Roma Nova* series) for her advice on all things Latin; my incomparable editor, Jo Field, in beautiful Devon; hugely talented graphic designer, for the cover artwork, Cathy Helms at Avalon Graphics, North Carolina; those lovely writers who've provided endorsements for the cover blurb; and the wonderful folk at SilverWood Books, responsible for the publishing process. But, mostly, my boundless gratitude goes to all of you who enjoy reading my stories.

And a particular acknowledgement here to those who contributed to the crowd-funding project and promotional work that made this publication possible. Thanks to all of you!

Peter Hensman
Wendy Murdoch
Heidi Chapman
Shelley Eaves
Penny Love
John Haywood
Sir Ian McCartney
Paul Forster
Anne Tweed
Brian Rimmer
Howard Metcalfe
Maija and Simon Robinson
Peter Worsfold
Solène Leti
Vanda Murray
Terry Dand
Steph Wyeth
Kat Bearman
Roisin McCormac
Joan and Tony Roberts
Luc Ricciardi
Marilyn Cronyn
Jake McCall
Paul Nowak
Steve McCall
Annie Wilde
Lord Ray Collins and Rafael Ballesteros
Tony Evans
Sharon and Nick Povey
Alan Simpson
Baroness Margaret Prosser
Liam Davies
Fred Taylor
Sharon Powell
Kim Withers
Peter Booth
Judy and Bob Jones
Jan Kearney
John Chapman
Chris and Pauline Grice
Susan Miller

Paul Jeorrett
Arthur Dixon
Roger Williams
Diane Hardy-Rose
Ian and Norah Lucas
Julie Tift
Ann McCall
Abi Davies
Gary and Charo Titley
Dylan Hughes and Sandra Gardner
Jeanne Milostan

David Ebsworth, February 2016